THE DREAM OF A DUCHESS

LINDA RAE SANDE

The Dream of a Duchess

V1.1

Edited by Katrina Fair

https://www.lindaraesande.com

ISBN: 978-1-946271-09-9

Library of Congress Control Number: 2018900862

Twisted Teacup Publishing, Cody, WY

PRINTED IN THE UNITED STATES OF AMERICA

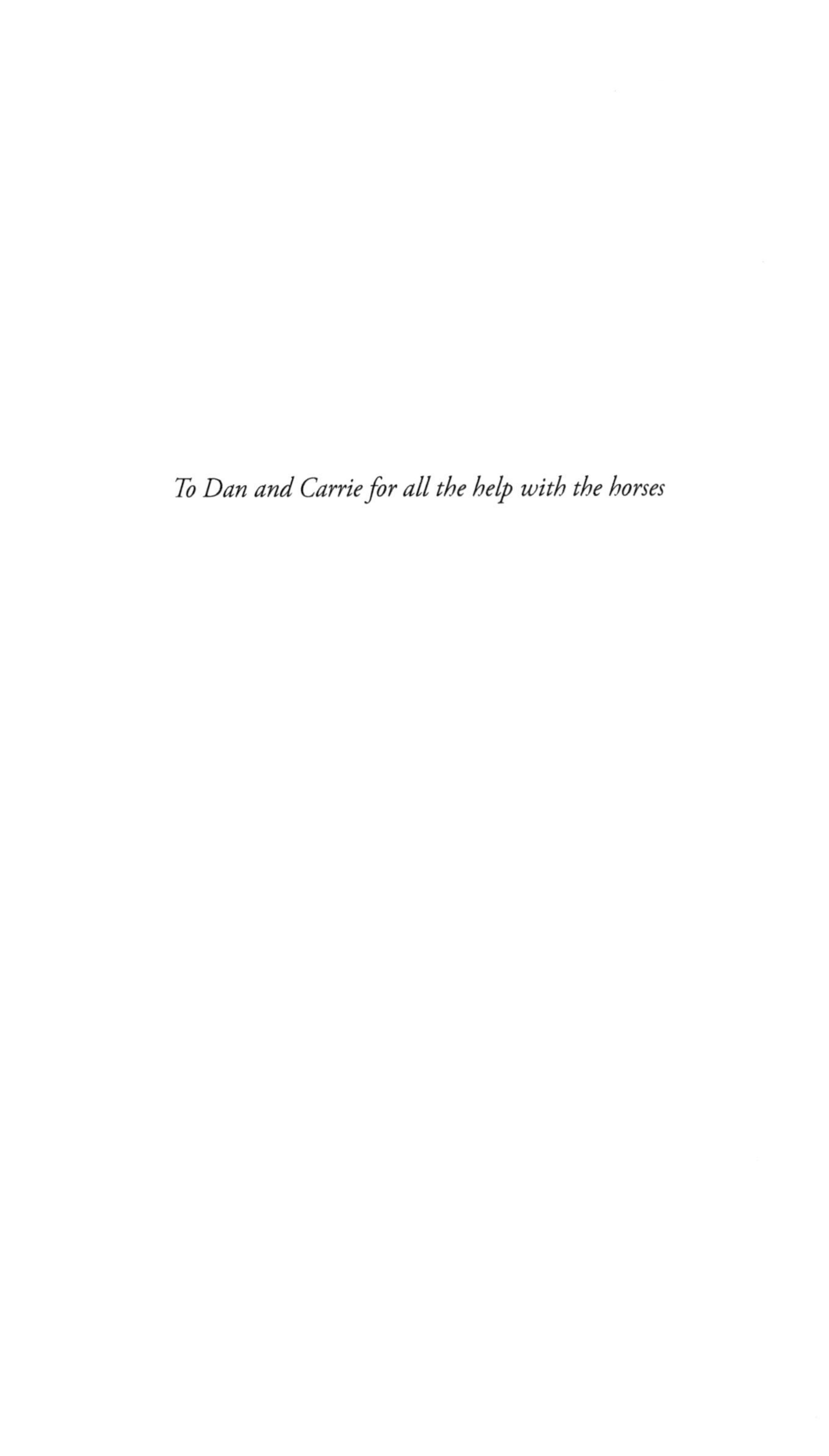

To Dan and Carrie for all the help with the horses

REGENCY ROMANCES BY LINDA RAE SANDE

The Daughters of the Aristocracy

The Kiss of a Viscount

The Grace of a Duke

The Seduction of an Earl

The Sons of the Aristocracy

Tuesday Nights

The Widowed Countess

My Fair Groom

The Sisters of the Aristocracy

The Story of a Baron

The Passion of a Marquess

The Desire of a Lady

The Brothers of the Aristocracy

The Love of a Rake

The Caress of a Commander

The Epiphany of an Explorer

The Widows of the Aristocracy

The Gossip of an Earl

The Enigma of a Widow

The Secrets of a Viscount

The Widowers of the Aristocracy

The Dream of a Duchess

The Cousins of the Aristocracy

The Promise of a Gentleman

The Pride of a Gentleman

The Holidays of the Aristocracy

The Christmas of a Countess

Chapter 1

AN ACCIDENTAL DEATH

April 1813, Craythorne Manor near Basingstoke

The seal had long ago been broken, the bits of dark red wax having fallen to a marble floor many miles away. There was no discernible impression left in the seal. Isabella wondered if there had ever been one as she turned the folded missive over between shaking fingers.

The first words she had already read several times.

My dearest Arabella, You will forever be in my thoughts, for I fear for your life. Mine may as well be over.

The simple "D" at the bottom provided little in the way of a hint as to whom might have written the missive, but then the message obviously required anonymity. The need for secrecy.

It seems fate has only been kind in one regard. Oh, how I wish I could be with you when that kindness is delivered. Let us hope it won't result in your demise.

Isabella read the last line over and over, confusion and fright building to the point she thought she might faint.

And she never fainted.

Why ever would Mum need to fear for her life? *Or whatever had Mum done to fear for her life?*

Isabella dipped her hand into the pocket of her riding habit, feeling for the pasteboard calling card her mother had given to her a long time ago. The corners were bent and frayed, but the print was still visible.

> *If something should ever happen to me, be sure to find this gentleman. He'll know what to do.*

The instructions hadn't come with a sense of foreboding, but rather had been made as if the man would be able to provide assistance in some way. Perhaps he was the solicitor assigned to her parents' estate, or an accomptant charged with seeing to their accounts.

Staring at the name, Isabella frowned.

David Fitzwilliam.

She glanced at the letter again, rereading the simple D at the bottom.

David.

D.

She slid the card back into her pocket, giving her head a quick shake. Certainly she would know this David Fitzwilliam if she ever saw him. He had probably been to the Craythorne estate on business in the past.

Or was *he* the 'D' from the missive?

The question had Isabella Tolson's heart racing as she carefully refolded the note and returned it to its hiding place in her mother's vanity drawer.

How long ago had the note been written?

The parchment was old, the scrawl that of a man's hand. She knew it was not her father's, as she would recognize the flourish of his script. Maxwell Tolson, Earl of Craythorne, had beautiful handwriting. Despite his beefy fingers, he took great care in how he formed his letters, in how his words lined up along imaginary lines across the page.

This missive was written by someone who was in a hurry. Someone who was fearful. Someone who was...

The creak in the floor behind her had Isabella turning with a gasp. She relaxed a bit at finding her mother regarding her, even if it was with a frown and crossed arms.

"Hullo, Mum," she managed, a bit sheepish as she dipped her head.

"What did I tell you about going through my things?" Arabella, Countess of Craythorne, asked as she continued into her dressing room. The light from the west-facing window bathed her in a golden glow, casting red glints in her otherwise dark hair. All the Brotherton women shared the hair coloring, along with an oval face, dark brows, long lashes, and a pert nose that together gave them an elegant appearance.

Isabella rather wished she had her mother's nose, but it was not to be. At least she had the oval face and the beautiful hair, although her curls were sometimes unruly.

"I'm sorry, Mum. I... I was bored," Isabella replied, hoping her sudden fear for her mother wasn't evident in her coloring. She was sure her face was bright red just from having been caught sneaking about in the dressing room. "I promise it won't happen again."

Arabella sighed, knowing full well her daughter wasn't interested in needlework, or drawing, or practicing the piano-forté. Having grown up with a younger brother, Isabella had become a bit of a hoyden, preferring horses to dolls and riding horses to more domestic pursuits. "Perhaps it's time we see to a Season in London for you," the countess suggested. At nearly nineteen, Isabella was past the age for her come-out, although she still didn't know all the dances performed at a *ton* ball. Having grown up at the Craythorne country estate near Basingstoke—her father had dubbed it Craythorne Castle—she didn't have the experience others of her age in London had when it came to socializing with daughters of aristocrats.

Or the sons, for that matter.

Isabella's eyes widened. "Truly?" she whispered. The idea of a Season in London wasn't so exciting because of the balls, or soirées, or garden parties, but rather because she wanted to attend another play at the theatre, and she wanted a chance to go to Tattersall's.

She had only been to the theatre the one time, but the evening had been exciting. A naval battle had been reenacted on stage, the ships actually floating in a tank of water as they exchanged mock gunfire. John, her younger brother by less than three years, had been so impressed, he asked if he could become a naval officer.

Isabella would never forget how his face fell when he was informed he couldn't join the British Navy. He was the only heir to the Craythorne earldom.

There was no spare.

As for Tattersall's, she just wanted to see the horses. Study their pedigrees and work up imaginary pairings. Study the shapes of their heads and watch how they walked. Compare colors and composition. Should her father decide to bid on one, she was sure she could provide him with the information to choose the best one to enhance his already impressive stables.

"Do you really think father will allow me a Season this year?"

Arabella angled her head to one side. "The earl has to go to London to attend Parliament. I see no reason as to why we cannot go along and stay in the terrace with him."

Well, she could think of one, but Isabella didn't need to know about him. "I'll speak to the earl about it during dinner this evening," she replied. "In the meantime, I do believe you're expected at the stables for your afternoon ride."

Nodding, Isabella gave a quick curtsy. "Thank you, Mum."

"Don't be long, though. Dinner is at seven, and you'll have to bathe and change, remember."

Suppressing the urge to roll her eyes at the reminder, Isabella murmured, "Yes, Mum," and hurried from the dressing room, her riding habit nearly catching on the corner of the door.

The countess watched as her daughter left the room. When she heard the girl's half-boots on the main stairs, she turned her attention back to her vanity and moved to open the drawer.

She knew Isabella had been reading one of the many letters she kept hidden in the drawer. Most were bundled with a satin ribbon—those from her friends or her late mother—but some were loose. Frowning, she pulled the one that looked as if it was out of place and winced when she saw the scrawl on the front.

"Bad news?"

The deep voice of Maxwell Tolson had her body jerking in surprise as she whirled around to find her husband regarding her with a scowl. He wore a loosely-tied robe, his bare feet apparent beneath the hem. "You frightened me," she accused, turning back around to slip the missive into the drawer. "As to the news, there wasn't any. Your daughter was simply reading the old letters from my mother and cousin," she added as she moved to place a hand on the earl's chest. "Are you already dressing for dinner?"

Maxwell regarded his wife for a moment, his brows still furrowed. The expression made him appear far older and more dangerous than he normally looked. "Not for a couple of hours or so," he hedged, his eyes suddenly darkening. "Until then, will you join me in my bed?"

Arabella blinked. Her husband rarely asked her to join him in his bed. When he was of a mind for conjugal relations, he usually came to her bedchamber, and did so well after dark. "I will," she replied with a nod, making sure she arched an approving eyebrow. She regarded him for another moment, wondering what he had in mind. "Except it's my lady's maid's day off, and she hasn't yet returned from the village. I don't expect her back until six o'clock."

His frown deepening, he gave a shake of his head. "I don't wish to bed your lady's maid."

Angling her head while managing an expression of contrition, she whispered, "Are you prepared to play lady's maid in her place? You'll need to undo the buttons on my gown." She turned around, her chin ending up on one shoulder as she presented her back to him.

"I think I can manage a few buttons," he claimed as he moved to stand behind her. The earl undid the first fastening, his large fingers struggling with the jet button. "Forgive me," he whispered before grasping the edges of the fabric in both hands and simply ripping it apart.

Arabella allowed a slight gasp of shock as the black buttons scattered over the Aubusson carpeting, dancing about until they came to rest on the master bedchamber and dressing room floors. She hadn't even managed to face the earl before he had the tapes of her petticoats torn apart. In the next moment, he had her in his arms and in the next, she was on his bed, left wearing only her corset and stockings.

Her breasts swelling in anticipation, Arabella tugged at the top of the fabric cups of her corset. She knew Maxwell found the action erotic, for he always paused to watch as she barely allowed her suddenly engorged nipples to escape the confines of the lawn fabric. When she moved her hands to the ties of his robe, he suddenly stilled them with his own, gripping her wrists in one large hand.

"Not yet," he whispered, his voice hoarse. He allowed his gaze to travel over his wife's corseted body, his attention settling on one exposed breast just as the afternoon sun suddenly bathed her entire body in a golden glow.

"Now?" she whispered, her breaths coming in short gasps. At one time, she cursed her body for its wicked reaction to his attentions. Now, she merely accepted the pleasures whilst imagining someone else providing them.

The earl shook his head, his lips suddenly descending onto the breast. Knowing he would expect a reaction, she lifted her chest just a bit and raked her fingertips into his unruly hair. Her purrs had him groaning as he moved his attentions to the other breast. She wasn't even aware of him spreading open his robe until he was suddenly inside her, filling her over and over again, his crisp, graying curls tickling her nipples whilst his tongue and teeth nibbled on an earlobe.

Maxwell's body might have been a bit large and his manner at times brusque and unforgiving, but Arabella had long ago learned he wanted her for more than just a mother for his heir. He had confessed his desires on many a dark night—at least he had after she had given birth to a daughter.

She often wondered if he suspected she had already given her heart to another. Her heart and her maidenhood. If so, Maxwell never asked her who might have ruined her. Never accused her of infidelity. Never put voice to doubt about the parentage of the girl who was now on her afternoon ride. Who was proving to be just as contrary as Arabella could be when stubbornness overruled good sense.

The earl allowed Arabella the occasional bouts of contrary behavior, but he was also quick to anger should she test his patience. Arabella simply learned when he was about to reach his limit and relented, usually throwing herself into his arms and begging forgiveness. The move would leave him momentarily confused, but distracted enough that his anger rarely disrupted the household.

Later, he would visit her in her bedchamber. Arabella never knew if he did do so to worship her body or to pretend to punish her for her insolence.

He had another child on her two years later. Their son, John, was away at Eton and would attend university in another year.

As for Isabella, a Season in London was on the horizon, although Arabella often wondered if there was a gentleman of the *ton* who could abide the girl's obsession with horses, one that might exceed his own.

Her attention was suddenly back on her husband, for when his entire body lifted from hers, he went rigid. She thought at first he was on the verge of his release, but his eyes were dark as they regarded her.

"What is it?" she asked in a hoarse whisper. "Why did you stop?"

Despite her attempts to hold onto him, Maxwell pulled his body from hers. "Who were you thinking about just then?" he asked, his voice gruff with menace.

Arabella blinked. "Why, you, of course," she whispered as one thumb flicked over chest, barely grazing a nipple. Usually the move brought at least a hiss or a grunt of satisfaction from him, but not this time.

She glanced around, wondering what had captured his attention. Why he might have thought she had been distracted.

Leaving the bed in a motion that belied his size, he wrapped his robe about his body and held it with one hand before stalking off. He had the bedchamber door open before Arabella realized what was happening. "Don't go," she called out. "Craythorne!"

Arabella managed to scramble off the tall mattress and was about to round the end of the four-poster bed when she stepped on one of the jet buttons that lay scattered about the carpet. Her stockinged foot slid sideways before she could gain her balance, sending her flailing to the floor.

When her head hit the maple footboard, the hollow sound had Craythorne turning around to find her on her back, her head twisted awkwardly to one side and her body lifeless.

A moment later, he was on his knees, begging her to wake up and shouting curses at the top of his lungs.

Chapter 2

A TWIN BROTHER'S SECRET

Meanwhile, in Kensington Gardens

The scent of roses had Clarinda Ann Brotherton closing her eyes and inhaling deeply, her expression one of pure bliss. Daniel Fitzwilliam adored seeing it, so he made sure she had occasion to display it every time she was in his company.

Even if it was for only ten or fifteen minutes at a time.

"They are your favorite, aren't they?" he murmured as he regarded the pink roses. Given the time of the year, there weren't too many in full bloom, but there were enough for Lady Clarinda. He had seen to the delivery of a dozen of them to Stockton House the day before. The Mayfair home of her father, the Earl of Heath, was also where Lady Clarinda still resided.

"Oh, indeed. Thank you for meeting me here again, Mr. Fitzwilliam," she said, her head angling so she could see if her lady's maid was watching them. Sometimes Missy grew bored and simply stopped watching the couple as they strolled through the gardens.

"I look forward to the days when I can do it every day," he replied, following her gaze to find her lady's maid intrigued by a garden of red tulips. Taking advantage of the opportunity, Daniel leaned in and captured Clarinda's lips in a quick kiss. "And that as well," he whispered, referring to the kiss.

"As do I," she countered with a grin. A slight dimple appeared in one cheek just as it bloomed with color.

"Will you marry me then?" Daniel asked as he reached into a waistcoat pocket and pulled out a ring.

Clarinda rolled her eyes, and her smile widened. "Yes, of course I will," she answered. Other than marrying in June, they hadn't discussed their impending nuptials at length, his proposal was expected. She was betrothed to the Earl of Norwick, after all, and had been since she was fourteen. "It's beautiful," she breathed as she watched him slide the gold band on her finger. Three bright blue sapphires glittered in the morning light.

Daniel had thought topaz a better choice given her aquamarine eyes, but Mr. Bridge had assured him sapphires were more valuable. Although the ring had cost him more than six months of his Norwick earldom allowance, he knew the expense would be worth it just to see her reaction.

"Will you wear it every day?" he asked.

Clarinda finally tore her gaze from the ring and nodded. "Of course. But what shall I say when people ask when we'll marry?" she queried. According to the contract her father and the late Earl of Norwick had signed eight years ago, she was to be married to the Norwick heir apparent by the time she was two-and-twenty. That birthday had already passed.

"Will June give you enough time to make arrangements?" Daniel wondered. "I don't want to rush you, but..."

"June would be perfect," she interrupted. "Father will be so pleased to hear you've finally proposed. I'm so pleased," she admitted with another grin. She suddenly sobered. "You do remember there are some other provisions that need to be met?"

Daniel winced, realizing she was referring to the businesses his brother, David, the current Earl of Norwick, still owned. Businesses that were inappropriate holdings for a man in his position. "I don't own either one of them," he said with a nod.

Clarinda's brows furrowed until a fold of skin appeared between them. Daniel was tempted to press a forefinger against it, a move he knew she wouldn't like one whit, even though she had done it to his knitted brow on more than one occasion. "I wonder why father made mention of them just yesterday then," she murmured. "Oh!" she added as she placed a hand over her mouth. "I wasn't supposed to hear his comment, of course, given he was speaking of a men's club and a... a *brothel.*" This last was said in a whisper, as if she wasn't supposed to know of such a business.

Shrugging, Daniel finally had to mention his brother. "David owns those businesses. Not me."

Her face brightening, Clarinda nodded. "I've forgotten you have a brother. A twin, is he not?"

"That's right," Daniel acknowledged, hoping beyond hope she didn't remember that it was David to whom she had been betrothed. A betrothal that stipulated David would divest himself of his unsavory businesses and marry Clarinda no later than her twenty-second birthday. Now that she was several weeks past turning two-and-twenty, Daniel was sure the contract for her marriage to David was null and void, which meant she could marry anyone.

Why not him?

He had felt affection for her since the first time he laid eyes on her. They had met in Hyde Park whilst she and her chaperone rode horses in the afternoons. They danced together at balls and soirées, sat next to one another at Lady Worthington's annual *musicales*, and rode horses during the fashionable hour in Rotten Row. Noting how David barely gave her a second glance when he attended the same entertainments, Daniel had decided Clarinda would be his wife.

About to kiss her again, Daniel allowed a sigh of disappointment when he realized the lady's maid was regarding him with a rather sour expression. "I fear our time is up," he murmured. "Will I see you here again?"

Clarinda allowed a smile. "Of course." And then, in defiance of her lady's maid's presence, she lifted herself on tiptoes and kissed Daniel on his cheek. "Until then."

Daniel gave her a bow and kissed the back of her hand before she hurried off, a sense of relief settling over him.

Now that she had accepted his proposal, the two of them could marry in June and all would be well.

Well, eventually.

Chapter 3

BREAKFAST INTERRUPTED

The next day, in Westminster, London, England

Octavius, Duke of Huntington, gave the footman a withering stare. "What is it?" he asked, obviously annoyed at being interrupted during his breakfast. Despite not having had more than two glasses of scotch the night before, a headache pounded at the front of his brain, and his mouth felt as if it were filled with cotton.

"A courier just delivered this for you, Your Grace," the footman said as he placed a sealed note on the edge of the table next to the duke's plate. "He said he is to wait for a reply," the footman added before straightening and standing at attention.

Annoyed, Octavius was about to make some comment about how long the courier might have to wait when he decided instead to simply read the missive and deal with it as quickly as possible.

Lifting the new note between his thumb and forefinger, he flipped it over to find a puddle of dark red wax impressed with a seal. *Norwick?* he guessed as he quickly lifted the corner and unfolded the paper.

Jesus! What could be so damned important on a Saturday morning as to require a courier?

He glanced at his chronometer, making sure it was still early morning and not the middle of the afternoon. Time had a way of slipping away from him these days, especially when he spent far too much time thinking. He didn't mind thinking so much during sessions of Parliament, but losing entire hours to his thoughts on days he could be out riding, or at Brooks's enjoying a game of hazard, or playing billiards with Lord Devonville, was simply unacceptable.

It hadn't been like this back when he had a wife, of course. A woman he had married because he felt affection for her—he had since they were young children—and whose absence due to death had him mourning far longer than most widowers.

The tiny child she gave birth to only moments before she died joined her in death—and in her casket. He couldn't bear to separate the two. *My heir*, he thought for at least the thousandth time since that awful day he was stripped of everything he held near and dear. Everything that mattered.

Well, everything except his dukedom.

Octavius swallowed suddenly, realizing it would be unseemly to weep in front of his footman. God knew he had done quite enough of it in the privacy of his bedchamber since that awful night.

His eyes focused on the messy script in the missive he held, and he began to read.

Hunt, I apologize for the ungodly hour, but your presence is requested at The Elegant Courtesan at your earliest convenience. Seems there's been a murder. I am in need of your counsel. Norwick.

Octavius blinked. And blinked again.

Christ! *A murder?*

The duke had a passing thought that the crime might have occurred at the upscale brothel David Fitzwilliam, Earl of Norwick, still owned in a tony section of Westminster, but the words 'seems there's been a murder' suggested the offense happened elsewhere. He reread the words twice before turning his attention to the footman.

"Tell the courier I will be there in an hour," he growled, pushing away from the table. Truth be told, he could be there in under thirty minutes if his groom could saddle his horse in ten. He was already dressed for a ride—he had planned to enjoy a ride in Hyde Park and possibly go as far as Chiswick before his luncheon. "And have the groom saddle my horse." At least he would get some exercise, although not for enjoyment, it seemed.

"Yes, Your Grace," the footman said, giving a bow before hurrying off toward the vestibule.

Fifteen minutes later, Octavius Whitney, Duke of Huntington, was on his way to *The Elegant Courtesan*.

Chapter 4

A WOMAN PURSUED

Meanwhile, at Worthington House in Mayfair

"Thank you for agreeing to see me. I know it's far too early to be paying a call," Clarinda Brotherton said as she made her way to a chair in Lady Worthington's private salon.

The older woman, obviously abed when Clarinda arrived, wore a deep red satin dressing gown over her rather elaborate night rail. Her blonde hair, still free of the grays of age, was brushed out and secured in a ribbon beneath her left ear, the style making her look years younger than her five-and-thirty years. "I've been awake for hours," Adele Slater Worthington claimed as she leaned over and poured a cup of tea for her visitor. She didn't add that she was awake because she had entertained her late husband's brother until five o'clock that morning.

Stephen Worthington's attentions had been a welcome respite from the confines of mourning, his discreet visits to Worthington House timed so that no one knew of their *affaire*. That he was a better lover than Samuel only enhanced his standing. As for how long their *affaire* would last, she found she didn't much care. She was quite sure the man was only paying her visits because Samuel had asked him to look after her should anything happen to him.

Such as death.

"Counting the days until I don't have to wear black or lavender any longer," she murmured.

Clarinda winced, a bit chagrined she hadn't considered Adele's situation when she decided to come for advice. "How are you, really?" she asked as she leaned forward to take the cup and saucer.

Adele gave a shrug. "Better than I could be, truth be told. And looking forward to life as an independent woman," the older woman added. "I've a house, a town coach and four beautiful horses, and a fortune to spend as I see fit. What more could I want?"

Clarinda dipped her head. "A man who loves you?" she ventured with an arched brow.

Blinking, Adele straightened on the settee and regarded her visitor for a moment. *Ah, the innocence of youth*, she almost said. "I take it Norwick has finally formally proposed?"

Nodding, Clarinda said, "He has. And my parlor is filled with pink roses." She pulled off her gloves and held out a hand. A ring of gold topped with three sapphires decorated her fourth finger.

Adele's eyes widened. "Finally," she breathed. "Where did he propose?" Rumors had persisted for years that David Fitzwilliam, Earl of Norwick, would make Lady Clarinda his wife, and not just because they had been betrothed since she was fourteen. Reports in *The Tattler* had the two meeting in secret in every square of the capital as well as having dinner together at Rules Restaurant. Sitings in Hyde Park along the Serpentine had also been reported.

"Kensington Gardens. He meets me there every other day for ten minutes," she whispered. "And he always manages a kiss or two before my lady's maid appears." She suddenly angled her head. "I wonder if he bribes her to stay back and give us a few minutes alone?" she murmured with a hint of concern.

Grinning, Adele allowed a sigh and decided not to address that particular comment. It had worked for other gentlemen who had little time to court the women they intended to marry.

Or ruin.

"Have you set a date?"

"Late June, although we haven't yet discussed a wedding trip," Clarinda replied, her brows suddenly furrowing.

"What is it?" Adele wondered, leaning forward to pour more tea.

"I can't help but think I'm being courted by two entirely different men," Clarinda whispered. "Do I sound utterly ridiculous for saying such a thing?"

Adele blinked. Then she inhaled sharply when she remembered there were *two* Fitzwilliams. "Are you quite sure you're being courted by Norwick and not by his twin brother?" she asked. She was tempted to add some brandy to her tea, if for no other reason than she would have to get some sleep once Clarinda took her leave. Given Stephen's frequent visits, she wasn't sleeping much at nights, and she planned to secretly attend the theatre later that night. If she sat in the back of her box, no one would notice her presence.

Clarinda frowned. "Which one is the earl?" she asked in a whisper.

Adele's brows lifted before a grin spilt her face. "David is the earl. Daniel—I think that's his name—he's the spare heir," she explained. "Although I don't think I've ever met him. I've probably seen him a dozen times and thought he was his brother," she added, her brows suddenly furrowing.

Apparently Clarinda hadn't seen the two men side-by-side. Adele had just the one time, although it was from across a crowded ballroom. With both men dressed in black evening attire as they had been, with their hair parted and combed exactly the same, it was impossible to tell the two apart.

"So, it *is* possible they're both courting me?" Clarinda hedged, a look of worry making her appear older than her two-and-twenty years. "Oh, but that cannot be. How can two men look so much alike that I wouldn't be able to tell them apart?"

"Because they're identical twins?" Adele responded with an arched brow. "But what does it matter? You're betrothed to the earl. Why would the other twin even bother to court you?"

Clarinda gave a sigh of relief. "Exactly. I knew you would have the answer," she said with a wan smile. "I was about to ask my godfather, but I really don't wish to bother Torrington with such a query. I'm his oldest goddaughter, and I shouldn't wish to seem... addle-brained."

Milton Grandby, Earl of Torrington, was her godfather and knew everyone in the *ton*, especially his one-and-twenty goddaughters and over a dozen godsons. That David Fitzwilliam wasn't among their company was only because the man had been born only a few years after Torrington.

Adele bobbed her head back and forth a moment before she remembered Clarinda's earlier words. *I can't help but think I'm being courted by two different men.* "So tell me, what made you think you were being courted by two different men?" she asked suddenly.

Her shoulders slumping, Clarinda wondered how to respond. "Some days, Mr. Fitzwilliam bestows the most wonderful kisses on me while other days he doesn't even attempt to show affection. Some days, he comes with pink roses, and other days, it's as if he doesn't know they're my favorite flower. Some days..." She paused, as if she didn't want to mention the next bit of information. "He seems old and cranky, while most days, he seems like the youngest, most darling man on the entire planet. Pray tell, how can that be?"

Having been married for over ten years, Adele could certainly agree that men were unpredictable, but explaining it to a woman who was thirteen years her junior and probably still a virgin would be difficult. "Men are fickle," she stated finally, hoping she wouldn't have to provide examples of just how fickle her late husband could be.

"More so than us?" Clarinda asked, incredulous.

Adele allowed a giggle, the musical sound filling the salon. "Oh, far more than us," she replied happily. She regarded the daughter of the Earl of Heath for a moment before adding, "Follow your mother's example, and employ a bit of patience," she suggested in a low voice. The Countess of Heath certainly had to have patience with the Earl of Heath. Albert Brotherton had been the worst sort of rake during his university days. Once he turned six-and-twenty, though, he settled down and finally married the woman to whom he had been betrothed since he was a child. "And all will be well."

Clarinda considered Adele's words for a time before finally allowing a nod. "Would it be acceptable to admit I love him?" she asked in a whisper.

Sighing, Adele angled her head to one side. "Give it a few months," she replied carefully. "Then, when you're sure of your heart, you can tell him anything you want. Just be sure to do so after he's pleasured you to within an inch of your life," she added with an arched eyebrow.

Clarinda blinked several times before finally allowing a nod, her face having turned bright pink at hearing Adele's words. "And, if by then, I've decided I *don't* love him?" she asked carefully.

Adele sighed. "Then let us hope he's gotten a child on you. Then you will have someone to love for the rest of your life." Not that she knew this first-hand. Samuel Worthington had never gotten a child on her, but then, he hadn't bedded her with the kind of fervor his brother employed in the bedchamber. *Good thing Stephen uses French letters*, she thought just then, for if she found herself with child, she didn't know what she would do.

Moving to get up, Clarinda held out a hand to keep Adele from rising from hers. "I'll let myself out. You get some sleep, and perhaps I'll see you at the theatre tonight," she suggested with an arched brow. "In the back of your box. Wearing all black."

Rolling her eyes, Adele gave a nod. "You know me too well," she said with an impish grin.

She watched as the younger woman took her leave of the salon, secretly jealous of Clarinda's younger age and situation.

Time and the opportunity to be a mother had already passed her by, she was sure. But a life of independence—the life of a Merry Widow—might be an acceptable alternative. Nights with Stephen were certainly suggesting that was the case.

Adele took her leave of her salon—brandy in hand—and headed back to bed.

Chapter 5

A TERRIFYING TALE

Back in Westminster

Holding onto Poseidon's reins with one gloved hand, the Duke of Huntington regarded the front door of *The Elegant Courtesan.* He wondered at the news that awaited him behind the white stone Palladian mansion. Having barely dismounted before a liveried stableboy ran up to take the Turk, he found he couldn't give Poseidon the small apple he had in his pocket.

"Good morning, Yer Grace," the boy said with a bow.

Octavius frowned before he tossed the boy a coin, wondering how the boy knew he was a duke. His horse didn't sport any silks bearing his ducal colors, and he hadn't patronized the exclusive palace of pleasure for nearly five years.

The duke wondered how much longer David Fitzwilliam would continue to operate the business. It was rather unseemly for an earl to even be engaged in trade—especially that of a brothel—although Octavius knew the man's twin brother, Daniel, saw to the books and the business side of the brothel whilst David did whatever it was he did as the owner.

"Morning," he answered, deciding not to take out his growing dislike of the day on the young stableboy. At least his headache had subsided. Poseidon had been most accommodating in getting him to *The Elegant Courtesan* in near-record time.

He walked up to stand on the top step between two Corinthian columns, thinking a butler would open the door before he would be forced to use the brass knocker. After a few seconds, he dared a quick glance around and simply used the handle to open the door.

Half-expecting to find several scantily clad females wandering about, he instead found himself regarding two fully-dressed young ladies, arm-in-arm, walking toward him. They looked as if they had been raised in the homes of gentlemen, their gowns and pelisses of the highest quality, and their bonnets quite fashionable.

"Ladies," he said with a nod, removing his beaver as he stepped aside.

"Your Grace," they said in unison as they each dipped a perfect curtsy. The two moved beyond him and took their leave of the house.

Octavius angled his head to one side and almost wondered if he had the wrong address. His arrival was obviously expected at the brothel, though, if both the stableboy and the two women who had just taken their leave knew he was a duke.

Glancing off to the side, he spotted the ornate hotel-like counter at which guests checked into *The Elegant Courtesan*. A young woman regarded him with an arched eyebrow.

"May I be of assistance, Your Grace?" she asked, her manner of speech suggesting that she, too, had been raised in a proper English home.

Perhaps she had.

"Is …" He started to say, "Norwick", but changed his mind. "The proprietor available?" He had heard rumors the earl would be divesting himself of his brothel and a gaming hell down the street in anticipation of his marriage to Clarinda Anne Brotherton. For the five years since David Fitzwilliam had inherited the Norwick earldom, it was expected he would sell the businesses because it was unseemly for him to hold such properties, even if said properties did a great deal to line his already rich pockets. And, according to the rumors circulating at Brooks's, the man no longer enjoyed any of the entertainments offered at his establishments. His involvement in both the brothel and the gaming hell were entirely professional.

The young woman behind the counter nodded. "I've informed Lord Norwick of your arrival. Would you like a brandy? Or a glass of whisky whilst you wait?"

Although he was sorely tempted to accept the offer of a whisky—he was fairly sure it was from Devonville's distillery just north of the border—he had a feeling he would need all his faculties for whatever awaited him. "No, but I do appreciate the offer."

When the woman merely nodded but made no move to leave her station, Octavius was about to ask that she fetch the earl when he realized she had probably already summoned him with a flick of her wrist beneath the counter. A series of wires were evident on the wall behind her, each one connected to a different room in the house. *The things you forget*, Octavius thought with a shake of his head.

This wasn't his first visit to the high-end brothel, of course. As a younger man, he had taken a great interest in spending time with one of its courtesans, a raven-haired woman named Ava who was especially beautiful and ever so patient while she taught him how to pleasure her. *You'll never keep your wife happy if you don't please her in bed*, she was fond of saying, as if her sole purpose in life was to see to his future wife's pleasure.

And she had. Although far too nervous at first, Octavius' late wife had finally taken a modest liking to the marriage bed, although she would never admit such a thing. At times, he refused to allow her to leave his bedchamber in the hopes he might be favored with yet another tumble before the dawn lightened the skies. Sometimes Jane even allowed it, although she did so grudgingly.

He had to push the memory aside lest he lose himself in

his thoughts again. His memories of the brothel came unbidden, though.

The Elegant Courtesan.

Expensive, exclusive, and ever so satisfying, his nights at the *Courtesan* had proved as educational as they were pleasurable. The resident courtesans were each employed for a different reason, a different proclivity. His choice of Ava hadn't been because he sought to improve his lovemaking skills but merely because he desired a beautiful woman with whom to enjoy a tumble until it was time he take his childhood friend as his wife.

At the time, he thought Ava's instructions misplaced. He was a good enough bedmate, he always thought—and he was paying a pretty pence for the privilege of having her exclusively for those weekly appointments—but after his visits increased in frequency, he found her requests to please her more challenging, more of a game he found he wanted to win every time they played. And then, one night, he arrived for his regular visit only to discover she was no longer in residence.

Married? he had repeated when the madame whispered the reason he would no longer be able to spend the night with Ava.

She left our employ a few days ago, the woman had said with a wan smile, her expression managing to display just how much she regretted having to disappoint the duke.

I do hope she married well, he remembered saying, deciding he couldn't feel too terribly upset about the loss of his favorite harlot. His only harlot.

A baronet, the woman had replied with a shrug. *I do hope you'll afford her all the courtesies should you come upon her at a ton event*, she added in a whisper.

Octavius blinked at that, wondering what the madame expected he might do should he come across Ava at a ball or soirée. Did she think he would give Ava the cut direct?

Or course he would not!

He had never seen Ava again, though, which suggested

the baronet had her sequestered in his country estate or in a hunting lodge, probably concerned her former clients would seek her out if he kept her anywhere near London.

Well, life as a baronet's wife had to be more respectable, he supposed.

The loss of a regular tumble, as well as turning eight-and-twenty, had him proposing to the woman who would be his wife only a week later. He had married her a few months after that.

Two years later, he buried her.

Silently chastising himself for once again becoming lost in his thoughts, Octavius sighed and wondered again about his reason for being at *The Elegant Courtesan* on a Saturday morning at almost ten o' clock.

"Huntington. Good of you to come so quickly," David Fitzwilliam, Earl of Norwick, said as he entered the large vestibule from a wide hallway.

Despite having been a regular customer for over two years, Octavius had never paid witness to the earl actually being on the premises before. The duke regarded the proprietor of *The Elegant Courtesan* with a nod. "You look like hell," he murmured.

David Norwick was usually well-dressed, well-groomed, and possessed of a confident air that served him well at the gaming tables at Brooks's as well as in Parliament. Although his manner of dress was appropriate, he looked a bit rumpled, and his face appeared rather haggard.

"I feel like it," David replied, not the least bit offended by the duke's remark. "I need you to meet someone, Your Grace," he added as he turned and led the duke down the hallway from which he had come.

"Is business always this slow on a Saturday morning?" Octavius wondered as he glanced around, not seeing any evidence of the resident courtesans or their clients.

"It is," David replied as he stopped in front of one of the last doors lining the hallway. Unlike the others along the Turkish carpeted corridor, there wasn't a painting of a doxy hanging above the door. Octavius surreptitiously glanced toward Ava's old room, knowing the painting of her had long ago been replaced with that of another woman, this one sporting blonde hair and not much else. A quick second glance had him realizing he had passed the young woman when he had first arrived.

How different women looked when they were fully dressed!

"We're closed until eight o'clock in the evening," David explained with an arched eyebrow. "Which gives us some time to sort this situation." He knocked twice on the door before letting himself into the room.

As with all the bedchambers in *The Elegant Courtesan*, the room featured a large bed, a floor covered with Aubusson carpeting, heavy drapes that blocked any light from the room's only window, and decor specific to whomever called the room their own. Noting the lack of accoutrements in this one, Octavius thought at first it was empty. But in the dim light of a lamp set on the bedchamber's only nightstand, he spied a young woman as she quickly stood up from the bed. Her riding habit suggested she had been riding just that morning, and at a great deal of speed. In the low light of the room, the velvet fabric appeared discolored, and most of her hair had escaped its pins and now fell in long, curly locks about her shoulders.

"I didn't mean to startle you, my lady," David said with a bow.

My lady? Octavius had to resist the urge to admonish the earl until he heard the young woman's response.

"You did not, my lord," she said before she curtsied. "I was afraid I might fall asleep, is all."

David reached over and turned up the gas on a lamp near the door. The room brightened to reveal the object of his attention.

"Octavius, Duke of Huntington, this is Lady Isabella," David said quietly. He turned his attention to the young woman. "He'll know what to do."

Dipping a curtsy to the duke's nod, Isabella murmured, "How do you do, Your Grace?"

What the hell? Octavius was about to say before he realized he had to keep his head about him. He was a duke now, even if he had only been one for a couple of years. It wouldn't be seemly to go about cursing in front of a gently bred young woman. He had barely finished that thought when he wondered why a gently bred woman would be in *The Elegant Courtesan.*

And then he remembered Norwick's missive.

It seems there's been a murder.

"Lady Isabella," he said with a nod, trying with all his might to remember if he had ever met her before. She still looked as if she should be in the schoolroom!

"Tolson," she offered, when she realized he was attempting to sort the rest of her name.

With a surname of Tolson, she might have been related to Maxwell Tolson, Earl of Craythorne. "What's this about?" Octavius asked as he moved closer to where she stood.

'Stood' might be giving her too much credit, he realized when he noticed how she seemed to require the support of the bed in order to remain upright.

He glanced around, deciding they should hold their conversation in the comfort of upholstered chairs. There were two near the fireplace, where a small fire provided heat and a bit more light.

"Come. Sit down before you fall down," he said as he indicated the wing chairs, noting how she seemed to be shivering despite the otherwise warm room.

Isabella quickly moved to one of the chairs, gripping the pull strings of her rather worn reticule between her gloved hands. She seemed to hesitate before sitting down, as if she feared her dirty riding habit would ruin the furniture. Meanwhile, Octavius glanced over at David, hoping the earl would provide a bit of context.

"I'll be in my office," David said before taking a step back and closing the door behind him.

Rather surprised at the earl's sudden departure—there was no lady's maid nor an older woman to act as a chaperone—Octavius once again turned his attention to the young woman. Although her riding habit was obviously of good quality—the cut and fabric suggested she was from a family with money—it now reeked of horse, and what he had first thought was discolored fabric was instead a good deal of nearly-dried mud splatters. What little he could see of her riding boots suggested they had suffered the same fate.

By continuing to stand, he realized the poor girl was probably as frightened of him as she seemed to be of whatever had her seeking refuge at the brothel. Octavius quickly took the other chair. Stunned by its comfortable upholstery, he thought to just sit a moment and think of what he should ask first.

Certainly something about why an aristocrat's daughter would come to a brothel. And he was about to ask just that when he discovered he didn't have to say a thing.

"I watched as my father killed my mother," Isabella said suddenly, as if she could read his thoughts.

Octavius blinked and nearly opened his mouth in shock. "When?" was all he could think to ask just then. Not 'who?' or 'how?' or 'where?' Any of those queries were probably the more logical questions with which to start such an inquiry.

Isabella glanced about the bedchamber, as if she were in search of something. "What time is it?" she countered. "Is it still … Saturday? Still morning?"

Rather alarmed at her response, Octavius pulled his chronometer from his waistcoat pocket. "It's nearly ten-thirty in the morning. And, yes, it is still Saturday," he replied carefully.

"Then, just yesterday. About four … four-thirty in the afternoon," Isabella said as her body rocked a bit in the chair.

The duke frowned, wondering too many things all at once. "Who is your father?" he asked before he shook his head. *Tolson*, she had said.

"The Earl of Craythorne," she whispered, barely able to get the words out.

Octavius did his best not to hiss. Craythorne had married one of the Brotherton females. Isabella's mother was probably a sister or aunt to Norwick's future wife, Lady Clarinda.

I suppose that explains why she's come to Norwick, Octavius figured. "Tell me everything. From the beginning," he ordered.

Isabella stopped rocking, well aware of the duke's sudden impatience. "My mother is … *was* Lady Arabella. Lady Craythorne," she added with too much emphasis on the 'was'.

Jesus! *The Duke of Craythorne killed his wife?*

Octavius inhaled sharply, but realized his expression must have startled the poor girl. "Go on," he murmured as he considered the character in her tale.

Arabella Brotherton.

That would be the sister of Albert Brotherton, Earl of Heath, he realized. Before he could think more on the victim's relatives, he realized he needed to concentrate on Isabella's story. For the first time that day, his inner thoughts weren't of his own tragic life, but of hers.

"I was about to go for a ride, but I realized I had forgotten my gloves, so I returned to Craythorne Castle intending to go to my bedchamber," Isabella explained. She gestured at her habit, wincing at the splatter patterns of dried dirt. "The stableboy took my horse, and I went into the house through the back door nearest the stables. I heard my father's voice—he was ... yelling. Shouting. Quite loudly. My only thought—two thoughts, actually," she quickly amended, "Were 'what had him so angry?' and 'where were the servants?' There were none about the halls. It's as if they had all taken a holiday or... or fled the house. I followed the sound of my father's voice until I found him in his bedchamber, his hands …" She stopped, her eyes suddenly closing as tears escaped.

"His hands?" Octavius prodded, rather enthralled by the young woman's tale.

"They were around my mother's neck, and he was yelling. Something about her disobedience. Her strong will," she whispered. Isabella's body once again rocked in the chair. "Her eyes were … white, her lips were blue. She was on the floor, and he knelt over her as if he was proud of what he had done," she managed to get out before a sob interrupted her words. "He has always had a temper," she whispered, her head shaking from side to side. "But I truly believed he felt affection for her."

Having heard the evidence of the Duke of Craythorne's temper whilst in sessions of Parliament, Octavius knew he could believe the girl's claim. "Go on," he said quietly, suddenly wondering as to the timeline of the incident.

Yesterday. Four o'clock in the afternoon.

Why had it taken so long for her to report the murder?

"I suppose he must have heard me," Isabella said in a quiet voice. "I must have made some sort of sound, for he suddenly looked up and saw me. The bedchamber door was open, you see, despite the fact that he was wearing his dressing gown." She didn't mention that her mother wore only her corset and stockings. "I was sure I would be next," she claimed in a hoarse whisper. She lifted her eyes to find the duke staring at her. "I ran back downstairs. I grabbed my reticule off a peg where I had left it the day before. I knew I would need money, I suppose... my gloves…" The images were replaying themselves in her mind's eye, now far more clearly than they had seemed the afternoon before, as if she knew she would need to tell of them to someone. "My horse was still saddled, of course. I didn't even need the mounting block. I simply ran and jumped up onto him, and we were off before my father had made it out of the house."

The duke regarded the young woman for a moment before allowing a nod. "And you rode to … to where?" he asked gently, his attention moving to her hands. Long fingers, ending in perfect oval fingernails, clutched her riding gloves and reticule as they rested in her lap. Both hands seemed to vibrate, though.

They shook as they rested on her thighs.

She was either freezing, or she was terrorized. Before he quite knew what he was doing, Octavius reached out and took the hand nearest him. Rather relieved she didn't wince or otherwise pull her hand from his, he regarded her with an arched eyebrow.

Where had she been before she made it to *The Elegant Courtesan?*

Isabella blinked. "I rode to... to here," she said with a wave of her other hand.

Octavius was about to ask why it had taken so long when it dawned on him that he didn't know where the murder took place. "From where did you ride?" he wondered.

"Craythorne Castle, of course," she replied simply.

The duke leaned forward, a look of disbelief settling on his features. Craythorne Castle was somewhere near Basingstoke! "That's … that's over forty... almost fifty miles away," he countered with a shake of his head.

"I know," Isabella replied with a nod. "My poor horse ..." Her tears began anew. "I think I may have ... he may have almost died. But he got me all the way here, and then he nearly collapsed when the stableboy came for him."

Shaking his head, Octavius was about to ask what kind of horse could have survived such an ordeal when he remembered that Craythorne was rather proud of his stables. The duke raced horses. Bred for endurance, there were several Arabians and probably a Thoroughbred or two that could have made such a trip. Why, Poseidon could make the fifty-mile trip to his country estate, Huntinghurst, in five hours.

"Hancock was a race horse, you see, bred for the steeple chases," Isabella offered, a sob interrupting her words. "But he's well past his prime."

Octavius continued to frown. Could the young woman read his mind?

He gave his head a quick shake. Could she really have

made it nearly fifty miles? In ... he considered how much time had passed since she had left Craythorne Castle. *Fifteen hours?*

Yes, of course it was possible. But in the dark?

Octavius decided there were far more important things to consider, however.

Such as Craythorne.

"Did he follow you? Your father, I mean?"

Isabella gave a look of fright. "I … I don't know. I couldn't hear anything after I rode away."

"Did you … hide?"

The young woman seemed surprised by the question. "Of course. Somewhat. We followed the path through the trees until it was too dark to see, and then we managed to …"

"We?" the duke repeated.

"The horse and I," Isabella clarified. "Hancock is very good in rough terrain, but we had to get onto the main road at Hook so I could see by the light of the moon."

Octavius blinked and shook his head. "It's a wonder you weren't set upon by a … a highwayman." He could think of other hazards, like wild animals, or the weather, or holes in the road in which a horse might trip and end up lame, but no need to make it sound any worse than it already had to have been for the poor girl.

"We were quick to ride off to the side of the road if anyone was coming our way," she countered defensively, as if she had realized he would grill her about every aspect of her story.

Rather impressed by the courage the young woman had shown in getting away from her father, Octavius realized there were still more questions that needed answering.

"Why come here?" he asked then. *Christ!* She had ridden straight to a brothel!

Isabella stared at the duke for a long time before tears again dripped from her cheeks. "Mother always said that should anything happen, I was to find David Fitzwilliam." She reached into her pocket and pulled out a white pasteboard calling card. The printing faded and the edges quite dog-eared, the card clearly showed the words, "David Fitzwilliam," in bold, black lettering along with some other information. She held it out in his direction. "She gave this to me several years ago."

Octavius furrowed his brows before remembering Norwick—or was it his twin brother, Daniel?—was betrothed to Lady Craythorne's relative, Clarinda Anne Brotherton. "Lord Norwick?" he repeated, just to be sure he understood.

"Yes, I suppose. When I reached the outskirts of London this morning, I asked at a coaching inn and was given instructions that got me here." She paused a moment. "Just … what is this place?" she wondered. "Is this a hotel, perhaps?"

Rolling his eyes, the duke could only imagine the misplaced humor the person at the coaching inn must have felt at giving the young woman instructions on how to get to a high-end brothel. If he ever learned the identity of the party responsible, he had half a mind to have them arrested and thrown into Newgate for their poor decision. "My lady, you are at *The Elegant Courtesan*, a rather upscale brothel, but a brothel none-the-less," Octavius explained with an arched brow.

Isabella blinked before allowing a nod. "Then, I am in the right place, at least."

It was the duke's turn to blink. "What did you say?"

The earl's daughter allowed a shrug. "My mother said Lord Norwick owned an establishment for courtesans. What better place to hide a gently-bred woman than a brothel?" she asked rhetorically. "She said he could provide protection for a time. He would do so because he is betrothed to marry my cousin, Lady Clarinda, you see."

Octavius wasn't about to argue the merits of seeking out a brothel for protection, especially since Lady Craythorne's instructions certainly proved their worth in this case. But what to do about the current situation suddenly had

Octavius displaying a look of concern. "Well, now the question seems to be what we're to do with you. You obviously cannot go home," he murmured. Anyone else would have packed her into a carriage and taken her back to Craythorne Castle. Her father was her protector, after all. But if Craythorne had truly killed his wife and thought Isabella had paid witness to the murder, then she could not go back there.

"He'll kill me," Isabella whispered in agreement. "I was the only witness to my mother's murder," she added as one of her ungloved hands moved to her mouth. Her riding gloves remained squeezed in the grip of the other hand, their kid leather fingers arcing out at odd angles that gave the appearance of a broken hand. Her body once again began to rock in the chair as her quiet sobs filled the room.

Octavius regarded the earl's daughter for a long time. *Do I believe her?*

He chided himself for even questioning the validity of her story. The girl was frightened. She looked as if she'd gone far too long without sleep. Her riding habit was a mess. Indeed, she looked as if she had been to hell and back.

Yet, despite her disheveled appearance, Octavius found her rather fetching. He closed his eyes a moment and attempted to block the inappropriate image he had just then imagined of her in a satin dinner gown with her hair piled high atop her head. Of her in his bed, her hair loose and splayed out on the pillows. Of her beneath him, naked, her head thrown back...

Octavius blinked. *Good God!* He hadn't given a single thought to bedding another woman since the death of his wife, and now he was imagining bedding a young lady! A frightened, bedraggled young lady.

She's probably ten years younger than me, for God's sake!

He gave his head a quick shake and returned his attention to the matter at hand, deciding two things.

Lady Isabella could not be returned to her father. Even if the man hadn't killed her mother, Isabella believed he had and would forever be fearful of him.

If Craythorne had indeed killed the Countess of Craythorne, then he would have no doubt killed his daughter if he thought there was any chance she would share her story with anyone. That or sequester her in a faraway place so that no one would either hear her tale or believe it if they did.

And having come to a brothel meant she was probably ruined as far as the *ton* was concerned. Although, when he considered how few people were about the establishment this morning, Lady Isabella might escape notice if they could sneak her out of the place.

"Are you betrothed to anyone?" he asked then, thinking he should send word to the gentleman. Perhaps a quick wedding could be arranged so that she would have protection from her father, although he realized too late she might not be of legal age to marry.

If she wasn't yet one-and-twenty, she required the permission of her parents. Permission that would not be provided given the circumstances. Octavius briefly wondered if Prinny might grant an exemption when he noticed the young woman's look of surprise.

Isabella's eyebrows arched up. "I haven't even had my come-out," she replied with a shake of her head.

This bit of news had the duke rather surprised. "How old are you?"

"I'll be nineteen in a week, Your Grace," she answered, her head lifting a bit with the claim.

Jesus! He had thought her at least two-and-twenty! A night spent riding and no sleep had aged her a good deal.

"What about any brothers... or sisters?"

Isabella's eyes widened. "John is away at school. At Eton. I have no other siblings."

Octavius gave the comment some thought, but realized the brother would be far too young to provide protection. Christ, he wouldn't yet know what had happened to his mother. "I'll see to it you can stay here for a day or two. You'll need to stay hidden, though, or you'll risk ruin. Or discovery," he added, realizing they had to keep her identity and location a secret so her father wouldn't discover her whereabouts.

On the other hand, they had to somehow determine if her claim was true.

Isabella nodded. "I sorted as much," she murmured, her head angling to one side. "I have never felt so spent in my entire life, Your Grace."

"You must be thirsty. You must be starving."

Lifting her head, Isabella shook it. "I fed and watered my horse in Egham while I helped myself to water from a pump," she whispered, remembering the stop because it had been the one refuge where she was completely hidden from the road, where she had felt safest despite the bright moon lighting the countryside with its ethereal glow. "But I do not think I could keep anything down right now," she added in a whisper.

Octavius nodded his understanding. "Did anyone see you? Besides whomever gave you directions at the coaching inn?"

Isabella regarded the duke for a moment, quite sure she had never met the man before. Blond hair, high cheekbones, a slight cleft in his chin—he looked every bit the aristocrat he was. His blue eyes appeared almost haunted, though, as if they belonged to a man far older than the one who sat gazing at her. Seeing her. Paying witness to her very real fright and exhaustion with a great deal of patience. A great deal of sympathy. "I don't think so. It was the middle of the night, and I was very quiet."

Well, she is resourceful, Octavius had to admit. He had never before heard of a single young lady who had done anything like she had done and been able to speak of it the following morning. But then, how many young ladies claimed to pay witness to their mothers being killed by their fathers and then riding fifty miles as if their lives depended on it? "You're exhausted, though," he countered with an arched brow. At her nod of acknowledgement, the duke stood up but indicated with a hand that she was to remain seated. “I’ll make the arrangements for you stay with Norwick. And …” He paused, not sure what else he could do just then.

If a missive was sent to Craythorne Castle asking about the well-being of the Countess of Craythorne, the earl would know his daughter was in London. Octavius decided he couldn’t risk the man discovering Lady Isabella’s whereabouts. Someone else would have to make the query, or pretend to pay a call on the countess.

Or perhaps confirmation of the countess’ death would reach others and make its way to London. Gossip usually traveled faster than race horses.

“I’ll have a modiste sent here with some clothes, and …” He glanced down at her half-boots. “Slippers,” he added.

“I have some money,” she said suddenly, lifting her reticule from her lap. “I apologize, Your Grace. I must look a sight,” she added, her brows furrowing.

Indeed, you do, he thought with a sigh, his body reacting in a way it hadn’t done for a very long time.

What the hell?

The poor girl had been to hell and back, and here his cock was responding as if she were one of the harlots in the employ of *The Elegant Courtesan!* He would no doubt end up in hell, but he expected he was already halfway there. Life without his wife had hardly seemed worth living, and here he was having lustful thoughts of what he might do with Craythorne’s daughter. Lustful and yet respectful, as well. He couldn’t imagine any of the daughters of the *ton* in London surviving such an ordeal, nor would any have the courage to do what she had done.

“I think I can afford whatever the modiste charges,” Octavius said gently, knowing full well it was entirely inappropriate for him to be buying clothes for the earl’s daughter. Hell, it was entirely inappropriate for her to be in a brothel! “I’ll stop by tonight to check on you,” he added before giving her a bow and taking his leave of the room.

He didn’t get far, though, as he used the door to the

bedchamber for support once it was closed. Leaning against the solid wood, Octavius took several breaths to clear his head. Decisions had to be made. An investigation had to be ordered. Arrangements for accommodation. A modiste.

Questions had to be answered as well. Isabella said she sought out David Fitzwilliam because she was instructed to do so by her mother. She had the man's calling card in her possession. True, her older cousin was due to marry the earl, but something else bothered him just then.

He hurried off to find Norwick to make his questions known.

Chapter 6

POST-PROPOSAL EUPHORIA

Meanwhile, in Mayfair

Daniel Fitzwilliam dismounted his gelding and regarded the front of Norwick House with a bit of jealousy. The fashionable mansion in Park Lane featured the *de rigueur* Palladian style architecture that had become so popular at the turn of the century. Grecian columns acted as sentries on either side of a large door and held up a portico above the landing at the top of the deep, shallow steps. A pair of topiary trees flanked the columns. Rows of arched windows were lined out on either side of the front of the house, various plantings at their base trimmed so as not to hinder the view from inside.

The effect was stately and elegant, a London-based home suitable for an earl and his wife in which to live and entertain. A home suitable for Daniel's older brother, the tenth Earl of Norwick. A mansion paid for from the funds the man had made from owning a high-end brothel. And a gaming hell, even if most knew it simply as a men's club.

Daniel was about to lift the odd knocker, a brass mermaid, but a butler opened the door and gave a start. "My lord, I didn't expect you back so soon," the butler said as he stepped aside.

"Porter," Daniel acknowledged with a nod. "It's me, Daniel, in search of my rake of a brother." He suddenly frowned, realizing what the butler had said. "Do you know where he went off to?" he asked, rather disappointed. He had rehearsed what he was going to say to David during the entire trip from Kensington Gardens. He was going to announce he was engaged to be married, and he was going to gloat about it. He still intended to, of course, but now he wouldn't be able to do it until his brother returned.

"A footman arrived rather early this morning. Something at *The Elegant Courtesan* required his immediate attention. He said he thought he would be gone the entire morning," the servant explained.

Frowning, Daniel wondered if something had happened to one of the employees. Despite the nature of the business, the brothel only admitted patrons who were rich, had been vetted, and who didn't cause trouble for the courtesans. "No hint as to what might have happened?" he pressed. He kept the books for the brothel and knew all the young women who worked there, if for no other reason than he was the one who gave them their pay every month.

His eyes darting to the side, the butler appeared rather sheepish when he said, "Apparently, an unexpected visitor arrived on the doorstep insisting she be allowed to see Lord Norwick. I only heard the words, 'bedraggled' and 'terrified' and something about a half-dead horse."

Knitting his brows, Daniel had half a mind to head to the brothel and discover the identity of the visitor for himself. But he thought better of it when he remembered this was a day he should be celebrating. He was betrothed to marry the love of his life. He would simply find his brother later and gloat about his engagement then. "I'll take my leave. Let him know I stopped in. I have happy news to share," he said as he made his way back through the vestibule.

Chapter 7

A CONFESSION EXPLAINS MUCH

A few minutes later Octavius found David Fitzwilliam in a salon at the end of the hall, staring at the dying flames in the room's fireplace. An empty tumbler dangled from the fingers of his right hand.

"Have you been awake all night?" the duke asked as he moved to the sideboard and helped himself to a whisky. He brought the crystal decanter along with his glass to place it on the side table next to David's chair.

The earl tore his gaze from the fire and turned it on the duke. His reddened eyes were either testaments to a night of too much drink, or the man had been crying. "Of course not. I might own this place, but I certainly don't spend my nights here," David replied, his voice sounding rather cross.

Octavius settled himself into the overstuffed wing chair, rather surprised at how comfortable it felt. He had half a mind to ask who had made the furnishings and then order new ones for his townhouse. "Seems we have a problem," he murmured.

"More like three or four," David countered in a whisper. The duke didn't yet know about the series of dominoes that were about to start tipping over in David's life.

First, there was Lady Clarinda. His identical twin brother, Daniel, had done him the favor of spending time with the woman to whom he had been betrothed since well before she was out of the schoolroom. Now that Daniel seemed on the verge of proposing marriage—if he hadn't already done so—David realized he needed to make it clear *he* would be marrying Clarinda. David supposed the contract for the arranged marriage between his father and Clarinda's father, the Earl of Heath, wouldn't hold up under current law, but if what Lady Isabella claimed was true—that Arabella Brotherton Tolson, Countess of Craythorne and aunt to Clarinda, was indeed dead—then he had every intention of marrying Clarinda as soon as possible—even if he had to steal her from his brother.

He was three-and-thirty, and he needed an heir.

Then there were his businesses.

The Elegant Courtesan and his gaming hell would have to be sold. Clarinda's father, the Earl of Heath, had seen to that proviso when he set up the marriage contract, and Clarinda had reminded him of the agreement on the occasion of their ride in Hyde Park during the fashionable hour just the week before. It was unseemly for an earl to own such businesses despite the monies they generated. At least he'd had them long enough to ensure his financial stability and that of the earldom's, probably for the rest of his life. That Clarinda knew anything about *The Elegant Courtesan* had David wondering who had told her. Certainly not her father.

The final domino was the one that had arrived on the doorstep of *The Elegant Courtesan* earlier that morning. She hadn't even been in the game until that moment. He didn't want Lady Isabella suffering anymore than she already had, though, and wondered what he might do to secure protection for her.

"Do you believe her?" David asked, his voice sounding weary in the quiet salon.

The Duke of Huntington nodded. "I believe she believes what she saw," he answered carefully. "She's frightened to death of her father. Can't say I blame her. Even if he didn't strangle his countess, Craythorne isn't exactly known for his even temper."

The earl shot him an angry glance. "Had I been there, I would have killed the bastard," he whispered hoarsely. He still might, if what the girl claimed was true.

Octavius gave a start at the vehemence he heard in David's vow. "Sounds as if you know more than I do," he prompted. When the Earl of Norwick didn't provide a reply right away, Octavius took a drink from his glass and closed his eyes. He tried to remember the last time he had drunk whisky before noon. It would have been during the year after Jane's death. *Probably the entire year*, he thought with a wince. "Pray tell, what do you know?"

David allowed a sigh. "She needs a protector. A place to stay. Clothes. A life away from Craythorne," he responded, as if he'd been writing the list in his head for some time. "Eventually, she'll need a husband." This last was said with a hint of despair, as if he couldn't stomach the thought of Lady Isabella with a man.

"Agreed," Octavius replied with a nod, rather impressed at the earl's recitation. He finished off his glass of whisky. "She said her mother told her to find you should anything happen. She has your calling card, Norwick. Why do you suppose Lady Craythorne would give her that instruction?"

David shook his head. "I suppose because I'm to marry Isabella's cousin," he murmured, his voice far too calm. *Jesus!* He hadn't even considered that particular connection until just then. He had struggled in vain not to think of the woman who had apparently been killed the day before. Once he gave into his memories, the pain would become real, as would the anger.

The tears had already fallen.

What was it about the Brotherton women that had him acting like a lovesick puppy?

He blinked suddenly. Arabella's family would soon figure out she had died. Someone would inform them, whether it be Craythorne, or the coroner in Basingstoke, or someone else. Then Clarinda would learn of her aunt's death, as well, and then tell him the circumstances. If she didn't offer the information of her own accord, he could always ask. Claim he heard it from someone at Parliament. He wondered how different the story would be from Craythorne compared to how it had been relayed by Isabella.

The girl had no reason to lie. No reason to falsely implicate Craythorne in her mother's death.

Did she?

The thought of how bedraggled she appeared that morning was his answer, of course. Of how bone-tired and frightened she sounded as she explained what had happened.

She had no reason to lie.

Octavius allowed David his brief woolgathering before he shook his head. "Those of us who have paid witness to Lady Clarinda's courtship *and* who can tell the difference between you and your brother know that *you* aren't the one courting Lady Clarinda," he accused suddenly. When David's attention finally turned on him, he angled his head. "I've seen your brother, Daniel, with her in Kensington Gardens. Several times. Since you're not the one courting her, perhaps you would be amenable to marrying Lady Isabella instead of Lady Clarinda." The words were out of his mouth before he considered the age difference between David Fitzwilliam and the young lady. The earl *was* a bit older than Octavius. Mid-thirties, perhaps? But marriages with age differences far larger weren't so uncommon. Sometimes they were even love matches.

But why did the thought of Norwick marrying Lady Isabella make him wince just then? Surely it wasn't just because the earl owned a brothel and a gaming hell.

"*I* will be the one marrying Lady Clarinda," David stated, his voice rather stern. "Daniel knows Clare and I have been betrothed since... well, since our fathers made the arrangements a long time ago."

The duke winced, wondering why David would allow his

brother to court the woman who was to be his wife. Couldn't Lady Clarinda tell the difference between the twin brothers? Perhaps not, if she was only allowed a few minutes of time in the company of a Fitzwilliam brother. Octavius was about to ask but decided not to anger David anymore than he already was.

Angered and hurting.

"Still, arranged marriages mean nothing these days. So ... why don't you marry Isabella? She's young, yes, but you're not getting any younger, and you need an heir ..."

"As do you."

Octavius nearly hissed at the simple words. The wounds of having lost a loving wife and a babe the year before were still too raw. Too fresh. It would be a long time before the widower would consider marriage again. Even then, he had made a promise to Jane to never love another. It wouldn't be fair to Jane. To his memories of her. "There must be a reason Lady Craythorne would send her daughter to find you," he tried again. "Perhaps she thought you two should wed—"

"I cannot wed Isabella."

The clipped words had Octavius straightening in his chair as David suddenly stood up from his and moved to stand before the fireplace. One of his hands gripped the mantle, as if he needed its support to remain upright.

Octavius stood up and joined him, wondering at the man's reaction to his simple suggestion. He raised himself up on the balls of his feet, attempting to match David's height. "What do you mean, you *cannot?*"

David's eyes darted to the left and finally returned to regard the duke. "She's my daughter."

The duke settled back onto his heels, his body giving a start as if the earl had slapped him across the face. "*What?*" he managed to get out, his brows furrowing in confusion.

The earl sighed and moved to retake his chair near the fireplace. "Isabella doesn't know, of course. That is, unless Arabella told her, and I rather doubt she would have said anything to anybody. Especially not to Craythorne."

Octavius stood before David another moment before slowly settling himself into the other chair. "What the hell? When ... how ...?"

"Well, the usual way, of course," David answered with a shake of his head, his manner rather gruff. "Arabella and I had an *affaire* when I was at university. She wasn't yet married to Craythorne, of course, but ... she was betrothed to him." The last came out as a whisper, almost as if he hesitated to admit anything more than he was forced to just then. He paused a moment. "I suppose you could say I am rather attracted to the Brotherton women," he added with an arched eyebrow, daring the duke to make mention of it.

Octavius shook his head, still rather stunned by the news. There had never been a hint of gossip about David and Arabella, which meant the two had kept their *affaire* a secret from everyone.

"Heath doesn't know?" Octavius ventured, referring to Clarinda's father, the Earl of Heath. His older brother, the prior earl, had been Arabella's father.

"God, no. Neither did his brother," David replied with a shake of his head. "Truth be told... you're the only other one besides me who knows," he murmured, his brows furrowing in sorrow.

Octavius considered the information, rather impressed the earl had taken him into his confidence, although given the circumstances, he had been forced to do so.

"So, we're still in a quandary," Octavius said in a low voice.

Lady Isabella needed protection, protection best supplied by a husband. Without her parents' consent, though, she couldn't legally wed until she was one-and-twenty.

Well, she could, but banns would have to be read in her parish as well as the parish of her future husband. Craythorne would surely learn of the impending nuptials and protest. Then he would demand to know where his daughter was staying.

The duke briefly wondered if he could find a bishop

willing to perform the ceremony. If a special license were purchased, he would have to swear he had her father's permission, though, since Isabella wasn't yet of age. Octavius didn't think he could do such a thing.

Worried that word might get back to Craythorne had him rethinking the strategy. The earl would probably react in a violent manner. Pistols at dawn might be the least of the man's vengeance.

"What about Heath? He's her grandfather. Certainly he can provide protection..."

"Stockton House will be the first place Craythorne will look for her," David countered, referring to the Earl of Heath's mansion in London.

Realizing the earl was right, the duke gave a shake of his head. "Well. This is a quandary. Who else do we know who needs a wife and can hide her until she's old enough to marry?" Octavius asked, his question almost rhetorical.

The earl didn't pause a single moment before saying, "You."

The duke turned to stare at David, his brows furrowed. "Me?"

David nodded. "As her real father, I cannot think of a more advantageous marriage for her," he murmured. "You can send her to your country estate in Sussex. She loves horses. You can provide protection. You have the resources. You need an *heir*," he added, one eyebrow arching up. "She's not a milkwater miss, Hunt. She's... she's brave and resourceful, and I'm quite sure she will be much easier on the eyes once she's out of the bath she's probably taking this very moment."

Octavius couldn't help the thought of a naked Isabella that formed in his mind's eye just then. She was young, yes, but in a couple of years—two years—she would be one-and-twenty. More beautiful. More mature. Old enough to marry without her parents' permission. Old enough to be a wife. Old enough...

What the hell am I thinking? he chided himself. *I certainly cannot marry the chit, nor anyone else for that matter.* It wouldn't be fair to any woman given the grief he still felt over the death of his wife and son. Besides, he certainly couldn't marry someone who wanted anything more than a marriage of convenience. He had made that promise to Jane. A promise never to love another. The moment before the light behind her eyes dimmed and her body went slack. The moment before their son joined her in death.

I still need an heir.

But can I afford to wait another two years to marry? he wondered with annoyance.

Two years?

No. Maybe. Yes.

He wouldn't marry Isabella, though. But he could at least provide protection and a place for her to live. A place to hide her away until they could learn more about what had happened to her mother. Until she was old enough to marry.

She will simply be my ward, Octavius decided. Who else could David trust to provide protection for her? Especially given the current circumstances?

She's almost nineteen, he reminded himself. Neither he, nor anyone else, for that matter, would be able to take her as his wife anytime soon. When someone did, Craythorne would discover her whereabouts. She was still the man's daughter as far as everyone else knew. She was Craythorne's to do as he pleased, and at the moment, he was either intending to end her life so that she couldn't spread word of her mother's murder, or he was experiencing a good deal of regret at what had happened and was hoping to beg for Isabella's forgiveness.

All the same, Octavius didn't care one whit about Craythorne or what he might want. When the chit reached one-and-twenty, she would be married, he decided. Until then, he had an estate in the country where she could hide.

A mostly-staffed estate with horses.

He regarded the Earl of Norwick for a long moment before finally giving the man a nod. "With your permission, she'll be my ward. She can live at Huntinghurst until she's either reached her majority or until Craythorne dies."

David furrowed a brow before he finally nodded in return. "Agreed." He paused a moment. "I have a cousin. In Boxgrove. She sees to one of my entailed properties."

The duke furrowed a brow. "Fair Downs?" he questioned.

"Indeed. My uncle used to keep it up on my father's behalf, and now his daughter does so on my behalf." At the duke's quizzical expression, he added, "As a châtelaine of sorts. I'll see to it she befriends Isabella."

Crossing his arms, as if he were about to argue, Octavius regarded the earl before finally saying, "Are you sure that's a good idea? I thought we were supposed to be keeping her a secret."

David gave a shrug. "Connie will. She's good at keeping secrets," he murmured, not about to add that she had kept his involvement in the death of a horse thief a secret since the night of her come-out. "And she's sees to the horses at Fair Downs."

Octavius straightened. "Race horses?" he countered, suddenly interested in learning more.

"One was. Two, really. None that I know of now, though," David replied.

Giving his head a quick shake, Octavius asked, "How is it you don't know your own stables?"

Taken aback, David replied, "Because the horses at Fair Downs are not mine. They are Connie's," he explained. "I gave them to her upon the death of my uncle, Edward. They were his, anyway, so I made sure they were part of her inheritance."

He was suddenly reminded he needed to see to refilling the coffers for Fair Downs. Constance Fitzwilliam had been good about keeping up the property with a small staff, but she did so on very little in the way of funds. She believed the money she found hidden in nooks and crannies and beneath loose floor boards was money her mother had hidden before her death years ago. Money she said her mother had squirreled away in an effort to keep it from her husband, Edward.

Addicted to gambling, especially when it came to horses, Edward Fitzwilliam had lost everything his race horse had won and more. But David had seen to it that more money was stashed away in less likely hiding places, like the bottom of the flour container and in the cushions of the parlor chairs. Behind books and at the bottom of vases. In the hems of bedchamber drapes and under mattresses.

Now that Isabella would be housed nearby, he would have an excuse to visit Fair Downs.

David suddenly frowned. "And look who's accusing me of not knowing my own stables. When was the last time you had a nag in a horse race?"

Octavius allowed a sigh. It was true he had lost all interest in his hobbies upon the death of his duchess. Upon the death of their newborn son. He figured his interest in his horses would be piqued again in due time, though. Perhaps in a year or so. "I don't have a contender this year," he replied with a shrug. "No three-year-olds, and certainly no six-year-olds."

David gave a snort, not believing the duke's claim. "I admit to having other issues on my mind this year," he replied. Selling his businesses, taking a wife, and seeing to Isabella's well-being were just a few. Once he was married, things would settle down, and he would have leisure time once again.

"How long can Lady Isabella stay here at *The Elegant Courtesan*? Without being discovered by the clientele?" Octavius wondered.

Frowning, David thought of the brothel's servants and who could be trusted. Thought of the bedchamber Isabella was in and if she could go out the back door without being seen. Thought of the girls who would insist on befriending her if they knew she was there. "A few days, I suppose. No more than a week." He didn't add that he would have to close the brothel before he married Clarinda. One of the reasons there was a bedchamber available for Isabella was because the former occupant had married. He didn't want to hire another given the limited time *The Elegant Courtesan* would remain in business.

"Find me when it's imperative that she leave. I'll do what I can in the meantime to make arrangements for her travel. I have to let the butler at Huntinghurst know, of course. And she'll need clothes..."

"I've seen to a modiste," David interrupted. "She'll be here on the morrow."

This bit of information had Octavius wondering if David kept a modiste on retainer for the brothel. "Anything else?"

David nodded. "She'll want her horse with her."

Octavius frowned. "I suppose we can make arrangements to have it brought down once she's settled."

"She won't leave London without Hancock."

Rolling his eyes, Octavius was about to put voice to a curse, but realized he was of a similar mind about Poseidon. Even if he didn't ride the beast at least part of the way down to Huntinghurst, he still saw to it the horse was tethered to his coach. "Fine. We'll bring the horse," he finally agreed.

His hands rubbing the sides of his face, as if he were wiping away tears, David nodded his thanks. "In the meantime, I'll find out what I can from Clare. See if her family has been notified of the death. If I so much as hear Craythorne is anywhere near London, he won't be long for this earth."

Straightening at David's vow, Octavius decided to take his leave of *The Elegant Courtesan*. Given the earl's sour mood, the duke wondered if another murder was imminent.

Chapter 8

TALK OF A NEW LIFE

Later that day

"Huntinghurst?" Lady Isabella repeated, doing her best to control her breathing lest she faint. Although she had eaten a bit of breakfast and napped for several hours in the bedchamber to which she had been taken that morning, her head still felt as if it were filled with cotton. If she didn't hold them clasped together, her hands would tremble. "Where is that?"

David Fitzwilliam regarded his daughter for a moment, a bit of pride filling his chest. Despite the horror of what she had endured just the day before, she was holding up far better than most men would in the same situation. "The Duke of Huntington's country estate. It's not quite as far as Chichester. Down in Sussex," he explained. "You won't know anyone, but then, the fewer that know you're there, the safer you'll be," he added as he leaned forward and rested his elbows on his knees.

Isabella nodded, her long, dark hair falling forward over her shoulders, the ends curling in a haphazard fashion. Given the need for secrecy within the brothel, only a few servants knew of her presence. None of them were lady's maids, though, and so she had only been able to comb out her hair after that morning's bath. An ill-fitting gown had been loaned to her. The owner could obviously boast of a bust more generous than Isabella's, for the bodice was far too large. "Has there been word yet from Craythorne Castle? Word of my mother's death, my lord?" she wondered.

Shaking his head, the earl said, "Not yet. It's a bit soon, though. It's not as if anyone else would make the trip to London like you did," he murmured. "I assure you, there will be inquiries made to the coroner and to anyone else who handles the body." Even if it looked as if Arabella's death was by strangulation, it was doubtful the Earl of Craythorne would be brought up on charges. As an aristocrat, he was nearly beyond the reach of the law.

"I understand," Isabella replied with a nod. Earlier that day, any mention of her mother would have tears collecting in the corners of her eyes, but at the moment, she felt drained. "My brother? Has word been sent to him?"

David winced, not sure what to admit. "He will be notified when word of your mother's death reaches others in London," he hedged, not about to tell her they had decided not to inform him directly. Should word come from him or from the duke, Craythorne would sort very quickly where his daughter had gone.

"I have a bit of money. I need clothes. Would it be...?"

"A modiste has been arranged to visit tomorrow morning at ten o'clock," David interrupted. "She probably won't have time to make anything for you, of course, but she'll bring some ready-mades for you to try. And some underclothes, and a night rail and such," he added, wondering why he felt a flush suddenly color his throat. He saw women in various states of undress all the time. He had seen nearly every inch of every courtesan in the building at least once. Why speaking of a woman's underclothes would have him blushing just then, he didn't know.

She's my daughter, he reminded himself. *Even if she doesn't yet know it.*

"You needn't be concerned with the cost," he stated

suddenly. When her brows furrowed in question, the earl gave a shrug. "*The Elegant Courtesan* will see to the bill."

Her eyes darting to one side, Isabella seemed about to ask something else. When she finally did, her voice was nearly a whisper. "Do you really own this establishment, my lord?"

The Earl of Norwick nodded. "Until such time as I am to marry your cousin, Clarinda, and then I shall either sell it or close it," he replied. "I agreed to those terms as part of the betrothal."

"So... in a couple of months?" she clarified. "I suppose that's not so very soon. It's not as if Clare will be expected to wear mourning clothes for her aunt's death."

Giving a start, David realized Isabella knew more than he had thought about his impending wedding.

Probably more than he knew.

"I wasn't aware a date had been set," he hedged. At Isabella's widened eyes, he straightened in his chair. "Pray, tell me what you know from your cousin."

Isabella blinked before giving him a frown. "Clare sent word that you two were to marry in June," she explained, wondering why her future cousin-by-marriage was staring at her as if he was about to faint. "Which was a bit of a surprise considering Parliament will still be in session."

I can imagine, David didn't reply, realizing Daniel had suggested the month knowing that particular detail. He would have to either miss a month of Parliament or delay the wedding trip until late July. "The roses will be especially fine then," he murmured, not sure what else he could say about the choice of wedding date.

"Clare wondered if you owned a hothouse in addition to your other business concerns, seeing as how she keeps receiving roses."

David closed his eyes, realizing his twin brother, Daniel, had been courting Clarinda far more seriously than he had first thought. If he wasn't careful, Daniel would be saying his 'I will's', as well, and Clarinda would be lost to him.

He wasn't about to lose another Brotherton girl to another man, even if that other man was his brother.

"I do not," he said in answer to the mention of owning a hothouse.

The first hint of a grin he had ever seen on Isabella suddenly appeared, a grin that finally had her looking her age. And looking quite fetching. Any man would be lucky to have her features lighting up the breakfast parlor in the morning. "What is it?" he asked as he allowed one of his own.

"She likes your kisses, too. She wrote that they were 'delectable'," Isabella said in a hoarse whisper, her grin widening at the same time a blush colored her face.

The hint of a grin on David's face disappeared in an instant. He had never kissed Clarinda, which could only mean one thing.

Daniel had.

And apparently more than one time.

"She wrote that?" he asked in disbelief.

Isabella suddenly straightened in her chair. "She did. I thought... I apologize. I suppose I shouldn't speak of such things. I just thought.. seeing as how you'll be marrying my cousin..." She stopped and allowed a sigh, the humor gone from her face as quickly as it had appeared.

"Perhaps I should see to bestowing some more of them on her before our wedding," the earl commented with an arched brow, attempting to lift the mood to what it had been just a moment ago. "Thank you for letting me know."

A bit confused, Isabella allowed a nod. "When do you suppose I'll be leaving for Huntinghurst?"

Realizing the moment of humor was gone for good, David sighed. "No more than a week from now."

"May I take my horse, my lord?"

Bristling at her continued use of 'my lord', he nearly admonished her before he remembered he hadn't told her she needn't address him as such. "Indeed. Huntington has agreed to arrange a place for him in his stables. The stableboy here says Hancock has a slight limp, but otherwise he seems to be recovering. An amazing feat for a horse of his age. He must have a good deal of Arabian in him."

"Oh, Hancock does," Isabella said with a nod. "He made an excellent steeple chaser one year, but now Father..." She paused and blinked. "*Craythorne* is only interested in the shorter races."

David couldn't help but hear the derision in her voice, especially when she said the name 'Craythorne'. But then, she believed the man had killed her mother. Had killed her mother and was going to get away with having done so given his status as an aristocrat.

Not if I can do anything about it, David thought as he considered when he might make a trip to Basingstoke. First, he had to be sure Isabella was safely hidden away at Huntinghurst. And then he had to be sure Clarinda was going to marry him and not Daniel.

Isabella's comment about steeple chasing suddenly brought him up short. "What do you know of horse racing?"

Isabella's eyes widened, as if she just realized she shouldn't have put voice to her claim about Hancock. "I've attended a few races," she hedged.

"And?" he prompted.

Giving a slight shrug, Isabella wondered how to respond. "I study the lineages of the horses. I try to sort which studs and mares might produce the best racers."

"Indeed," David whispered. He straightened. "I rather imagine you'll appreciate the stables at Huntinghurst. The duke raises his racers there, although he hasn't had a contender in a couple of years." *Ever since his wife died*, he didn't add.

Her face brightening, Isabella looked as if she might not be able to stay seated. "Oh, do you suppose I might be allowed to visit his stables?"

David blinked. Her excitement at hearing there were race horses at Huntinghurst had her disposition changing once again. *Christ, if he doesn't, I'll build another set of stables just for you*, he thought. *And give you a few horses while I'm at it.* "I don't see as how that will be a problem. Besides, Lord Huntington is rarely in residence. He goes there to hunt and sometimes hosts a house party." Although, now that he gave it some more thought, David realized the duke hadn't hosted a house party there since his duchess had died.

"Oh," Isabella responded, as if she wasn't sure how she should react to this bit of information. "But you'll ask him on my behalf?" she pressed.

The earl nodded. "Of course." He dared a glance at the clock on the mantle and gave a start. "I must take my leave of you. I have an appointment in St. James Street." He stood up and gave Isabella a bow, pausing as if he might finally tell her the truth about him. But when she dipped a curtsy and seemed at a bit of a loss, he thought better of it.

She was still reeling from the loss of her mother. How would she react when she learned Craythorne wasn't her father?

Relieved, he could only hope.

As for David, mourning Arabella meant spending the entire night and most of the next week becoming too familiar with the bottoms of several bottles of scotch.

Chapter 9

NEWS OF A DEATH REACHES LONDON

A week later

Clarinda stared at her father for a very long time before she blinked and asked if she might sit down.

"Of course," Albert Brotherton, Earl of Heath, said in a whisper, indicating the chair across from his desk. "I should have told you yesterday, but you were still so happy about Norwick's proposal, I couldn't abide being the bearer of bad news."

Dropping into the chair, Clarinda's eyes brightened with tears as she stared at the earl. "When did she die?"

Heath cleared his throat as an attempt to hide the annoyance he still felt by how long it had taken to be notified of his sister's death. "A bit over a week ago. She slipped and fell. Hit her head on a footboard. Craythorne wrote that she was probably dead before she hit the floor."

"And you believed him?" Clarinda queried, a combination of sorrow and anger giving her the appearance of a woman far older than her two-and-twenty years.

Giving a slight shake of his head, Heath wasn't about to admit he had already dispatched a courier to Basingstoke with instructions to learn what he could of Arabella's death. Craythorne's account had seemed plausible, of course, but given the man's temper and the fact that Arabella hadn't been back to London in an age had Heath suspicious. "I don't yet know what to believe, but I am determined to learn the truth. Especially..." He paused, not sure he should mention the rest of what Craythorne had written about in his letter. From the blotches scattered about the perfectly penned missive, Heath realized the man had probably been crying whilst he wrote the words that described not only the loss of his wife, but of his daughter, as well.

She paid witness to her mother's death, or at least the immediate aftermath, and was overcome with grief. The groom said she rode off on her favorite horse, Hancock, and she has not been seen since anywhere near Basingstoke.

"Especially?" Clarinda prompted as she leaned forward.

Heath sighed. "Lady Isabella is missing. She... saw her dead mother, and she took off on a horse."

"And went where?" his daughter asked, incredulous.

Shaking his head from side to side, the earl finally said, "We've no idea. She was still missing when he penned this," he said as he lifted the pages of the Earl of Craythorne's letter. "By now, she's probably returned to Craythorne Castle," he said with some hope.

Leaning back in her chair as if she had been slapped, Clarinda allowed a cry of sorrow. "He killed her, didn't he? She saw what he had done to Arabella, so he had to kill her to keep her quiet—"

"Clare!" Heath admonished her. "We don't know that," he said, rather surprised Clarinda would seem so sure her uncle-by-marriage was a murderer. Her reaction was in line with his, though. If Parliament wasn't in session, he would make the trip to Basingstoke himself.

"He'll get away with it, too, won't he?" she whispered, her front teeth denting her lower lip as she tilted her head back. She stared at the coffered ceiling, losing her battle to keep the tears from falling in front of her father. She knew he hated it when women cried, but she couldn't help the sorrow she felt just then.

The Earl of Heath dropped his chin to his chest, rather wishing he had held off telling Clarinda about her aunt until after the courier returned from Basingstoke with some kind of official word. It was possible that even if it was murder at the earl's hands, the coroner had been paid to claim it was an accident. "Even if he's not brought up on formal charges, Craythorne will suffer for what he's done. You can be sure of that, Clare."

His daughter nodded, a lacy hanky already held against one cheek. "Should I tell Norwick we have to delay the wedding?" she asked, ready to reschedule her nuptials if necessary. She really should mourn her aunt.

Heath shook his head, already expecting she would offer to reschedule the wedding. He was determined to have her wed, though. Another man had already written claiming he wished to offer for her hand if Norwick didn't marry her 'by the deadline'. He supposed the would-be suitor referred to Clarinda's twenty-second birthday, but how many knew about that provision in the betrothal contract? "No. Arabella would want you to go ahead. You've already been delayed quite enough through no fault of your own," he replied, his annoyance at the Earl of Norwick's late proposal evident in how he said the words.

In fact, since his daughter wasn't wed by the time she turned two-and-twenty, Heath had been about to send a letter to Norwick telling him the terms of the contract were null and void. And then the letter from Craythorne had arrived at the same time his man of business was telling him Norwick had a contract to sell his gaming hell to Frank O'Leary and that an agent was seeing to the sale of the mansion in which *The Elegant Courtesan* conducted business.

Given his daughter's frequent trips to Kensington Gardens and the pink roses that scented the front hall of Stockton House, it seemed Norwick was intent on marrying Clarinda. Now that she was displaying a rather expensive sapphire ring, Heath decided he would allow Norwick to wed his daughter. In fact, he would insist on it.

"I think just a small ceremony, then," Clarinda managed to get out before a sob robbed her of breath.

The earl secretly thrilled at hearing the words. Her dowry would drain one of his accounts as it was. "Whatever you think is best," he agreed with a nod. "Courage, daughter," he added in a solemn voice. "And don't worry too much about Izzy. She's probably already returned to Craythorne Castle."

"Has Cousin John been informed? He's away at school. I shouldn't want him to learn of his mother's death from... from a classmate," she said as her eyes widened. From her father's reaction, Clarinda realized he hadn't given a thought to her youngest cousin.

"I should think Craythorne has already written to him. No need for you to be concerned, especially with your upcoming nuptials," he commented. Before Clarinda could put voice to a protest, he turned in his chair and regarded a piece of correspondence on a silver salver.

Realizing she was being dismissed, Clarinda gave a curtsy and took her leave of her father's study.

She had a wedding to plan.

Chapter 10

AN EARL CLAIMS HE'S GOING TO CLAIM A COUNTESS

A week later

David Alexander George Fitzwilliam regarded the missive he had penned the night before, wondering how the words would sound when Clarinda read them aloud. The letter included condolences on the death of her aunt. A comment as to how long he had known Arabella (but nothing of their *affaire*). Assurances her niece, Isabella, was probably in good health and simply hiding from her father. A mention of looking forward to their wedding day and an offer to delay the nuptials should she wish more time to mourn her aunt.

He didn't include the information that Isabella was his daughter or any word of the girl's true whereabouts. According to his brief visit with Huntington at Brooks's, Isabella was settled into a guest suite at Huntinghurst and thrilled she was allowed access to his stables. Her horse had his own stall and had recovered from whatever injury had him limping the morning the two had arrived at *The Elegant Courtesan*.

What had David suddenly grinning just then was the mention by the duke that Isabella was so pleased with the arrangements, she had hugged Huntington and kissed him on the cheek. A bit flustered by the show of affection by his new ward, the duke had merely nodded and set off for London with word that he would return in a few weeks.

Poor man probably hasn't had a woman touch him since his wife died, David thought with a sigh.

He sobered as he returned his attention to the letter he had written to Clarinda. Would she notice his handwriting was a bit different from Daniel's? Had she received notes from his brother that would provide a comparison?

He rather hoped not. The argument he'd had with Daniel the night before had nearly led to blows. They might still have a mill at Gentleman Jackson's boxing saloon if Daniel didn't give up his pursuit of Clarinda Anne Brotherton. They were both abysmal boxers, so at least it would be an even match.

"You cannot marry Lady Clarinda," David had stated before he was even halfway through the vestibule of the townhouse Daniel maintained in Bruton Street. The batman had attempted to see to his coat and top hat, but David didn't pause long enough to remove them.

"Why ever not?" Daniel Jonathan Andrew Fitzwilliam countered when he appeared in the hall just beyond the vestibule. "You certainly don't appear ready to marry her."

David angled his head to one side, as if he were addressing a recalcitrant child, attempting to ignore the fact that looking at his brother was like seeing his own reflection in a looking glass. "Because she's betrothed to *me*, and has been since she was... twelve, I think it was."

His twin brother, younger by mere minutes, crossed his arms and gave a quick shake of his head. "Fourteen. You know *nothing* about her," Daniel said quietly.

"I know everything I need to know," David countered, his frown making him appear far older than his brother. "Jesus, Danny, how could you *do* this?"

"I love her."

Still wearing his great coat, David dropped into a wing-back chair as if he'd been punched. He scrubbed his face with a hand, wincing at the growth of whiskers that had already made themselves apparent despite his valet having shaved him that morning. It wasn't even six o'clock in the evening. "Obviously, since you've apparently been providing her with 'delectable kisses'," he accused.

Daniel moved to a sideboard and poured scotch into two crystal tumblers. He offered one to his brother, scowling when David seemed to hesitate before taking it. "I didn't poison it, if that's what you're thinking," he said as he set it on the side table. He took the adjacent chair, a smug expression suddenly giving way to a grin.

"How can you find this funny?" David asked in dismay. He downed the scotch in a single gulp, immediately regretting the move as he nearly choked on the smoky fluid, his throat burning as it made its way down.

"How can I not?" Daniel countered. "I finally have something in my life that is not *yours*."

David stared at his brother, rather wishing they didn't look so damned much alike. "She is not *yours*," he whispered. "Father arranged a betrothal with the Earl of Heath. We were all there in the same room when the contract was completed. They signed it. I signed it. *She* signed it," he explained, exasperation nearly robbing him of breath.

"Betrothals are breakable," Daniel countered with a shrug. "It won't hold up in a court, and you know it. Besides, Clarinda is already two-and-twenty. You were supposed to marry her *before* her birthday. *And* you made a promise you would divest yourself of the brothel and the gentlemen's club, and ..."

"The club is under contract. An agent is seeing to the sale of the brothel. I'll simply close it if I don't have a buyer by the end of June," David interrupted, ignoring the comment about Clarinda already having turned two-and-twenty. He had forgotten about that particular clause in the contract, so he hoped the Earl of Heath had as well.

Daniel stared at his older brother. "Who's buying the club?" he asked, his expression displaying his shock at this bit of news. Surely he would have heard about an impending sale from someone at Boodle's.

"Frank O'Leary. He's looking to expand his gaming concern to this side of London, and the club will allow him to do that," David explained, not bothering to add that he had been the one to approach the owner of *The Jack of Spades* with news he was was willing to sell at a discount.

He still couldn't believe he was nearly done with the club. The monies it generated allowed him to purchase any number of accoutrements necessary for life in the capital. A fully-furnished house in Mayfair that he had since renamed Norwick Place. A sporty phaeton with a matched set of greys. A town coach at Tillbury's. A wardrobe suitable for a member of the *ton*. An account at the Bank of England that would see to his wife's future and their children when he died.

And a dowry for Isabella.

He wondered then if he would ever have to mention his daughter to Clarinda. Given the two were so closely related, he realized it was only a matter of time after he told Isabella before Clarinda would know of his *affaire* with her aunt. He would have to tell her before that happened. *After Isabella, though*. He owed his daughter that much.

Or would it be better to tell Clarinda first? he suddenly wondered. *Christ!* How would she react when she learned of the *affaire?*

David thought about mentioning Isabella to Daniel just then—she was the man's niece, after all—but thought better of it. Give the man the opportunity to absorb the news related to his businesses. He would tell him about Isabella later.

Maybe after he told Isabella he was her father.

"*The Jack of Spades* Frank O'Leary?" Daniel asked, still in shock.

Pulled from his brief reverie, David stared at his brother and blinked. Christ, he was getting as bad as Huntington when it came to bouts of melancholy. "Yes. He'll keep the place up better than most. He runs the best Faro parlor of anyone in London."

"Jesus, Davy. When were you going to tell me?"

David sighed, realizing he was pulling the rug out from under his brother in more ways than one. "I just did. It's partly why I came tonight," he replied. "As for *The Elegant Courtesan*, I rather doubt I can find a buyer in the next month or so. I'm thinking I'll simply shut it down… I've hired an agent to see to selling the property, though."

"Can you live without that income?" Daniel interrupted.

Angling his head while he regarded his brother, David sighed again. "You tell me. You're the one who keeps all the books." He suddenly frowned. "And may I remind you, I do have an earldom that generates a bit of income—"

"Very *little* income," Daniel interrupted just before he finished his scotch. His inheritance upon their father's death had been proof of that. Although he had enough to live on if he never married, he wouldn't be able to support a wife and family without the monies he earned from his accounting and clerical duties for the Norwick earldom.

"And some race horses that might earn a purse or two."

Daniel gave him a quelling glance. "Those damn horses cost you more than you'll ever win at a racing match," he reminded him. "But, yes, I suppose you're set for life with what you've earned with the club so far." He paused a moment, his brows furrowing. "Seems I'll be out of a job, though." The thought had him wincing in more ways than one. His income depended on David's. The money he earned from keeping the books was money he planned to use to support his life with Clarinda.

David's brows shot up. "How so?"

Daniel waved an arm toward the desk. "I won't have any books to keep."

"Nonsense," David countered. "I'll still have the expenses of Norwick Park, and Norwick House, Fair Downs, and the earldom. Tenant cottages and such. Seed. Maintenance on the plows." *A wife.* Her dowry alone would sustain them if the earldom no longer generated any income. "I hope you'll continue to keep those ledgers, as I really don't wish to employ a secretary."

One advantage about having a brother who was good with numbers meant David didn't need to keep an accomptant for the businesses. He rather hoped Daniel would be amenable to simply continuing what he'd been doing but on a smaller scale.

Or larger, if Clarinda proved to be an expensive wife. At least he would be gaining a dowry upon their marriage.

Furrowing his brows until a fold of skin developed between them, Daniel finally nodded. "I suppose I can do that," he agreed. "But I'm not giving up Lady Clarinda."

About to tell Daniel about Arabella Brotherton Tolson's death, David realized he wouldn't be able to do so without sobbing. So he merely nodded. "Perhaps we should allow Lady Clarinda to decide," he finally suggested.

Daniel's eyes darted to one side, as if he were trying to sort just how Clarinda would know to choose him should both brothers be in the same room with her at the same time. They looked so much alike, she might not realize who was who.

He was never allowed to spend more than a few minutes at a time in her company—there was always a lady's maid with her—but he did have the advantage of having courted her. He knew her favorite flower. He knew what caused her to blush. He knew how to kiss her when the maid wasn't looking.

David doesn't know all that, he reasoned. "Perhaps we should," Daniel agreed. "May the best man win."

David frowned. "No. May the one that needs a wife and an heir be the one that wins," he countered. He blinked then. "But not for a couple of days."

"Why?"

Shifting in his chair, David hesitated before answering. "I'm heading down to Boxgrove tomorrow. To see Cousin Connie," he said quietly.

At the mention of Constance Fitzwilliam, Daniel suddenly stiffened. "Is something wrong at Fair Downs?" The memory of what had happened to Constance on the night of her come-out had him remembering that was also the night David had killed a man at Norwick Park—the thief whose attempt to steal a race horse had been thwarted by Constance, but at the expense of her virtue. Although the woman wasn't yet old enough to be on the shelf, he rather doubted she would ever gain an advantageous marriage. Besides, Boxgrove didn't offer much in the way of eligible bachelors. Most of the men in the small village were Benedictine monks.

The earl gave a shake of his head. "No. Nothing that I know of, at least. But it's past time I pay a visit to Fair Downs. See how she's doing." He didn't add that he wanted their cousin to pay a call at Huntinghurst and befriend Isabella. His daughter needed a confidante, and Constance's interest in horses was a match for Isabella's. "But when I return, we shall both pay a call on Lady Clarinda. At the same time," David said with a nod.

Daniel leaned back in his chair and finally nodded in return, wondering at the sudden pall that seemed to settle over him just then. For when Clarinda was faced with both Fitzwilliam brothers at the same time—and was told which was which—would she know to choose him?

Or would she choose the earl?

Chapter 11

A PROPOSITION COMES FROM AN UNLIKELY SOURCE

Two days later in Boxgrove, Sussex

Constance Fitzwilliam knelt next to her favorite horse, tears collecting in the corners of her eyes until they finally spilled down her cheeks. Favor, better known as *Twins' Second Favorite* to those who followed the horse races in England, lie with his head pressed against her knee. For a moment, he seemed to gaze up at the woman who had ridden him since the day he had been put out to pasture, his racing days over and his time as a stud just beginning. That had been over seven years ago, and during that time, he had seen to the creation of several generations of Thoroughbred horses in the stables at both Norwick Park and Fair Downs.

One of them became a racer. Even won the Derby at Epsom Downs.

Too bad father gambled away all the winnings, Constance thought as she regarded the dying horse through watery eyes.

Edward Fitzwilliam, brother of the Ninth Earl of Norwick and a widower, had been an inveterate gambler. The winnings from Favor, and later, from Mr. Tuttlebaum, only provided more grist for the gambling mill.

And then Edward had died, leaving his only daughter with enough funds to run Fair Downs, pay the servants, and make it to her majority. Given she was just two-and-twenty, it would be another three years before she could expect to receive her inheritance.

The man's nephew and owner of Fair Downs, David Fitzwilliam, Earl of Norwick, never took Favor or Mr. Tuttlebaum—or any of the other horses—back to his stables at Norwick Park. *They are yours*, he had told her following the brief graveside service for Edward. *Part of your inheritance. I will be sure you have clear ownership of them all.*

The earl never visited Fair Downs after that—at least, not that she knew of. He only wrote on occasion to ask after her and her favorite horses. Now that he was set to marry Lady Clarinda in a month, Constance rather doubted she would hear anything more from her eldest cousin. She was sure he would prefer to forget about her, if only because of what he had done on her behalf the night of her come-out. What he claimed he'd had to do.

Constance squeezed her eyes shut, the tears beginning anew for an entirely different reason.

The sound of Favor's labored breaths finally ceased, and Constance no longer suppressed the sob that robbed her of breath. The tears streamed freely down her cheeks as she dropped her head until her chin rested on her chest.

"Oh, Miss Fitzwilliam, I am so sorry," her lady's maid said from where she stood several feet away. She had been on the hunt for her mistress for some time, rather surprised to discover Constance wasn't in her bedchamber or in the stables but in the middle of the pasture behind Fair Downs' manor house.

Constance sniffled. "Thank you, Simmons." She took a deep breath before using the backs of her hands to wipe the tears from her cheeks.

Simmons was quick to offer a hanky from her own pocket. "I realize it's not a good time, but Mr. Cruthers has paid a call. He wonders if you might have a moment to see him."

Frowning, the expression forcing a fold of skin to appear

between her eyebrows, Constance regarded her lady's maid a moment.

Mr. Cruthers?

Constance attempted to take a breath as she realized what her lady's maid had just said.

Why ever would the vicar be paying a call today of all days?

She rather doubted the man knew Favor was to die on this day, and even if he did, she didn't think a vicar would be amenable to performing a service on behalf of the beast. "I'm hardly dressed to receive visitors," Constance murmured, wincing when she realized her round gown would be stained from the grass upon which she knelt.

The lady's maid gave a slight shrug. "Perhaps he's thinking to court you," Simmons suggested.

Reeling as if she'd been struck in the face, Constance stared at Esther Simmons. She blinked and made a most unladylike sound, something between a snort and a sniffle. "I rather doubt that. He's old enough to be my *father*," she replied, finally deciding she had to get up. The prickling sensation in her legs, more pronounced now that she had been kneeling for so long, would only get worse, and then she would be unable to stand and walk without assistance. She dared another glance at Favor before lifting a hand toward Simmons. "Help?"

Grasping Constance's hand, the maid gave it a quick tug and stepped back until her mistress was on her feet. "Yet, the man is wearing his very best suit," Simmons countered, her voice kept low as if she thought someone might overhear her.

Not about to ask Simmons how she would know such a thing, Constance gave her a quelling glance. "Then I suppose I shall have to change into an appropriate gown," she replied, wrapping her shawl about her shoulders against the sudden chill that crept down her spine.

"I showed him to the parlor, and one of the maids is seeing to tea," Simmons explained as they headed toward the house.

Wondering at her lady's maid's comments about the

vicar, Constance decided she didn't want to know more. She wanted a chance to mourn Favor. "Could you let the groom know about Favor? I'd like him to arrange for a grave digger and a burial for him. I think a small headstone would be appropriate."

The lady's maid stopped and stared at her mistress in shock before she realized Constance would have no patience for an argument just then. "Yes, my lady," she replied with a nod. She dipped a curtsy before she hurried off toward the stables.

The early spring morning was still chilly, the sun having just burned off the fog surrounding Fair Downs. As she made her way toward the main house, Constance allowed her gaze to sweep the horizon. The steeple in nearby Boxgrove was finally visible, as was a bit of blue sky. Perhaps it wouldn't rain as it had for the past few days, although she felt her tears had been a close substitute on this day.

A sob had her hiccuping as she entered the house, startled to find Mr. Cruthers standing in the hall directly in front of her. *Why isn't he in the parlor?* she wondered as she gave a quick curtsy, Simmons' hanky held to her nose. "Mr. Cruthers," she said with a nod. Remembering the condition of her gown—and noting his gaze was about to take in the grass stains down the front—she added, "Please pardon my absence from the house. I've had a rather trying morning."

The vicar moved to take her hand, bestowing a kiss on the back of it. "Miss Fitzwilliam. Let me be the first to say how sorry I am you are having a poor morning," he offered, his bushy eyebrows furrowing in concern. "Why, you look as if you've just received word of a death in the family."

Pulling the shawl from her shoulders, Constance held it in front of her stained gown and wondered how to respond. "Something like that," she murmured.

She had half a mind to make the man continue to wait whilst she went up to her bedchamber to change gowns, but decided she didn't want him left by himself downstairs. Not that he would have made off with any of the silver—Christ!

He was a vicar—but she couldn't help but think he would begin snooping through the drawer of the escritoire if given half a chance. Then she wondered how long the man had been left unattended while Simmons searched for her.

He's probably been through all the drawers in the parlor and was on his way to find some more in another room, Constance thought with a sigh.

"We missed you at Sunday services. I do hope you were not ill," the vicar said, his head angled as if he almost hoped she would claim she was.

Constance stiffened, trying her best to hide a flash of annoyance. "Thank you for your concern. I was quite well, but one of the mares was foaling at the time. I elected to be with her until such time as I could ensure she and her filly would survive."

This last had the vicar's eyes widening. "I would have thought your groom could see to a horse," he responded, the words said as if he were scolding her.

Bristling, Constance had half a mind to ask the vicar to take his leave. "But then *the groom* wouldn't have been in attendance at your service," Constance countered, rather glad to see the look of utter confusion that seemed to settle over the man's features as he tried to weigh the significance of one absence over the other.

Uncomfortable with holding the conversation in the hall, she waved a hand toward the parlor at the same moment she noticed the maid coming from the kitchen with a tea tray. "Will you join me for tea?" A spot of tea would at least make the vicar's visit more tolerable.

"Yes, yes, of course," Mr. Cruthers replied as he stepped aside and allowed Constance to precede him into the parlor. The vicar gave a nod to the maid before he followed, settling into an upholstered chair once Constance had taken a seat in the middle of the settee. She had spread out her shawl so it covered her lap and hung down to hide the grass stains.

"My lady's maid says you have come with news," Constance prompted, hoping the man didn't plan to stay long. She poured a cup of tea and added sugar before offering it to the vicar.

"Why, yes," he answered, apparently surprised by her words. "My esteemed colleague in Cocking has informed me there is a young woman among his flock who is in need of a... a friend," he hedged.

Constance paused in stirring her tea, her attempt to withhold a sour expression from appearing having failed. This wasn't the first time the vicar had prevailed upon her to befriend some young woman. Just the year before, an unmarried girl from Chichester had been sent to live with an aunt only a mile from Fair Downs. She had visited the girl on several occasions, and despite their lack of common interests, they enjoyed several afternoons of tea and conversation. Once the pregnant servant finally agreed to marry the footman responsible, though, Constance never saw her again.

"Oh?" she managed, not particularly interested. "And who might *this* one be?"

The vicar helped himself to a Dutch biscuit. "A girl of quality, it seems. She has recently moved into Huntinghurst, in fact. A ward of the Duke of Huntington," he explained before nibbling the edge of the biscuit. His furrowed brows made him look as if he had never tasted spiced shortbread before. *Probably has only ever eaten English shortbread,* Constance thought, resisting the urge to roll her eyes.

Intrigued by the mention of a ward of the Duke of Huntington, though, Constance angled her head. "I wasn't aware the duke had any family," she murmured, her brows furrowing when she remembered talk of his late duchess. The petite, blonde woman, who had been in possession of a complexion so pale she had probably never set foot out of doors, had died in childbirth. The baby boy died, as well, leaving the duke in a state of melancholy in which some claimed he still suffered.

Constance knew the couple had been childhood friends —her cousin, David, had mentioned it in a letter when he wrote that their marriage had been arranged long ago and was apparently a happy one. That Jane Ludlow would die in childbirth was no surprise, though. None of her older sisters had survived the childbed.

"Oh, I don't believe she is his *family* member," Mr. Cruthers corrected her.

Several guesses as to whom the girl might be came to mind, but Constance did her best to wait for the vicar to provide more information before she jumped to any unsavory conclusions. When he didn't offer more information, though, she was forced to ask, "If not a family member, then how is it she became his ward?"

At this, Mr. Cruthers stiffened. "Why, I was hoping *you* might discover the information when you meet her," he replied. "My colleague assures me she is of utmost quality. A daughter of the *ton*—an orphan—with no place else to live. Since you are so closely related to an earl, I immediately thought of you and mentioned your close proximity—"

"Close proximity?" Constance interrupted. "Huntinghurst must be... six miles away," she argued, remembering the duke's country estate was somewhere between Cocking and Singleton.

"True, but you are a woman with horses. Surely you could make the trip in an hour in your gig," he countered.

Constance stared at the vicar is disbelief. Yes, she could make the trip in an hour, probably less if she simply rode one of her mares. Simmons would have to come along, though, and her lady's maid wasn't an accomplished horsewoman.

Far from it.

Which meant she would have to drive the gig.

"Is there some other reason besides my relation to Lord Norwick that has you requesting that I ... I befriend this girl?" she wondered, deliberately using the word 'girl' since she had decided the duke wouldn't be housing a woman—unless said woman was his mistress. Propriety wouldn't allow it.

When the vicar's eyes darted sideways, Constance realized

there was a reason even before he finally said, "She spends all her time in the stables."

Her brows arching up in surprise at this bit of information, Constance gave a shake of her head. "You say that as if it is a flaw in her character."

He took a breath and held it a moment. "Well, my *colleague* is of the opinion it is," he replied, immediately wincing when he realized his words would annoy his hostess.

Straightening on the settee, Constance regarded the vicar with a steely gaze. "Should you see your *colleague* in the next day or so, please inform him that I shall be paying a call on this girl. I shan't be disabusing her of the idea that it's unseemly to spend too much time in the stables, however," she warned. "Besides. What else is a girl to do with her days out here in the country?"

She meant her question to be rhetorical, of course, but the vicar's eyes widened before he blinked. "Why, embroidery, of course. Painting. Drawing. Learning French. Playing the piano-forté."

It was Constance's turn to blink. The man had a point. It just didn't seem to apply to her or apparently to the young woman who was sequestered at Huntinghurst.

"Nevertheless, a woman who knows horseflesh and who can ride should be considered a valuable asset to any marriage-minded man," she stated as she got to her feet.

Caught off-guard, the vicar struggled to stand. "I was not familiar with that mandate, my lady," he managed when Constance made it clear their time in the parlor was over by making her way to the door.

"Well, now you are, Mr. Cruthers. Good day, and thank you for coming," she countered as she held out her hand but not in a manner that would allow him to kiss the back of it.

The vicar shook it rather lightly. "Good day," he replied as he bowed.

He took his leave of Fair Downs, rather disappointed he wasn't granted the time to state his true intentions for making the call in the first place. He had hoped he might propose marriage and secure a positive response from the headstrong woman. Now that he gave it some more thought, though, he realized the two of them would probably never suit for the very reason that Constance Fitzwilliam seemed intent on putting her horses first. Since there were six of them in the stables at Fair Downs, that would mean he would end up in seventh place in her affections. And seventh place was a few pegs too low for his taste.

Chapter 12

AN EARL PAYS A CALL ON A VICAR

A half-hour later

Elijah Cruthers eyed the glossy black coach parked in front of his vicarage and wondered who might be paying a call. He directed his horse to the mews that served most in Boxgrove and dismounted, relieved when a stableboy raced up to take the reins.

"You weren't gone long," the boy commented, making conversation in the hopes of gaining a shilling from the vicar.

His attention directed to his house, Elijah shook his head. He absently pulled a farthing from his waistcoat pocket and tossed it to the stableboy. "No, unfortunately," he murmured before taking his leave of the mews. Seems he wouldn't be making plans to wed in a month.

The stableboy regarded the farthing a moment before watching the despondent vicar head off. "Your visitor looks like quite the gentleman," he called out.

Elijah paused and finally turned around. "Did you recognize him?"

Shaking his head, the boy said, "Only that he's been here 'afore. A day or two ago."

The vicar nodded and hurried to his house, realizing his visitor could be only one man.

David Norwick. At least, that's the name the gentleman had used when introducing himself. The name was even on the calling card the man had given him on his first visit. Even so, Elijah had reason to suspect the name was really an alias, as if the gentleman didn't want his true identity known. He was the one who had sent him on the very errand from which he was just now returning.

Had the man spied on him? Followed him to Fair Downs and watched as he made his call on Miss Constance Fitzwilliam?

Frowning, Elijah had just stepped through his front door when his housekeeper hurried up to him.

"He's here again. That gentleman," she said, her eyes wide but her voice kept to a hoarse whisper. "He's even wearing a *silver* waistcoat," she added as she stepped aside. "So elegant."

The vicar nodded, resisting the urge to roll his eyes at the mention of the man's waistcoat. Their visitor was obviously a man of some means. "I couldn't help but notice the coach parked out front," he answered with an arched brow.

Taken aback by this bit of information, the housekeeper dared a glance out the front window and gasped. "He's got to be a rather wealthy gentleman," she murmured. "Don't you suppose?"

"Now, now, Mrs. Fletcher. Whether he is or he isn't, I rather imagine I shouldn't keep him waiting," he commented, an expectant look on his face. When the housekeeper didn't immediately reply, he added, "What have you done with Mr. Norwick?"

The housekeeper blinked. "Oh! I put him in your study," she replied. "Then I took in some tea."

Elijah nodded. "Very good. Now let's see what I can do for him." He wasn't about to say something about already having done something for the visitor—for a rather hefty tip. Even though Mrs. Fletcher hadn't been working the day the gentleman first paid a call, she had obviously learned about it from someone in the small village.

The vicar opened the study door and stepped through, relieved to find his visitor gazing out the study window. "So sorry to keep you waiting, Mr. Norwick," he said as he gave a short bow and made his way to his desk.

"Quite all right, Mr. Cruthers. I was headed back to the capital and thought I would inquire as to whether or not you might have had a chance to see to that matter we discussed yesterday."

The vicar gave a nod, still wondering if he'd been followed to Fair Downs. "Just returned from paying a call on Miss Fitzwilliam, in fact," he replied. "Although she seemed a bit... suspicious when I made the request, she assured me she would pay a call on the young lady at Huntinghurst."

David Fitzwilliam, Earl of Norwick, took a quick breath, relieved to hear that his cousin hadn't rebuffed the vicar. He would have paid a call on Constance and made the request she befriend Lady Isabella himself, but then he would have had to explain his interest in the young woman. He rather doubted he could avoid telling Constance the truth—that he was Isabella's father—but he still hadn't wed Clarinda, and he didn't want her learning about Isabella by way of gossip or an anonymous letter.

He wasn't ashamed of what had happened with Arabella Brotherton all those years ago. The heart wanted what the heart wanted, it seemed. He had spent the past nineteen years hoping Craythorne might succumb to an early death by illness, or lose his life in a duel, or suffer a coronary whilst riding one of his damned horses so that David could claim Arabella as his wife.

Her untimely death had shocked David to his very core. Sure he would die of a broken heart, he was prepared to simply remain unmarried and allow his twin brother to inherit and marry his intended.

But he didn't die. Even after a week spent downing the contents of every bottle of spirits in Norwick House. Even after a week of wishing he could join Arabella in death, although he supposed that was mostly due to the hangover he experienced when he had finally finished off all the liquor.

His brother had been the one to insist he sober up and return to Parliament. When Daniel's words weren't enough, his right fist to David's jaw had done the trick, the sharp pain permeating his addled brain.

Jesus, Davy. Your damned jaw 'bout broke my hand, Daniel had complained.

He hadn't responded to his brother's words—at least, not verbally—but his head had cleared for the moment when he realized life would go on. That he had a daughter—one tangible result of his love for Arabella Brotherton—and, therefore, a reason to live. An earl to visit—time hadn't lessened his desire for vengeance, and initial reports from Basingstoke only mentioned that the untimely death of the Countess of Craythorne was due to an 'unfortunate accident'.

Duty called. There were the entertainments of the Season to enjoy—balls, soirées, and musicales. Sessions of Parliament to attend. A future wife to court. Heirs to sire.

David's attempt to pay a call on Maxwell Tolson, Earl of Craythorne, had been met with news that the earl wasn't at Craythorne Castle and had not been for over a week. *He's quite bereft at the loss of his countess,* the butler said in a quiet voice. *And now his daughter. She went for a ride and never returned. We fear she has died, as well.*

Although he had been tempted to assure the man that Lady Isabella was still alive, David kept mum and instead pressed the butler for more information on the cause of death. *She fell and hit her head, my lord,* the butler responded. *It is said she died instantly.*

When David paid a call on the coroner in Basingstoke, the man merely shrugged. *Terrible accident,* he agreed.

Any evidence of strangulation? David asked carefully.

The coroner frowned. *Can't say if there was or wasn't. I never saw the body.*

When the coroner couldn't provide information as to

whom might have seen the body—whom might have prepared Arabella's body for burial—he gave another shrug. *I was in Portsmouth at the time.*

Frustrated, David made his way southwest to a coaching inn in Chichester, intending to pay a call on his cousin. The idea of recruiting the vicar to approach Cousin Connie came to him when he overheard the man mention his avocation during his luncheon at the coaching inn. He followed the vicar to his small cottage and made his acquaintance a few hours later.

"Are you unwell, Mr. Norwick?"

The sound of the vicar's voice brought David out of his reverie with a start. "I apologize. Something you said had me woolgathering," he claimed. He sighed. "You say she seemed *suspicious?*" he repeated.

The vicar took a seat and poured more tea into the earl's cup before he poured one for himself. "She has reason to be. The last time I asked her to pay a call on a lonely young woman, it was because the chit was... well, she was in the *family way*, but she wasn't yet married, you see. Then the young man who was responsible appeared and married her the next day. *Poof*, and they were gone back to the home where they were both servants. With nary a fare-thee-well, I might add."

David gave a nod. He rather wished Arabella had hidden somewhere so that he might have married her. Craythorne would have been furious, but...

He shook the thought from his head. *No more living in the past. No more regrets*, he thought as he regarded Mr. Cruthers for a moment. "I rather imagine Miss Fitzwilliam wasn't too happy to lose a new friend."

"Probably not," the vicar agreed, not bothering to mention that Miss Fitzwilliam was actually rather annoyed by the whole affair. "But I told her what you said about the horses. That seemed to get her curiosity up. I rather imagine she'll be paying a call at the duke's estate in the next day or so."

The earl finished his tea, contemplating this bit of news. "I do appreciate your help in this matter," David said as he moved to stand up. He paused at the vicar's next words, though.

"I fear my arrival occurred at a rather awkward time, however."

David blinked. "Oh?" He sat back down.

"Seems her favorite horse died this morning. Twins..." He shook his head. "Something Favorite?" he offered as a possible name.

The earl's eyes widened. "*Twins' Second Favorite*," he murmured, the memory of the colt's birth suddenly in his mind's eye. He and Daniel had watched the foaling, and they had both declared the horse to be their second favorite of all that had been born that year at Fair Downs. Their first favorite, a consummate racer, was now well past his prime and had been put out to pasture at Norwick Park. "I'm sorry to hear it," he added with a shake of his head.

Realizing his visitor must have known more about Miss Fitzwilliam than he first let on, Elijah said, "Perhaps you could do me the favor of... *recommending* me to Miss Fitzwilliam?" If Miss Fitzwilliam held this Mr. Norwick in high regard, then perhaps a good word would have him moved up a few pegs in her estimation. At the earl's sudden frown, he added, "I went there today to do your bidding and to ask if I might court her, you see, after I had secured her assurances she would see to the young lady at Huntinghurst. But the death of the horse had her in a most melancholy state."

No doubt, David almost said. "You would be wise to consider someone else to be your wife, Mr. Cruthers," he warned suddenly.

"Oh?" the vicar responded as he straightened in his chair, one eyebrow arching up in question. For once, the man appeared as if he might have a backbone.

"I rather doubt Miss Fitzwilliam will ever agree to be anyone's wife. Unless you are a man with a stable full of horses, trust me when I tell you this, she would not make a suitable wife for you." And with that, David Fitzwilliam stood up, bowed, and took his leave of the vicarage.

Elijah Cruthers was left staring at the tea tray, wondering how it could be a woman would love horses more than him.

Chapter 13

A VISIT TO HUNTINGHURST

The next day

"How early do you suppose a daughter of the *ton* would be up and about?" Constance wondered from where she sat in the small breakfast parlor at Fair Downs. Although the morning sun had just begun to light the cheery room, it was still rather early in the morning. Instead of wearing her usual riding habit—she frequently exercised one of the horses just after breakfast—she had chosen to wear a sprigged muslim gown in a pale blue. A darker blue redingote and matching hat would make for an appropriate ensemble she could wear to pay a call at Huntinghurst.

Simmons helped herself to another rasher of bacon and joined her mistress at the table. Although she usually had breakfast with the other servants of Fair Downs in a small room off the kitchen, Constance had requested her company on this day. "I'm quite sure I wouldn't know," she replied. Not ever having worked in service in an aristocrat's home, she was unfamiliar with the schedules. "Why ever do you ask?"

Constance considered how much to tell her maid. "The day looks as if it will be a fair day for a drive. I'm thinking of paying a call at Huntinghurst." She waited a moment, wondering how Simmons would react. Sometimes the lady's maid behaved in a most timid manner, afraid of everything and everyone.

"Huntinghurst?" Simmons repeated, her eyes widening in shock. "Doesn't a duke live there?"

"Sometimes," Constance replied, quite sure he was there during the hunting season. As for this time of year, she had no idea. Now that Huntington's ward lived there, perhaps the duke would be there more often.

The more she thought about the young woman who was apparently Huntington's ward, though, the more curious she became. If Mr. Cruthers hadn't mentioned the chit's propensity for spending time in the stables, she wouldn't have considered paying a call. "I need someone to ride with me, either in the gig or on horseback."

Realizing her mistress was offering to take her along as opposed to the stableboy, Simmons' face lit up. "May I join you? It's been an age since we went to Chichester," she said with some excitement.

Constance resisted the urge to remind her lady's maid they probably wouldn't be stopping in the largest town in the immediate area. "Then I'll have Jenkins hitch up the gig. Can you be ready to go in an hour? I shouldn't want to arrive too early in the morning." She probably shouldn't even plan to be at the front door of Huntinghurst before one o'clock in the afternoon, since morning callers in London were said to arrive about that time.

Why ever call them 'morning calls' when they occurred after twelve o'clock? she wondered.

Constance was about to answer her own question with a thought as to when aristocrats might enjoy a luncheon, but Simmons was nearly bouncing in her chair.

"Oh, yes, my lady," Simmons assured her, a smile splitting her face. She suddenly sobered. "You've said nothing of his visit yesterday, but may I inquire as to what happened with Mr. Cruthers?"

Taking a drink of her coffee and wincing at how weak it

tasted—cook was probably running low again—Constance considered how to respond. She really didn't want to tell the servant about the odd conversation, but she could share at least one important bit of information. "Well, he did not ask to court me, if that's what you were expecting," she replied, about to add, *Thank the gods*, before she thought better of it.

Her eyes rounding in disbelief, Simmons suddenly blinked several times. "I... I was so sure," she murmured. "It's just that, you're..." She stopped and stared at her plate.

"I'm what?" Constance wondered.

Her lady's maid seemed to slump in her seat. "Not getting any younger," she whispered. "You'll be considered *on the shelf* in just a few years..."

"I'll reach my majority in just a few years, at which point I can claim my inheritance," Constance corrected her, one eyebrow arching up with her claim. "If I marry, my inheritance becomes my dowry, and I will have no claim to it at all."

Simmons stared at her mistress in shock. "Don't you *want* to be married?"

The younger woman allowed a sigh, not quite sure what she wanted just then. One thing was certain, though. She didn't wish to be courted by Mr. Cruthers. And given most of Boxgrove's residents were the Benedictine monks who lived at the local monastery, she rather doubted she would be courted by anyone else. It was time she consider living the life of an independent woman for the rest of her life.

After all, hadn't she already been doing so?

"It's not a matter of what I want or don't want," Constance finally answered. "But a matter of *availability*. Should a man ever wish to marry me, it will be because he appreciates my horse sense."

And he'll have to have some, too.

The lady's maid allowed a sigh that made her position on the matter quite clear, but then she also knew the funds to continue running Fair Downs might run out before Constance could claim her inheritance.

Despite her mistress' late mother having hid money throughout Fair Downs in an effort to keep it from being gambled away, it was becoming harder to find the meager treasure. "I'll tell Jenkins about our need for the gig, and then I'll change into a gray gown," Simmons said as she stood up, gave a quick curtsy, and took her leave of the breakfast parlor.

Less than an hour later, the two were climbing onto the bench of the small gig. Mr. Jenkins turned over the reins to Constance with a reminder that the black shire didn't require the use of a crop, and that he would be taking the wagon to Chichester to pick up the household's latest order of provisions.

Simmons carried a basket filled with bread, cheese, apples, and a bottle of ale. Her sewing basket dangled from one arm. In the event she would be left with nothing else to do while Constance paid the call at Huntinghurst, she could spend the time repairing clothing. The lady's maid sincerely hoped she might meet a maid or two at the manor house—or even a footman, for that matter—but she wasn't counting on it. How many servants would even be on staff at a hunting lodge?

Daring a glance at her chronometer, Constance was relieved when it was just a bit past eleven when the shire pulled into the semi-circular drive in front of Huntinghurst. If what the vicar had said was true about the duke's ward, then the girl would certainly be up and about by now.

The manor was far larger than she expected—she had always thought it was supposed to be a hunting lodge—and she nearly had the gig making a U-turn before they reached the imposing Ardingly sandstone structure.

Although most manor houses appeared to grow straight out of the ground with little in the way of landscaping at their base, Huntinghurst obviously employed a full-time gardener. The row of Palladian windows along the ground floor were set off by square-cut boxwoods, and spiral topiaries flanked the front door. In front of the boxwoods, newly-bloomed red tulips decorated the entire length of the house. A row of tiny white flowers provided a contrasting edge at the base of the tulips.

"It's three stories tall," Simmons remarked, her mouth left open after she made the statement. "There must be hundreds of flowers."

"I'll bet it has wings out the back," Constance remarked as she pulled the shire to a halt just shy of the front door. If so, there was most certainly a garden out back—kitchen gardens, if nothing else—and probably a pond. She was about to consider the possibility of a folly, but before she could secure the reins, the front door opened, and a butler stepped out.

"Good morning," the man said with a bow before offering a hand to assist them.

"Good morning," Constance said as she stepped down from the gig, giving her skirts a quick shake. "I do hope I am not too early to pay a call."

Peters paused just as he was about to assist Simmons from the conveyance. "If you're here to see the duke, my lady, I'm afraid His Grace is not in residence," he replied, his manner a bit guarded.

Constance angled her head, rather relieved to hear it. "I'm actually here to pay a call on his ward. Is she in residence, perhaps? I am Miss Fitzwilliam from Fair Downs."

The butler seemed rather surprised, his brows furrowing as if he wasn't quite sure how to respond. He motioned them toward the front door before saying, "Lady Isabella is in residence, but she's not exactly *in* right now."

Arching a brow, Constance had to suppress the urge to grin. Butlers could be ever so confusing. "So, she is out?"

Sighing, the butler nodded. "Out at the stables."

Constance allowed the grin. "Do you suppose I might be allowed to join her there? And would there be somewhere my lady's maid could wait whilst I visit with Lady Isabella?" At least she had a name for the ward—and she was fairly sure the girl was an aristocrat's daughter given how the butler referred to her as 'Lady Isabella' as opposed to 'Miss Isabella'.

"You're sure you don't mind, my lady?"

The butler seemed ever so surprised by her request. *Surprised, and was that a bit pleased?* she wondered. Was Mr. Cruthers' colleague correct in his supposition that the ward didn't have regular callers? "Not at all, seeing as how I've made the trip from Boxgrove, Mr…?"

"Peters," the servant replied with a nod. "I'll escort you there and have the stableboy see to your horse," he said as he turned and led them into the house. "Your lady's maid is welcome to stay in the servant's dining room."

Apparently overhearing the butler, a footman suddenly hurried off down the hall, and Constance wondered if he was off to fetch the stableboy. No other maids or footmen were apparent from where they stood in what might have been the vestibule—had it not been such a large and open space. Her gaze had her taking in the rich paneling—what little of it she could see. There were so many paintings hung on the walls, hardly any of the woodwork showed!

Constance did her best not to boggle at the sight of the painted ceiling or the chandelier that looked as if it could hold a hundred candles or more. Straight ahead, a wide staircase led up to a landing where the stairs split and went off in opposite directions. Above the landing, a huge window did little to provide light for the stairs. The glass seemed to have discolored, or perhaps it had been made unclear on purpose.

"This way," Peters said as he led them down the hall to the left before turning again to the right.

As they passed a few open doors on their way to what seemed to be the center of the house, Constance dared a glance toward what appeared to be a salon filled with floral upholstered furniture—a bit of a surprise for a hunting lodge, she considered. The odors of vanilla and vellum wafted from another room—the library, no doubt—while another room looked as if it might be a study.

Although she had spent a good deal of her youth at

Norwick Park, the country estate of the Norwick earldom, that property had nothing on Huntinghurst when it came to marble floors, paneled walls, and painted ceilings. The artwork on display—huge paintings and marble busts mounted on fluted columns—lined the hall through which the butler led them.

When Constance realized she hadn't seen a single animal's head mounted on any of the walls, she decided Huntinghurst wasn't a hunting lodge at all but rather a country estate.

Peters paused when a housemaid appeared from one of the rooms, murmuring instructions that soon had Simmons leaving their company with the maid.

Upon exiting another large door, Constance nearly stopped in her tracks. Her guess about the house having wings was confirmed when she realized they were exiting close to where the east wing jutted out from the main house. A crushed granite path, parallel to the east wing, led south. A quick glance to the right showed another set of doors near the west wing along with a matching path.

As for gardens, there seemed to be several of them tucked into the three-sided courtyard. The kitchen garden ran the length of the east wing, that structure apparently providing protection from the elements. Another long garden ran the length of the west wing, a riot of color already on display despite the time of the year. Climbing vines laden with bright green leaves and pink blossoms nearly hid the lower story of the stone walls from view.

Constance's attention was captured by what lay ahead, though, for the most colorful garden was the farthest from the main part of the house. A parterre design of clipped boxwoods surrounded a series of evenly spaced clusters of flowers. The six wedge shapes formed by the boxwoods pointed to a small marble fountain in the center.

The crushed granite path took them past the garden as it veered to the left. Once the path cleared the east wing, the crushed granite was replaced with a series of what appeared to be freshly installed flagstones that led directly to the stables.

Constance couldn't help but feel a bit of envy at seeing the large structure. Built of the same Ardingly sandstone as the main house, it looked as if it could house at least two-dozen horses.

"Tell me, Mr. Peters. Is Lady Isabella expected to live here at Huntinghurst very long?"

The butler seemed to stiffen as he walked, as if her question triggered a warning. "I've not been apprised of the long-term plans for the young lady," he replied carefully. "However, she was introduced to me as His Grace's ward."

Constance considered the answer. Certainly a ward wouldn't yet be one-and-twenty. "I only ask because I was hoping she and I could become riding partners. I don't have one, you see, and..." Her words were cut off when a loud curse suddenly emanated from the stables.

A curse voiced by a female.

A most unladylike curse.

Peters pretended he didn't hear the shout of 'you hellion!' and continued. Meanwhile, Constance had stopped in her tracks and was now hurrying to catch up to the servant, half-tempted to ask if a woman was berating a man or a beast.

When she peeked around the open door to the stables and paid witness to a dark-haired woman tugging on the bridle of a yearling, she knew immediately who the hellion was.

"Lady Isabella, may I present Miss Constance Fitzwilliam? She has come to pay a call," Peters announced from where he stood just inside the entrance. He turned and gave their visitor an arched brow. "I'll have tea brought to the parlor," he said before giving a bow and taking his leave of the stables.

"Oh," Isabella said as all the air seemed to go out of her. Curiosity had the yearling giving up his fight with Isabella, and he now walked of his own volition to join their guest.

Constance stared at the horse, stunned at how much he

looked like *Twins Second Favorite* must have looked, back when the racer had been but a yearling.

"I apologize. I'm sure I must have sounded like a shrew just then," Isabella said as she came alongside the horse. "It's very good to meet you, Miss Fitzwilliam," she said.

Constance finally tore her gaze from the yearling and angled her head to one side before dipping a curtsy. "My lady, it's so kind of you to receive me," she managed, not adding that the ward didn't seem to have much of a choice. The butler could have had her wait in the vestibule and made the trip to the stables without her. But then she wouldn't have had the opportunity to pay witness to the well-designed interior of the stables.

"You look as if you've seen a ghost," Isabella said as she glanced back and forth between the horse and Constance.

"I think I am seeing him right now," Constance whispered. She gave her head a shake. "I have reason to believe he looks just like *Twins Second Favorite* did at that age. And he's probably just as stubborn."

"Hermés is that," Isabella agreed. "Although he seems fascinated by you," she added as she continued to watch the two. "Who is *Twins Second Favorite*?"

Constance lifted a gloved hand to the horse's head and very gently slid it up to where a white diamond interrupted the rich brown coloring of the bay. "He was a racer, although not as fast as his brother, *Twins Favorite*. *Twins* is still alive—he has at least another year or two left in him I should think. He lives at Norwick Park. But after that..." She allowed the sentence to trail off as she gave her head a shake.

Isabella blinked at hearing a reference to Norwick Park but then winced at the woman's implication for the future of the horse. "How many studs do you have in your stables?"

Lifting her hand from Hermés' head, the visitor gave her head a shake. "*Mr. Tuttlebaum* and *Mr. Wiggins* are the last, I'm afraid, but they are true brothers. All the rest in my stables are mares and their foals. I dare not breed them together," she said with a shake of her head. She didn't add that Mr. Tuttlebaum's and Mr. Wiggins' sire had been borrowed from a nearby viscount's country estate. Bounder, one of the horses that spent their days in a pasture a few miles from the ones surrounding Fair Downs, seemed glad of the attention Constance bestowed on him and simply followed her to Fair Downs one spring day. He immediately took to her favorite mare, Amasia. Their first colt, Mr. Tuttlebaum, went on to win her father a good deal of money by winning every race in which he was entered. A few years later, and this time with the permission of the viscount, she once again bred Bounder to Amasia, producing Mr. Wiggins. He had been born the same night as her come-out. "This boy will make an excellent stud some day," Constance remarked as she studied the yearling.

Watching how Hermés seemed so calm in the woman's company, Isabella leaned in and asked, "Would you be amenable to a trade, perhaps?"

Constance eyed the younger woman for a moment. "What... what kind of trade?"

Biting her lower lip, Isabella reconsidered what she was about to say. The grooms had both claimed they could do nothing with Hermés. She was determined to find a suitable stud for Artemis—the mare was ready for motherhood, she was sure—and bringing a new line into the stables might be better than the line breeding she was considering. Especially if Miss Fitzwilliam's horse was from a line of racers.

Isabella didn't even stop to think what the duke would say. It was his horse, although the man didn't seem to give a whit for what happened in his stables. "Your Mr. Wiggins for a day in exchange for him," she said in a whisper.

Blinking, Constance wondered if the chit was daft. This yearling was a perfectly formed horse, obviously from good breeding stock. "But, why ever would you get rid of such a darling?" she asked as she smoothed her hand over Hermés' withers. The yearling knickered in response, moving a bit closer to Constance.

"He adores you," Isabella said in a whisper, a bit of jealousy making her wonder how the woman did it. "But he's picking fights in the pasture. He bites ears. He's stubborn as a mule, and the groom hasn't been able to get shoes on him."

Constance allowed a grin. "He's just testing you. He obviously wants to be the dominant male in the stables."

"Well, he'll have to age a few years before *that's* going to happen," Isabella countered. "There are already several ahead of him."

Mr. Tuttlebaum was too old to be a dominant stud these days, Constance figured. The yearling would have the opportunity to share the pasture with mares he might one day impregnate. "Are you sure?" she asked, her gloved hand returning to the yearling's head.

"I suppose I should see this *Mr. Wiggins* and his pedigree charts," Isabella replied.

Constance nodded. "Agreed. I don't have the charts with me, of course, but I have them in my memory." She glanced around the interior again. "These stables are magnificent," she breathed.

Isabella nodded. "Indeed. Apparently the duke used to race a few of these horses, but one of the grooms says he hasn't done so since his duchess died." When her visitor seemed perplexed by this bit of news, she added, "I'm hoping I can see to some contenders for the coming years. For when he regains his interest." She crossed her arms and regarded the yearling again. "As for you, young man..."

"Where were you taking him?" Constance asked.

"I was going to tie him to a post near the parterre garden. Teach him some patience whilst we have tea. Or perhaps he just needs to run."

Constance took his lead, and they headed back to the gardens. Hermés stayed close and halted as she tied the lead around a metal ring attached to the side of the orangery. "It looks like you do this often," she commented, noticing a pail of water set against the sandstone building.

"Just started, actually. I've only been here a couple of weeks. Given there are only two grooms and a stableboy, there isn't time for them to train every horse for riding. So I do what I can." She turned toward the house. "You will join me for tea, I hope?"

Smiling, Constance nodded and gave Hermés a light tap on his nose. "I'll be back to check on you in good time."

The horse knickered as the ladies made their way back to the house.

"Are you a friend of the duke?" Isabella wondered, thinking perhaps the woman expected to find Huntington in residence.

"Oh, no. I've never met the man," Constance replied with a shake of her head.

Isabella had to resist the urge to stop in her tracks. "Have you visited Huntinghurst before?" she asked, wondering what had the young woman paying a visit.

"I have not. The vicar in Boxgrove—Fair Downs is just outside of the village—he paid a call yesterday with news of you. Said you could use a visitor."

Isabella paused before she opened the door, wondering how a vicar in Boxgrove would know anything about her. She was about to ask when Constance added, "He claimed his colleague in a village up the road told him about you."

"Oh," Isabella replied, rather surprised by this bit of news. She hadn't attended church services since her arrival, but she had located a small chapel in one corner of Huntinghurst.

But how could a vicar have known of her presence?

They made their way to the parlor, where a tea tray had been left on the low table in front of the settee. Momentarily at a loss, Isabella waited until her guest was seated before she settled onto the settee. "Forgive me, but I haven't served tea in a very long time. How do you take yours?"

"With milk and sugar," Constance replied, secretly thrilled she could have sweetened tea. She rarely indulged given how expensive sugar could be. "I cannot be your first caller since your arrival."

"Oh, but you are," Isabella replied as she poured the tea.

"If I didn't speak to the horses and the maid who sometimes helps with my buttons, I wouldn't say anything more than 'good morning' or 'good night' all day long."

Constance considered her hostess' words, realizing life in the manor was probably as lonely for Isabella as Fair Downs could be for her at times. At least she had a lady's maid in Simmons to help keep her company. "Where did you used to live?"

Isabella handed her guest the dish of tea and wondered how to respond. "Near Basingstoke. The duke took me in when my mother died." She managed to get through the words without a lump developing in her throat, but she hoped they could speak of something else. "Miss Fitzwilliam—"

"Oh, do call me Connie," her visitor interrupted. "I am quite sure we'll become fast friends."

Isabella allowed a grin. "Isabella, then. And I do hope Fair Downs is not too far away. I should like us to ride together. You do ride?" This last was said as if she feared the woman was only interested in raising horses—not riding them.

"Of course I do, although I fear Fair Downs isn't close enough for us to meet every day. It's six miles south, and I think a bit east of here," Constance explained, one gloved finger drawing a map in front of her. "Maybe twice a week?" she offered, noting Isabella's sudden expression of disappointment.

Obviously excited by the prospect of having a riding partner, Isabella's eyes widened. "Meet halfway?"

Constance furrowed a brow as she considered where that might be. "Or I could just tether a horse to my gig and come all the way here. My horses all need exercising," she murmured.

"You would come all the way here? Twice a week?" Isabella queried.

"How old are you? And how often is the duke in residence?" Constance countered, one eyebrow arching as if that should answer the question.

"Nineteen. And I have no idea. He accompanied me the day I was brought here and said he would be back in a few weeks. He only stayed a day before he left to return to London."

Constance frowned, rather surprised to hear that the duke had left his ward with little in the way of company, and apparently no companion. "With stables like his, it's a wonder he doesn't just live here," she replied. "What keeps him in London, I wonder?"

Isabella blinked. "Parliament, I suppose. The Season's entertainments." She wasn't thinking of a mistress when she made the comment about entertainments, but wondered if Constance did when Isabella noticed how the woman's eyebrows arched up. "London probably has more to offer than Chichester."

Not having spent time in London, Constance didn't offer a rejoinder. And she thought it better she not suggest the duke probably kept a mistress in London. Didn't all aristocrats? She was fairly sure her cousins both did. In fact, David owned a brothel, a fact she shouldn't have known but did because she had once overheard her late father speak of it.

"What of your husband...?" Isabella stopped, remembering how Constance had been introduced. "Pardon me, Peters said you were *Miss* Fitzwilliam." Her eyes widened when she remembered the name.

Was she related to Lord Norwick? She must be! She had mentioned Norwick Park.

"I am not married," Constance stated with a shake of her head. "Happily not so. I am merely biding my time until I reach my majority and can collect my inheritance."

Isabella frowned before lifting the teapot to offer more. "But... what will you do?" she asked as she refilled both cups. Isabella couldn't imagine a future without a husband. Without children. Without horses.

Well, Constance would at least have horses, she reasoned. Perhaps that was enough.

"I shall have funds enough to run Fair Downs as it should be. I wish to add onto the stables and raise racers," she explained, not about to admit she would have to seek permission from her cousin, the Earl of Norwick. Fair Downs was an entailed property of the earldom, after all.

"Me, too!" Isabella claimed, setting down her tea as she leaned forward. "It's been my dream ever since I came here and saw just how grand stables could be." She didn't mention that her father's stables were extensive, as well. She had thought them rather grand until her first day at Huntinghurst, when the duke had taken her for a tour of the house and stables.

Her visitor grinned. "As for a husband... I rather doubt I shall ever marry," Constance claimed. "I am already two-and-twenty with no prospects in sight. Most of the men in Boxgrove are monks."

Isabella blinked. Other than how Constance had described its location earlier in their conversation, she had no idea where Boxgrove was—she'd never even heard of the village—but the thought that there were no prospects for marriage hadn't crossed her mind when she agreed to Lord Norwick's plan that she move to Huntinghurst.

"Lord Norwick made the arrangements with the Duke of Huntington for me to stay here at..." She stopped and angled her head to one side, once again remembering how the woman had been introduced. "Are you related to Lord Norwick, by chance?"

Constance straightened in her chair, rather stunned to hear her cousin's name only a moment after she had paid him a thought. "I am. Lord Norwick is my cousin, in fact." Her eyes widened and she suddenly slumped a bit, a sigh escaping. "I believe I have just sorted how it is the vicar knew of you," she said in a quiet voice.

Isabella's eyes darted to one side. "I did wonder since I haven't yet been to church. Pray tell, what do you know?"

She had a brief moment of fear when she thought her presence at Huntinghurst had already become common knowledge among the locals. Locals as far away as Boxgrove. At this rate, it wouldn't be long before word of her location reached Craythorne Castle.

"David is my oldest cousin. The next oldest is his twin brother, Daniel. I owe David much, as he allows me to run Fair Downs as I see fit. He conveniently forgets about us, you see." *Mostly because I don't want him to remember me.* "But if he is the one who saw to it the duke took you in as his ward, then I'm quite sure he is the 'colleague' who informed the vicar of your presence here." She didn't add that David had probably bribed the man to pay the call on Fair Downs yesterday.

So much for Simmons' idea that Cruthers wants to court me. What a relief!

Isabella allowed a sigh. "I do hope that is the case." She dared not tell Constance everything just then. Perhaps after they had met a few times for rides around the estate, then she would confide in the woman.

"What of the duchess?" Constance suddenly asked. "There must be a new one. How often is she in residence? We never hear of her."

Shaking her head, Isabella leaned forward and whispered. "There isn't a new one. The only one died in childbirth. I think His Grace is still quite bereft over her loss. He loved her, you see." She paused a moment, one brow furrowing. "The servants claim the duchess never even made the trip to Huntinghurst."

Constance boggled at this news. "Then she was a fool," she said, her gaze wandering about the beautifully appointed parlor. "Have you ever been in the room that would have been her bedchamber?"

Blinking, Isabella dared a glance at the open door before she leaned forward and said, "Once. It's gorgeous, although the drapes are always pulled shut so it's very dark in there. She had her own bathing chamber, as well. All marble with a copper tub." The thought of taking a bath in that tub had crossed her mind several times since the day she had discovered the bathing chamber off the mistress suite. A day when it had rained the entire day and left her with nothing to do but explore Huntinghurst.

"I don't believe aristocrats love their spouses," Constance said suddenly. "Maybe they feel a bit of affection for one another. But certainly not love. Not when their marriages have been arranged since before they were out of leading strings."

Isabella frowned. "But it's not like that anymore," she claimed with a shake of her head. She continued to frown, though. Well, it was that way for her parents. At least, that's what she believed as she grew up watching her father forgive her mother's frequent bouts of contrary behavior. And although she was quite sure her father had felt affection for her mother, she was now wondering if the beast ever really loved Arabella Brotherton. If he had loved her, then how could he kill her? Strangle her to death? Over... what?

Isabella blinked, remembering that afternoon of only a few weeks ago. She had been in the dressing room reading her mother's correspondence. Had Craythorne discovered the letter from 'D'? Thought perhaps Arabella had taken a lover and then killed her in a jealous rage? She was about to allow her mind to wander more but then remembered she had a guest.

Isabella gave her head a shake, determined to wipe away the questions she had about her father. "Your cousin claimed he is to marry Lady Clarinda. *The Tattler* always featured articles about those two secretly meeting in Kensington Gardens."

Angling her head to one side, Constance wasn't about to counter the young lady's claim. It was true David was betrothed to Lady Clarinda, but given the lady was the same age as Constance and the deadline for their nuptials—Clarinda's twenty-second birthday—had already passed, Constance thought perhaps someone else might be courting Clarinda by now. "I cannot imagine David escorting anyone in Kensington Gardens. Daniel would, of course. He's the romantic twin," she murmured, her expression changing entirely with the mention of the younger twin brother. "If David does finally marry her, I will send a letter welcoming Lady Clarinda to the family," she added with a sigh. "And then I shall pity her for the rest of my life." This last was said with a good deal of humor, as if Constance knew something about her cousin that most did not.

Isabella merely grinned, suddenly realizing the cousins were probably happy to know one another. She grinned even wider after a moment, happy to have a new friend.

Chapter 14

AN EARL PAYS A CALL ON FAIR DOWNS

Meanwhile, in Boxgrove

Spotting the glossy black coach parked in front of Fair Downs, Mr. Jenkins knew immediately who was paying a call. Having just returned from Chichester with that month's food stuffs, the groom quickly parked the wagon behind the coach, gave a small apple to each horse, and made his way to the front door.

"Lord Norwick?" he called out as he reluctantly stepped through the front door. Normally he would enter through the back, but with everyone else gone, he didn't want to startle the visitor.

The tall earl poked his head out of the parlor. "Hello, Jenkins," David said. "Any idea where the lady of the house might be?"

The groom gave a bow. "She's paying a call over at Huntinghurst. Don't expect her back for another hour or so, though," he said. "Can you stay that long, my lord? I can see to some tea whilst you wait."

"Won't be necessary," David said as he approached the groom. He held out a ten pound note. "I was just here to pay the staff and check on the place."

His eyes boggling at the sight of the money, Jenkins hesitated a moment before taking it from the earl. "This is for all of us then?" he asked, thinking the ten pounds would be split among all the servants.

"That's for you. I've left another one for Miss Simmons on her bed, one for the housekeeper—it's on the desk in her office—and one in the kitchen for the cook. Where is she, by the way?"

Jenkins' face seemed to pink up a bit. "Down at the coast. Her husband's ship came in day 'afore yesterday. We don't expect her back until tomorrow," he added with a waggling brow. "The scullery maid has been doing the cooking in her stead."

David nodded his understanding. "Conjugal visit, of course." He angled his head to one side. "Housekeeper?"

Jenkins shook his head. "Haven't got one. Miss Fitzwilliam has been seeing to it herself."

Wincing at this bit of news, David peeled off another bank note from a roll he held in one fist and gave it to Jenkins. "Give it to her. Tell her she has to hire a housekeeper," he demanded, his words a bit harsh. He suddenly sighed, realizing the groom agreed with him about the need for another servant.

"Oh, I will," Jenkins said with a nod. "I'll see to it she doesn't squirrel it away with the rest of her mother's money."

David frowned before he realized what money the groom was referring to. "Well, give my cousin my regards, then. I'm off to London. I'm about to finally take a bride, Jenkins."

The groom blinked. "Lady Clarinda, by chance?"

The earl gave a start, rather surprised the groom would know of his intended's name. "How did you know that?"

Jenkins gave a shrug. "Simmons reads us *The Tattler* during dinner some nights. I must say, the roses are a nice touch, my lord." He glanced down at the bank note he held and his eyes widened. Holding the ten pound note as if it were pure gold, Jenkins shook his head. "My lord, Miss Fitzwilliam already pays us a salary," he said in a quiet voice, not adding that it was far less than what the earl was giving out.

"Mr. Jenkins, Fair Downs is an entailed property of the Norwick earldom. Salaries are my responsibility," David stated, almost as if had said the words many time before.

The groom merely nodded. "She appreciates it, my lord. Really, she does. She's just... proud, is all."

Allowing a sigh, David finally nodded. "Well, if the funds should grow short again, you might mention the possibility of some of her mother's money behind the books in the study," he suggested with a wink.

Jenkins blinked again, the air going out of his lungs in a *whoosh*. "Yes, my lord. I won't tell it was you who left it there."

"I appreciate your discretion." David was about to take his leave of the house but paused. "I was very sorry to learn of *Twin's Second Favorite's* passing," he said in a quiet voice. "I know he was her favorite."

Lowering his head a bit, Jenkins finally nodded. "He was my favorite, too, my lord. But now, Mr. Tuttlebaum has that honor."

David gave a nod, remembering how Mr. Tuttlebaum had managed to win every race in which he was entered. Too bad his younger brother, Mr. Wiggins, hadn't been listed in Weatherby's *Giant Stud Book*. At three years of age, he would have been eligible for last year's races, David considered. Perhaps he would see to it Constance could enter him in the Ascot when he turned six. If Mr. Wiggins won, then Constance would have the winnings along with her inheritance and be set for life.

A capital idea, David thought has he climbed into his coach for the trip back to the capital.

Chapter 15

DOUBLE THE CHOICE, DOUBLE THE CONFUSION

Three days later

Clarinda Anne Brotherton dared a glance at the ornate mantle clock in her bedchamber and wondered how much longer she would have to wait before the butler appeared. Open on the vanity was the missive she had received shortly after waking that morning.

My dearest Lady Clarinda,

A matter most urgent requires your attention. A reckoning, if you will, for you have a decision of utmost importance to make. Please accept my call at four o'clock this afternoon. Should you require an excuse to meet with me, say it is to ride in Hyde Park during the fashionable hour, for you may require the time to make your decision.

Yours very truly,

D

The handwriting was familiar, of course. She had received other missives from 'D'. She was betrothed to the man, after all. But this one mentioned something urgent, and other than the plans for their upcoming nuptials, she could think of nothing else requiring *urgency.*

Despite expecting it, she still gave a start when the sound of a sharp rap came from the door. "Come!" she called out. She dared a quick glance in the mirror in front of her, rather hoping her riding hat didn't hide too much of the coiffure Missy had managed to create just the hour before. Her dark hair, wound into a simple chignon and secured with flower-tipped pins, would have been suitable for a ball, dressed as it was.

The butler stood with his gloved hands behind his back. "There are two gentlemen calling on you, my lady," he said as he held out white pasteboard calling cards.

Angling her head to one side, Clarinda frowned before getting up from the vanity. "Two?" she repeated. "But I was only expecting...." She was about to say 'D', but thought better of it. "Norwick."

His eyes darting to one side, the butler seemed at a loss as to how to respond. "One of them is Lord Norwick, I am sure," he replied carefully.

Clarinda took the calling cards, examining each a moment before raising her eyes back up to meet the butler's. "Oh, dear," she murmured quietly. For in her hands, she held identical cards. Identical except for three letters. Or just one, depending on how one arranged the letters.

"I apologize, but I do not recall which one gave me which card," the butler murmured, his manner most apologetic. "Not that it would have done any good, though, seeing as how they're dressed exactly the same."

Frowning so a fold of skin developed between her brows, Clarinda gave her head a quick shake. "I don't understand."

Allowing a slight sigh, the butler straightened. "You will when you see them, my lady. I've shown them both to the parlor. I'll bring tea in a moment."

"Bring the scotch, too," she ordered.

Or maybe I'll have brandy.

Clarinda hurried from the bedchamber and watched as the butler made his way to the back stairs. She had to slow her steps as she reached the top of the main stairs. Lifting the skirts of her riding habit, she carefully lowered herself down each step and was nearly at the bottom before she remembered her hat. She was about to go back up, but male voices sounded from the parlor, and they were tinged with a hint of anger. Or perhaps it was merely anxiousness. Nevertheless, curiosity had her proceeding to the parlor doors.

About to breeze in as she would with any of her lady callers, Clarinda stopped short before she was one step beyond the threshold.

She blinked.

She managed to bob a curtsy.

She even lifted both hands as the two gentlemen callers lowered their lips to the back of her knuckles and brushed identical kisses over them.

But that's as much as she could do before a gray cloud seemed to replace the images of the two men who stood before her.

Two identical men.

"She's fainting," one of the men said as he moved to get an arm beneath hers. The other followed suit, and soon the two had her half-sitting on the settee.

"Do you have any smelling salts, Danny?" David asked as he found a fan and began waving it in front of her face.

"Of course not," Daniel replied, his manner betraying his annoyance with his brother. "But you should have known this was going to happen," he accused. "The least you could have done was come prepared."

"Should I loosen her corset?" David asked, leaning over as if he intended to undo the buttons down the front of her riding habit.

"No!" Daniel replied. "The butler said he would be bringing tea..." He stopped, rethinking his protest. If his brother was caught with his hand down Lady Clarinda's corset, his chances at being the one chosen by her to be her husband would probably be significantly reduced. "Although, I suppose if you must..." he suddenly encouraged.

David gave his brother a quelling glance. "I have to do

something," he argued, his gaze taking in the beauty whose head was leaning back against the top of the settee. Her swan-like neck, fully exposed, led to an oval face featuring a peaches-and-cream complexion with just a faint dusting of freckles on her pert nose. The high cheekbones weren't as evident in repose, but her long, dark lashes were. He had half a mind to kiss one of her eyelids. *God, she is beautiful*, he thought, rather shocked he hadn't noticed before. *She looks like Arabella*. Behind those eyelids, he knew her eyes were green. Or blue. Or both.

Deciding to find out, he leaned over and gently kissed both her eyelids.

"David!" his brother admonished him. "What the hell?" But his protestations stopped when he realized Clarinda's aquamarine eyes were fluttering open. She was staring at his brother with an expression that easily betrayed how besotted she was with him at that moment.

David lifted one of her hands in his and held it a moment. "My beautiful bride," he murmured before leaning over to kiss her palm.

Rolling his eyes, Daniel was about to put voice to a complaint when he realized Clarinda had turned her gaze on him. "Hello, Clare. I do hope you're feeling better."

She angled her head and took a quick glance at both of her visitors. "Who are you?" she asked.

Feeling as if his stomach had dropped to his feet, Daniel sighed. "The man who wants to make you his wife, of course," he replied. "The man who has courted you in Kensington Gardens. Given you dozens of pink roses. Bestowed a sapphire ring on your finger," he said as he moved to lift the hand on which the ring was displayed. "I wanted to give you our grandmother's ring, but our mother, Dorothea, is still wearing it."

Clarinda furrowed her brows at his claim and pulled her hand back before he could grasp it. "Norwick?" she asked, her question betraying her confusion.

"At your service," David replied with a bow.

Smiling, Clarinda angled her head and said, "I knew you had a twin brother, but you didn't tell me he looked *exactly* like you," she admonished lightly.

David gave a slight shrug. "Which is why I thought to bring him along. So that I might introduce you."

Clarinda turned her attention to Daniel, whose expression betrayed the murderous thoughts he was having of his older twin brother just then. "Have you been in town long?" she asked, her inquisitive expression faltering just a bit as she paid witness to the man's sudden anger. *What had he said about Kensington Gardens?* she wondered, finally feeling as if she had recovered from her fainting spell. Seeing two Norwicks in the parlor was enough of a shock, but it didn't help that her lady's maid, Missy, had tugged her corset strings a bit too tight. She could barely breathe!

Daniel's chest compressed just a bit. Despite her attention on him, she didn't seem to *recognize* him. Didn't seem to realize that *he* was the one who had been courting her. That *he* was the one who bestowed the stolen kisses on her in Kensington Gardens. That *he* was the one who gifted her with pink roses. "Of course, I have," he replied. "The entire time I've been courting you, in—"

"The entire time *I've* been courting you," David interrupted, still holding onto one of her hands.

Daniel was about to say something like, *What, two minutes?* but realized Clarinda was gazing at his brother with a look so besotted, she might have been a girl fresh out of the schoolroom and not the woman of two-and-twenty she was.

How can this be happening? he wondered, his chest compressing so he actually winced. *Am I having a coronary? What the hell?*

"You're looking a bit peaked, brother," David said suddenly, his face betraying a hint of concern that actually looked genuine. "Are you ill?"

"That was my thought, exactly," Clarinda chimed in, her gaze finally resting on Daniel. "The tea should be here any moment, but perhaps you could use some brandy. I think there's a bottle here—"

"That won't be necessary, my lady," Daniel said with a shake of his head. He moved to get up from the settee, a combination of anger and hurt—nay, betrayal—providing the strength he needed.

He would deal with David in private.

His hand still hurt from when he had punched his brother just two weeks ago, but more important, he didn't want Clarinda paying witness to his lack of skills as a pugilist.

Chapter 16

A DUCAL VISIT TO A WARD

Two weeks later

Timing is everything, Octavius considered as he regarded the luncheon that had been set before him. *The Angel*, one of the oldest coaching inns in all of England, was the perfect place to rest his horse and enjoy a pint of ale with his food. Just behind him, a burly driver had taken a seat along with a servant, the liveried man putting voice to a complaint about how much longer their trip south would take. When the man mentioned Craythorne, the duke paid closer attention.

"Don't fash yourself. I'll get you there 'afore nightfall," the driver said just as the tavern maid delivered their pints of ale.

"And you know where this cottage is?" the servant pressed. "I've not been to his lordship's seaside retreat before." The manner in which he said 'seaside retreat' was most facetious, Octavius thought, which had him wondering where this particular servant usually worked.

The driver made a sound not unlike a snort. "Outside Southampton, of course. Not too far from civilization."

Octavius realized just then that the liveried servant certainly wasn't from Craythorne Castle in Basingstoke—

Guildford was in the wrong direction if they were headed to Southampton.

"Trust me, you'll like it better than London in the summer," the driver continued. "And seein' as how the earl won't be going back to London anytime soon, it's either work at the cottage or you'll be seein' to finding a new position."

"I suppose," the servant replied, rather dejected. Any further talk was interrupted by the delivery of their meals, and a moment after that, word that the horses had been changed out on their coach, and that they needed to leave.

Octavius dared a glance at the two servants as they took their leave of *The Angel*, half-tempted to follow them to Craythorne's cottage. He remembered his own coach, though, still somewhere on the way to Guildford from London—he had passed it a half-hour out of Guildford—and decided to continue to Huntinghurst.

Once he finished his early luncheon, Octavius was about to take his leave when his coach pulled into the yard. He grinned at the driver and groom, giving them a wave as he set Poseidon on the road south to Cocking. The change of coach horses would take just twenty minutes in the inn's yard, but he had no intention of waiting.

The coach had departed the duke's townhouse more than an hour before Octavius took his leave on Poseidon. He had given instructions to the driver to wait for him at Guildford. Octavius had thought to ride his horse only halfway to Huntinghurst and then spend the rest of the trip in the coach, but the fine summer day and Poseidon's determination to run on this day—apparently the entire distance to Huntinghurst—had him changing his mind.

Curious as to the endurance of his mount, he wondered how long Poseidon could last. The beast had been restless of late, and with so many mares in season in the city, the beast seemed more anxious than usual. A few days at Huntinghurst after a hard run could only help his disposition.

And perhaps his own as well. Mourning Jane was making him maudlin. Old.

Nowadays, he spent his early mornings riding along the Serpentine. He spent his days in Parliament—the current session wouldn't end until mid-July. He spent his late afternoons in Kew Gardens, staring at the red roses Jane had said were her favorites. He spent his evenings reading. He spent his nights fighting nightmares.

And of late, he had been spending far too much time wondering how he was going to tell his ward the story of how her mother had died. At least, according to Craythorne.

Perhaps she already knew, he considered. The newspapers in London had finally included the death notice, buried on the page with the rest of the obituaries. The Earl of Craythorne hadn't made an appearance in London since the death of Arabella, his few letters to associates mentioning his heartbreak at having lost his wife to a horrible accident.

Arabella tripped and hit her head on the footboard,

Craythorne had written to his late wife's brother, the Earl of Heath.

Despite my attempts to revive her, she was already lost to me. I had her buried in the family plot on the Craythorne grounds.

That letter had been written just a few days after Isabella was dispatched in a ducal carriage to live at Huntinghurst. When Octavius approached Albert Brotherton, Earl of Heath, to give him his condolences, he wasn't surprised to learn Heath was rather suspicious about the circumstance surrounding his sister's death. *I cannot help but believe he had something to do with her death*, Heath offered as he indicated the letter he had received.

When Octavius asked if he might read Craythorne's account of the tragedy, the earl immediately handed him the missive. *I sent a man to investigate*, Heath said in a quiet voice. *But the servants all told him Craythorne grieved for two days—first for Arabella and then for his daughter—and then he disappeared from Basingstoke.*

Do they suspect he was complicit in her death? Octavius asked then. Should they be willing to talk, servants could be a wealth of information about their masters and mistresses.

Heath took a deep breath and let it out slowly. *Not a one. Those who were willing to speak at all said Craythorne was in love with Arabella. Devoted to her.*

Octavius remembered frowning at the comment. Isabella had never mentioned Craythorne's devotion to her mother. Had the shock of seeing the man leaning over Arabella, his hands around her neck, completely obliterated any good memories she might have had of her father?

But he couldn't give the question further consideration when he realized Heath was regarding him with a quizzical expression. *You are suspicious as well?* he asked.

Octavius allowed a noncommittal shrug. *Did your man interview anyone who handled the body? Could he confirm she died of a wound to the head?*

Shaking his head, Heath allowed another sigh. *He could not.*

After taking his leave of Stockton House, Octavius found Norwick at Brooks's and passed along what he had learned from Heath. *We may never know the truth,* he warned the earl.

Octavius would never forget Norwick's response.

I will. If it takes killing the man, I will learn the truth.

Octavius was nearly to the turnoff for Huntinghurst when he spotted two mounts heading in his direction. Slowing Poseidon to a canter, he watched as the two riders made the same turn he would be making in another few hundred yards.

Isabella, he realized, with another woman. He watched as they continued, apparently unaware of his approach. Both rode with practiced ease, their backs straight and the skirts of their riding habits spread in perfect arcs along one side of their mounts.

Poseidon reared his head, apparently unhappy with the slower pace. "Settle down, you beast," Octavius murmured as they made the turn. The women were already around the next bend, but Poseidon soon had them back in sight just as the two mounts stopped in front of Huntinghurst. He could hear the women chatting as they slowed their mounts.

"Hello!" Octavius called out, Poseidon cantering until he was nearly abreast of the women. Octavius pulled him to a halt.

The older woman seemed surprised at his sudden appearance, and not in a good way. Then Isabella's face lit up with a brilliant smile. "Your Grace!" she called out, halting her horse.

"Your Grace?" Constance repeated in a hoarse whisper meant only for Isabella to hear as she halted her own horse next to Isabella's mount. "Oh, dear," she whispered, not at all prepared to meet the Duke of Huntington.

Octavius was quick to dismount and hurry over to the women. "Allow me," he said as he placed his hands at Isabella's waist and lowered her to the ground.

"It's so good to see you, Your Grace," she said as she stood on tiptoes and gave him a kiss on the cheek. When she stepped back, she dipped a curtsy and said, "Your Grace, Duke of Huntington, I wish to introduce you to my new friend, Miss Fitzwilliam."

Octavius was sure his face reddened at Isabella's greeting—he was never kissed on the cheek by anyone but his mother—but he was quick to let go of her and move to the other horse. The duke tipped his top hat, thinking Isabella's new friend seemed familiar. "Good afternoon," he said as he reached up to Constance's waist.

"Your Grace," she said with a nod as she held her crop in one hand and placed her other hand on his shoulder before he lowered her to the ground.

"Miss Fitzwilliam sees to Fair Downs on behalf of Lord Norwick," Isabella said. "She is gracious enough to make the trip to Huntinghurst so that we might ride together two times each week," she added, just then noting that the duke hadn't been out for a pleasure ride. His boots displayed a layer of dirt, as did his top coat, that suggested a much longer journey.

"It's an honor to meet you, Your Grace," Constance said as she dipped a curtsy.

"You must be Norwick's cousin," Octavius commented as he offered an arm to her. "Poor thing," he added with a teasing grin.

A bit tongue-tied, Constance merely nodded and finally placed a hand on his arm, noting how Isabella had already helped herself to his other arm. The three made their way toward the front door.

"From where did you ride, Your Grace?" Isabella wondered, her attention going to the side of the house where George, the stableboy, was racing out to see to the horses. He had parked Constance's gig at the end of the drive and had unhitched her draft horse earlier that morning.

"London, in fact. Please excuse my appearance. I intended to ride in the coach for part of the trip, but my mount seemed up to making the entire trip at a near gallop."

"All that way?" Constance remarked in disbelief. She was about to say something about how saddle sore he must be, but thought better of it.

"Indeed. Poseidon has been most restless of late."

Isabella angled her head in his direction. "'Tis the season, Your Grace," she murmured with a smirk.

Frowning, Octavius was about to ask what she meant when George let out a shout. The duke turned around and cursed, his body tensed to move quickly.

The two women whirled around, their attention going to Poseidon. The stallion had mounted Constance's horse, and although the mare didn't seem particularly bothered, Constance let out a cry of shock.

"Christ!" Octavius said under his breath. "Forgive my curse," he managed then, his head shaking from side to side.

Although she had paid witness to horses mating in the past, Isabella inhaled sharply at seeing the huge beast atop the Thoroughbred bay Constance had brought from Fair Downs. "Oh, Connie, I do hope you didn't have breeding plans for Amasia this season," she murmured as she watched George lead her own mount away from the other two horses.

"I didn't have a stud in mind for her at all," the older woman replied, her breaths coming in short gasps. She seemed on the verge of tears.

Octavius turned to regard her, his brows furrowing. "Poseidon has an exceptional lineage," he stated, his words suggesting he was offended by her manner.

"Of that, I have no doubt," Constance replied with a shake of her head. "He's a magnificent beast, Your Grace. Perfect composition. Excellent head shape and wide-spaced eyes. Long legs, high withers, deep chest. Seventeen hands tall. Maybe more," she said as she continued to watch the horses.

Rather stunned to hear her recitation of his horse's perfect features, Octavius turned to regard her. "So, what, pray tell, is at issue, my lady?"

Constance lifted her gaze to him and gave a slight shrug. "I'm quite sure I cannot begin to afford the stud fee," she said with a sigh.

At first rather surprised by her comment, Octavius finally allowed a grin. And then he chuckled, which had Isabella turning to regard him with a tentative grin. "Let us agree this one time is gratis," he announced with a nod. He allowed a sigh before he realized the two young women were watching horses mate. "Why don't we go inside for some refreshment?" he suggested, rather embarrassed to have two women flanking him as they watched his horse have its way with the smaller Thoroughbred.

"Peters said he would see to tea and cakes in the parlor," Isabella replied.

After a quick glance in George's direction, and seeing that the head groom had joined the young stableboy to help with the horses, Octavius once again offered his arms to the young ladies. "Let's try this again," he said as they made their way into the house.

About to excuse herself and claim she needed to get back to Fair Downs, Constance realized it might be some time before Amasia would be available to leave.

Settling herself into her usual chair in the parlor, Constance watched as both the duke and Isabella seemed rather tentative with one another. She had paid witness to Isabella kissing the duke's cheek, but as his ward, she supposed it was a proper greeting. That he didn't return the greeting the same way had her wondering, though.

"I do hope you get to stay a few days," Isabella said as she poured tea. She added milk and sugar before offering the cup and saucer to Constance.

Octavius angled his head to one side. "Just a day or so," he replied. "Parliament is still in session. But I've news from... from the Earl of Heath," he hedged, wondering if she had shared her reason for being at Huntinghurst with Constance.

If she suspected the news was truly news about her mother, Isabella didn't show it in how she responded. She handed him a cup of tea and was about to ask, "And how is my uncle...?" when she realized the query would tie her in a familial way to the earl. "How is Lord Heath these days?" she asked instead.

Taking a sip of the tea, his eyes widening at how sweet she had made it, Octavius dared a glance at their guest. "Heath is rather happy his daughter is finally going to marry." His news was far more serious, but he didn't dare bring up the matter of Craythorne's letter to Isabella's uncle in front of Constance Fitzwilliam.

Isabella allowed a brilliant grin. "I rather imagine Lady

Clarinda is of the same mind." She turned her attention to Constance. "Your cousin will be most fortunate to marry her," she said, *sotto voce*, her face lighting up in delight as she said the comment.

Octavius blinked, and not because of what she said but rather how she said it. How her face lit up. How genuine she seemed with her enthusiasm.

Had Jane ever shown such delight when relating happy news? *Perhaps she had never had such happy news to share*, he considered.

"I am glad for them both, but I must admit to a bit of surprise that Lady Clarinda was still agreeable to the match given Norwick missed his deadline," Constance replied.

"Me as well," Octavius agreed, rather surprised the woman knew about that particular clause of the betrothal contract. "They plan to wed in a couple of weeks, but they won't go on their wedding trip until after Parliament ends in July."

"I hear tell Lady Clarinda wishes to see Italy," Constance said, not about to mention Simmons had read that particular item in the latest issue of *The Tattler*. "Will you attend the wedding?" Constance asked, her query directed to Isabella.

The younger woman shook her head. "Oh, no. There was a death in her family recently, so I'm quite sure Clare would prefer they be married in a small, private ceremony."

So, she hasn't shared too much, Octavius realized, although he winced at her use of Lady Clarinda's nickname. "I've a mind to go just to be sure Norwick actually says his vows," he teased. He regarded Constance for a moment, wondering at her age and her circumstances. Surely if she wanted to marry, there would be an eligible bachelor somewhere around Chichester willing to have her. She was a handsome woman, her dark hair wound into a top knot from which a riot of curls erupted. Her fitted riding habit promised a pleasing figure beneath. And if she was as accomplished a horsewoman as Norwick suggested, then surely a man could appreciate her skills with a horse.

Well, some would. Not all men had an appreciation for horseflesh.

"I really should be taking my leave," Constance said suddenly, her attention on the Rococo clock on the mantle. "I had no idea it was so late."

The duke stood up, affording a bow to her deep curtsy. "Do you have an escort, Miss Fitzwilliam?" he asked with some concern.

"My lady's maid, of course," she replied with a nod.

"Very good. I look forward to your next visit," Octavius said as he took her gloved hand and brushed his lips over her knuckles.

A bit surprised by the gesture, Constance gave a nod. "It's kind of you to host me, Your Grace." She decided it best not to say anything about Amasia.

Isabella joined her, giving the duke a curtsy. "I'll see Miss Fitzwilliam to her gig and return in a moment," she said to the duke. At Octavius' nod of acknowledgement, Isabella escorted Constance, arm-in-arm, to the front door. "I do hope you're not too terribly vexed about what happened with Poseidon," she said in a quiet voice, just before she directed a footman to see to summoning Simmons from the servants' dining room. "If she should carry his foal, it will be magnificent."

Constance leaned in and gave a wink. "I'm counting on it."

And with that, Constance Fitzwilliam took her leave of Huntinghurst.

Isabella turned to head back to the parlor, hoping the duke was still there. She knew he intended to tell her something about her uncle, but he obviously couldn't given her visitor. About to make her way up the stairs, she stopped when she realized he was descending them. "Your Grace," she said as she dipped a curtsy.

"In my study," he stated, his manner most severe.

Stunned by his curt words, Isabella hurried to keep up,

pausing on the threshold of the dark paneled room. "What is it?" she asked in a whisper.

He gestured to the chair in front of a massive oak desk. "Shut the door."

Isabella did as she was told, gingerly taking a seat in front of the desk as if she expected an inquisition to take place. "What's wrong, Your Grace?"

"What does Miss Fitzwilliam know? About you? About your circumstance?"

Relaxing a bit, Isabella realized he was only worried about how much Constance knew. "Lord Norwick asked that she befriend me. She knows he's to marry Lady Clarinda, of course, but she doesn't know I am related to Clare. She thinks me an orphan."

Octavius regarded her for a long time before he finally allowed a sigh. "You're quite sure she doesn't know more than that?"

Furrowing her brows, Isabella gave her head a shake. "If she does, it's because Lord Norwick told her. We only speak of horses."

He arched a brow at the claim. "You spend hours in her company, riding horses, and you only speak of horses?" he asked in disbelief.

Isabella wondered at the disbelief in his voice. "Yes. Well, we did talk a bit about the latest issue of *The Tattler*. But I'm not familiar with the subjects of the articles, so it's really of no interest to me."

Octavius blinked. Even the men at White's and Brooks's took an interest in *The Tattler*, London's premiere gossip rag. Perhaps Isabella was still too young to involve herself in gossip. "I've come because your uncle received a letter from Craythorne."

Isabella stiffened and held her head up. "And?"

The duke sighed. "He described a scene in which Lady Craythorne fell and hit her head on some furniture. Claims she was dead before she hit the floor." He watched Isabella carefully, gauging her reaction and not a bit surprised at how she jerked in response to his callous words.

"His hands were around her neck," she whispered hoarsely.

"Did you see... did you see any blood? From a gash? A wound to her head? Any evidence at all of her having hit her head?"

Isabella shook her head back and forth and continued to do so as she said, "No. No. No. He was *strangling* her. He had his hands around the base of her neck, and he was yelling at her and shaking her."

Octavius held up a staying hand. "Lord Norwick will be paying another visit to Craythorne Castle. He intends to discover the truth for himself, even if he has to interview those that saw to your mother's body. At some point, the truth of the matter will revealed," he assured her.

He didn't tell her Norwick had already attempted to speak with Craythorne. The letter in Heath's possession and news from the man he had sent to investigate only confirmed what Norwick had reported—the bereft Craythorne had left the castle. What neither knew was that Craythorne was sequestered in a cottage near the coast, and Octavius only knew that because of what he had overheard a driver say whilst he ate his luncheon at *The Angel*. No one had seen the man since the day of Arabella's funeral.

A single tear made its way down Isabella's cheek. "Thank you, Your Grace. I do appreciate you having made the trip to tell me in person," she managed to say without a sob interrupting her.

"How are you getting on otherwise?"

Straightening in the chair, Isabella allowed a nod. "Very fine, I think. It helps to spend time in your stables. I simply *adore* your horses."

Octavius gave a start as to how she said the last words. He had never wondered what it might be like to be *adored* by someone. To be held in such esteem as to have someone speaking in glowing terms and displaying an expression of obvious appreciation as Isabella was doing this instant.

Had Jane adored him? Octavius furrowed his brows, thinking her affection far more than simple adoration.

At least, he hoped it had been.

"As long as you don't spoil them rotten," he finally replied.

Isabella blinked. "Oh, besides an apple now and then, they shall only have my attention," she claimed with a shake of her head.

They'll be spoiled for certain, the duke thought with a sigh.

Chapter 17

A WEDDING BREAKFAST

Late June, 1813

For an affair that was to have been on the intimate end of the social spectrum, David Fitzwilliam was rather surprised at the number of guests that assembled in Stockton House for the breakfast following his wedding to Lady Clarinda.

"How does it feel to be leg-shackled?" Milton Grandby, Earl of Torrington, asked as he helped himself to a glass of champagne from a footman's tray.

David regarded his fellow earl for a moment and nearly rolled his eyes. The older earl had managed to avoid marriage, opting instead to escort a different widow every Season to the various events. A quick glance around the parlor didn't reveal a woman that fit the bill, though. "How does it feel to be the last of us to be a bachelor?" David countered with an arched eyebrow.

Milton straightened and seemed to give the question some thought before saying, "Like I've won some kind of contest, and I'm just waiting for my prize."

Giving the Earl of Torrington a quelling glance, David downed the rest of his champagne. "A larger bank account is your prize," he murmured. "I fear mine is about to be drained when I begin receiving the bill's for my wife's modiste."

Frowning, Milton leaned in closer. "Now see here, Norwick. You're speaking of my very first goddaughter, and I'll have you know she's not a typical spoiled chit," he admonished the younger earl. "Heath wouldn't have allowed it. Besides, she came with a rather large dowry that should see you quite flush, probably for the rest of your life. That is, unless you're planning to take up gambling."

David shook his head. "I am not. But I am rather glad O'Leary took over the gaming hell, even if I let him have it at a steep discount. An agent has seen to the sale of the property that housed *The Elegant Courtesan*—"

"Which will be sorely missed," Milton interrupted.

"And Lord Pettigrew has taken one of the girls as his mistress. He needed a townhouse for her, and I just happened to have one to let," he said with an arched brow. "So the sting of losing my cash flow is not so great."

Lord Torrington rolled his eyes. "You'll appreciate having more time to spend at your club. Time at home with Clare. She adores you."

David swallowed, thinking of how many times he wished his brother had objected during the reading of the banns, or had simply stepped in and taken his place at the altar. Despite his need to be married, he still wasn't sure he wanted to be married.

And then Clarinda was suddenly standing next to him before the altar, glancing up at him with a teasing expression that had him thinking she was Arabella. The moment left him a bit discombobulated, much like when she had first opened her eyes after he kissed the delicate skin of her eyelids the day she had fainted.

Any thoughts of Daniel stepping in to replace him flew from his head as he stood and said his vows. No, she wasn't Arabella. But she was so much like his first love—in how she looked, in how she spoke, her demeanor, her soft giggle—he found he was a bit smitten. "I do feel affection for her," he murmured. "But I think it will be some time before she... trusts me," he added.

"Heard about that, did you?" Milton asked in a hoarse whisper. "I have to say, she was quite serious when she said she wouldn't put up with a philandering husband, but I never expected she would hire a Bow Street Runner to see to it you stayed monogamous." He paused a moment. "Whatever tipped you off?"

David spotted his new bride in conversation with Lady Worthington and winked, which had her dimpling and her face turning a pretty shade of pink. "The invoice from the agency," he replied with an arched brow.

Milton guffawed, which had several nearby guests glancing in his direction. "Despite what you're thinking now, it will all be worth it. Get a child on her and enjoy your life whilst you can," the older man advised. He glanced around the room. "Now, what have you done with your twin brother?"

Frowning, David did a quick survey of the guests from his taller perspective, but Daniel was no where to be found. "Licking his wounds, I suppose." At Milton's perplexed expression, he added, "He claimed he loved Clarinda. Wanted to marry her. Even proposed to her," he said with a sigh.

The older earl's bushy eyebrows furrowed into a single caterpillar across his forehead. "And here I thought that was you," he said quietly.

"Only sometimes," David admitted, both brows rising up on his forehead. His gaze once again found Clarinda in the crowd, and instead of simply winking at her, he watched her until she finally joined him and the earl. He leaned over and kissed the side of her head. "Hullo, beautiful," he whispered.

Milton took her hand and kissed the back of it. "Send for me if he does something you don't like," he said, *sotto voce.*

Clarinda's face bloomed with color before she gave a nod. "It's your turn to marry, you must know," she countered.

The older earl grimaced. "Not quite yet. A couple of

years, perhaps, when I finally decide which one," he said. Despite his words, his gaze followed one particular woman through the breakfast crowd, and although Clarinda tried to guess just whom it might be, she soon gave up in favor of listening to her new husband's quiet words of affection.

Chapter 18

AN EARL PAYS A CALL, A DUKE PAYS A VISIT

The following April, 1814

The trip from London had been far more pleasant than Octavius expected. The weather outside was fine—not a cloud in sight—but given the letter he had received from Peters, his butler at Huntinghurst, he expected to find a different climate inside Huntinghurst.

He had timed his arrival perfectly, for he had lunched at the last coaching stop just to be sure he was at the front door of the estate no earlier than three o'clock in the afternoon. Given this was Peter's usual day off, he let himself in and stood just inside the front door, listening intently.

He found he heard nothing at all.

Octavius frowned, an expression he realized he was prone to do far too frequently these days. *Why was the news never good?* he wondered just then, his hand moving to the pocket where Peter's most recent missive rested. Besides a brief accounting of the household expenses, the butler included a rather unusual addition to his weekly report.

Your Grace, I fear your charge has become a hoyden, her behavior most uncharacteristic of young ladies of quality. Although Lady Isabella hosts a handsome woman (in the company of her lady's maid) for tea and to go riding on occasion, she continues to exhibit tendencies to toil in a most unladylike manner. Why, just last week, I paid witness to her brushing a horse in the stables...

At that point in reading the letter, Octavius had been interrupted by the butler of his Mayfair townhouse with news that he had a visitor. For once, the duke actually welcomed the diversion, even if it came in the form of David Fitzwilliam, Earl of Norwick.

Or maybe because it was Norwick.

Welcome back to London. How was the wedding trip?

David angled his head first to one side and then the other. *Diverting*, he finally replied. *I have had my fill of Italy and Greece, however. Entirely too hot, but Clarinda never complained. Never tired at looking at old stuff, either.* Upon his arrival, David had given the duke more than a simple nod, nearly bowing when he appeared in the doorway to the study. *I hope I haven't come at an inconvenient time,* he added, moving to the chair Octavius indicated with a wave.

Arching an eyebrow at the comment, Octavius wondered if that was usual for Clarinda or if she had simply been on her best behavior. *A trip sounds like a perfect diversion for me right about now. You've managed to time your arrival just right. I've just received a complaint and was pondering what to do.*

His brows furrowing, David regarded the duke a moment before he allowed a sigh. *What has she done now?* he asked in dismay, realizing almost immediately the duke referred to Isabella.

Toiling, it seems, Octavius said as he tossed the letter onto his desk.

David blinked. *What?*

Peters paid witness to her brushing a horse, Octavius stated, barely able to hide his humor behind his mock astonishment.

David nearly blinked again, but his sigh of relief was quite evident. *Jesus, Hunt, you had me wondering if I was going to have to send her to a finishing school on the Continent,* he groused. *I take it your butler has never worked in a London household. Otherwise, a young lady brushing a horse wouldn't seem so scandalous. Christ, I've paid witness to Mayfield's daughter brushing her horse,* he claimed, referring to Julia Harrington.

Have you told your countess about her yet?

Even knowing the duke would ask again as to whether or not he had shared his secret with Clarinda, David still felt a hint of annoyance. *I have decided I will do so on the occasion of either Isabella's twenty-first birthday or Craythorne's death,* he said in a quiet voice. *Which ever comes first. Clare will no doubt mention something about the date and Isabella's mysterious disappearance. And then I'll have my prompt to explain that she's under your protection. If she presses and wants to know more, well, then I'll mention I'm her real father,* he said with a shrug.

Coward, Octavius countered, retrieving the decanter of scotch from behind his desk. He poured a finger's worth into a couple of tumblers and handed one to David.

I admit I am on tenterhooks here, the earl replied, taking the scotch with a nod. He waited until the duke had taken a sip before he did so. Then he waited for the smoky fluid to burn his tongue a bit before swallowing. *I thought it would be easy to tell Clare because...* He stopped and allowed a sigh.

What is it?

I aways thought she and I would get on, of course. She's a very agreeable woman. But I didn't expect to... He stopped again, his gaze finally rising to meet the duke's questioning glance.

To what?

Feel affection for her, David nearly whispered, his expression looking as if he were doing an imitation of one of his hound dogs.

Octavius blinked. And then he blinked again. *Be careful, or before long, you'll be in* love *with your wife!* he accused, rather surprised the mention of loving a wife didn't have a lump building in his throat.

From the way the duke had said the words, David didn't know if the man was appalled or impressed. *I rather doubt that. And I rather doubt she'll ever be in love with me*, he argued. When he paid witness to the duke's sudden grin and heard an accompanying chuckle, he added, *It's not funny, Hunt! This is... quite unexpected!*

The duke sobered then. *Soon you'll know how your brother, Daniel, feels,* he warned in a quiet voice. He took another sip of his scotch. *Where is he, by the way? I haven't seen him since your wedding.*

David dipped his head. *He's gone back to Norwick Park. He's still seeing to the books, of course—*

Bleeding you dry, I imagine. That's what I would do if I was acting as accomptant for a brother who stole my true love from me.

But he says he cannot abide being in the city knowing Clare is married to me, David went on, ignoring the duke's verbal jab.

Octavius sighed. *Such are the vagaries of being the second son, I suppose,* he murmured. Since he had never had a younger brother, Octavius didn't know how he might have reacted if he found his affection for Jane challenged by a brother. He was about to consider the topic another moment, but David waved a hand through the air. The duke blinked and gave a nod. *What is it?*

When you next go to Huntinghurst, will you take something for me? David asked as he pulled a small box from his topcoat pocket. He reached over and placed it on the desk, holding it a moment before pulling his hand away.

Octavius regarded the pasteboard box as if it might explode. *And whom should I say is giving it to her?* he wondered, his tone suspicious.

Oh, you can let her know it's from me, of course. And Clarinda. A birthday present.

But I thought Clarinda was under the impression Isabella is dead?

David rolled his eyes. *I'm sure you'll sort what to say exactly,* he countered. *I just... I want her to know someone is thinking of her.*

Octavius gave a nod, not about to admit he spent time thinking of Isabella. Far too much time.

Octavius continued to listen to the quiet in the front hall of Huntinghurst, wondering where the servants might be. He didn't bother trying to soften the sound of his boot heels as he finally made his way down the hall that led to the courtyard. Perhaps everyone was outside, or in the village. He nearly stopped in his tracks when he remembered it was market day. Allowing a rather loud sigh of annoyance, he decided to make his way to the stables. He was already out the door and on the crushed granite path before he realized there was someone in the parterre garden.

And something with her.

Pausing, he angled his head to one side and watched as Isabella walked through the paths between the boxwood hedges. Wearing an apple green muslin gown and short gloves, her hair gathered into a bun atop her head, she looked as if she could be any one of a dozen chits he might pass in Jermyn Street whilst shopping, except instead of holding onto the handles of a hat box or shopping bag, she held onto a rope that encircled the neck of a colt.

Isabella had nearly reached the end of one row and was coaxing the colt to turn onto the next row in the pattern when she suddenly glanced in his direction.

Resuming his walk toward her, Octavius watched as Isabella had the colt turning onto a path that would allow her and the colt to exit the parterre and head in his direction. He met her just as the colt cleared the boxwood-lined path.

"Your Grace! What a pleasant surprise," Isabella gushed as she pulled the colt to stand alongside her. She dipped a curtsy and, instead of offering her gloved hand, she stepped forward, wrapped her free hand around the back of his neck, and bestowed a kiss on his cheek. Next to her, the timid colt finally overcame its initial fear of the duke and showed a bit of curiosity by sniffing at his pockets.

A bit surprised by her greeting, Octavius managed to capture her free hand as she stepped back. He brushed his lips over the back of it. "For me, as well," he replied, wondering at her affectionate greeting. *Had she been taught a version of the French way to welcome an old friend?* No one was about the grounds to see what she had done, though, so he decided not to admonish her. "Who do we have here?" he asked, rather stunned to see a colt so soon in the spring.

"This is Hermés. He's proving to be as ornery a colt as his older namesake was."

Octavius arched both eyebrows, rather surprised to hear the assessment given she had a lead around the colt's neck. And the colt had seemed to follow her through the garden without trampling the plantings. "Yet he seems to be behaving right now."

"It's early," she countered with a grin. "Pray tell, do you have something in your pocket?" she asked. "I'm afraid I'm all out of carrots, and he seems to think you have a treat," she added as she noted how the colt was nosing his topcoat.

Remembering he carried the pasteboard box David had given him, he was about to pull it out of one pocket and hand it to her, but thought better of it. Instead, he reached into the other pocket and pulled out a small apple. He had intended it for his own mount, thinking he would go for a ride since he had spent the entire trip to Huntinghurst in the coach. He offered the apple to the overly curious colt.

Isabella rolled her eyes as the horse knickered and proudly downed the apple. Hermés was about to reach over and continue sniffing at the duke's topcoat when Isabella said, "No, you've had quite enough," as she pulled back on the lead.

Hermés' stubbornness became apparent, though, and Isabella finally undid the lead from around his neck. "I've had enough of you today. Off to your mum," she said as she placed a hand against the side of his head and gave a slight push. "It's probably his dinner time anyway," she added as she returned her attention to the duke.

Octavius watched as the colt, realizing it was free of the rope, hurried off to join Maia. The mare was tethered to a post just beyond the parterre garden.

"Other than the fact that she's outside of the fence, why is Maia tied up?" Octavius wondered as he squinted in the direction of the brood mare. A descendent of several racing horses, she had the perfect lines and profile to be one herself, but he had never trained her for the track. He rather doubted she had ever had a saddle on her.

"She's finally learning patience," Isabella replied as she turned her attention back to the duke. "She manages to be the first at everything, you see."

Octavius resumed his walk toward the stables, offering an arm to Isabella as he contemplated her mention of Maia being first at everything. *Could she have been first at the finish line?* he wondered. Well, it was too late given her age. She was well past six years, the top age for any of the races that took place in England. "For example?" he prompted, rather entertained by Isabella's comment.

"She's first at the hay, first out of the stables in the morning, first with the stud, first to foal..." She allowed the sentence to trail off as she placed her hand on his arm and walked alongside the duke.

"I must admit I didn't expect to find any foals this early," he said. "How many more will there be, do you suppose?" Ever since Jane's death, he hadn't given half a thought to the stables at Huntinghurst. Knowing Isabella took an interest and seemed amenable to spending time with the horses allowed him to continue his ambivalence.

"Just three," Isabella replied with a sigh.

Octavius frowned at her response, not because of the number she mentioned but rather how she said it. "You sound disappointed."

Isabella dared a glance up at the duke's profile, wondering if he was disappointed in her. Although they hadn't discussed her involvement with his horses, she had simply taken over some of the duties a more involved owner would do—overseeing the match ups of studs with mares, halter-breaking the foals, and documenting pedigrees. "Mr. Reeves says you're no longer entering them in the racing circuit," she replied. "You have at least two that could beat Craythorne's best this year," she added, hoping he would show some interest. They had just entered the stables, pausing to allow their eyes to adjust to the darkened interior.

"No doubt," he responded as he glanced about. "Perhaps next year," he murmured, his gaze taking in the empty stalls. All had been mucked, and new straw bedding covered the dirt floors. Impressed at how clean everything appeared, he glanced around in search of one of the grooms so he could compliment them. "I take it the horses are all out in the pasture?"

"Indeed," Isabella replied. "I made sure three were exercised this morning, though, including my own. Thank you for allowing me to board him here."

Octavius regarded her with a hint of surprise. "Of course." Then he frowned. "With you doing so much in here, I have to wonder what my employees are doing."

"Oh, they're working, Your Grace. But they have gone to town today. Mr. Campbell wanted to find a new topcoat, seeing as how he wishes to court someone," Isabella said with an impish grin.

"Mr. Campbell must be at least fifty!" the duke countered in surprise.

"I rather imagine the Widow Fraser is at least that old," Isabella countered. "And Mr. Reeves is in search of some tools. One of the tines on the pitchfork broke last week, and George has been making do with the gardener's rake."

Octavius frowned, although he knew if a broken pitchfork was the worst of the stable's problems, then things were running smoother than usual. "And what of George? I don't see him about," he asked. The stableboy rarely left his post.

"He's probably seeing to your coach," Isabella replied. "I saw him run off toward the front of the house when I was leading Hermés to the garden walk. Thought perhaps the mail coach had come."

The duke nodded. "Have you plans for this afternoon?"

Isabella gave a shake of her head. "Other than untie Maia, I do not." She glanced about, realizing she was alone with the duke. "Would you like to join me for tea? Or a lemonade? Cook made a batch this morning."

"I had a luncheon in Petworth, but I could do with a lemonade," Octavius said, rather surprised to learn of fresh lemonade. "Pray tell, from where did cook get the lemons?"

Isabella grinned as she turned to head back to where Maia was tethered. "From the orangery, of course. We've had lemons for months."

Octavius blinked, rather stunned to learn he had an orangery. "Since I'm rarely at Huntinghurst, could you remind me where that might be?"

Isabella let out a giggle, the musical sound bringing a grin to Octavius' face. She pointed to the brick and sandstone building next to where the mare was tied up. Hermés had apparently had his fill and was resting in the clipped lawn next to the mare. "I'm not sure that's what you intended for its use, but when cook received the gift of a lemon tree from a suitor, we made use of it."

"A suitor?" the duke repeated. Goodness! Were all his servants about to be leg-shackled?

"Only for about a month. When Mrs. Cooper made it clear she wasn't about to give up her *independence*, Mr. McDonald married a servant up in Cocking," Isabella explained as she moved to undo Maia's tether.

"Here. Let me get that," Octavius offered as he stepped up to undo the slipknot. The rope came free, and Maia reared her head before turning toward the pasture. Caught off-guard, Hermés struggled to stand up and then hurried off to follow his mother.

Octavius noticed how the rope had been threaded through a metal ring attached to the side of the orangery. A simple slipknot held it in place. Giving it a quick tug, the rope came completely free. He held it out and angled his head. "Did you know she could have escaped had she wanted to?" he asked with an arched brow.

"Of course," Isabella replied. "I tied it that way on purpose." She took the rope from the duke and retied it to the metal ring. "She doesn't even try to break free," Isabella added with a shake of her head. "She perceives she is unable to escape, so she doesn't bother to try."

Arching a brow, the duke gave a shake of his head. "Is anyone else scheduled to learn patience?" he asked with a hint of humor.

Isabella was about to admit *she* was in need of a lesson, but thought better of saying so to the duke. "Probably Hermés," she murmured with a grin. She hadn't yet told the duke what had become of the older Hermés, or about the stud that would be seeing to at least one of the mares in the next few weeks and again in a year or so.

"Come. Let's get you out of the sun. You're not even wearing a bonnet," Octavius admonished her, a bit surprised at how comely she looked with a few freckles sprinkled about her nose and cheekbones.

Isabella gasped and suddenly headed for the stone bench at the edge of the parterre garden. A broad-brimmed straw hat decorated with tiny flowers on one side had been tossed onto the bench. She quickly positioned it on her head and rejoined the duke. "Hermés likes to chew on it," she complained, her comment enough to explain why it hadn't been on her head whilst she led the colt about the garden. "How long will you stay this visit?" she asked as she placed her hand on the duke's arm for the walk to the house.

"I thought to head back tomorrow." At her mewl of what sounded like disappointment, he added, "Or the day after. Depends on what needs to be done, I suppose." He opened the back door into the house and stepped aside so Isabella could pass. "I'm never sure how things are here at Huntinghurst until I come in the autumn for the bird hunting."

"It's such a beautiful house, I cannot imagine why you

don't come more often," she countered, and then her eyes suddenly widened as she whirled to face him. "It's not because *I'm* here, is it?"

Octavius couldn't help but see the look of hurt that appeared on his ward's face just then. That she would even think such a thing set off a twinge of regret. "Of course not," he said quickly. "Huntinghurst is just one of several houses I own. With the Season already started, though, I must be back in London for Parliament. I do what I can to visit the houses within a day's journey when I'm able to get away from town."

The explanation seemed to appease Isabella. "I'll go pour us some lemonade and meet you in the parlor."

"What?"

Isabella gave a shrug. "Mrs. Cooper is at market, as is the scullery maid. If we're to have lemonade and biscuits, then I need to see to it," she explained. She dipped a curtsy and was about to head for the kitchens when Octavius was suddenly at her side. "I'll help," he said when he noticed her look of surprise.

"Have you ever been *in* the kitchens, Your Grace?" Isabella teased with an arched brow.

Octavius was about to answer when he realized that he hadn't been. At least, not as an adult. "I used to sneak in there late at night when I was a boy," he admitted. "Midnight snacks of roast beef or bacon," he added with an arched brow.

"Ham," Isabella said, her impish grin giving away her guilt.

"Apple tarts," Octavius countered, his grin widening.

"Chocolate," Isabella whispered.

"Chocolate?"

She nodded. "Sometimes cook leaves a pot on the stove when she knows I'm still out in the stables after dark."

As soon as she made the comment, Isabella realized she had made a mistake. "Which is rare. It only happens when a mare is foaling," she added quickly.

Octavius suddenly displayed a frown of disapproval. "I employ grooms and a stableboy for a reason, Isabella. You shouldn't be out in the stables—*working*—especially after dark."

Isabella angled her head to one side. "But I don't mind, really, Your Grace. I enjoy being with the horses."

Deciding not to argue with her on the point, Octavius changed the subject. "So, where do I find the biscuits?"

She pointed to a ceramic container on a shelf as she took two glasses from a salver and set them on a tea tray. She followed it with a small silver salver. "Biscuits go here," she said before she turned to open the cold box in which the pitcher of lemonade could be found.

"You don't expect me to place biscuits onto this little tray?" he half-asked with feigned derision. "Do you?"

Isabella was about to pour the lemonade but instead gave him a shrug. "I suppose not. Just bring the jar," she suggested as she lifted the tray and took her leave of the kitchens—with the entire pitcher of lemonade.

Blinking, Octavius regarded the ceramic container for only a moment before hoisting it into one crooked elbow. He made his way out of the kitchens, daring a glance in both directions before hurrying after Isabella, as if he thought he might be caught with his hands in the biscuit jar.

Isabella took a seat in the middle of the settee and poured the lemonade. She offered a glass to Octavius, who was contemplating what to do with the biscuit jar. She cleared a space on the tray and he settled it in place before removing the lid.

"What have we here?" he asked as he leaned over and peered into the jar.

"Dutch biscuits, shortbread, and something the cook learned how to make from her grandmama in Norway," Isabella commented, helping herself to some shortbread.

Octavius examined a *serinakaker* before finally taking a small bite. His eyes widened before he finished chewing. "Oh, my," he said with a sigh.

"You'll not be able to stop at just one, Your Grace," Isabella warned, a grin splitting her face.

"Good thing there are several in here," he countered, leaning over to help himself to another. He settled back in his chair and regarded his ward for a moment. "I received a letter from Peters. He is... concerned."

Straightening at the mention of the butler, Isabella resisted the urge to roll her eyes. Although the two had never quarreled, she was quite sure she and the butler would come to blows if they did. Peters obviously didn't approve of her spending time in the stables, but what else was there for her to do all day? "He has no need to be," she replied, finally drinking her lemonade. "At least, not about me."

"Probably not," Octavius agreed. "But, nevertheless, I thought it best to pay a visit just to see how you're getting on."

Angling her head to one side, Isabella allowed a sigh. "I like it here, Your Grace. "I love the stables and most all of the horses—"

"Most?" the duke teased before he suddenly sobered. "You mentioned Hermés is a bit ornery. Is there another you find difficult?"

Isabella's eyes darted to the side. "Ares, but I think I will be as stubborn with him as he is with me."

The duke shook his head. "You shouldn't be spending any time at all with that beast."

"He just needs training."

"And I employ grooms for that," Octavius insisted.

"They won't go near him," Isabella countered. "Besides, they don't have the time given all their other responsibilities."

"Then he shall remain a wild horse," Octavius stated, as if there was nothing else to be said about the horse. "I understand you've been receiving a frequent visitor. Is it Miss Fitzwilliam?"

Rather stunned at the sudden change of topic, Isabella blinked. Obviously Peters had been writing of the fact that she had a frequent caller in his missives to his master. "Yes.

You'll remember Lord Norwick's cousin. Miss Fitzwilliam still comes to ride with me, although not as often these days."

"Miss?" he repeated.

"She is still unmarried. Three-and-twenty and looking forward to spinsterhood, which I suppose is good since she claims the only bachelors in Boxgrove are monks."

Octavius furrowed his brows. "If I remember correctly, she is a horsewoman?" he half-asked.

"An accomplished one, yes. She sees to the stables at Fair Downs, and although it is an entailed property of the Norwick earldom, the horses are all hers."

This had the duke's eyes widening. "Good God! How can she afford them all?"

Isabella gave her head a shake. "She received a small inheritance when her mother died, and she will inherit her dowry when she reaches her majority," Isabella explained. "She claims her inheritance will allow her to expand the stables and raise racehorses."

Octavius regarded his charge for a moment before responding. "You say that as if you think it's a suitable plan for an unmarried woman," he accused.

Blinking, Isabella straightened on the settee and wondered if she should tell him the truth or feign indifference. "I cannot say if it is or it isn't. I know I should like to do it myself." At the duke's sudden look of shock, she added, "I would love to have my own stables, Your Grace. My own horses. I wouldn't necessarily raise them to be racers, but if one or two could run the Ascot or the entire circuit..."

"I cannot believe what I am hearing," Octavius claimed with a shake of his head. "What about a husband? Children?"

Isabella angled her head first one way and then the other. "I think I should like a husband and a few children—I certainly don't aspire to be a spinster—but any man I marry will need to be a horseman. An accomplished rider. With enough funds to help me with the expenses of owning horses, of course."

"Of course," Octavius agreed, although his words were said with a hint of sarcasm. "And where do you suppose you're going to find such a man?"

Isabella blinked. *Why, right in front of me*, she almost said, as shocked by the realization as she knew the duke would be if she put voice to the words.

The Duke of Huntington would make the perfect husband for what she had planned, she thought. He already had the stables, although they would have to be expanded. He owned plenty of pastureland. The perfect house from which to run such an operation. He had the connections to the Jockey Club in Newmarket.

And he was handsome.

"At Tattersall's, perhaps?" she offered meekly.

It was the duke's turn to blink. "Perhaps," he replied, a sudden twinge of disappointment making him wonder why he found the idea abhorrent. "This... plan of yours—"

"It's just my dream, Your Grace. Something I think of when I imagine how I would like my future to be," she murmured. She inhaled and let the air out slowly. "Will you be joining us for dinner this evening? Cook will be returning from market soon. I'm sure she'll have the ingredients for a rather grand meal."

At the suggestion of having dinner at Huntinghurst, Octavius' countenance seemed to lighten. "That sounds capital," he replied. He glanced around the parlor, rather happy to find it appeared recently cleaned. "In the meantime, I have to see to some correspondence, so I'll be in my study." He stood and bowed. "I'll see you at dinner," he added as Isabella curtsied.

He was about to head toward the door when he remembered the box from Norwick. Pulling it from his topcoat pocket, he gave it a quick glance before handing it over to Isabella. "This is for you. From Lord Norwick." He didn't add that he hoped it was the earl's admission that he was the girl's father. Even though the man had been married to Clarinda for nearly ten months, he claimed he still hadn't made his countess aware that her cousin was also her step-daughter.

The coward.

"He and your cousin have finally returned from their wedding trip," he added, realizing the box might contain something the earl had acquired during his travels.

"Thank you," Isabella murmured, studying the white pasteboard box. "Should I… should I open it now?"

The duke shrugged. "Whenever you like." Not particularly curious as to what might be in the box, Octavius took his leave of the parlor.

Chapter 19

A BOX REVEALED

A few seconds later

Isabella stared after Octavius for a moment before returning her attention to the box. A bit on the heavy side for such a small container, she gave it a shake, quite sure she heard something metallic inside. Her curiosity piqued, she opened the lid. A folded paper popped out and nearly fell to the floor before she could capture it in her free hand. The bottom of the box was littered with a variety of coins.

Setting the box of coins on the parlor table, she unfolded the missive and struggled to read the scrawled words.

Dear Lady Isabella,

I hope this letter finds you in Good Health.

His Grace informs me you have settled into Huntinghurst and continue your appreciation of his stables by riding his horses. Since he seems to have forgotten them, it is fortuitous you are there.

I write from London, where I am finding marriage to your cousin, Clarinda, an agreeable situation. It is as much of a surprise to me as to her, I believe. Brotherton women seem an agreeable bunch, and given you are the daughter of one, you may count yourself among their ilk.

The wedding trip to Italy and Greece was well received by Clare. Unlike me, she didn't mind the oppressive heat and loved the opportunity to shop for small trinkets to bring back as gifts. (I had to remind her on only two occasions of the size of our trunks, unaware she had included an empty one amongst her luggage. The minx.) One such trinket is included for you. She mentioned how much you would want one.

Having received a letter from my cousin, Constance, expressing concerns that you seem to lack suitable riding habits, I am including some pin money for such an expense. I expect the bit of pin money you once had has probably long since been spent, and I rather doubt Hunt has thought to see to refreshing your funds.

When I am next in Sussex, I hope to pay a call. Until then, I am yours in service.

Norwick.

Isabella reread the difficult script several times before she was sure she understood the earl's every word. She glanced back in the box, thinking there was probably at least twenty pounds in various denominations of coins.

Riding habits? Why, she could have a local modiste make a dozen or more! Then she thought of her worn riding boots and her lack of suitable dinner gowns and realized she would need to limit what she spent on riding clothes.

As for a modiste, she figured Constance could help her locate one.

Then she remembered his reference to a trinket and searched through the box again. Near the bottom, a gold charm in the shape of a horse revealed itself from among the coins. Holding it between her thumb and forefinger, she nearly teared up when she realized Clarinda had been thinking of her. She was almost about to write a 'thank you' letter to her cousin when she remembered she could not.

Clarinda believed she was dead.

But Lord Norwick is my cousin-by-marriage. How thoughtful of him.

Helping herself to another biscuit, she finished her lemonade and contemplated her future.

Chapter 20

AN UNEXPECTED AFTER DINNER GUEST

Later that night

Octavius regarded the remains of the dinner he and Isabella had been enjoying for nearly two hours. "You were correct about cook having the ingredients to make a rather grand dinner," he commented as he set aside his napkin.

"I don't think I've eaten this much since the last time you were in residence," Isabella replied. Her glass of claret stood empty, and she couldn't help but notice the duke's port was gone. "Would you consider a walk? I know it's dark, but—"

"A capital idea," he replied, pushing back from the table. "Do you need a shawl or pelisse?" he asked, once again admiring her dinner gown. He knew it couldn't have been made in London—it was far too plain to have been created by a modiste in the capital. Although it lacked ornamentation, it suited his ward perfectly.

"I do not," she replied as she stood up. "It's been rather pleasant these past few nights." They made their way through the portrait gallery and left the house by way of the door that led to the parterre garden, the duke helping himself to a lantern. "Despite the rather harsh winter, it's been beautiful here," she commented as they made their way.

"I often wish I could take all of Huntinghurst and simply drop it into the middle of London," Octavius said suddenly. "And then I remember how large it is, and realize I would still have a long way to get to Parliament."

Isabella giggled. "You are speaking of all the lands as well as the house, then?" she asked.

"Indeed. Someday I'll take you to where it's possible to see it all," he said as they entered the garden. The scents of newly-turned earth and greenery assaulted his nostrils as he took a deep breath and grinned. "But for now, this is what I think of when I think of Huntinghurst," he said as he waved an arm to indicate the parterre garden.

"The garden?" Isabella responded in disbelief. "Not your stables, or the hunting grounds, or... or the house?"

"You needn't sound so incredulous," he replied with a smirk. "I had the gardener do it several years before I married Jane. So it would be ready when she..." He allowed the sentence to trail off, just then remembering that Jane had never seen the garden. She had refused to make the trip to Huntinghurst, sure it would be too rustic for her tastes. Too far from a city.

"'Tis a beautiful garden," Isabella said, wondering at his sudden quiet. "And the blooms continued until the snow fell last winter," she went on. "I hadn't seen snow in years. The horses loved it, of course. They loved playing in it."

Octavius angled his head as he listened to her words, rather stunned at how beautiful she appeared in the dim light from the lantern. How she seemed to glow as she spoke of his horses. When her face suddenly took on a different expression, one of curiosity, he was jolted from his reverie.

A soft knicker had his attention going to a horse that was making its way in their direction and doing so rather quickly. "Whatever are you doing out of the stables?" Isabella asked as she stood up and moved toward the yearling, the light from the lantern on the stone bench casting her long shadow so the horse was partly hidden from Octavius' view.

The duke watched in alarm, wondering how a horse

could have escaped its stall—unless it hadn't been put into its stall. Then he wondered if something might be wrong with George.

The yearling knickered again, its head bobbing up and down as it approached. Isabella reached out and pressed her hand against the side of his neck. "Something's wrong," she said as she turned to find the duke directly behind her. "Perseus would never leave his stall at night unless something spooked him," she claimed, not about to add that the yearling had learned how to lift the latch so he could take his leave whenever he pleased.

Octavius was about to head for the stables, but remembered the lantern and went back for it. "Stay here," he ordered, his quick steps and long strides taking him past her and the horse before she could put voice to a protest.

Left in the near-dark—only a quarter-moon lit the western sky—Isabella kept her hand on the horse and moved to where the flags were evident. She watched as the duke disappeared into the front door of the stables, a chorus of knickers and neighs greeting him. The lantern's light cast an eerie glow through the stable's open door, occasionally disappearing for a moment before flaring to a golden yellow.

"Did you manage the latch yourself? To get out of your stall?" she whispered to Perseus. Thoughts of the horse escaping on its own were replaced with one where his escape was assisted by someone. Fear had her imagining the worst—a horse thief intent on taking as many of the beasts as he could set free all at once.

What if he had a pistol?

Her eyes widened before she took a hasty breath, wanting desperately to cry out and warn the duke. Perhaps if she moved a bit closer to the stables...

The noise from within the stables grew as the horses voiced their displeasure at whatever was going on. A moment later, she heard George's voice join the fray before she saw him run past the stable door. A few shouts, a few more neighs and then... nothing.

Taking a few more steps toward the stables, she was nearly beyond the east wing when Perseus made a sound of protest. "What is it?" she whispered softly, realizing Perseus sensed her fear.

She turned her attention back to the stables, gasping when she realized the duke was silhouetted in the doorway. He carried the lantern in one hand as he made his way toward her, something dark cradled in his other arm.

"What happened?" she asked as she rushed to meet him. "And what is that?"

Looking a bit disheveled, Octavius allowed a sigh. "A dog, I think," he replied. He attempted to hold the creature so Isabella could see it, but it burrowed into his bent arm.

"A puppy," she said in awe. "But... but where's the mother? Is it from one of your hunting dogs?"

Octavius dipped his head. "No. There are no bitches in the kennels, and this one's mother is dead. Seems she thought that Perseus' stable would be a good place to leave this one, but I think she was kicked at some point."

"Oh, dear," Isabella murmured as she reached out to take the puppy from the duke. "Do you suppose there are others?"

"George is looking now, but I fear they may have been born somewhere else. Probably in the forest. She was no doubt in the process of moving them into the stables when one of the horses took exception to her presence." He directed his comment to Perseus, thinking the yearling had been the one to do the kicking since it was his stall in which the puppy had been deposited.

Isabella's attention was on the black and white ball of fur she held, rather surprised to find the creature's eyes wide open and its pink tongue peeking out. A quiet whine sounded followed by a yawn that displayed a row of sharp, white teeth. "Well, I suppose we need to find a nurse for this one." But if none of the duke's hunting dogs were female...

"I rather doubt it's going to make it through the night," Octavius warned quietly.

Her attention suddenly back on the duke, Isabella allowed a gasp. "Isn't there something that can be done?"

Grimacing, as if he knew she would persist with wanting to save the puppy, Octavius said, "I suppose he could be bottle fed—"

"I can do that."

The duke regarded his ward for a moment, momentarily struck by how she looked cradling the puppy in her arm. Her silk dinner gown made her appear far more elegant than he had ever seen her. Far more mature. An image of what she might look like cradling a baby had an odd sensation gripping his chest. He had to blink when he realized she was staring at him. As if she might be thinking the same thing.

Perhaps if she had to spend time seeing to the puppy, she wouldn't spend as much time in the stables. "Let's see if Mrs. Cooper can be of assistance," he offered, referring to the cook.

And with a command that he return to the stables, Perseus hurried off in that direction while Isabella and Octavius made their way back to the house.

Chapter 21

A PUPPY CHANGES EVERYTHING

M*idnight*

When Octavius finally made his way to his apartments several hours later, he wondered if he had made a mistake with the puppy. He could have simply moved it outside and left it to die—he was sure there were more pups somewhere nearby left to the same fate—but there had been the thought that Isabella could do with a distraction. A companion.

That he felt a bit of jealousy when he saw how she held the dog—in how she murmured quiet assurances and smoothed a finger over the top of its head—was simply a reminder of how Jane's affections had been transferred from him to the unborn baby she carried. Although he had thrilled at knowing she might be carrying his heir, he remembered the sense of loss he felt when Jane no longer afforded him the same intimacies they had shared prior to her pregnancy. Then, when she died in the childbed, his loss was doubled.

Octavius shook away the memory, determined not to dwell on that particular moment in his past.

When he had left Isabella in the parlor, she was feeding the puppy. Hungrily sucking on the makeshift nipple the cook had managed to create to cover a bottle of goats milk, the little beast was staring at his new mother as if he were memorizing everything about her.

If Isabella ever held him like that, he would do the same, Octavius considered.

Although Peters seemed appalled at the idea of the puppy spending the night in the house, he saw to it a footman was dispatched to locate a wooden crate in which the dog could sleep while a housemaid saw to an old blanket.

"He'll likely cry and whine all night for his mum. Keep you awake, he will," Thompson warned Isabella when she left the tattered quilt with her.

"I expect he will," she replied, just then wondering about the messes the dog would no doubt leave until it was trained. "I don't suppose there are such things as nappies for puppies?" Isabella queried.

"None that I know of, my lady, but I think we can find some old rags to use in the bottom of the crate." The maid paused for a moment. "Does he have a name?"

Isabella furrowed her brows as she thought of the names that Constance had mentioned from *The Tattler*. "Nelson, I think," she replied, remembering something about a naval commander with that name.

"What will the poor thing do during the day, though? Whilst you're out riding?"

Isabella considered the question for a moment before allowing a grin. "I shall take Nelson with me. If he's going to be my dog, then he will have to learn to be with horses all day. And they shall have to learn to be around him."

As Octavius stared at the canopy above his bed, his cockstand tenting the bed linens, he inwardly groaned when he remembered hearing Isabella's edict from where he stood outside the parlor. Now he wondered why it bothered him. Isabella was his ward. Nothing more. Just because she tended to greet him with a kiss on the cheek didn't mean there was anything between them. How could there be? She was his ward.

Or was she really his châtelaine?

The châtelaine of my stables, he thought just then.

He gave a quelling glance down the top of the bed linens and quietly cursed. Just a ward, indeed. And now she was a ward with a pet named Nelson.

Chapter 22

PILLOW TALK

Late July 1814

Clarinda sounded a mewl of disappointment when her husband finally pulled himself from her body and landed on the bed next to her, his own groan filling the otherwise quiet bedchamber. He snaked an arm behind her shoulders and pulled her over so she ended up nestled next to his side, the palm of one hand pressed atop his chest. He covered the small hand with one of his own.

"May I stay?" he wondered after a few minutes. Although he usually spent most nights with Clarinda in her bed, he still felt it necessary to ask.

"I'm not about to let you leave," Clarinda countered in a whisper. "Especially if you still intend to be off to Sussex in the morning." She almost asked if she might join him, but the thought of spending an entire day bouncing about in a coach held little appeal.

Unless they spent the time bouncing about engaged in sexual congress.

That might be rather exciting, she thought, trying to imagine a position that would ensure neither bumped their heads or left their bottoms exposed. When she thought of riding him astride, her knees on either side of him as he sat pressed into the squabs, her face lit up.

Clarinda was about to ask if she could come along when David suddenly turned his head in her direction.

"Would you make me go back to my own bed if I wasn't leaving for Norwick Park in the morning?" He hadn't visited his country estate in some time, but decided it was time he check on his own stables as well as his brother. Ever since the wedding, Daniel's communications had been rather terse and only about business.

Lifting her head from his shoulder, Clarinda regarded him in the dim light from the tiny flames that licked about inside the fireplace. "Of course not," she replied. "Besides, you tossed all my hairpins onto the carpeting when you removed them this evening. If I let you leave this bed, you'll wake the entire household with your curses when you step on them."

David blinked and regarded his wife for a moment, a grin finally splitting his face. "I love you," he said in a whisper.

Clarinda regarded him a moment, rather shocked to hear him say words she never expected to hear from him since their wedding. "You do?" she murmured as she moved to sit up in the bed, the bed linens falling from the front of her to reveal her breasts. Angling her body to look down at him, she bit her lower lip with an eyetooth.

Unable to ignore her engorged nipples, still red from what he had done to them with his tongue and teeth only moments ago, David flicked a crooked finger over one of them. "I didn't think it would be such a surprise for you to hear me say it," he replied, sliding his other hand along her side until he heard her slight inhalation of breath as his thumb brushed the side of a breast.

"I was sure you loved another," Clarinda whispered, one of her hands attempting to cover his.

His brows furrowing, David gave his head a quick shake. He raised himself up to sit against a pile of pillows as he pulled her so she sat astride and atop him. Having recovered from their earlier lovemaking, his erect manhood was left pressed against her belly. "A long time ago," he finally admitted. "But she's gone, and now... now there's only you."

Clarinda angled her head, and several locks of her long, brunette hair fell to hide her breasts from his view. "And you don't have a mistress." The words didn't come out as a question, but then, she had reports from a Bow Street Runner assuring her he did nothing more than attend sessions of Parliament and visit his men's club when he wasn't in her company.

"No need to have one," he said with a shrug, a crooked finger sliding through one of the locks of hair. "Not since before I finally married you. Something I realize now I should have done a long time ago."

Clarinda swallowed, and gasped again when the back of his finger brushed over her breast again. She lowered her torso to rest atop his, her head ending up in the small of one of his shoulders as she slid her hands along his sides and sighed. She sighed again when David pulled the bed linens up and over her back, reminded of how he had held her so close the day after her miscarriage.

He had been in the study when she realized what was happening, her anguished cries turning to sobs so violent, David claimed he thought she would die. He had stayed with her in her bedchamber the rest of that day and that night, ordering Missy, her lady's maid, to leave and arguing with the physician over her care. He finally collapsed in exhaustion the following morning, wrapping his body around hers in what she remembered as a cocoon of comfort and warmth.

Clarinda supposed she should have known then that he loved her. But they hadn't spoken the words. Not since before their wedding day.

Just the one time in Kensington Gardens, the moment he had bestowed her with the sapphire ring. Clarinda sighed and closed her eyes, a wan smile lifting the edges of her lips.

They lay like that for several minutes, David's fingers

trailing over the bumps of her spine and over her long thighs where they were tucked against his sides. "I have been meaning to tell you something," he whispered. When she didn't respond, he kissed the top of her head. "It's about... it's about your cousin, Isabella. She's alive and safe, but she paid witness to her mother's murder. I am going to Norwick Park tomorrow, but I am also going to Basingstoke. Again. Craythorne has managed to avoid seeing me when I've attempted to pay a call. He hasn't been back to London since Arabella's death. It's past time he explain himself. Pay for what he did to Arabella," he murmured.

He waited a moment, rather surprised Clarinda didn't respond. He kissed the top of her head again, frowning when she still didn't say anything. When he finally angled his head and took note of her closed eyes and even breathing, he realized she had fallen asleep.

Allowing another sigh of disappointment, David dropped his head into the pillows. *Well, at least I tried*, he thought, knowing the duke would still call him a coward if he mentioned the attempt to inform Clarinda of his relationship to Isabella.

What would the Duke of Huntington call him if he learned David had seen to Craythorne's demise?

Chapter 23

A DUKE PREPARES FOR A TRIP

August 1814

Half-tempted to make the trip to Huntinghurst on horseback, Octavius, Duke of Huntington, realized he would have to ride at least part of the way in his traveling coach. He had letters to read and decisions to make. Although he thought he was better at thinking from the back of a horse, he couldn't read whilst riding.

He had tried. It hadn't worked.

These days, if he didn't pay mind to Poseidon, the old horse simply stopped walking. Or else he cantered. Octavius was sure Poseidon cantered as a means to annoy him when he was lost in thought, the steps jostling him until he was nearly unseated and awoken from his stupor.

"I have the small trunk packed. Shall I make the trip with you, Your Grace?" Watkins wondered from where he stood next to the cheval mirror. Given it was still dark, the valet had lit all the candle lamps in the room. He held a waistcoat on one arm, and a topcoat was draped over the other. He was prepared to offer the garments when his master was ready to finish dressing.

"No need, Watkins. Spend a few days with your wife," the duke said from where he regarded his image in the master suite's cheval mirror. *Damn! When did I grow so old?* "One of the footmen at Huntinghurst is angling for a promotion. Claims he can sew, so I'll give him a go," Octavius murmured as he helped himself to the waistcoat.

"Very good, sir," the valet responded, his dispassionate voice hiding his surprise at learning he once again wouldn't be expected to make the journey south. He moved to help the duke with buttoning the waistcoat, but the duke was already seeing to the fastenings.

"I'm to remind you there is a standing invitation to visit His Royal Highness, the Prince Regent, in Brighton, should you make it there, Your Grace."

Octavius scowled, remembering he had been the one to speak of the invitation as a sort of afterthought to his last trip to Sussex. "I won't make it that far south," he vowed. He had no intention of going beyond Huntinghurst. He had a stable of horses to review and a certain young lady to visit. One he had been avoiding for several months, partly because he had no news to share, but mostly because being in her presence had him befuddled.

Bewitched.

At twenty years of age, she was headstrong and coltish, angry and sad, happy and delightful, and the most beautiful creature he could imagine. He knew because his mind conjured her nearly every night before he fell asleep. Although he wasn't twice her age, at three-and-thirty, he was still a good deal older than Isabella. Older than what she might want in a husband—if she was even hoping to marry. He had no idea of her desires these days.

His last visit had been cut short before the two could finish their first argument. She had tested him from the moment he appeared in the stables. Shocked at seeing wooden braces secured around the front legs of a colt, he had ordered they be removed immediately. Isabella insisted they remain on Endymion for at least another week, claiming they would help to straighten his legs. Although somewhat intrigued by her idea, Octavius found he couldn't immediately agree—he had never heard of such a treatment and thought merely to have the colt put down. Isabella pushed and pushed as she tended to do, and he refused to give in. He wanted time to think on it. But her stubbornness had him frustrated and angry. Why, he had half a mind to tie *her* to the metal ring attached to the orangery! Instead, he had simply turned on his heel and left Huntinghurst for the immediate trip back to London.

Later, his driver mentioned she had run after the coach, not stopping until they had turned onto the road to Cocking.

He couldn't decide if he should be angry at her for such unladylike behavior, or honored that she would chase down his coach in an effort to apologize.

Jane wouldn't have done such a thing, he thought. Of course, they never argued the same way he and Isabella did, but he knew Jane would have been capable of doing so. She just knew not to argue.

He suddenly straightened, at once shocked that he could even compare Jane with Isabella. He was also a bit surprised when he realized he hadn't given Jane a second thought in some time. As if time had memories of her fading in his mind's eye.

Jane could be headstrong when she wished to be, but then, she was far more spoiled than Isabella would ever be.

Octavius blinked, remembering Isabella's comment about her mother being too headstrong, and knowing Arabella had been just as beautiful as Clarinda, and Isabella nearly as comely, he suddenly understood Norwick's fascination with Brotherton women.

Apparently, so did his manhood. He allowed a sigh when he realized how uncomfortable his breeches had become as Watkins held his topcoat open for him.

Now that a number of foals had made their appearance in the pastures surrounding Huntinghurst, Octavius was determined to meet each and every one. He hadn't had a horse in the racing circuit for nearly four years and thought perhaps it was time he pay closer attention to his stables. He had learned on his last visit that several of his mares were pregnant. When he asked as to the identity of the studs, his head groom had given him a rather nervous look.

Your ward has been keeping the papers, the man had said. Rather startled by the comment, Octavius asked why Mr. Reeves hadn't been doing so.

I cannot read or write, but she can, Your Grace.

Well, he supposed it made sense the head groom would trust Lady Isabella to complete the pedigree sheets for his new colts. He hoped she understood how they were to be completed for the *Giant Stud Book*.

Those at the Jockey Club in Newmarket were probably wondering what had become of his once-prolific stables. After the death of Jane, he had simply lost interest in racing. Lost interest in his stables. Lost interest in anything but his duty to his dukedom and attending sessions of Parliament. Since he was rarely at his clubs, he was sure his friends thought he was sequestered in his London townhouse with a mistress.

Or spending his days in a drunken stupor.

Well, he had done that on occasion, the liquor dulling the pain of loss. But his bouts had become less frequent once Isabella was sequestered at Huntinghurst.

Had it already been a year? *Longer*, he realized.

For the past year, Octavius believed Maxwell Tolson would meet his death at the hands of David Fitzwilliam, Earl of Norwick. Despite having married Clarinda Anne Brotherton—and claiming he was quite content with his new wife and their life at Norwick House now that they had been back from Europe for a few months—Norwick always seemed as if he were trying to control a deep-seated rage.

Octavius secretly knew the earl had already killed a man, a thief who had apparently attempted to make off with one of the horses from his stables at Norwick Park. The duke often wondered if there was more to the tale, but if there was, Norwick remained mum on the topic.

So did his twin brother, Daniel.

Heartbroken that Clarinda had married David instead of him, Daniel had left London shortly after the wedding. He relocated to Norwick Park in Sussex and continued his work as the earldom's man of business.

In the meantime, no one knew if David had ever threatened Craythorne, although if he had, his *affaire* with Arabella might become known to the other earl.

If Craythorne didn't already know.

Perhaps Craythorne had learned Isabella was not his own daughter, and that had been the reason he had become so enraged, he was capable of killing her mother.

We may never know, Octavius thought with a sigh, wondering if Craythorne was still sequestered in a seaside cottage near Southampton.

"Will there be anything else, Your Grace?" Watkins asked, his manner rather hesitant. Although he was used to having to interrupt his employer's frequent bouts of melancholy—he had been told to do so if it appeared the duke would miss an important engagement—the valet hadn't been forced to do so for many months.

Octavius gave his head a shake, silently cursing himself for the momentary lapse. "No. Let the butler know I'll be departing shortly," he said as he placed his signet ring on one finger and checked the decorative links securing his cuffs. "With any luck, I can be there in time for luncheon."

"Very good, sir," Watkins replied, giving a bow before taking his leave of the master suite.

Within a half-hour and just as the sun was lightening the eastern sky, the Huntington coach made its way south.

Chapter 24

HOMECOMING AT HUNTINGHURST

Later that day at Huntinghurst

Upon entering the large vestibule of Huntinghurst, Octavius knew in an instant that something was different. The entry to the multi-winged manor home had always been a bit on the dark side. A bit forbidding. He glanced up and studied the walls, suddenly sure the color on the plaster was lighter. A quick look at the transom above the door showed it was still there, although the glass was no longer as opaque with age and years of accumulated dirt.

"Has a colorman been here?" he asked as the butler hurried to take the great coat from his arm.

"Indeed, your Grace. Her ladyship thought it time for a new coat of paint." The response was delivered as if the man were holding his breath, sure the duke would be annoyed at the change in the vestibule.

"Well, it certainly improved the place. And I can actually see you, Peters," Octavius said with a grin. "Don't know if that's an improvement or not."

Peters allowed a wry smile and gave a deep bow. "It's good to see you again, Your Grace," the butler said as he moved to take Octavius' top hat. The duke had shed the great coat he had worn whilst riding, rather surprised at how much warmer it was in Sussex compared to when he had left London that morning.

"I trust all is well here?" Octavius dared a look beyond the vestibule, wondering if he would see evidence of a subtle change in the rest of the house.

The butler offered a shrug. "For the most part," he hedged, almost as if he were a bit afraid to say anything else.

Having stepped beyond the vestibule, Octavius did a quick visual sweep of the two halls that jutted off to either side. Finding no evidence of anything different, other than maybe the paneling appeared newly polished, he dared a glance up the central staircase. Like the windows in the transom, the mullioned windows at the first landing appeared almost clear. Light poured in, illuminating the patterned carpet that covered the stairs all the way to the bottom.

"And what part would not be well?" Octavius countered as he turned his attention back on the butler.

Peters dipped his head, as if he regretted his words. "Lady Isabella has been..." He paused and gave a quick shake of his head. "A challenge, I suppose," he finally managed to get out. At the duke's sudden frown, which made the man appear even more imposing, if that were possible, the butler added, "She's become friends with the maids, and she allows the dog to sleep in her bedchamber."

Octavius couldn't help the sense of relief he felt just then. He had imagined the butler about to claim the chit was a challenge because she was sneaking off at night, or imbibing in the liquor he kept in the study, or locked up in her bedchamber in a perpetual state of melancholy. *She would have learned how to do that from me*, he thought suddenly. "The house certainly doesn't seem to have suffered for it," he remarked.

"When it rained last week, I discovered her cleaning the windows alongside the maids," Peters whispered, the manner in which his bushy eyebrows arched up giving him the appearance of someone who had been thoroughly scandalized. "Said she had to do *something* since she couldn't go on a ride."

This last had Octavius frowning more than learning Isabella had been discovered cleaning windows. "Has a favorite mount, does she?"

His eyes darting to the side, Peters nearly nodded before angling his head first to the left and then to the right. "Oh, other than her own horse, I don't believe she has a favorite, Your Grace."

The response had the duke even more alarmed. "Where will I find Lady Isabella right now?"

"The stables, no doubt. She spends most of her days out there, sir."

Although he would have liked to get a bit to eat and have a cup of tea, Octavius elected instead to check on his ward. "Seems I'm headed out there then. See to a luncheon for us."

"Of course, Your Grace," the butler responded before giving a bow. "I'll let Cooper know you've arrived. He'll act as your valet whilst you're in residence."

Glancing back at the vestibule, tempted to go out the way he had come in, Octavius instead headed down one of the halls to the short passageway that led to the back of the house. The entire way, he was aware of how much cleaner, nay, newer, the place seemed.

Lighter.

Faith!

Had the chit hired a colorman to paint the entire house? If so, he hadn't received the bill, which had him wondering if it had been done. And then he realized he couldn't smell any evidence of new paint. Certainly the place would have reeked of oils.

Upon closer inspection, he realized the walls in this hall weren't painted at all, but covered in silk fabric. The mouldings at the top and the baseboards at the bottom hid the edges, making it appear as if the fabric was wallpaper.

Octavius gave a shake of his head. *When have I ever paid a mind to the wall coverings before?* he wondered.

He took a breath and continued on his way out the back door, nearly stopping at the sight of the riot of color that made up what he had at one time hoped would be his wife's favorite garden. Although he employed a gardener or two for the property, he hadn't paid much attention to the grounds since Jane's death. He hadn't the patience to review the gardener's plans, nor the desire to see the results knowing they would only remind him of what he had lost. Remind him of Jane and the life he once had. The life they should have been enjoying right now.

Octavius stared at the boxwood hedges. Perfectly trimmed into a pattern of curved hedges, they met in the middle from which a fountain erupted. Inside of each set of bright green hedges, rows of red tulips and bluebells filled in the remaining space. From the windows above, he realized the central part of the garden would have looked like a six-petaled flower. Rhododendrons in white, yellow, and pink lined the sandstone walls of the house, and smaller flowers surrounded the crushed granite path that encircled the parterre.

Try as he might to avoid it, he couldn't help but allow his gaze to settle on the stone bench in the south corner. There was a similar stone bench in the garden behind his Grosvenor Square mansion. Where Jane had been seated when she told him she was expecting their first child. He squeezed his eyes shut at the memory.

He should have known she was too frail to bear a child. Too frail to make his duchess. She wasn't strong enough for the role, even if she was stern enough to stand up to those who found fault with her. Hell, the coronet was even too big for her head, he remembered just then, the memory of her attempting to wear it bringing a grin to his face.

Dammit.

Octavius shook his head, chastising himself over having

allowed the memories to consume him. If he wasn't careful, he would begin weeping.

Resuming his trip through the garden on the crushed granite path, he noted the imprints of smaller boots, and for a moment he wondered who had made them.

Lady Isabella, of course. She probably took this same path to get to the stables if she truly spent as much time there as the butler claimed.

When he emerged from the garden and cleared the back wing of the house, he realized the path continued in the lawn. A series of flags led straight to the stables. He couldn't remember having used them before, and now he wondered how long they had been there.

A groom was seeing to removing the saddle from Poseidon as a stableboy held the reins. The boy gave a bow when he realized the duke was upon them. "Yer Grace," he said as he kept his attention on Poseidon.

Well, at least he had a healthy respect for the beast.

The head groom stood up and gave a nod. "Yer Grace."

"Where might I find Lady Isabella?"

The groom and stableboy shared a quick glance. He couldn't help but notice how they stiffened at hearing the query. "Probably in the meadow by now," Reeves replied, although his manner suggested he was a bit nervous. "She likes to ride there." When Octavius gave him a questioning look, he added, "About a mile west of here. The one with the pond in the middle."

Octavius straightened. Isabella wasn't the only one who liked to ride there. He almost asked how she had discovered it, but figured one of the grooms would have led her there. Although it was nearly surrounded by trees, there was a well-worn path leading into the clearing. The pond was the perfect place to water a horse on a hot day. "Then I suppose I'll need my horse," Octavius stated.

"Of course, sir," the groom replied, immediately seeing to securing the saddle.

A moment later, Octavius was mounted and heading

west, rather hoping he would simply come upon Isabella as she and a groom made their way back to the stables. But he made it all the way to the meadow without seeing anyone.

When he cleared the trees, his gaze immediately went to the pond. Next to it, Isabella stood with her back to him. Facing a horse nearly as large as Poseidon—just as black, too, although he couldn't determine exactly which horse from this distance—she was holding up one gloved hand as she took a step back. Meanwhile, her dog seemed to be sleeping in a bit of shade next to the pond.

"What the...?" He watched a moment as she took another step back, still holding her hand up. When the horse tossed its head, she paused in her retreat and moved forward, the hand apparently moving to rest on its forehead. He could hear a soft whinny before he watched her repeat her retreat again, her hand held up as if it could stop the horse from following her. This time, she managed to make it several steps away from the horse before he once again tossed his head, this time letting out a whinny of complaint that had Poseidon giving a jerk of his head.

"Steady, boy," Octavius murmured as he glanced around. *Where the hell is the groom?* Certainly she would know to have a groom or a footman join her when she was on a ride!

And then he remembered how nervous the stableboy and Reeves had been back at the stables. As if they knew one of them should have been with her.

Dammit!

Poseidon must have sensed his annoyance, or he simply grew impatient at standing still, for he tossed his head.

Octavius spurred the beast into a quick walk, his attention on Isabella as she continued whatever it was she was attempting to do with...

Ares?

A jolt of fear shot through Octavius just then. Even as part of him realized the beast was saddled and that she had to have ridden him to the meadow, he also knew the three-year-old had never been broken.

At least, he hadn't been when Octavius was last at Huntinghurst.

He dismounted even before Poseidon had come to a complete halt, calling out her name as he took several steps in her direction. "Isabella!"

Ares tossed his head again, and his ears suddenly flattened just as Isabella turned to discover who had called her name. Grinning, she held up her hand again in Ares' direction, gave him a quick beseeching look, and turned to run in the duke's direction at the same time the dog raced ahead, his tale wagging.

"Your Grace!" she called out, her face alight with a huge smile. Her arms wrapped around his shoulders as her body collided with his.

Nearly bowled over, the duke took a step back as he was forced to lift her a bit and turn in a half circle or end up on his bum. There was a moment of awe at her enthusiasm, a moment of happy surprise at how she embraced him. At how she seemed so pleased to see him. At how good it felt to have her body pressed against the front of his. To inhale the scent of honeysuckle and citrus from her hair. To simply hold a woman for a moment before her feet touched the ground.

And then the moment was suddenly over. Even the dog had simply come to a halt and now sat regarding him with his tongue hanging out of his mouth.

He was completely unprepared for the heady combination of conflicting thoughts he experienced just then—fright, joy, anger, surprise—that he said the first thing that came to mind.

Or shouted it, rather.

"What the *hell* do you think you're doing?"

Stunned by the curse—by the anger she witnessed in his face and in his voice—Isabella Tolson immediately stepped away from Octavius, her expression displaying a combination of confusion and dismay. She took another step back as if she'd been punched in the stomach. Well aware Ares had begun pawing at the ground, Isabella held out the flat of her hand in his direction but kept her attention entirely on the duke—on how he scowled at her. She held out her riding habit to the sides and dipped a deep curtsy. "I... I apologize for... my reaction, Your Grace," she managed, still not exactly sure why he seemed so angry with her.

Perhaps she'd been too forward with her embrace, she thought. It was an improper greeting for a duke, of course, but it was hard to think of him in that way. Not after living under his protection for so long.

Even if she rarely saw the man.

For a moment, she was sure he returned her hug of welcome in equal measure. She was sure his arms had tightened around her to pull her as close as possible. Even his dour expression seemed to have softened a bit for that moment her boots had left the ground. Now he was glaring at her and giving his head a shake as if *he* were the impatient horse she was trying to finish breaking.

"That's not why I'm angry..." Octavius started to say, his gaze going to the black horse who looked as if he might bolt at any moment. "Christ, you're out here alone with..." He stopped again as Isabella seemed to ignore him.

"I am not alone. Nelson is here." Turning to Ares, Isabella allowed an audible sigh and moved to recapture the reins. "Really, Ares, you must practice patience, or you'll be forever frustrated," she said in a hoarse whisper, rather relieved the beast hadn't taken his leave of the meadow. "Trust me, as I've certainly had to," she added in a quieter whisper.

Ares could have bolted, she knew. He had done it the first time she had brought him here as she rode one of the older horses. Ares had fought the lead rope around his neck until he realized he was about to get some exercise. Once in the meadow, where the pond offered a source of water and the clearing a place he could run in a circle, he had done so once, twice, three times before he had finally slowed and rejoined her and the other horse.

And then only because she held out an apple as a bribe.

It was two more weeks before she could get a bit on him, and she'd had to do that in the small corral next to the stables.

"Come, Ares. You're in the presence of the Duke of Huntington. You must show him your very best bow," she said as she gripped the reins and pulled them down until Ares finally capitulated and lowered his neck until his nose was nearly in the tall grass. She loosened her grip on the reins, relieved when Ares didn't rear his head but rather slowly raised it up. She could swear he added a bit of a nod at the end.

Octavius watched in wonder as the horse responded to Isabella's command. He probably would have, too, given how her gloved hand smoothed over the side of Ares' head and down his neck. He noted how she barely touched the beast, and a frisson shot down his back when he imagined her fingers doing the same to his bare skin.

Jesus. How long has it been since I've been with a woman?

He blinked away the thought, stunned he would think such a thing in the middle of a meadow. And with such a young woman! She was his ward! Even if there wasn't a contract making it official, Norwick had seen to it his daughter was under Huntington's protection.

"You have managed what even those in Parliament are unable to do," Octavius murmured then, closing the space between them with a few steps. Poseidon followed even though the duke had let go of the reins when he dismounted.

Isabella regarded him a moment, her posture ramrod straight, her shoulders pulled back to reveal what he realized had to be a perfect figure beneath the fitted riding habit. "Anger you, apparently," she offered in reply, her eyes suddenly downcast. All the fight seemed to go out of her just then as her shoulders slumped and her breath left in a long sigh.

"Render me speechless, actually," he countered with a sigh. "I spend most of my time in Parliament angry."

Isabella lifted her eyes to meet his, wondering if he was

teasing her. "I didn't bring a groom with me because... because there are only the two now, and I would feel awful that they have to work a longer day because I have kept one of them out here whilst I see to training a horse." The words came out in a rush, frustration evident in their tone. "Besides, they can be such a distraction with their comments—"

"Why are *you* training my horses?" Octavius interrupted, his scowl firmly in place.

Isabella flinched, mostly because the words came out in a sort of disbelief of her ability to do such a thing. "What else would I do all day?" she countered, one hand going to a hip in a rather indignant manner. The move only accentuated the tight fit of her riding habit.

"Wash windows, apparently," he remarked with a hint of disgust. "You're a *lady*, Isabella. The daughter of an earl. You cannot be doing the work of the housemaids and footmen," he admonished her.

Isabella rolled her eyes, clearly annoyed with the duke's words. "The windows looked as if they hadn't been cleaned since the day the house was built! Besides, it was raining. The whole day! I couldn't go for a ride. I was *bored*, Your Grace. What would you have me do instead?"

Octavius shook his head, stunned by her arguments. "Embroidery, perhaps? Read a book. Write letters." The last words were out of his mouth before he remembered that other than him, she really had no one to whom she could send correspondence. At least, not as long as they were keeping her whereabouts a secret. "To me," he added, a bit too late.

Blinking, Isabella was ever so glad she had Ares to lean back against just then. "Would you read them?"

It was the duke's turn to blink. "Of course. I read all my correspondence."

"Then, in the future, I shall do that on the days when it rains," she replied with a nod.

"Good," Octavius replied, his curt nod matching hers.

Although he should have felt a bit of satisfaction at having won this particular argument with the headstrong chit, he couldn't help the niggling feeling he had missed something important.

The clause in the contract, of course.

She had only agreed to write letters on the days when it rained. She hadn't agreed to cease training his horses or working with the servants, and he was about to bring up the point when he noticed Ares give a snort.

Isabella allowed a sigh and rolled her eyes as Ares dropped his nose to her hip. He nudged her until she was forced to take a step sideways. Well aware the duke was poised to do something should Ares continue his impertinent behavior, she reached into her pocket and pulled out an apple. Holding it on her outstretched palm, she gave Octavius a shrug as the horse helped himself.

"That reminds me," Octavius said suddenly, rather stunned at how confident she was with the beast. "I'm starving. I told Peters to see to a luncheon. Will you join me?"

Isabella's eyes widened in surprise. Despite admonishing her for the past ten minutes—both with his words and with the way he scowled at her—the duke suddenly seemed friendly. She nodded. "Of course, Your Grace." She turned to the dog. "Come, Nelson."

The puppy hurried to her stand before her, his tale wagging. She lifted him onto Ares, straddling him over the front of the saddle before she slipped a boot into the stirrup and mounted the horse. It was then Octavius realized the saddle wasn't a sidesaddle and that her riding habit had been designed for riding astride.

He couldn't help the combination of shock and arousal he felt just then. She was still a maiden. She shouldn't be riding a horse like that! What if—?

"I only ride sidesaddle when I'm riding with Miss Fitzwilliam," Isabella stated from her perch atop Ares, well aware he was about to put voice to a protest. And with that, she kicked her heels into Ares and allowed him the run he had been waiting for all morning.

Cursing under his breath, Octavius jumped onto Poseidon and raced after her, not quite sure he wanted to catch up.

He rather liked the view of her from behind.

Chapter 25

LUNCHEON WITH A DISTRACTED DUKE

Twenty minutes later

Isabella dared a quick glance out her bedchamber window, worried the duke was admonishing the head groom with whom he had been in a discussion since his return from the meadow.

He didn't seem angry as they stood facing one another, but then it was hard to tell from this far away. At least Octavius wasn't waving his arms about. And she couldn't hear him bellowing at the man. Not that he would bellow. He was entirely opposite of her father in almost every way.

If Reeves lost his position because of her, Isabella would feel awful. Watching the two a moment longer, she noted how Poseidon occasionally pawed at the ground, his head tossing until the duke seemed to do something to settle him. Missing whatever it was—one of his hands was blocked from her view—she made a note to ask.

She was sure Octavius would have caught up to her whilst she made the return ride to Huntinghurst. Ares was fast, of course, but she didn't allow him full rein knowing Octavius would probably lecture her on her poor judgment. Instead, she had forced the Thoroughbred to keep to an easy run. Poseidon should have been able to outrun Ares given the duke's experienced riding skills. There was another reason, as well, but she didn't follow the thought as she washed her hands in the basin and then saw to a repair of her hair. Several pins had escaped during her ride.

A quick sniff of her riding habit had her undoing the buttons down the front and stepping out of it in favor of wearing a sprigged muslin gown. She had left the pale yellow frock splayed out on the bed in anticipation of wearing it for tea later that afternoon. Spending most of her day in a riding habit, she rarely changed clothes.

Isabella was in the middle of pulling on the gown when one of the household maids appeared in the open doorway.

"Why, my lady, the duke is back in residence. You really must remember to shut your door," Thompson whispered.

Stunned she hadn't closed the door to her bedchamber—had she really been in that much of a hurry?—Isabella gave a nod. "Could you help me with my boots?"

The maid was quick join her, making sure the door was latched before moving to pull off the riding boots. After a struggle, the two finally managed to get them off. "I think it's time the duke buys you a new pair," Thompson commented as she studied the soles. She aimed them in Isabella's direction. "You've a few holes."

Isabella sucked in a breath. After more than a year of almost daily wear, they were in need of repair. "Indeed," she replied. "Do I look... presentable? I'm having luncheon with His Grace."

Her eye's widening, the maid gave a nod. "Well, you'll need some slippers," she hinted, disappearing into the dressing room.

Isabella took the opportunity to move to the vanity. Studying her reflection in the mirror, she wondered if she would be considered a handsome woman in London. Would a young buck find her attractive? Not gorgeous like her mother, certainly, but pleasing to the eye?

She remembered the moment she had met Constance Fitzwilliam—and the odd sensation she had felt at seeing herself alive and five years older in another woman. Although a bit disconcerting, she thought she rather liked the idea of one day looking just like Constance. Sophisticated, but not as proud as she remembered her mother appearing. She conjured the image of the woman in her mind's eye, wondering if any of their features matched. Other than the color of her hair and the shape of her face, Isabella possessed only a passing resemblance to her mother.

The image of her mother dissolved into her watery reflection when the maid reappeared and stood staring at her.

"Oh, there's no need to cry, my lady," Thompson said. "I'll just get that smudge removed, and you'll be right as rain."

Smudge?

The maid knelt and held the slippers until Isabella stepped into them. Then she hurried off to find a linen.

Turning her head to discover what the maid had noticed, Isabella wondered how she had missed the rather indecorous smudge of dirt that discolored her left cheek. She sighed in dismay, wondering if it had been there when the duke found her in the meadow. Before she could put voice to a complaint, the maid had returned and was seeing to its removal.

"Right as rain," Thompson stated.

"And my hair?" Isabella wondered, taking the linen so she could wipe the rest of her face.

Angling her head to one side, Thompson reached up and plucked a pin from the bun. A lock of hair unwound and fell past Isabella's shoulder, the slight curl at the end resting just above her collarbone.

The memory of Constance Fitzwilliam flashed before her eyes. *Sophisticated*, she thought with a slight grin. "I like it," she said in a whisper. She gave the maid a nod and said, "Thank you for your help. I know it's not part of your position to play lady's maid."

Grinning, the maid gave a curtsy. "Och, I don't mind a

bit, my lady. We'll have to see what we can do with your hair for this evening's dinner."

Isabella blinked. "Dinner?" She hadn't given a thought to the duke being at dinner that evening.

Given his reaction to her greeting in the meadow, she wondered if she had done something unforgivable or if she would be able to return to his good graces with better behavior. At least the man hadn't immediately left to go back to London like he had done the last time he visited.

"Aye. His Grace has requested a dinner be served."

"For how many?" Perhaps he had invited others to join him at Huntinghurst.

The maid blinked. "The two of you, of course," she replied.

Isabella's eyes widened. She supposed he planned to tell her at luncheon, the reminder of which had her gasping. "I have to go down. Now," she said, hurrying to the window. The duke was no longer speaking with the groom, which meant he had probably come into the house and was waiting for her.

The maid curtsied as Isabella took her leave of the bedchamber, nearly colliding with the duke as she did so.

"Pardon me, Your Grace," she managed as she dropped into a deep curtsy.

Octavius blinked, his brows furrowing so he appeared far older than his three-and-thirty years. He glanced at the doorway from which she had emerged before returning his attention to her and then giving her a nod. "How is it you've managed to change your clothes, your hair..." He dared a glance down at the hem of her gown. "And your shoes in the five minutes since you left the stables?" he asked, clearly incredulous. *Jesus! Did I lose track of time again?*

It was Isabella's turn to blink. "I believe it's been more like fifteen minutes, Your Grace," she countered. "I didn't wish to keep you waiting." When he continued to stare at her, the look of disbelief still quite evident, she added, "You said you were starving."

The reminder had him giving another quick nod. "Indeed." Holding out an arm, the duke gave her another quick glance before leading her down the stairs and to the dining room. "Am I to believe the level of light in the house is entirely due to cleaner windows? Or did you have the servants add more candles?"

Inhaling sharply, Isabella nearly stopped walking. "I would never do such a thing, sir," she claimed. "They're far too expensive—"

"I'm teasing," Octavius said with a sigh before suddenly stopping just outside the dining room. "I wish to apologize for my outburst earlier. I think you... *misunderstood* just why it was I raised my voice."

Isabella furrowed a brow. "It wasn't because I behaved like a... hoyden?" she asked in a quiet voice. She knew there were two footmen just inside the dining room waiting to begin their luncheon service, and she certainly didn't want them overhearing the duke admonishing her.

Octavius frowned again. *Did she think her greeting was inappropriate?* It was, of course, or rather would have been if they had been in the presence of anyone other than the two horses and the dog who were watching them. "I admit I was rather surprised by your manner of welcome," he hedged. "I always am. But pleased, in fact." At Isabella's widened eyes, he added, "My arrivals don't usually involve young women throwing themselves at me."

Her mouth dropped open in an effort to put voice to a protest—by no possible measure had she *thrown* herself at the duke, even if her feet had left the ground for a moment—Isabella found she had to swallow her complaint. Octavius had placed a finger on her lips and leaned a bit closer.

"I am teasing," he whispered.

Isabella took a deep breath and allowed a nod.

"My reaction was entirely due to the fear I felt at seeing you alone with Ares."

Isabella's eyes widened again. "*Fear?*" she repeated, her

mouth once again about to drop open. She clamped it shut lest the duke put his finger there again.

Not that she minded him touching her. A sort of buzzing sensation along the surface of her lips had been set off by his last attempt to quiet her.

"Fear, yes. At what might have happened given there was no one with you out there. The last time I was in the presence of Ares, he was an unbroken beast capable of trampling anyone who got within ten feet of him."

Swallowing, Isabella remembered all too well how difficult it had been to get close to Ares. After days of trying, she found she had to pretend to ignore the Thoroughbred so it appeared to be his idea to approach her.

Thank the gods he liked apples.

When she didn't respond to the duke's comment, he led her to the opposite end of the dining room. Pulling out the chair to the right of his carver, he waited for her to be seated before he said, "I know you must be..." He paused before remembering her comment to Ares. "*Frustrated* with me. I haven't visited as often as I should have, especially these past few months. I apologize for that."

Isabella watched as a footman hurried to help the duke with the carver, but she waited until the servant had taken his leave of the dining room before saying, "You needn't apologize. I am well aware you have your duties in London."

Octavius regarded her a moment, a bit startled by her words. He did have affairs to see to in London, not the least of which was Parliament. But since she had been moved into Huntinghurst, he found more excuses to stay in London rather than face her. And face the memories of what his life had at one time been like when Jane was still alive. He was just about to recall a particularly charming luncheon with his late wife—the one during which she hinted that she might be expecting a babe—when he realized Isabella was staring at him. Staring at him as if she were expecting him to say something.

Had he missed a comment? Had she put voice to a

query? He had thought he was beyond his extended reveries, but apparently he had been lost in thought just then. *The chit probably thinks I'm a candidate for Bedlam*, he considered. "What is it?" he asked.

"Did you fire Mr. Reeves?" Isabella asked in a whisper, ready to argue on behalf of the overworked servant.

Octavius gave a start. "What makes you think I would do such a thing?"

"I saw you speaking with him, and I worried you might have blamed him for something I did entirely of my own volition."

The duke gave a sigh of frustration. "Reeves is in charge of the stables. It's his job to look after my horses. That means he has to be responsible if you take one of my horses on a jaunt—"

"It was not a *jaunt*," she interrupted, immediately regretting her words. "Your Grace," she added with a pained expression. *If only the floor could open up and swallow me whole,* she thought. She dared a glance at him, rather surprised he didn't seem angry just then. Instead, he was regarding her with an expression that suggested he was lost in thought.

A footman settled a plate on her charger, the surface covered with a cold collation of piped ham and peas. He did the same for the duke whilst another footman saw to the delivery of a loaf of sliced bread fresh from the oven whilst yet another footman poured wine and water.

She was sure the three footmen were all there were in the entire household!

"Leave us," Octavius ordered.

Suddenly afraid, Isabella stiffened in anticipation of running from the room. Although his order hadn't been said with a hint of menace, Isabella had no idea what the duke intended to do once they were alone in the dining room. She hadn't spent enough time in his presence to know his moods. To guess what he might do next.

Now, if she were standing and facing him, she was sure

she could hold her own in an argument with him. And she would know when to let him think he had won. Not like last time, when she had pushed just a bit too hard and had the man stalking off in anger over her insistence that what she was doing with one of the horses was the best for its care.

A colt had shown obvious signs of developing crooked front legs, and Constance had explained how to treat the affliction. But the duke was obviously unfamiliar with the wooden braces she had made for Endymion. Quite incensed, the duke and she had argued, and then she had watched while he stalked off, unaware he simply continued to where his coach was still parked in front of the manor, stepped in, and ordered the driver to head back to London.

When she realized what was happening, she immediately realized she needed to apologize, but the coach was already pulling away from the front of Huntinghurst. Despite her effort to run after it—to catch it before it made the turn to Cocking—she was too late.

For the first time since her arrival at Huntinghurst, Isabella retreated to the first story salon, took a pen to paper, and wrote a letter of apology.

Dear Duke of Huntington,

I write with a heavy heart, made so from our Unfortunate Encounter this afternoon. Despite my attempt to apologize in person (my stockinged ankles were on display as I chased your coach all the way to the main road with the hope your driver might see me and stop), I was unable to do so.

I wish to Apologize for having upset you. It is never my intention to vex you so, but it seems I manage to do so with your every visit. I am left to wonder if all ladies are a vexing problem for you, as I cannot believe I am the only one who speaks her mind when she holds certain beliefs near and dear.

My mother, may she Rest In Peace, taught me that when I am certain of my position, I must stand and fight for it lest tyranny be allowed to prevail. (Not that I believe you to be a tyrant, for I do not hold that opinion of you. At least, not usually.)

Please believe me when I tell you that I hold your horses in high esteem, for they are magnificent beasts, and I only wish to see them Healthy and Happy and Prepared for when you are once again interested in the Horse Races. If my plans work as I believe they will, you will have at least two horses ready for next year and two more the following year. Perhaps three.

As for the reason for our argument, the colt is already showing signs of improvement. I will return him and his dam to the pasture when his legs appear straighter.

Despite the way in which I argued with you, I hold you in high esteem as well, for I do not know where I would live or what I would do with my days if it wasn't for your stables.

Thank you for taking me in. Thank you for use of the beautiful bedchamber overlooking the stables. Thank you for providing me protection from Craythorne. I cannot help but believe I would be dead if not for you.

Despite what you may think, I look forward to when you return to Huntinghurst. Please believe me when I assure you I only have your horses' best interests at heart. Even Ares.

Very sincerely yours,
Isabella Tolson

The duke's response had arrived only four days later, the words written in an even, easy-to-read script.

Dear Lady Isabella,

You are forgiven.

Most ladies hold their tongues except in matters of gossip. You are the only one who vexes me.

I have never before been accused of being a tyrant.

I am glad Endymion is recovering despite your unorthodox treatment.

You are welcome.

Hunt

Post scriptum: Do not waste your efforts on Ares.

When Isabella had read this last line, she took it as a challenge rather than an edict. Now she realized he was quite serious with his words.

Once the three servants disappeared from the dining room, Octavius took a sip of wine and regarded his plate before turning his attention back to Isabella. "I did not fire the groom, nor would I. Apparently, he's the only one left out there besides George since no one informed me the *other* groom had left my employ some six weeks ago." The measured tone of the words suggested he was doing everything to contain his annoyance—his anger—at having just learned of the situation with Mr. Campbell.

Isabella regarded Octavius for a moment, stunned by his comment. "Mr. Campbell left your employ because he *died* Your Grace," she said in a soft voice. "Quite suddenly. I'm certain he would have given notice had he known he was about to expire. He was very loyal servant."

Staring at her as if she had suddenly grown another head, Octavius gave his own head a sudden shake. "Now you're teasing me," he accused.

Isabella shook her head. "I most certainly am not," she countered. "I didn't attend his funeral, of course, but we did have a small gathering here at the house on his behalf. His intended cried the entire time, poor thing. They were due to marry next month."

Replaying the head groom's words in his head, Octavius realized he had completely misunderstood the man's comment. "So, when Mr. Reeves said Mr. Campbell had 'gone', he meant he... he *died?*" Jesus, he had thought the man had run off with Mrs. Fraser, the widow he was courting!

Isabella winced at hearing how Mr. Campbell's passing had been described by the head groom. "Indeed. When I inquired as to when he might hire a replacement, Mr. Reeves claimed he didn't have the authority. So we've simply made due with the three of us." When it appeared as if the duke wasn't going to press the issue, Isabella returned her attention to her plate and resumed eating.

"You don't find it... *unseemly* to work in the stables?" Octavius finally asked. "You're a lady..."

"I am happy to do it, sir. Truly," she said quietly. "Besides, training horses is hardly work. Other than Miss Fitzwilliam and Nelson, the horses are my only friends. Who else can claim to spend their days in the company of their best friends?"

Octavius could think of a few ne'er-do-wells in London who spent their days with so-called friends, but he didn't put voice to his thoughts just then. Instead he concentrated on his meal until he realized Isabella was regarding him with a look of concern. "What is it?" he asked as he set down his fork.

"May I ask what you did to calm Poseidon? When he seemed unsettled earlier?"

Furrowing his brows, Octavius thought for a moment and then wondered how she knew he had needed to calm the beast. "I gave him an apple," he said with a shrug.

"Oh, of course," Isabella responded with a nod. She supposed she should expect Poseidon and Ares to be similar in their temperaments—and their likes—given their lineage.

"What do you mean by that?" he asked, careful to avoid looking directly into her eyes. Her gaze would have him mesmerized, thinking of what it might be like to have those eyes watching him from the other side of a ballroom, or from the other end of a dining table. What it would be like to wake up with those eyes watching him every morning. As if she could see into his very soul.

She would learn entirely too much if she did.

"Ares will do anything for an apple," she claimed, deciding it was the perfect time to bring up the matter of Ares. "Poseidon and Ares are brothers, are they not?"

Octavius gave a start, wondering how she knew. "They are. I suppose Mr. Reeves mentioned it?" he half-asked, never intending for her not to know of common pedigree of the headstrong horses.

"He didn't have to," Isabella replied with a shake of her head. "I've been studying the lineages of your horses. Ares and Poseidon share so many of the same traits. Earlier, in the meadow... when they were facing one another, it was like seeing them in a mirror," Isabella explained. "Were you the one who broke Poseidon?"

The duke nodded. "About killed me, which is why I realized Ares was a mistake. I never should have allowed Poseidon's sire and dam to mate again."

"Ares is not a mistake," Isabella said softly. "He's the fastest horse in your stables."

Sighing, Octavius furrowed a brow. "How... how *did* you break him? Without him breaking you?" She had never shown signs of being injured by a horse. No broken bones or obvious limping. No scars or bruises.

Isabella allowed a wan grin. "By making it his choice to be broken," she replied. At the duke's look of confusion, she gave a shrug. "Every morning, I exercise three horses. I start by going into the stables carrying a bit and a lead. All the horses watch as I choose one I haven't ridden in a few days. I put the bit on, all the time making small talk and praising the horse. Then I lead it out of the stables to where George has a saddle ready. Within a few minutes, I'm off riding. Fifteen minutes later, I'm back, and I repeat the process with another horse."

Octavius shook his head. "Where is Ares during all this?"

"In a stall. Right near the door."

"How did you get him in a stall?" the duke asked, obviously surprised the beast would tolerate an enclosure.

Isabella gave a one-shouldered shrug. "He wants to be with the other horses, of course, so when I call them in for the night, they come and each go to their own stall. Ares is always the last, of course, so I make sure he can go directly into the first stall. Then, in the morning, he has to watch as each horse parades by for their opportunity for a run. Once three horses have run, I let them all go out to the pasture for the day," she explained.

"How did you get a bit on him?"

At this, Isabella inhaled and then frowned. "One day, I chose him as my third horse. I held the bit up like I do with any other horse, and I started to put it on him."

"He allowed it?" Octavius asked in surprise.

"Oh, goodness, no. He backed up. Shook his head. Complained bitterly. You would have thought I had tried to strangle him. So I went to the next horse, who was more than happy to have the opportunity at a run." She paused a moment. "It took five more tries before I got it on him," she admitted with a wry grin. "But then, I knew I couldn't have George put a saddle on him. So I led him to the enclosure, and George brought another horse—Enyo—to help settle him. I rode Enyo in the pen while he raced around in circles."

"How long until you got him saddled?"

"A few weeks, but by then, he didn't mind the idea so much."

Octavius dipped his head. "Lots of patience, then," he commented, remembering he hadn't had the time for it with Poseidon. He wanted a horse suitable for London traffic, figuring he would leave the coach-and-four for his duchess to use when she went about her calls. When his last mount came up lame, Poseidon seemed the obvious choice as a replacement. Once he was broken, he proved perfect for the task. Breaking Poseidon nearly proved the duke's undoing, though.

"A lot of apples is more the thing," Isabella replied, a dimple appearing. "Rather fortuitous you have an orchard on your property."

Octavius allowed a grin. "Indeed. However did you manage the first ride?" he asked, remembering how Poseidon had bucked and fought until they were both exhausted.

"I wasn't the first to ride him, of course. Mr. Campbell managed it. I was on Enyo at the time, and he's always been rather sweet on her, so I think he allowed it just to show off." At Octavius' snort, Isabella gave him a quelling glance. "The first time I took him to the meadow, he was saddled, but I was riding Enyo," she claimed. "He followed us the entire way. Never tried to run off. Just ran around the meadow as fast as he could once we got there. Showing off, I tell you," she claimed. "Then, when he finally settled down, he came closer and watched as I trained Enyo to canter and to back up. After a few days, he came even closer and started doing what she was doing. After that, she was the one watching while I trained Ares."

Finally allowing a nod, Octavius sighed. "That's how you do it with the others then, too?" he wondered.

Isabella bobbed her head back and forth. "Most are quicker to accept a bit, mostly because I get one on them when they're younger. They seem to want to learn when they see the racers being timed on the track. Why, when three of them are racing side-by-side with the grooms and George on their backs, all the horses in the pasture hurry over to watch. It's as if they want to race, too."

Octavius stared at Isabella, awed by her enthusiasm and by the way her face lit up whilst she described his horses. He wanted nothing more than to be one of those horses she exercised in the mornings. Wanted nothing more than to have her undivided attention. Why, he would even welcome having to stand next to the orangery for a half-hour or so learning patience if it meant she would come and untie him and lead him back to his stall at night.

He gave his head a shake.

What the hell?

"Has something happened?" she asked then, wondering at his odd expression.

Octavius gave a shake of his head. "No," he replied. "Other than the need to find a replacement for Mr. Campbell, all is well, actually. I'll see to it a notice is posted in Chichester. Peters can see to the particulars."

"Miss Fitzwilliam might know of someone," Isabella

suggested. "Someone with... with a suitable character, of course," she added, realizing the duke wouldn't allow just anyone to be employed in his stables.

This had him giving a nod. "When is she next due to join you on a ride?"

"Day after tomorrow. Can you stay that long?"

Octavius thought the question odd until he remembered he rarely stayed more than one day at Huntinghurst. The last time, he had left—in a huff due to their argument—without even spending the night. He later cursed himself for his shortsightedness. The coach had been forced to stop at *The Angel*, a coaching inn in Guildford, when it was too dark to go on to London. He realized he could have simply gone to his apartments at Huntinghurst and spent his time sequestered there, avoiding Isabella until they could discuss the issue of Endymion's treatment in a more calm manner.

"Perhaps." He paused a moment. "I was ready to forbid you from going near the stables when I last left you," he added suddenly. At Isabella's look of shock—fright, even—Octavius allowed a wan grin. "But I figured you would simply vex me more by running away."

Isabella realized then he knew her better than she thought he did. "You have the right of it," she admitted with a sigh. "Tell me, Your Grace. Is it really so unseemly for me to spend time with your horses? To train them? It gives me joy and a sense of... a sense of accomplishment when I'm able to ride a horse I've broken."

Octavius finished off his wine and regarded her for a moment. "Let us come to an agreement," he suggested. "You can continue to do what you do with my horses, but you must also see to your training as a lady."

Isabella blinked. "Training?" she repeated, her eyes wide.

"Do you know how to dance?"

"Of course." She paused a moment. "Although I've not had occasion to do so since my arrival. And I do not know the steps of the new dance, the waltz, that is becoming so popular in the capital."

Arching a brow, Octavius briefly wondered how she even knew about the waltz and then remembered *The Tattler* was a source of information in Miss Fitzwilliam's household. "Then you shall learn it. After dinner this evening," he announced. "What about serving tea?"

Isabella blinked, allowing a slight shrug. "I do it twice a week with Miss Fitzwilliam," she replied with a nod.

"Can you speak French?"

"*Oui, monsieur. Bien que je n'ai pas l'occasion de m'exercer à le parler*," she managed to say. *Although I don't have the occasion to practice speaking it.*

"*Peut-être que Miss Fitzwilliam peut aider à cet égard.*" *Perhaps Miss Fitzwilliam can help in that regard.*

Isabella gave a nod. "*Peut-être. Je vais demander.*"

Octavius allowed a grin, realizing Lady Craythorne had at least seen to teaching her daughter some of the skills she would need to manage as the wife of an aristocrat. "Do you paint?"

"Poorly."

"Embroidery?"

"Fair. I know all the stitches, of course. I just don't have the needle and threads to practice it here."

The duke realized he hadn't seen to it she had a sewing basket. Since Jane had never stepped foot in Huntinghurst, there probably wasn't one she could use.

"What about drawing?"

Isabella angled her head to one side. "I can do a very good representation of a horse," she offered.

Octavius sighed. "Of course, you can," he replied, realizing he should have expected the response. "Have you other... *talents* a lady might find useful?"

Straightening, Isabella nodded. "I know the recipe for making shortbread biscuits," she announced.

Octavius frowned. "Since your cook would be the one to make biscuits, that hardly seems useful."

"But, what if she takes ill and cannot make them?"

Isabella countered. "I shouldn't expect a scullery maid to know how."

Giving his head a shake, Octavius decided to try a different tack. "How do you spend your evenings here? When it's too dark to be out in the stables? What do you usually do after dinner?"

"I read, of course," she replied. "Your library has excellent references on horses and horse breeding."

"How many have you read?"

"All of them. Some twice." She didn't mention the other books she had read, some with topics she was sure she wasn't supposed to have known anything about just yet.

Octavius blinked, realizing that she probably knew more on the subject than he did. "Are horses really *all* you think about?" he asked, somewhat rhetorically.

Not about to admit she thought of *him* far more than she should, Isabella gave a shrug. "I do concern myself with the running of the household. When Peters doesn't seem to know how to direct the maids. There's no housekeeper, you see—"

"I didn't see fit to hire a replacement for the last one."

Isabella's eyes widened. No wonder there hadn't been a housekeeper at Huntinghurst for the entire eighteen months she had been there. "She didn't get along with Peters, either?" she questioned.

Octavius rolled his eyes. "Something like that," he allowed, suddenly wondering if perhaps the butler was as vexing for the women of the household as Isabella was to him. "Since you have already been acting in the capacity of châtelaine, and given your age—you're hardly a ward—perhaps it would be best if we consider that your position here."

Isabella blinked. *The mistress of the castle?* She stared at the duke for a moment. "I would be honored," she replied with a nod.

The duke wondered for a moment if he was making a mistake but finally nodded in reply as he pushed away from the table and moved to stand. "I have some correspondence to see to," he said then. "I will see you at dinner."

Nodding again, Isabella rose and dipped a curtsy. "Your Grace," she said as she took her leave of the dining room.

If she was expected to dance with duke after dinner, she wanted to be sure she had something appropriate to wear.

Chapter 26

A VISIT TO THE STABLES

Later that night

Having spent the entire afternoon in his study at Huntinghurst, Octavius emerged from the walnut-paneled room in search of sunlight and a bit of fresh air. He headed out the back door and made his way to the stables, not particularly surprised to find another horse tethered to the side of the orangery.

Leading two horses out of their stalls, Mr. Reeves gave a bow as the duke entered.

"How long has he been out there?" Octavius asked as he waved toward the yearling.

Mr. Reeves cast a glance in the direction of Perseus, giving his head a quick shake. "Half-hour at most, Your Grace. Truth be told, can't say I thought it would do much good, making a horse stand still for a time like that, but it seems to help."

Octavius furrowed a brow. "In what way?"

The groom allowed a shrug. "Calms 'em when they're in their stall for the night. Don't rub their tails as much, neither."

Giving a grunt, Octavius nodded and made his way into

the stables, his quick steps taking him past a series of empty stalls, all mucked and ready for new straw. Only one stall at the end was occupied, a bay mare and her colt watching him intently from where they stood. The colt retreated behind his mother, but his lowered head allowed him to peek out from beneath her belly.

"Aphrodite? Is that you?" Octavius asked in a quiet voice as he reached for the latch.

The mare regarded him for a moment before moving toward him, her head lowered.

"It is you," he whispered. He knelt so he could better see her colt. "You always throw the best looking colts," he added, reaching out to place a hand on her withers. Aphrodite knickered in response, which had the colt poised for a quick retreat. "Have you named it yet?" he asked, as if the horse might provide him with a response.

"Anteros, if Your Grace is in agreement," George said from where he stood in the middle of the building, a pitchfork in one hand.

Octavius turned his attention to the stableboy, his head angled to one side. "I don't think the name has been used for one of her colts before," he agreed.

"Lady Isabella has been keeping track of the names, Your Grace. She's good at that."

"Is she now?" the duke replied, his attention going back to the colt. He wondered how Isabella was keeping track. Back when he paid any mind to his stables, he kept detailed pedigrees for each and every horse. Pedigrees he then sent on to the Jockey Club in Newmarket. He had to if he had any intention of entering a horse in the racing circuit.

"Oh, yes, sir. She's quite particular about details. Knows her horses, that one."

Arching an eyebrow at the comment, Octavius angled his head and finally allowed a nod. "I suppose that means she spends a good deal of time with them."

George nodded. "Oh, she does, Your Grace. Every day."

He paused a moment. "Well, except when it's raining too hard. Then she keeps to the house. Otherwise, she's out here or riding."

Octavius considered the stableboy's comment for a time before allowing a nod. "You don't... mind her spending so much time in the stables? Getting in your way?"

George shook his head. "She's never in the way, Your Grace," he claimed with a shake of his head. "When I came down with an awful cough last month, why, she made me stay in bed, and she mucked the stalls."

Blinking in shock at hearing the boy's tale, Octavius allowed a sigh of frustration. "I do hope you afford her all the courtesies she's due as a lady," he said, his voice rather stern.

"Oh, but I do, sir. But sometimes, when she's training the beasties, it's hard to think of her as a right proper lady. If you catch my meaning, Your Grace."

Octavius rolled his eyes and turned his attention back to Aphrodite. Her colt had latched onto a teat and was helping himself to a late lunch. "I don't suppose you think of her as a lady, either," he accused.

Aphrodite pretended to ignore his question, a soft knicker her only response.

"He'll be a racer," George stated, his attention on Anteros. "Lady Izzy says prob'ly the longer distances."

Frowning at the stableboy's use of a nickname, Octavius gave a shake of his head. "I guess we'll know in a few years," he responded. After a moment, he asked, "If I let Perseus loose from the orangery, what will happen?"

George allowed a shrug. "He'll come to his stall straight away. I just put some hay in there," he replied. "He sorted how to work the latch to let himself in. Then he'll head out to the front pasture for the rest of the day."

Octavius angled his head. "He won't... run off?"

Giving a short laugh, George shook his head. "None of your horses run off, Your Grace. None of them would risk the wrath of Lady Izzy. Uh, Lady Isabella, I mean to say," he corrected himself.

The wrath of Lady Izzy?

Well, Octavius knew he had at least one topic of conversation for dinner that evening.

Chapter 27

A DANCE AFTER DINNER

Later that night

The dinner service was impeccable, Octavius thought as he watched a footman remove the remains of the dessert course whilst another delivered a glass of port to him and a glass of champagne to Isabella. Although conversation had been a bit stilted with the young lady—especially after his question about what constituted 'The Wrath of Izzy'—they had finally reached a level of comfort where conversation seemed to flow with ease.

"I never beat them," Isabella said suddenly. "I don't whip them, either."

Octavius frowned, wondering why she felt it necessary to put voice to the claims. "I didn't think you did," he replied.

"When George talks of 'The Wrath of Izzy', he's merely referring to my raised voice," she explained. "I... I tend to... curse when a horse is being particularly difficult. Before I tie it up to the orangery."

Doing his best to suppress the grin he felt coming on just then, Octavius said, "I see."

"I am not the only one who curses in your stables," Isabella said in a quiet voice.

"I rather imagine not."

Isabella sighed. "You're about to admonish me for something. I can tell. Just... just say what ever it is that has you vexed."

"You really don't have to muck stalls when George is ill," Octavius replied quietly. At the moment, it was difficult to imagine her doing so, what with the way her hair was styled and the manner in which she was dressed. Despite its lack of lace or furbelows, her sapphire dinner gown made her appear every inch a lady. The white kid gloves she had worn into the dining room had been surreptitiously removed, revealing long fingers devoid of rings. One wrist featured a gold chain with a horse charm dangling from it, though.

Isabella's eyes widened, as if she wondered who might have tattled on her. "I know," she responded. "But I don't mind. Really. Miss Fitzwilliam does what she must with her stables at Fair Downs," she added, as if she were using Constance as a model for how to run a stables.

"Miss Fitzwilliam is not the daughter of an aristocrat," Octavius responded just before he took a sip of port. He was rather surprised the port had been delivered to him while Isabella was still in the dining room. He had expected she might excuse herself and make her way to the parlor, but then he realized she would have no one to keep her company there.

"There are days I completely forget I am one," she replied, just before she took a sip of champagne. Her eyes widened before she allowed a grin. "Now I understand what Monsieur Perignon meant."

Octavius cocked an eyebrow. "Are you referring to the French monk who discovered champagne?"

Isabella nodded. "It is said he claimed drinking champagne was like tasting the stars," she murmured.

Octavius allowed a grin of his own. "At least you have an appreciation for champagne. Given your work in the stables, I feared you might have taken up drinking ale with your dinners," he teased.

Isabella gave him a quelling glance. "Ale is far too sour

for my taste," she countered. "But I appreciate a glass of claret with dinner now and then."

"As long as you're not helping yourself to the scotch... "

"Of course not!" she replied in mock horror.

Octavius regarded her for a time before he leaned forward. "How are you? Getting on here, I mean?" He had struggled through the entire dinner wondering when she might put voice to a grievance. They had certainly argued enough times during his visits, although it had always been about the horses. If he could stand it, this might be his longest trip to Huntinghurst since her arrival. On the occasions of his other visits, he had always found an excuse to leave after a day, as if he thought spending any more time would give her an opportunity to unleash a string of complaints having nothing at all to do with the stables but with her lot in life.

Or beg for some frippery. Or a bauble. Jane had done that on occasion. He had always been happy to oblige her, of course. She was his very best friend. His wife. He had been determined to keep her happy.

Octavius had to give his head a quick shake, knowing if he allowed his memories of Jane to continue, he would be lost in thought for a long time.

Isabella blinked at hearing the question. The duke had never before asked how she found life at Huntinghurst. "I am... well, Your Grace."

"Huntington," he stated. "Or... Hunt," he offered. "It seems unnecessary for you to refer to me so formally after all this time."

Apparently trying out his name in her mind, Isabella allowed a frown. "Hunt seems terribly... informal," she murmured.

"No more so than 'Izzy'," he countered with an arched eyebrow. "Which is how George referred to you earlier today." He pushed his carver away from the table in anticipation of standing.

Isabella allowed a grin as she did the same, realizing

they were about to go for a walk. "He's become somewhat of a younger brother to me." From the duke's quelling glance, she knew he didn't approve. "He's an orphan, so he doesn't have any family of his own," she argued as she surreptitiously shook out her skirts and pulled on her long gloves. She made sure to pick up her glass of champagne when she noticed the duke lifting his glass of port from the table.

"As long as you don't have him moving into one of the guest suites," Octavius murmured as he offered an arm.

"Of course not. Besides, he's rather happy with his room above the stables," she replied. "He said he used to sleep out of doors after his mum died."

"Which is why I had Mr. Reeves see to a position for him. The urchin seems to know his way around a horse, and he's certainly willing to work." Watching for her reaction, Octavius was pleased to see Isabella's surprise at his comment. Ever since she had mentioned the word 'tyrant' in her most recent missive, he found he was determined to prove he was anything but.

They made their way to a nearby salon, where Octavius deposited their glasses onto a sideboard. "When was the last time you danced, my lady?"

A frisson passed through Isabella at the thought of dancing with the duke. With just the two of them, they could hardly perform a longways dance, which meant...

"The waltz?" he added with an arched brow.

Isabella's eyes widened. "Well, I've watched my mother dance it with Craythorne," she replied.

"You'll need to know it when you return to Society," Octavius said as he stood before her. "Your left hand here, your right hand here," he ordered as he held out his arm and set a hand at her waist. Isabella gave a start, but did as she was told. "The count of the music is a bit different," the duke warned. "One, two, three, one, two, three. When I do..." He pushed against the hand he held in his. "You step back with your right foot." Isabella did as instructed. "Now your left, and then on the next count, bring your right foot to your left."

Tempted to look down, Isabella found she couldn't when Octavius lifted her chin with a hooked finger. "Head up. I'll be watching over your shoulder so we shan't bump into anything."

Isabella held her head high. "Aren't we a bit... close?" she asked as he had her repeat the first three steps.

Octavius waved a hand between them, making a square pattern. "This is the space that will keep us separated," he said, interrupting his murmured, 'One, two, three'. "You'll not step into this space, nor will I. Now you're going to step forward with your left foot..." He pulled her hand at the same time he gave the instruction and stepped back. "Your right foot comes forward, and now bring your left foot to your right."

Stutter stepping a bit, Isabella finally understood what he meant. "So, it's backwards from the first three steps," she hedged.

Octavius considered her words. "Yes, except you'll be moving forward whilst I move backward." He had her do the steps again, continuing his quiet counting. "Now do those six steps all together." He began the count and Isabella held her breath as they completed the shape of a box. "Very good," he said as he gave a glance about the room. "We could just do this here, but it's a far more elegant dance if I lead us about in a larger circle."

Before Isabella had a chance to respond, he had her performing a slow version of the dance, his lead taking them in an arc about one side of the salon.

"It's much more enjoyable with music," Octavius said as he steered them around a low table.

"Perhaps Connie can play for me whilst I practice," Isabella murmured, mentally counting.

"Does she play piano-forté?"

Isabella blinked. "I... I don't actually know. I suppose I shouldn't assume such a thing."

"Do you play?" he asked, returning them to their original location.

"Of course. Although I have not done so lately. I've been spending most of my time with the horses." Her eyes suddenly widened. "*Perseus!*" she exclaimed, just then remembering she had left the poor beast tethered to the orangery. Whirling to head for the door, she intended to run from the salon and out to where Perseus was tied up when she was suddenly spun backwards and around and found herself pressed against the front of the duke. "Oh!" she gasped, blinking when she realized he hadn't let go of his hold on her hand.

"I let him go an hour before dinner," Octavius said, gazing down at her large eyes. Brown eyes. Dammit, but they seemed to swallow him whole just then. Mesmerize him so that he could do nothing else but stare into them. Do nothing else but kiss the lips that were left slightly open from her expression of shock.

He had his lips lowered to hers even before he quite realized what he was doing. Even after they touched, ever so lightly, he wasn't sure if he was imagining it or if he was truly going to kiss Isabella. And then she lifted her free hand to his shoulder, as if for support, and their lips locked in the gentlest of kisses.

Barely there, soft and sweet, her lips molded to his as he deepened the kiss. He was aware of how she seemed to press harder against the front of his body, as if she needed more than just his shoulder for support. The hand that held hers let go to move to the side of her waist. Free of his hold, the gloved hand moved to the back of his neck, smoothing through the ends of his silken hair until a frisson seemed to pass through his entire body.

The sensation had him breaking the kiss with a gasp of surprise, but his hands still clung to her waist, as if he needed her for support. Unsure of what to say—he knew he should apologize for his unseemly behavior—he was spared having to say anything right away.

"Is that why vouchers are required to dance the waltz? Because they end in kissing?" Isabella asked in a breathless whisper.

Frowning at the odd question, Octavius finally realized to what she was referring. "Not… not exactly," he managed, hoping his hardened manhood hadn't made itself too apparent as it strained against the placket of his breeches and against her soft middle. "Vouchers are only required at Almack's. The subscription dances are Wednesday nights, you see, and a young lady is not allowed to dance a waltz unless she is in possession of a voucher."

Isabella continued to regard him with wide eyes. "So I don't require one if I'm waltzing somewhere else, such as at a… a rout or a ball?"

The duke nodded. "Exactly." He pondered what to say next when he realized she was regarding him—or rather his lips—with a rather hungry expression.

"Then the kissing isn't part of the waltz?" she wondered, one elegant eyebrow arching up.

Octavius swallowed. "It is in private, of course, but not… not in public." Despite wincing while he put voice to the white lie, he was sure she believed him.

Isabella regarded him through her dark lashes, her face flushed from both the dance and the kiss. "I think I should like to dance another waltz," she murmured, her brown eyes once again seeking his.

"Perhaps it would be best if we… we got some air. Walk with me?" he asked as he finally gave up his hold on her waist to offer an arm.

"Of course," Isabella replied, hoping the disappointment she felt wasn't too evident in her voice.

Neither of them said a word as Octavius led them down the hall to the back of the house. Remembering it would be dark, he helped himself to the lantern near the back door and held it in front of them as they made their way. "I do hope you're not in the habit of going outside after dark. At least, not without an escort."

Once they were through the door, the still summer night enveloped Isabella in warmth. Despite the cut of her gown, she was sure she never felt warmer in her life. "I've only been out to the stables at night if a mare was foaling," she assured him. "I always try to move a pregnant mare to the foaling stall when it's evident she is about to drop her foal."

Octavius considered her words as they walked the path that led into the parterre garden. "Still, you should have an escort," he said, his voice tinged with a scold.

Isabella ignored his comment in favor of inhaling the scents of newly-turned earth and flowers. "Is this garden anything like Lord Weatherstone's garden?"

Rather surprised by her question—how would she know to ask about Lord Weatherstone's garden?—Octavius pretended to glance about the dimly lit parterre. "Not a bit," he replied with a shake of his had. At Isabella's gasp, he added, "Although I have not been in those gardens for some time, they are far larger, and I remember they had rather tall hedgerows—"

"To hide behind?" Isabella interrupted. "Whilst kissing?"

Octavius furrowed a brow. "I think they are intended to act as walls between the various collections of flowers," he countered, not about to admit that most couples used them as she was imagining. "There is a fountain of Cupid in the middle where you can toss a coin and make a wish."

Isabella wondered what she might wish for should she ever find herself in the famous gardens. Horses, surely. A large stables in which to house them. Pastureland. "What did you wish for?" she asked as she took a seat on the stone bench.

Blinking at the memory that suddenly filled his mind's eye, and not just because it might bring tears, Octavius gave a short laugh. "That my betrothed would be pleased with my choice of a townhouse in Westminster," he murmured as he took a seat next to her. "I bought it about a month before Lady Jane and I were to be married."

"Was she? Pleased, I mean?" Despite having lived at

Huntinghurst for a year-and-a-half, Isabella knew little of the late duchess. The servants rarely spoke of her—none of them had met her since she was never in residence at the country estate, but they seemed to hold her in high regard.

Octavius dipped his head. "She was not." At Isabella's soft gasp, he added, "It didn't have a ballroom, and she thought the parlor entirely too small." He grimaced, not having remembered Jane's initial reaction to the townhouse he had occupied since her death. He had been so intent on pleasing her, he didn't give it a second thought when she claimed to have a different property in mind. One that cost nearly twice what he had paid for the first townhouse. One that featured an excellent address in Grosvenor Square and neighbors of high rank and flush bank accounts.

He moved into the first townhouse when he couldn't bear to go back to the mansion. Not after Jane had died there. Not after their son had joined her in death.

Now that he had given up on ever returning, an agent was seeing to its sale.

"I think I would be very pleased with a townhouse in Westminster," Isabella said with a sigh. "Although I have only ever been inside my father's, and just the one time."

"So you have been in London. Before..." He allowed the sentence to trail off, not intending to bring up that day when she had appeared at *The Elegant Courtesan* with the tale of her mother's death.

Isabella nodded. "A long time ago. I was ten, I think. Mum was excited to see her friends and her family. She had invitations that kept her out and about for the entire fortnight we were there." She allowed a sigh. "I watched the parade of aristocrats in Hyde Park during the fashionable hour, not realizing they did it nearly every night. We went to Sadler's Wells Theatre."

"To see a naval reenactment, no doubt," Octavius commented.

"Indeed. I was entranced, although the crowd was particularly raucous."

"Did you go to the pleasure gardens?"

Isabella shook her head. "No, but we went to Kew Gardens. The roses were in bloom. I had no idea roses could be so many colors." She waved a hand to indicate the roses that were featured in the parterre garden. Although most were red, there were yellow, pink and peach roses, as well.

The mention of roses in Kew Gardens had Octavius swallowing. Hard. "The red ones were Jane's favorite," he managed to get out.

Not sure how to respond, Isabella waited a moment before saying, "I have heard she was a very lovely woman."

Octavius swallowed again, finally clearing his throat. "She was very... pretty," he said, the word chosen a bit too carefully. "Gorgeous, really."

Isabella caught the way he said the word 'pretty' and wondered if he really meant his late duchess was clever or cunning. "I am sorry for your loss. She sounds as if she was the perfect duchess."

Stiffening on the bench, Octavius didn't respond. He squeezed his eyes shut, willing himself to think of something else—anything else—other than Jane. He didn't know how much time had passed before he felt lips kiss his cheek and heard her whispered, "Good night, Your Grace."

Inhaling sharply, he opened his eyes to find Isabella taking her leave of the bench. He reached out and captured her hand before she stepped away. Coming to his feet, he pulled her into a hug, his arms wrapping about her waist and shoulders.

Isabella bit back the gasp that would have given away her surprise—fear, even—at being gathered into his arms when she heard his whispered plea.

"Allow me this impropriety. For just this moment."

Relaxing into his hold, she was about to ask if he was well when he suddenly removed his arms and straightened.

"Forgive me. I... there are times..." He gave his head a shake.

"There are times when one needs to be held." *Times one*

needs to hold onto someone, she nearly added. “You are forgiven, of course,” Isabella murmured. She regarded him another moment before she lifted herself on her tiptoes and kissed him on the cheek. “I should not mind if it happens again.” Dipping a curtsy, she once again stepped away from the duke and made her way back to the house.

Octavius watched her as she disappeared, half-tempted to chase her, capture her in his arms, and repeat what had just happened. Instead, he remained in the garden and stared at the fountain, his thoughts of Jane replaced with thoughts of Isabella.

Chapter 28

THE TRUTH REVEALED

Late April 1815

Constance Fitzwilliam was in the stables when a glossy black coach pulled up in front of Fair Downs, its four matched black shires giving the equipage a regal bearing despite the lack of markings on the coach door. Having just returned from a ride with Isabella, their spirited conversation about the pros and cons of line breeding, she was ready for a hot bath and a cup of tea.

The bath would have to wait, it seemed.

"Oh, my lady, the earl's come a calling," Simmons said as she hurried into the stables, her eyes wide and her manner suggesting she considered him as important as the king of England.

There were times when David Fitzwilliam was indeed more important than the king—he owned Fair Downs, after all—but on this day, Constance merely thought of him as her cousin. "Tell His Highness I'll be right there," Constance replied as she moved to hang up some tack and put away the brush she had just used on her mount. She was about to head for the house when she realized she wasn't alone in the stables. Whirling around, she gasped at the sight of her taller cousin.

"Or His Highness can simply join you in the stables," David said, his manner rather droll.

"Norwick," Constance said with a sigh. "I apologize. I shouldn't have said such a thing to my lady's maid."

David allowed a grin. "You're forgiven," he said just before he pulled her into a hug. "Besides, I rather like the idea of being a king," he teased.

Constance resisted the move at first, but soon relaxed against the front of his body. "Are you here on business?" she wondered as she stepped away, giving him an assessing glance from top to bottom. As usual, her cousin was impeccably dressed, although he wasn't wearing a top hat just then. His hair was always cropped rather short, but he had allowed his mutton chops to grow a bit longer, which should have made his face appear more haggard, and yet he looked younger than the last time she had seen him.

"No. This is just a social call. And just how is it you knew it was me and not my brother?" he wondered. For some reason, Constance never seemed to have trouble telling the two of them apart.

"Danny's hair is a bit darker, and he has that little scar next to his eye," she replied as she waved a finger next to her own eye.

"That's it?" he countered, rather disappointed in her response.

Constance furrowed her brows. "What did you expect? You two still dress alike, don't you? Still wear your hair short and your tails long?"

Well, she had him there. "What will it take to get a cup of tea and a biscuit, my lady?"

Turning to the stable door, Constance held out a hand and beckoned him to join her. "Your presence in the parlor. But I'm sure I smell like horse, so you'll have to wait—"

"There's no need for you to change clothes, Connie," he interrupted. "I've been riding in the coach for the entire fifty miles from London. I probably have as much dust on me as you do," he claimed, despite the fact that his clothes appeared recently brushed. "Were you at Huntinghurst, by chance?" He opened and held the back door as she passed over the threshold.

"I was."

"And?" he prompted.

Constance angled her head as she made her way into the parlor. Simmons had already seen to delivering a tea tray, and Constance couldn't help but notice it featured the very best china teapot and cups. "Lady Isabella has become quite the lady of the house," she stated as she took a seat and checked the pot. "She's got every servant but the butler wrapped around her pinky. She's got every horse but one trained for riding. She's got one of the groomsmen acting as a jockey for the two she seems convinced can run in races."

"Can they?" David asked as he accepted a cup of tea and helped himself to a shortbread biscuit. Nothing of what Constance had said seemed to surprise him.

"Probably," she hedged. "She finally got a saddle on Ares, so he will be the sure bet."

Unfamiliar with a horse named Ares, David took his cousin's word for it. "Any suitors?" he wondered with an expectant look.

Constance gave her head a shake. "None that I know of, but..." She allowed the sentence to trail off when she thought better of what she was about to say.

"But?" David prompted.

"I can't help but think she's sweet on the duke. He's been in residence a couple of times whilst I was there, and she always greets him in a rather familiar manner. Kisses him on the cheek," she whispered as she leaned forward, one eyebrow arching up.

David gave his cousin a quelling glance. "Haven't been to Paris, have you?" he asked rhetorically.

"Neither has she," Constance stated, her head held in a manner suggesting she had one-upped him.

"Touché, cousin," he said with a sigh. "Is there any reason you think the duke shouldn't consider her to be his duchess? He needs one, you must know. Along with the heir and spare and a dog or two to complete the ducal portrait."

Constance regarded David for a few seconds before she said, "She's seems awfully young for him, but then, I think it's good for him to be around someone who is younger. He's certainly not as old as he appears. It's almost as if he wants everyone to believe he's... elderly."

"It *is* a bit of an act," David agreed, just then realizing that his cousin's words were true. Odd how he hadn't noticed it himself.

"I can't imagine Huntington marrying his ward, though."

"Why ever not?"

Constance blinked, rather stunned at how offended David seemed just then. She was about to remark on his response but thought better of it. "Those two have a... a sort of push-me, pull-you kind of relationship," she hedged. "She pushes and pushes, and just when he's about to explode, she retreats, almost like she knows just how much he'll endure before he's ready to pull her over his knee and give her a good spanking." Constance ignored David's look of shock at hearing her words and continued. "But then, he doesn't let her get away. He pulls her in. Gets her to capitulate. To agree with his way."

"And if she doesn't?"

"He leaves for London."

David regarded his cousin for a time as he considered her words. He had a clear memory of how Arabella used to behave. Always testing the limits of whomever she was with, and then, at the last minute, just before she was beyond redemption, she would give in and apologize for her behavior. She was always forgiven, of course. Who wouldn't forgive such a beautiful woman with eyes that could see into a soul?

Just like Clarinda's, he suddenly thought. But Clarinda wasn't manipulative. Not like Arabella had been.

Isabella had obviously learned the behavior from her mother. Learned it and was using it to confusing effect on Huntington.

"He's a duke. She knows it. She just needs reminding at times," Constance remarked.

David's brows suddenly furrowed. "Have you paid witness to this... behavior?" he asked, thinking most of what Constance was saying wouldn't have happened with an audience present. The duke knew better. So did Isabella.

"Of course not." Constance rolled her eyes, realizing that other than having paid witness to Isabella kissing the duke's cheek, she was passing along what she'd been told by her lady's maid.

And a few tidbits Isabella had shared.

She was never quite sure if Isabella only did so to gauge her reaction or because she truly wished to know if what she was doing was proper or not. The poor girl had never spent time with others her own age, nor had she been to London for a Season. "Simmons rides in the gig with me on the days I go over to Huntinghurst. Then she spends the afternoon in the servants' dining room listening to the Huntinghurst servants gossip about their master and his ward," she whispered. "There aren't that many servants given the size of the household. It's a wonder they can keep it up as well as they do."

David continued to frown as Constance described life at Huntinghurst. He had been to the estate home several times, usually for house parties, or to go hunting with the duke, but he had never noticed the lack of staff.

"Is your interest in her because you're married to her cousin?" Constance asked then. "Or... is there more? I cannot help but think she's hiding something—"

"She paid witness to a murder," David stated suddenly. He swallowed, realizing he was bringing her into his confidence. Again. "So Hunt agreed to offer a place for her to live until she either marries or reaches her majority."

There.

He took a breath and let it out, rather shocked he spoke what he had kept secret from everyone but Huntington and Isabella.

A moment later, and he couldn't believe how *relieved* he felt at having told someone else about Isabella's circumstance. Constance wouldn't tell anyone—not even her maid. He knew this because she had never told anyone what she had witnessed that one awful night at Norwick Park. What he had done to the despicable man who dared to enter the stables intending to steal a horse. Who dared to take a young woman's virtue on the night of her come-out ball.

"She's never said a word," Constance whispered as she struggled to breathe. She furrowed her brows. "Who are you hiding her from?"

"Her father."

Constance's eyes widened with fright. "Jesus, Davy! We could have been seen by someone who knew her—"

"Rather unlikely," David interrupted. "Basingstoke is far enough away. Craythorne kept Arabella and Isabella sequestered in his castle for most of her life. Only let her ride horses and spend time in his stables."

Constance felt the hairs on the back of her neck prickle, and she suddenly straightened in the settee. "Arabella?" she whispered. "Not 'Lady Craythorne'?" One of her eyebrows arched up in either query or accusation.

David dipped his head. "I knew her a long time ago, Connie. Loved her, even."

"Loved her enough... to get a child on her?" Constance whispered, tears collecting in the corners of her eyes. She took a quick breath and let it out, as if she were struggling to get air. "Oh, my God! No *wonder* she seems so familiar, Davy," she wailed, her voice kept low lest a servant overhear their conversation. "Why didn't you just tell me? Why did you have to send the vicar—?"

"Because I haven't told Clare," he stated in a hushed voice.

She blinked, just then realizing how awkward it would be for him when he finally did. Arabella had been Clarinda's aunt. "Does... does the *duke* know?"

David nodded. "I told him the morning Isabella first

arrived in London. The morning after she paid witness to the murder. I wanted him to marry her, you see. Provide protection for her. His wife had died and, like me, he needs an heir. As a duke, he could have thwarted any efforts Craythorne might have made to get her back. Or to see to it she was declared incompetent, or sent to Bedlam so she couldn't implicate him in Arabella's death. I couldn't let that happen."

Constance sniffled, one of her hands searching her pocket for a handkerchief. David offered one before she could pull it out, and she took it with a nod. "She's a relation to me, and yet she's never said a *word*," she repeated, almost as if she were upset with Isabella.

"That's because she doesn't know," David whispered.

Blinking in disbelief, Constance stared at David for a very long time before she gave her head a shake. "You're going to tell her," she stated emphatically. "Aren't you?"

A flash of annoyance crossed his features, her edict sounding ever so much like Huntington's. "I plan to, of course. On the occasion of her twenty-first birthday."

Constance finally nodded, although it was apparent she didn't agree with his plan. "If I were her, I think I would want to know my father was someone other than the man who murdered my mother," she whispered.

David stared at her for a very long time, rather wishing it was that simple. If he wasn't married to Clarinda, he would tell Isabella. Would have told her the day she appeared at *The Elegant Courtesan* holding the dog-eared calling card with his name on it.

"You're more worried about what your wife will think of you, though, aren't you?" Constance suddenly accused. "Which means..." She straightened on the settee and allowed a slight gasp. "You're worried you'll lose her. That she'll leave you."

"Of course, I am," David retorted, his annoyance still evident.

"You love her."

"I do."

This seemed to surprise Constance enough that she was left without an immediate response. After a moment, though, she said, "If she loves you, Davy, then you've nothing to fear."

David regarded his cousin with an expression that reminded her of a rather sad hound dog. "I don't yet know if she does or she doesn't," he whispered.

Nodding her understanding, Constance refilled his teacup and sat back in the settee. "Will you spend the night? There's plenty of room for you and your grooms."

Apparently surprised by the invitation, David finally nodded. "I will. But I must be off for Southampton in the morning."

"You'll stop at Huntinghurst on the way?"

David considered the question for a moment but finally shook his head. "No. I only would if Hunt is there," he replied. "It wouldn't be seemly."

"Coward," Constance accused with a grin.

"There's that, too," he agreed with a roll of his eyes, wondering if Huntington had used the term to describe him whilst she was in his company. He drank the rest of his tea as he considered what he would be doing the following day. Paying a visit to the man who had murdered his first love. Who had murdered the mother of his daughter. He knew where to find him, thanks to Huntington's mention of a cottage near Southampton.

The man will not be long for this earth, he vowed to himself.

"Do let me know how it goes," Constance whispered. "And should you need to do something... *awful*, know that I will keep it in confidence. You shouldn't have to bear it alone, Davy. Makes you old, you know." *Makes me old*, she didn't add.

David nodded and gave a sigh of relief. "One day, you're going to make a very good wife for a man who needs one," he murmured.

Constance gave a most unladylike snort. "I can't imagine who that might be," she replied with a watery grin.

"Oh, I can. An earl or... a marquess. Yes. That's it. A marquess in search of a woman who will put up with his love of horses," he went on, his amusement growing by the minute. "A man who will appreciate your affection for horses." He suddenly sobered, almost as if he had one in mind.

Shaking her head in disbelief, Constance could only smile at his ridiculous claim. After all, there wasn't a marquess within thirty miles of Boxgrove.

Unless he was a monk.

Chapter 29

AN EARL PAYS ANOTHER CALL ON A DUKE

Early May 1815

Instead of heading directly to Norwick House when his coach returned to London, David Fitzwilliam, Earl of Norwick, paid a call at Huntington's Westminster townhouse and requested an audience with the duke. Octavius had him brought to his study, sure the man simply wanted to know how Isabella was fairing at Huntinghurst. Even before the scotch was offered, though, Octavius realized this visit was different from all the others when David said he had just come from Southampton.

"Please tell me I'm not complicit in an earl's death," Octavius said in hushed tones. He had just returned from having spent three days at Huntinghurst. The visit had given him a new perspective on life, a reminder that life in the country was far different from life in the capital.

He already missed it.

Or perhaps he was missing Isabella.

David frowned, realizing word of Craythorne's death hadn't yet reached the capital. "You are not," he stated. "But he did die. While I was there. The physician said it was consumption, but I know now he died of a broken heart," David said quietly.

Octavius finished pouring the scotch into two crystal cups before he nodded his understanding. "I was beginning to wonder why we hadn't seen him in Parliament these last few years." Although he hadn't paid a call at Craythorne Castle himself, other aristocrats had claimed to have made the attempt and been told by the butler that the earl wasn't even in residence and wouldn't be accepting callers due to a 'protracted illness'.

Did guilt count as such? he wondered.

"He said it was an accident—that Arabella really did fall and hit her head—but he did admit he was... he was a bit angry with her at the time. He said he caused the fall. She slipped on some buttons, he said." David shook his head, still trying to make sense of what the dying earl meant with his confession.

Octavius winced. "What ever did she do to make him angry?"

David swallowed and cleared this throat, as if speaking of Arabella still brought tears to his eyes. "Me, I suppose. He was sure she had cuckolded him at some point—said he always thought she was thinking of someone else whilst he bedded her—but he loved her anyway." He paused a moment. "He never knew it was me," he added with a shake of his head.

"Did he know the truth about Isabella?" Octavius wondered. Christ! How had Isabella so misjudged what she had seen that day? She had been so frightened of Craythorne, she had risked life and limb to get herself to London and then agreed to stay hidden from everyone until she was either old enough to marry or Craythorne died. Surely what she saw had to be brutal.

Shaking his head, David sighed. "He only said he missed her terribly. Missed her... *enthusiasm*, he called it. Missed her help with the horses." He paused a moment, as if he had to take a breath in order to continue. "I told him she wasn't dead. I told him she was safe. And then... then he died."

The duke stared at David for a long time before he gave

his head a quick shake. He certainly understood the dying man's words about Isabella. If she wasn't at Huntinghurst, he would miss her. Miss her enthusiasm. Miss her kiss on his cheek when she greeted him.

"Will you tell her now? Octavius asked suddenly. "Tell Isabella the truth? Because if you don't, I will," he warned with an arched brow.

"Clare still doesn't know."

"Don't you think it's past time you told her?"

"Tell her... what? That her younger cousin is also her step-daughter?" David countered with a sigh. It was bad enough Clarinda still believed she had been courted by him those few months before they finally married. When—or if —she figured out Daniel was the one who had escorted her in Kensington Gardens, she might refuse his overtures. Other than her expression of disbelief, she hadn't responded to his claim that he loved her that night before he left for Sussex.

Did he dare risk losing her? He had already waited too long to start his nursery. Clarinda's miscarriage only made the situation more worrisome. His need more immediate.

Even when he should have been courting Clarinda, he had instead allowed his brother, Daniel, to squire her about on short excursions, not realizing at the time that Clarinda had fallen in love with his brother. That Daniel never seemed convinced David would marry Clarinda had been short-sighted of the spare heir, for when Clarinda did marry David, the broken-hearted Daniel left London for Norwick Park. Determined to forget his lost love, he rarely paid a visit to London. When he did, he was all business and avoided the social scene.

Heartbreak and bitterness did that to a man.

David gave his head a shake, realizing he was as guilty as Huntington when it came to getting lost in his thoughts. "What do I say? 'Oh, I thought you should know you have a stepdaughter'..."

"Yes. Or something like that," Octavius replied, offering the earl one of the crystal cups.

David took it and downed the contents in a single gulp. "Do you think Isabella can keep it a secret?"

Octavius downed the scotch and frowned. "I don't think she should have to. Jesus, Norwick, she deserves to know the truth. They're cousins. And what are you so damned afraid of?" He turned to stare at the earl, stunned to find David looking far more haggard—old, even—than he had ever seen him. Even though he hadn't killed Craythorne, he looked like a guilty man whose conscience was getting the better of him.

"I love her, Hunt." He shook his head as if in warning, as if he thought the duke was about to say something pithy. "I never expected to feel anything more than affection for Clare. After Arabella... I was so sure she would be my only love." He paused a moment, lifting his gaze to meet the duke's. "But the heart wants what the heart wants, it seems, and this heart has decided on Clare."

Inhaling slowly, the duke considered David's words. That's how it was sometimes. A man's hardened heart sometimes developed soft spots that allowed a woman to worm her way in there and work her magic. Bewitch him. Make a man feel younger. Valued.

Desired.

"Do you love her more than you loved Arabella?"

The question had David's face contorting in anger before he suddenly took a seat in the nearest chair. He might have fallen down otherwise. "Damn you," he whispered. He drew the back of a hand across his mouth before fisting it. "If I had loved Arabella as much as I love Clarinda, I suppose I would have defied my father and Craythorne and seen to it I made her my wife," he admitted at the same time the duke took the chair across from his. "But I did not."

"Despite my accusations to the contrary, I truly do not believe you a coward, so... perhaps you only felt lust for Arabella," Octavius offered, the words cautious. "Many did. You *were* much younger back then."

The problem with men who had just experienced epiphanies was how they dealt with the aftermath of their sudden insight. Sometimes messy, sometimes not, but always life-changing, the realization of something *important* seemed to leave the male of the species reeling.

"The Brotherton women are all gorgeous," David hedged, his eyes lifting to find Octavius staring into his scotch. "I suppose you've noticed that about Isabella."

The duke blinked. Jesus, he'd have to be blind not to find Norwick's daughter beautiful! "Even when she was bedraggled and covered with mud, she was comely," Octavius replied. "She's two years older now." Two years more beautiful. Two years more stubborn. Two years more desirable.

Lifting himself from his chair, David stepped over to where the decanter of scotch stood on a silver salver and stared out the study's only window. After a moment, he allowed a sigh. "Let's make an arrangement then," he said as he lifted the decanter and poured a finger's worth into his cup. He turned to add the same amount to the duke's. "I'll tell Isabella everything if you make her your wife."

"You have a deal," Octavius announced, downing the scotch much like David had done only a moment ago.

Blinking, the Earl of Norwick took a step back and stared at the Duke of Huntington for several seconds before asking, "Have you... have you *ruined* her?"

Offended by the question, Octavius recoiled. "Of course not." He didn't add that he had wanted to on several occasions. That he had imagined all manner of ways he could bed Isabella. Imagined how he might strip her bare and cover her body with his. How he might use his tongue and teeth to bring her to ecstasy before finally—finally—seeing to his own by taking her virtue.

He had already kissed her far more than he should have, but her real father didn't need to know that.

"When?"

"When?" Octavius repeated, his brows furrowing.

"When will you marry her?"

The duke allowed a shrug. "I suppose after I court her for a time..."

"You needn't. She'll accept your proposal."

Octavius angled his head to one side before one of his brows furrowed in suspicion. He was quite sure the earl hadn't paid a call at Huntinghurst, and if he had been writing letters to Isabella, the chit was keeping them hidden and their contents to herself. Not something he would expect of Isabella. She craved friendship. Craved news. Craved companionship, although probably not as much now that she had Nelson following her about. "Have you already spoken with her?" he asked in a whisper.

"No," Norwick replied with a shake of his head. He inhaled before turning to regard the duke. "But my cousin, Constance, continues to pay calls on her. The two share a love of horses, you see. I know Connie is rather lonely down at my property in Boxgrove." She had little hope of landing a husband given the lack of eligible bachelors in the area. And he certainly didn't want her to marry the vicar, Elijah Cruthers. The man was old enough to be her father.

Octavius straightened at the mention of Constance Fitzwilliam. "Lady Isabella is rather taken with Miss Fitzwilliam," he said quietly. "She's been a good friend. A steady friend."

"And Connie is an expert horsewoman."

"As is your daughter," Octavius countered, tamping down the sudden arousal he felt at remembering Isabella riding astride on Ares.

This news seemed to surprise the earl. "In what way?" he asked as his brow furrowed.

"In every way. She knows how to breed them, break them, ride them, and race them. I expect a winner in at least two horse races this year."

Norwick stared at the duke. "I knew she loved horses, but..."

"Perhaps you could pay a call on her with that as your excuse. Have her give you a tour of the stables at Huntinghurst, and then tell her the truth. You would be proud of what she's accomplished in only two short years. I know I am."

Frowning at the duke's assessment of his daughter, Norwick finally allowed a nod. "I shall write a letter and pay a call next week," he promised, suppressing a wince when he remembered this was the week he hoped to spend more time with Clare. He needed to get another child on her, and he hoped she wouldn't miscarry this time. "Will you propose in the mean time?"

"Possibly." At the earl's intense stare, he added, "I should think a ring is required for such a proposal, but I cannot be assured of finding an appropriate one on display in a goldsmith's shop," he explained in a huff. "I may have to have one crafted for her." The thought had him wondering if Stedman and Vardon could create something with horses in mind.

Norwick was about to claim that the man's ducal ring would suffice, but he rather doubted the duke would part with the symbol of his station in the peerage. "I believe a bauble is in order for my own wife. To soften the... blow, so to speak."

The duke shook his head as he stood up. "Your wife will not be the least bit surprised you have a daughter," he claimed. "In fact, she will be relieved to learn Isabella is not Craythorne's daughter." With that, he turned and refilled his cup with more scotch.

Tempted to punch the duke for his impertinent words, Norwick simply held his fists at his sides and glared at Octavius. "I know you think I merely married Clare because I had to. Because we've been betrothed since she was in the schoolroom. But I do love her," he stated emphatically. "Within the first ten months of our marriage, I felt as much affection for her as I did for Isabella's mother," he added in a whisper. "And now I love her even more."

Octavius turned around to find the earl's eyes bright with unshed tears. For that brief moment, he actually felt sorry for Norwick. But when he remembered the man would soon be his father-in-law, he straightened in an attempt to match the man's height. "Then let us hope you prove it to her every day you are blessed to have her in your life."

The Earl of Norwick nodded. "I do," he replied with a nod. "At least, I try very hard to." He paused a moment and finally allowed a sigh. "Thank you for the scotch. Do let me know how it goes."

With that, the earl took his leave of the duke's townhouse and made his way as quickly as he could to Norwick House.

He had a wife he loved, and he needed to get a child on her.

Chapter 30

NEWS OF A LATE EARL FROM ANOTHER EARL

The following afternoon

The arrival of the Duke of Huntington at Huntinghurst had been entirely unexpected. Usually Peters was apprised of his impending arrival through the Royal Mail, but with the Earl of Norwick's news and knowing it wouldn't be long before the London newspapers printed an obituary, Octavius thought it best to deliver the news of Craythorne's death in person. Given the circumstances and the time of day, he made his way directly to the stables, expecting to find Isabella there.

Mr. Reeves gave a shake of his head when asked about Isabella. "She was here all morning. Exercised several horses and then said she had some correspondence to write," the groom explained.

Hearing Isabella was writing letters had him rather surprised. "Anything I need to know? Is the new groom working out?" Octavius wondered, his attention on a group of horses in a nearby pasture.

For the next few minutes, Mr. Reeves apprised the duke of what had happened in the stables since his last visit, including the hiring of a groom from Cocking and the death of the oldest horse in the stables.

Saddened at hearing of the loss of Apollo, a horse he had ridden on hunts during his college years, Octavius gave the groom a nod before he made his way back to the front of the house.

There was no one to greet him when he made his way into the main hall. A deep growl emanated from the top of the stairs, though, and when Octavius glanced up, he was stunned to see a rather large black and white dog with long hair staring down at him.

"Nelson?" he wondered, bewildered. "Is that you?" The last time he had seen the beastie, the pup didn't reach the top of his boots. Now the dog looked as if its head would reach his hips.

His tale suddenly wagging, Nelson bounded down the stairs and came to a rather unsteady stop before the duke, his shaggy tail wagging in giant circles. Octavius bent over, curious as to how the beast could see anything given how much hair covered its eyes. "Are you even in there?" he asked as he reached out to pet the dog on its head.

"Nelson! Where are you?"

The sound of Isabella's voice came from somewhere upstairs, and the thumps of running feet had Octavius allowing a bit of a grin as he imagined her racing about in search of her pet.

Nelson gave a soft 'woof' as he continued to wag his tail.

When she suddenly appeared at the top of the stairs, Octavius was forced to straighten and stare. Dressed in an elegant carriage gown, her hair done up in a smooth chignon, she looked as if she was the mistress of Huntinghurst.

Well, she was, he supposed.

"Hunt!" Isabella said with a good deal of awe. Making her way down the steps as fast as her half-booted feet would allow, she flung her arms around him. "We didn't expect you," she whispered before she kissed him on the cheek. She made the move to step backwards, intending to curtsy, but Octavius had wrapped an arm around her waist and held her a moment.

"You look as if you're going somewhere," he murmured, a hint of disappointment in his voice.

She shook her head. "I've only just returned from Fair Downs, in fact. And a bit of shopping in Chichester," she added when the duke didn't immediately release his hold on her. "You look well."

Octavius stared at her a moment, tempted to kiss her rather than explain his reason for being there. "I am," he replied finally, his arms dropping away. "It appears Nelson is as well. I would not have expected him to grow quite so large, though, given how tiny he was when I found him."

Isabella allowed a brilliant smile. "Nor I. Mrs. Cooper used to complain about him, but he does such a good job cleaning up the kitchen floor, she gives him all the scraps she used to leave for the scavengers," she explained. "Peters still doesn't approve, of course, but Nelson knows to stay out of his sight." She paused a moment. "May I escort you to your apartments? I had the linens in your bedchamber changed out last week. You must be tired from your travels."

Rather surprised at how much older she seemed than when he had last seen her, Octavius gave his head a shake. "Have you had a luncheon... or tea yet?"

She shook her head. "No, but Mrs. Cooper is seeing to one right now. I'll let her know you've arrived..."

"I'll come with you," he interrupted, offering an arm.

Isabella blinked, rather surprised by his odd manner. She placed a hand on his arm and gave him another glance. "May I ask as to the reason for your visit? I do hope it's not because you've received bad news." The bad news certainly couldn't be about her. She and Peters had been getting along quite well these past few months, as if the butler had finally come to terms with her presence in the household, perhaps because the duke had mentioned her station as châtelaine to the servant.

Or else Nelson had simply taken her place as something about which to complain.

Octavius wondered how to respond just then. "Let's talk about it over luncheon, shall we?"

Well aware of how he paused in his response, Isabella struggled to keep up a happy demeanor despite the ominous response. "Of course."

"How is Miss Fitzwilliam?" Octavius asked as they entered the kitchens. "Norwick informs me she is keeping Fair Downs in good order."

"She is well. One of her favorite mares is due to foal sometime in the next few weeks." She didn't add that the mare was Amasia and the sire had been Poseidon.

Mrs. Cooper's jaw dropped at seeing the duke in her kitchen, but she remembered to drop a curtsy as well. "Yer Grace," she managed as she moved a pan of baked bread from the oven onto a counter.

"Mrs. Cooper, I've come seeking sustenance," Octavius said in a teasing voice. "And some water in which to wash my hands."

"Well, I'm not too sure about *sustenance*, Yer Grace, but I'll have a right proper luncheon ready for ye in a few minutes." She motioned to the water pump. "I'll get you a clean linen," she added as she opened a cupboard door and withdrew a cloth. She handed it to him.

"Much obliged." He finished drying his hands and offered his arm to Isabella again. "Shall we?"

More and more perplexed by the duke's behavior, Isabella simply responded with a nod. They made their way into the dining room. A footman was already seeing to a second place setting while another poured wine.

Once the two were seated, Isabella regarded Octavius for a moment. She was about to prompt him for his news when a footman entered with plates of lamb cutlets, carrots, and the newly baked loaf of bread. When the servants finally disappeared, she allowed a sigh. "I was about to write you a letter."

Octavius regarded her a moment. "You have news?"

Isabella suddenly looked as if she might cry. "Apollo

died," she said. "He'd been missing for a couple of days, and George finally found him this morning. At the edge of the farthest pasture."

The duke's attention seemed to settle on his plate for a time before he finally said, "As has Craythorne. Norwick brought word from Southampton yesterday, which is why I made the trip here today. I wanted you to know as soon as possible."

He hadn't meant to tell her over luncheon. He had thought to spend some time in her company first. Learn what she might wish to do once she was no longer required to live at Huntinghurst. Provide her a list of options for whatever she might do now that she no longer had to fear for her own life. But the topic of death had already been brought up. The opening had been perfect for him to simply say the words he had spent the entire morning rehearsing in his head.

He figured she would excuse herself from the table and request some time to weep. Surely she would give a moment to mourn the man she had known as her father, even if she believed he had killed her mother.

So he was entirely unprepared for her response.

"Thank the gods!" she whispered as one of her hands went to her chest. Her eyes suddenly widened when she realized she had said the words aloud. "Oh, forgive me, Your Grace. I just feel such... such *relief*," she murmured, her attention returning to the duke. "Southampton?" she whispered before she gave her head a shake. "Oh, the cottage, of course," she added then. "We used to go there for a few weeks during the summer." She took a breath and let it out. "My brother? Where is John?"

Octavius blinked, rather stunned by her comment. Of all the reactions he had imagined, relief was not one of them. She had asked about her brother before—many times, in fact—and he'd only had minimal news of him.

Now John was the Earl of Craythorne. At least, he would

be once he petitioned the Lord Chancellor for a writ of summons to the House of Lords.

"He's been summoned from Cambridge," Octavius stated. "To London. He'll live at the Craythorne townhouse, of course, until the transfer is complete."

"May I see him?"

Now there was a question he was prepared to answer. "Eventually," he hedged. "I think it's best to wait until after the funeral and the writ of summons is complete." He watched as Isabella's shoulders slumped. "Lord John believes you are dead. Craythorne gave up looking for you over a year ago. Perhaps it would be best to..." He paused, knowing his suggestion would seem heartless. "Write a letter to him."

Isabella was about to put voice to a protest, but knew the duke was right. What would John think if she simply showed up on his doorstep? It had been a few years since they had seen one another.

Would he even recognize her?

Will I recognize him?

"That's an excellent idea," she said, returning her attention to her meal.

Octavius blinked. "It is?" He couldn't help the hint of incredulity that sounded in his voice.

"Isn't it?" she countered, her fork pausing in mid-air.

Resisting the urge to laugh, Octavius merely nodded. "I expected you would argue," he murmured.

Isabella sighed. "I almost did," she admitted, giving him a rather sheepish expression.

The duke allowed a wan grin and was about to resume eating when he remembered the box Norwick had given him. "I have something for you from Norwick," he started to say.

"Oh?" she responded, her curiosity evident. The duke rarely mentioned the Earl of Norwick, but he was the only other aristocrat who knew of her predicament.

Octavius pulled a small box from his coat pocket and held it out to her. "He asked that I give this to you."

Isabella regarded the white pasteboard box for a moment. "What is it?"

The duke shrugged. "I've no idea. He gave it to me when we spoke yesterday."

Taking the box from Octavius, Isabella angled her head before finally lifting the lid. A folded paper nearly popped out of the box as it attempted to unfold on its own. Isabella captured it in one hand before it could fall to the floor. Beneath it, a gold band topped with a single diamond lay in the velvet-lined box.

Isabella nearly dropped the box. She recognized the ring. Her mother had worn the ring every day of Isabella's life.

"What is it?" Octavius asked, his own curiosity forcing him to lean over the table so he could see into the box.

"My mother's ring. But... but how would Lord Norwick have possession of it?" she asked as she regarded the half-unfolded missive as if it might bite her. She finally set the box on the table and gave the duke a glance.

Octavius closed his eyes, realizing what must have happened when Norwick finally called on Craythorne. To confront him about the day Arabella died. "I'm sure he has explained it in his letter," he murmured, now wishing he had opened the box. He had no idea how much the earl would admit in writing. But Octavius would be furious if the man admitted to being her father without doing so in person. Norwick owed her that much.

"May I read it now?" she asked. At his hesitant nod, she opened the note.

After a few moments, Octavius wondered if she was having difficulty reading the earl's writing. Rolling his eyes, he realized she probably couldn't make out half of Norwick's scrawl. "I may be able to help if you're unable to read it. His penmanship is abysmal," he said gently.

Isabella shook her head but finally passed the letter to Octavius. "I... I think he's trying to claim Craythorne didn't kill my mother," she whispered.

Octavius sighed. “That’s because…” He stopped and instead began to read the letter out loud.

“Dear Lady Isabella,

From the moment I learned of your reason for showing up at my place of business two years ago, I never doubted your claim about having paid witness to your mother’s murder. I wanted to believe it, you see, because I have carried a special hatred for Craythorne simply because he had claim to the woman I wanted to marry.

You see, I loved your mother.

I knew if I went to Basingstoke to find your father that very day, I could be found guilty of murder, for I was well prepared to kill the man for what he did to your mother. Hunt knew it as well, and prevented me from going. His cooler head reminded me others would learn the truth of your mother’s death soon enough.

It has taken some time, but reports from Basingstoke, and finally, from your father directly, have me convinced your mother’s death was not by his hands at all, but from a terrible accident—”

“No!” Isabella interrupted. She stood up from the dining table and whirled around, her eyes blazing. “I *know* what I saw!”

Ignoring her outburst, Octavius remained seated and continued to read.

“According to Craythorne, the horrible scene you described did indeed occur. However, he wasn’t strangling your mother, but rather attempting to revive her. His shouts and curses were because she had slipped and hit her head, rendering her dead before she fell to the carpet. He was frightened and saddened. Broken, really.

I know this account will seem unbelievable to you. It did to me, as well, although the injury to your mother was finally corroborated by the coroner who saw to her body. There was no evidence of strangulation, but there was a large gash on the side of her head."

Despite Isabella's whispers of, "No, no, no," Octavius continued.

"Craythorne remembers seeing you that day when you watched what appeared to be him strangling her. He claims he was too bereft to go after you, to explain to you what happened. He remained in a fugue state for several hours, refusing to speak with anyone. When you didn't return from your ride that afternoon, he was convinced he was cursed by the devil himself. He lost much that day, and has finally died of consumption, although to hear him tell it, he wishes he had died that day as well.

He was ever so relieved to learn that you were alive, and of course, he cursed me for having kept you from him these past few years. He loved you very much despite your headstrong manner. He knows you inherited that particular trait from your mother, and he claims he rather liked the challenge of two women who sometimes knew better than him. Women who were worthy of their place in the aristocracy despite his attempt to keep you from the temptations of London."

Aware of Isabella suddenly cringing at hearing her described as 'headstrong', Octavius paused and arched an eyebrow. "You are that," he murmured. When Isabella didn't respond, but merely settled back into her chair, he continued.

"He is of the opinion you will have a horse in the Ascot before the decade is done. If that is the case, you must have others set for all the other races as well. Since I have a contender or two, we shall see you at the finish line.

As for the bauble you find in this box, you will no doubt recognize the ring as your mother's wedding ring. Craythorne couldn't bear to bury it with her and thought to give it to your brother for when he takes a wife. Once he learned you were alive, however, he insisted you have it."

The duke placed a hand over Isabella's, giving it a gentle squeeze when he heard her quiet sob.

"I have more to tell, but wish to do so when I can meet you in person. I trust Hunt will continue to provide protection until we can sort what to do next."

"I will, of course," Octavius murmured before continuing.

"On a happier note, when I married your cousin, Clarinda, a couple of years ago. I will admit I did not expect to love another woman in my lifetime. Certainly not as I loved your mother. I had believed others who claimed there is only one love for any man in his life. However, I am betw..."

Octavius stopped and sighed, unable to make out the strange word.

"Betwaddled?" Isabella offered, tears already dripping from her eyes.

"Must be," he agreed with a smirk. He continued reading.

"However, I am betwaddled to discover I am in love with Clarinda. What is it about Brotherton women, I wonder?

I pray you will remain well and continue to vex Hunt to distraction. He needs the challenge. Until we meet again, I am yours in service.

Norwick."

Isabella's teary eyes widened at hearing the closing words of the letter. "Why ever does he believe I vex you?" she asked in dismay, turning to regard Octavius as if she thought him guilty of sharing his frustrations with the earl.

The duke dipped his chin a bit, not about to accuse her of having done so since he agreed to act as her ward. "I am guilty of having mentioned that you vex *Peters*," he finally admitted. "As for how challenging you can be... he does have a point. When you do not obey me—"

"When have I *ever* disobeyed you?" she interrupted, suddenly indignant. Furiously wiping away the few tears that remained on her cheeks, she glared at him.

Octavius sighed and dropped the letter to the table, a bit dismayed that Norwick hadn't admitted he was Isabella's real father. At least he had mentioned having loved Arabella. Perhaps Isabella would sort the rest for herself.

The revelation of what had caused Arabella's death—a simple accident—meant they had spent the past two years blaming a man who was essentially innocent, even if he was an unlikeable man. A disagreeable man. Octavius had spent the past two years harboring Isabella when it probably would have been safe for her to remain at Craythorne Castle.

Unconsciously, he gripped the back of her hand a bit harder until he felt it flinch in his grasp. He stared down at his hand, wincing at seeing the lines of his bones in relief, at the signs of how much he had aged since Jane's death.

As for what she had just asked, Octavius suddenly winced. It was true she hadn't ever truly disobeyed him. He had never thought it necessary to order her to take a groom along on a ride, or to stay out of the stables so that the grooms could do the jobs she had made her own. Other than Ares, he had never forbidden her to stay away from his horses, for that matter, and now he had a worthy herd for riding and racing.

He had never forbidden her from helping the maids with their duties. He hadn't thought it necessary. Now he had a country estate once again capable of hosting house parties and hunts.

He was about to apologize when he realized she was staring at him, apparently waiting for him to answer her question.

When have I ever disobeyed you?

"Other than your dealings with Ares, you have not," he whispered as he shook his head.

Isabella finally allowed a nod. "He is not a bad horse," she murmured. "A bit headstrong, but then, apparently so am I," she whispered. She drained her glass of wine and finally turned her attention back to Octavius. "Oh, dear," she murmured. "What's to happen now?"

Allowing a sigh, Octavius wondered how to respond. "Life goes on," he said with a shrug. "As for where you'll live..." The duke stopped and realized he hadn't rehearsed this particular offer. Until yesterday—until his conversation with Norwick—he had always thought that if Craythorne died or she reached one-and-twenty, he would simply offer her transport to London and the Craythorne townhouse, thinking she could be mistress of that household until her brother took a wife.

Although the arrangement seemed perfectly reasonable when he devised it, he found it unacceptable now. Especially now that he remembered what Reeves had to say about Isabella. Now that he realized Peters hadn't sent a word of complaint about her in the past six months. Now that he realized Huntinghurst was better off with her as mistress of the house. Now that he realized he would be better off with her as his wife.

The improved state of the interior as well as the revived gardens were because she had taken an interest. The condition of the horses in his stables—Christ, he might have a contender for next season's races!—was even of more import.

"I wondered if perhaps..." He paused again, giving a sigh of frustration. *How do I ask her to stay on as my châtelaine? Permanently?*

Isabella stilled herself. Given how much time she spent in the stables and the satisfaction she felt while working on possible bloodlines for a future generation of race horses, she no longer considered where else she could live.

What else she would do with her days.

She would go stark raving mad if she couldn't spend her days with horses. *I'll be a candidate for Bedlam within a month*, she considered. "Perhaps?" she prompted, her brows furrowing as she imagined the worst—being sent to London to live with a brother who had no idea why she fled Craythorne Castle.

"Would you be amenable to staying on here at Huntinghurst? Continuing to act as its châtelaine?" It wasn't exactly what he wanted to ask, but he knew what her answer would be even before he put voice to the question.

Isabella's eyes widened before she allowed a brilliant smile. "Oh, of course I'm amenable!" she replied happily. She suddenly sobered. "You're not... teasing me?"

Octavius wondered at the sense of relief—nay, joy—he felt just then. Seeing how his proposal had her lighting up like a thousand candles had his chest contracting, much like Jane's words had that day she confirmed she was with child. "I am not teasing," he confirmed with a shake of his head.

"What about the stables? May I continue to train the horses?"

"If I said, 'no', would you stop?"

Isabella blinked as she stared at the duke, stunned by the simple question. What options would be available to her if she didn't continue to work in his stables? She could only think of Constance Fitzwilliam, wondering if perhaps the woman might allow her to live at Fair Downs. "Probably not," she hedged.

"You mean, *most certainly not*, I expect," Octavius countered.

"Probably," she agreed, rather careful with her response.

Octavius allowed a grin. "Then I suppose you'll continue training the horses. However..." He held a finger in warning.

Isabella held her breath a moment. Of course there would be a condition. There was always a condition.

"I wish to see these pedigree charts you've apparently been keeping. Reeves tells me you plan to send copies to Newmarket in anticipation of registering the foals born since you arrived. *My* foals," he added with an arched brow.

Wincing at his comment, Isabella had to resist rolling her eyes. "I wasn't going to send them in without your consent," she claimed. "I cannot. They require your signature and your seal. Besides that, there are some names of grandsires and damsires missing from the records."

Octavius was about to argue that his records were complete when he realized he hadn't given the paperwork much attention these past few years. Not since Jane had died. "Then we shall have to see to making them complete," he stated. "After we're done here, perhaps?"

Resisting the urge to suggest a different time—the pedigree sheets were spread out on every available surface in the upstairs salon along with the notes of her research—she finally agreed. "All right," she replied. "But after that I must see to some time with one of the mares."

Frowning, Octavius angled his head. "Is something amiss?"

Isabella shook her head. "No. But Enyo is due to foal any day. It's her first, and..."

"There are pregnant mares?" Octavius asked in alarm. He had forgotten to ask Reeves if any studs had been turned out with the mares last spring.

"Five of them, Your Grace." At the duke's look of alarm, she added, "I've been very careful as to their breeding..."

"Have you?" he interrupted, his ire suddenly apparent. "Who gave you the right to..." He suddenly stilled himself as one of her hands moved to rest atop the one that had fisted on the table. He stared at it for a moment before he sighed.

"No one, Your Grace," Isabella whispered, as if she knew he could be calmed with soft words. Jane had learned that trick even before they were wed. "You've had other, more important concerns, I'm sure." She was about to tell him about the trade she had made with Constance—the one that was responsible for one of the future foals—but thought better of it. "If you were to have contenders in the races in eighteen-seventeen and beyond, there had to be some colts foaled this year." She almost added, "And last," but decided he would see the yearlings soon enough. Whenever he paid a visit to the pasture just beyond the stables.

Or saw their pedigree charts in the salon upstairs.

"I suppose I'll need to be sure no one from Tattersall's learns about you," Octavius said under his breath.

"Tattersall's?" Isabella repeated.

The duke allowed a sigh. "London's auction house for horse flesh," he murmured.

"I've heard about Tattersall's, of course," she claimed. "I've always wanted to go there."

"And, no, I will not take you there," he added with an arched eyebrow.

"Well, I rather doubt they would have suitable Thoroughbreds for racing," she countered, her chin thrust out in defiance.

Octavius blinked. Truth be told, he hadn't attended an auction at Tattersall's in ages. He really didn't know what they featured these days. Matched pairs for phaetons and curricles to be sure. Horses for town coaches and Broughams and landaus.

But horses capable of winning the Ascot?

"Only if someone found themselves in extreme debt and in need of immediate funds," he agreed with a nod. He returned his attention to his food, rather surprised he had nearly cleared his plate.

"Have *you* ever bought a horse there?"

The duke blinked as he considered her question. "Once. I found my last mount there," he replied. "Got him from a baron who didn't know what he had. The man needed blunt, and I needed a horse suitable for London traffic."

Isabella's eyes widened. "Are there many like that?"

Octavius frowned. "Like what?"

"Men who don't know the value of their horseflesh?"

Nearly laughing at her shocked expression, Octavius suddenly sobered. "Probably more than I know about," he murmured. "You must remember that it *is* an auction house. Some horses go for far more blunt than they should, and others are a steal. It simply depends on the audience and the horses for sale."

Isabella concentrated on her meal for a time before finally asking, "Would you take me there if I promised not to bid on a horse?"

Octavius gave her a quelling glance. "What did I say not five minutes ago?" he asked rhetorically.

Sighing, Isabella displayed an expression of disappointment. "I was merely curious, is all," she whispered.

Almost feeling sorry for her, Octavius rolled his eyes. "When I take you to London to meet your brother, perhaps we can go. Just to observe, though," he warned when he saw how her face lit up.

God, was she beautiful when she lit up like that!

"Thank you," she responded. "I should like to know how horseflesh is valued by those in London," she added.

Furrowing his brows, Octavius wondered at her comment. "But, why?"

Suddenly nervous, Isabella gave a shake of her head. "Merely curious, is all." She dared not admit there might be one or two colts too many after foaling was complete this spring.

Or tomorrow. She was sure Enyo would be delivering twins at any moment. If the foaling went well and both foals were delivered alive, then one of those colts might provide the duke with a bit of unexpected income in a year or two.

"What aren't you telling me?" Octavius suddenly asked as he straightened in his carver.

Her shoulders slumping as if she thought she'd been caught in a lie, Isabella said, "One of the mares is carrying twins, I'm sure of it."

Octavius blinked. "Twins?"

Isabella nodded.

"Sired by..."

Her eyes widening in fright, Isabella thought to claim she didn't know, but the pedigree charts in the salon were already inked for both potential colts. "Ares," she whispered.

Leaning back in his carver, Octavius gave a brief glance at the ceiling in an attempt to control his immediate reaction. Ares was headstrong. Ornery. Dangerous. Not the traits one wanted in a race horse. Or any horse, for that matter.

"He's *fast*," Isabella claimed. "And Enyo is agile. She has a good temperament and excellent lineage. Together, they can produce a racer, I'm sure of it," she continued, arguing her point as she leaned in the duke's direction.

"But who will break them?" he countered in a rather loud voice.

"*I* will."

The duke blinked as he regarded the young woman, realizing he shouldn't be so stunned by her claim. Mr. Reeves had been rather generous with his praise about Isabella's ability with the horses. "You're sure?" he asked.

"I broke Ares. I broke every yearling you had in your stables the first year I was here," she added with a shake of her head. "And what I didn't know, I learned from..." Here, she stopped, wondering if she should mention Constance Fitzwilliam.

Octavius arched a brow. "From?"

"Miss Fitzwilliam," she replied with a sigh, her gaze dropping to her plate. The last of her luncheon lay untouched, and yet as hungry as she had been when they first entered the dining room, she now found her appetite had gone. "She's been an excellent teacher. She knows so much about horses and horse breeding."

The duke stared at her for a few moments, not about to

counter her claim. According to Norwick, Constance Fitzwilliam was an accomplished horsewoman. She owned all the horses at Fair Downs, and she had obviously taught Isabella the finer points. It was doubtful Isabella had learned so much on her own given her age.

"I am glad you have a friend in Miss Fitzwilliam," he said. "Have you met anyone new this past year? Had any visitors?"

Isabella thought for a moment. "The mail coach driver is new," she replied lightly. "Rather young, but he has a good command of the ribbons."

Octavius blinked. *Are horses all she thinks about?* "Young, as in...?"

"Only two-and-twenty, Your Grace."

Wondering if the young man had propositioned her, an annoyed Octavius was about to ask when Isabella offered, "His wife lives in Milton and is expecting their first child later this year."

Octavius wondered at the sense of relief he felt just then. Was that jealousy that had him initially annoyed at learning there was a new mail coach driver stopping at Huntinghurst a few days a week? Or was he just annoyed at the thought that Isabella was impressed with the driver's command of the ribbons?

"He's not the least bit handsome," Isabella said then, a grin barely touching her lips.

Frowning, Octavius gave his head a shake. "That you would put voice to such a claim has me wondering..." His eyes widened. "Did he...?"

Grinning more broadly, Isabella shook her head. "You have nothing to be concerned about, Hunt," she said. "I only noted his command of the ribbons."

Octavius furrowed a brow. "You were teasing me," he stated.

Angling her head to one side, she allowed a sigh. "There are times I truly wonder what might have your interest and what might have you perplexed."

"Have you sorted it?"

Isabella shook her head. "I have not."

Feeling a bit too much relief at her simple response, Octavius finished his food and leaned back in the carver. "Then let us see these pedigree charts you have been constructing," he replied.

Keeping her expression as impassive as possible, Isabella nodded. "Would you care for a glass of port or another glass of wine before we go up?"

Nearly grinning at her stall tactic, Octavius shook his head. "I shall wait until after dinner to have a glass of port," he replied. "Shall we?"

And with that, he pushed himself away from the table at the same time Isabella stood up, feeling ever so much like she was about to be admonished. Again.

Chapter 31

NAVIGATING THE CHARTS

A few minutes later in the salon at Huntinghurst

"You needn't look as if you're heading to an inquisition," Octavius said as they reached the partially open door to the upstairs salon.

Isabella gave a start, her mind having drifted to Enyo and when she might foal. She couldn't believe she had told the duke the mare was pregnant with twins. She was sure he was incensed enough when he learned she had bred Enyo to Ares.

"Promise you won't..." she started to respond before letting out a sigh of frustration.

Octavius furrowed a brow, about to ask why she would need him to make a promise when his attention was suddenly drawn to the inside of the salon—and the sheets of parchment seemingly scattered over every available horizontal surface of the room, including the floor. "What the...?"

"It's not as bad as it looks," Isabella interrupted, wincing a bit when she realized he was on the verge of cursing.

And it really was quite messy if one didn't know there was a reason the papers were arranged as they were.

When his other brow arched up, as if to counter her claim, he exhaled what sounded like a grunt. "Enlighten me," he ordered in a harsh whisper.

Isabella gave a nod and glanced about, wondering which horse she should start with in her explanation. "Over here, then," she said as she led him to a single sheet at the end of what appeared to be a flattened pyramid of similar papers, splayed out across the length of the room. Some of the sheets angled off from the edges of the array, starting another series of similar sheets. "This will be the pedigree chart for Andromeda's foal," she said as she bent down and lifted a sheet on which was a blank line next to a pedigree chart. Already inked in were the names of the dam, Andromeda, and the name of the sire, Perseus, and their dams' and sires' names, the even lettering easy to read. One of those lines was blank, though, the name of the sire's sire missing. "Except I'm not sure of the grandsire. Mr. Reeves said he couldn't remember, that he doesn't have a good enough memory..."

"Zeus, of course," Octavius stated. "Well, Zeus the Third, actually," he corrected himself, remembering when his father had restarted the naming sequence his great-grandfather had started more than a century ago.

"Oh, that makes sense," Isabella remarked as she hurried over to the escritoire and took a seat. Octavius watched as she dipped a quill into the ink pot and carefully lettered in the missing information. "Perseus has the same coloring as Apollo. Same temperament, too," she remarked with an arched brow as she got up and placed the sheet back from where she first picked it up.

Octavius was already studying the charts beyond the one she had updated, his head shaking a bit as he seemed to chew on the edge of his thumb. "I didn't realize Artemis had been bred," he murmured. "And I don't recognize this sire," he said, a bit of alarm sounding in his voice. He picked up a sheet next to the one he held and studied it. "Or the grand-sire. Nor the granddam."

Isabella swallowed. "That would be because *Mr. Wiggins* isn't from your stables."

There were times Isabella knew she was in the presence of a duke. From the way Octavius' posture seemed more erect than usual, from how he squared his shoulders, from the way his head canted slightly—as if he knew his pointed stare could be made more intimidating by the pose—Octavius had her realizing *now* was one of those times.

The Duke of Huntington did his very best impression of a duke. "And from just whose stables would he be?"

Isabella nearly flinched but did her best to appear nonplussed. "Miss Fitzwilliams' at Fair Downs."

Although the words were delivered in a clear voice, Octavius was sure Isabella's lips were trembling. He had paid notice to those lips of late, and his gaze was once again captured by them. There was once again the odd thought of what it might be like to kiss those lips again, to feel those lips kissing him. Kissing his chest. Kissing his...

Her answer finally permeated his consciousness and he gave a start. "Constance Fitzwilliam?" he repeated. He suddenly wondered if the earl had already paid a call on his daughter. Rode in on a horse and...

Isabella sighed. "We... we made a trade of sorts." She didn't add that she rather doubted Constance had told Norwick she was busy seeing to a generation of race horses for her own stables. How the poor woman managed without much help from the earldom was beyond her ken.

The duke once again stiffened. "How so?"

Isabella sighed as she nearly lost her resolve to stand up to the duke. "She brought her stable's only stud for Artemis, and in return, I gave her a yearling. Hermès." She was prepared for Octavius to erupt in anger, but instead he simply stared at her. "He was becoming... difficult," she went on. "He and I never got along. He was picking fights in the pasture. Biting ears, and, well, Connie seemed to know how to work with him. How to make him behave."

"Does Miss Fitzwilliam have his pedigree information?"

Not exactly what she was expecting to hear from the duke—Isabella expected a rather loud curse and a blistering scolding—she nodded. "She does. I made her copies of all that I could find for Hermés, and she provided me with those," she added as she waved toward the line of sheets that continued for several generations back.

Octavius turned his attention to the sheet he held. "Do you know anything else about this stud?"

Isabella moved to stand next to him and pointed at the grandsire's name. "He won the Epsom Derby back in ninety-eight. Miss Fitzwilliam said Norwick used the winnings to build his men's club. And she..." Isabella moved her finger to the granddam on the other side of the line. "Won the Oaks in oh-two."

Stilling himself a moment, Octavius realized he had been in attendance at that horse race. The Oaks, made up entirely of fillies and run at Epsom Downs, was always a crowded affair with a huge purse. And, yes, *The Elegant Courtesan* had been built using the funds Norwick had won in that race.

"But has *Mr. Wiggins* won any races?" the duke wondered. He hadn't attended the races since Jane died, his enthusiasm for most idol pursuits having waned.

His enthusiasm for almost anything, for that matter.

"He hasn't been entered," she replied with a shake of her head. "In fact, Lord Norwick has only visited Fair Downs a few times since winning the Oaks, and Miss Fitzwilliam says he's never very interested in reviewing the horses since they belong to her."

Frowning, Octavius was about to claim the earl was still an avid horse racer, but realized any of his current race horses were probably stabled at Norwick Park. "Why breed this particular stud with Artemis?"

Isabella allowed a grin. "She's not only fast, but she can last."

"You're saying she has stamina?" he guessed.

"Indeed," Isabella replied.

Octavius was about to ask how she would know such a thing, but remembered how she had that one time ridden a horse nearly fifty miles, mostly at night, and lived to tell the tale. The fact that her mount had survived the ordeal was a testament to the Craythorne stables as well as to her skill at knowing when to push hard and when to allow the horse time to recover.

Suddenly interested in what she was trying to accomplish—breed a horse suitable for a longer race—Octavius returned the sheets to their place in the lineage. "You think her colt could win a race like St. Leger at Doncaster," he accused.

Allowing a one-shouldered shrug, Isabella finally nodded. "Except for one problem."

"Problem?" The duke turned to face her, another pedigree sheet in hand.

"None of your current horses are eligible to race this season," Isabella replied with a sigh.

"Why ever not?" he asked in alarm.

"They're not in Weatherby's stud book," she replied, moving to where an open book rested on the settee. She lifted it in her arms, the pages displaying the lineages of two of his horses. "This is a few years old, though. Have you summited papers for Artemis, Ares, Enyo, Hermés, Andromeda...?"

Octavius held up a hand as if to stop her questions. "It's true, I haven't been submitting the papers. Ever since..." He paused, stunned that he almost said his late wife's name out loud. "Since about four years now," he finally said.

Obviously disappointed at the confirmation, Isabella merely nodded. "Well, with Mr. Reeve's help, I've been able to trace most of your current stables back to the pedigrees I found, but there are some I've had to leave blank," Isabella explained, as she made her way down a line of parchments.

For the next hour, the two worked in tandem as Octavius provided names and Isabella penned them, making copies as she went.

"You could be a clerk," Octavius commented as he glanced over her shoulder. He dropped another sheet onto her escritoire. "But I think you may have made a mistake with this one."

Isabella stiffened when she realized which pedigree he questioned.

The one for Enyo's foal.

Make that *foals*.

She was positive the mare was pregnant with twins, and so she had drawn in two lines instead of one.

"Mr. Reeves agrees with me. Enyo is carrying twins," she claimed. She didn't add that she was sure they would arrive in the next day or so. The mare had grown restless and was displaying the tell-tale signs of impending labor. "We have her in a foaling stall in the stables."

The duke waited until Isabella had finished filling in a name before he said, "That's not the mistake I was referring to," he stated.

Isabella frowned. She picked up the parchment and reviewed the names, quite certain she had them all correct. "Then... what?"

"The sire. I just remembered it cannot be Ares. I ordered he be gelded. Probably two years ago. Back when he was a yearling, in fact."

Daring a questioning glance up at the duke, Isabella had to keep from letting out a 'huff' of disbelief. "He has not been castrated, I assure you," she countered with a shake of her head. "Besides, I wouldn't have allowed it. He's too important..."

"You countermanded my *order?*" The fury on Octavius' face had Isabella nearly cowering in fear. "He was a dangerous horse!"

"He is *not!*" she argued as she straightened in the chair. "He just needed training. And now that he's broken, he's an excellent ride." Realizing her words hadn't placated the duke in the least, she added, "I honestly wasn't aware you wanted him gelded."

Octavius was about to argue when he remembered a bit of what she had said. "Wait. What did you mean when you said, 'he's too important'?"

Her eyes darting to one side, Isabella lifted the sheet again and pointed to Ares' granddam on his sire's side. "She won the 2000 Guineas." She lowered her finger to the grandsire on his dam's side. "He won the Ascot."

Allowing a wan smile, the duke gave his head a quick shake. "The same year. I remember," he murmured.

She moved her finger to Enyo's line and pointed to her dam's name. "She won the St. Leger."

Octavius straightened, his eyes tracing back the two lines. There were a few names in common in both Enyo's and Ares' lines. "This is... this is *in-breeding*," he whispered, a look of worry furrowing his brows.

"It's *line* breeding," Isabella argued.

"Only if it works," he countered, his frown still firmly in place.

Isabella had half a mind to press a fingertip in the space between his brows, just to see what he might do. "It will," she insisted. She pointed to the blank lines where the foals' names would be written in. "One of these is going to win races. Maybe both of them."

Octavius was about to ask if she would make it a bet, but thought better of it. It was bad enough she knew more about his stables than he did.

It was worse that she was right about Ares.

And she would probably take him for half his annual income if he did allow her to bet.

Chapter 32

CONFESSION IS SUCH SWEET SORROW

Meanwhile, at Norwick House in Mayfair

Clarinda knew something was different the moment David entered her bedchamber. Although he wore the same robe he always did and even kissed her on the temple as she finished brushing out her hair, his manner seemed far more guarded than usual. "Did you have a good trip?" she asked as she pushed herself away from the vanity. "Southampton, wasn't it?"

The earl was quick to help with the chair, offering a hand as she stood up. "I did. I have some good news, in fact," he said as he led her to the bed. "Although, someone had to die for it to become possible for me to tell you." Her lady's maid had turned down the bed linens, so rather than making his way to the other side of the bed, he saw to removing her dressing gown before scooping her into his arms and placing her in the middle of the bed.

Clarinda allowed a gasp of surprise, covering her suddenly naked breasts with her arms. "Norwick," she gently admonished him. "I haven't yet put on my ni..." She swallowed the rest of her protest, though, curious as to what his good news might be. "Who had to die?" she wondered in alarm, just then realizing the rest of what he had said.

David had his robe off before he made it around to the other side of the bed, the sight of his naked body eliciting another gasp of surprise from Clarinda. Slipping beneath the covers and settling her against his side before wrapping an arm behind her shoulders, he allowed a sigh. "Craythorne died. Day before yesterday."

Clarinda angled her head from where it rested in his shoulder. She stared at him a moment, remembering again he had been in Southampton. "Were you... were you with him?" She almost asked if he had been the one who had caused Craythorne's death. It wouldn't surprise her given the rumors that had her husband killing a thief sometime in his past. She knew he disliked Craythorne. Had long before they married. "Did you...?" she stopped before she dared put voice to the rest of the question.

"I wanted to, Clare. I don't mind admitting it. For the past two years, I have thought of killing that man on more occasions than you can imagine," he claimed in a hoarse whisper, not adding that it had been more like twenty years.

"I can imagine a good deal," Clarinda countered in a matching whisper, her breaths coming faster and her heart beating a tattoo David could feel against his chest. "But, why?"

"Because I was sure he killed Arabella."

About to put voice to her thoughts on the matter—she had told her father she had the very same suspicions!—Clarinda wondered what reason he had to believe her aunt's death had been murder. "Did you kill him?" she asked, her breath held in anticipation of his confession.

"I did not," he said as he stroked a finger down her arm. "Craythorne described her last moments in great detail, though. Arabella died from a terrible accident—one in which he had a hand—but an accident none the less. He died... he died of a broken heart. Or consumption, if you believe the physician."

Clarinda stared at her husband for along time, wondering at the sorrow she heard in his voice. Maxwell Tolson was a despicable man, a bully, and a brute. How Arabella could abide marriage to the man had been a source of worry among the Brotherton women for years. Many had questioned Arabella's father's choice in a husband for his only daughter. He reminded the naysayers that his daughter would be a countess and mistress of her own castle.

A castle in which she would eventually meet her death.

"You said you had good news," Clarinda remembered.

"I do. My daughter will be marrying a duke," David murmured before placing a kiss on her forehead. He tightened his hold on her shoulders in anticipation of her bolting from the bed.

A fold of skin appeared between Clarinda's brows as she considered his words. "I... I wasn't aware you had a daughter," she said, attempting to lift her head from his shoulder.

"I love you, Clare. Please, please do not hate me for what I'm about to tell you," he pleaded.

Clarinda stiffened in his hold, her thoughts suddenly jumbled. "She's either illegitimate, or you were married... are you a widower?" she asked in alarm, managing to roll over in his hold so she could regard him directly. He was certainly old enough to have been married before, but she had never heard he was. He was famous for having mistresses, though. Had one of them given him a child? A daughter? A long time ago?

"No. Neither," he replied with a shake of his head before he allowed a sigh. He pushed himself up on the pillows a bit, pulling her up with him. "I was once in love, Clare. I had an *affaire*. While I was in university. I thought back then I would never love another, and... I didn't," he claimed in a quiet voice. "Until I married you and realized it was possible to have more than one love in a lifetime."

Staring at him for a long time, Clarinda struggled with how to respond. "With... one of your mistresses?"

"No, Clare," he replied with a shake of his head. He took a breath and held it. "I was in love with Arabella Brotherton."

Clarinda blinked before she frowned again. "My *aunt?*" she questioned, as if she needed to remind him of their familial relationship. "Before... *before* she married Craythorne?" Her attention suddenly seemed to focus on something beyond his shoulder.

"Of course," David replied, a bit offended she would think him capable of adultery.

"She was with child when she married Craythorne," Clarinda murmured.

"She was," he agreed, rather surprised anyone else knew Arabella was *enceinte* at the time of her wedding.

"My mother always thought Craythorne had ruined her. She hated that man."

"For good reason," he interjected. "He could be cruel."

Clarinda stiffened in his hold. "If he didn't kill Arabella, then did he kill Isabella?" she asked in alarm, struggling to break his hold on her. "Oh, my God—"

"He did not," David interrupted, steadying her body with his other arm. "I thought he killed Arabella because Isabella was sure he did." He paused, expecting she would put voice to a cry, but when she merely blinked, he went on. "Isabella did what she was told to do, you see. Arabella told her to find me should anything untoward happen."

"Find you? Where? When?"

David struggled to hold her close, still afraid she might dart out of the bed. "Isabella found me the day after Arabella's accident and claimed to have paid witness to her mother's murder. She was sure she saw Craythorne do it, saw him yelling at Arabella as she lay on his bedchamber floor, and Isabella believed he had strangled her."

Clarinda's eyes widened. "Isabella is *alive?*" she asked in awe. And then she furrowed her brows. "She's your daughter."

"She is."

"But... but, how? Where have you been hiding her?"

David sighed and pulled Clarinda into a tighter hold. "Huntinghurst. Since about a week after Arabella's death."

Clarinda blinked again. "The Duke of Huntington's hunting lodge?" she guessed, her expression indicating revulsion. "Poor girl."

"It's a beautiful estate, Clare. A wondrous manor home with a stable of race horses and lands as far as the eye can see," he countered, realizing Clarinda had never been invited to one of the duke's house parties. "She's been there for nearly two years acting as its mistress. Apparently vexing the butler and endearing herself to every horse on the property. Has a dog, too."

"Well, Izzy would certainly be at home in the stables," Clarinda said with a wan grin.

David allowed a grin of his own. "You know that about her?" he asked, amused at hearing his wife's nickname for Isabella.

Grinning, Clarinda used a fingertip to trace the contours of his chest. "She's always been a bit obsessed with horses," she said in a quiet voice. "As far as I know, she's only attended the Ascot once, but she swore she would one day have a horse of her own competing. Can you imagine?"

David pulled her head down to his, bestowing a gentle kiss on her lips that soon had her entire body settling onto the top of his. "I can," he whispered when he finally relaxed into the pillows. "She's my daughter, Clare. Which means she's your stepdaughter. And I intend to see to it her dream comes true." He closed his eyes a moment before he suddenly opened them "That is, if Hunt cannot."

Inhaling at hearing his vow, Clarinda finally allowed a nod as she regarded him for a time. "I wish you had told me she was alive." She frowned then, the fold of skin reappearing between her eyebrows. "Why didn't you tell me?"

David allowed a sigh of relief at the same time he wondered how to respond. "I love you, Clare. I admit, I didn't expect to. But when you had that miscarriage, I realized I was desperately, thoroughly in love with you. More than I ever was with Arabella. I feared if I told you about Isabella, you would hate me, and I... I couldn't abide that."

Thrilling at hearing his declaration of love once again, Clarinda allowed a nod. Then her eyes suddenly widened. "Does Isabella know? Does *she* know you're her father?"

David blinked. "Not yet. I've written a letter..."

"Coward," she accused gently. "How could you keep it from her?"

David grimaced at hearing the word, wondering if she had heard the duke call him that. Then he sighed at hearing the question. "I only explained what happened with Craythorne," he said. "Hunt was going to give her the letter when he got back to Huntinghurst—today, in fact. At some point, he's going to propose marriage."

"Coward," she said again, although her grin betrayed her happiness at hearing his words.

"I'll tell her I'm her father in person, of course. I'd like you to come along if you would. Tomorrow?"

Clarinda gave a nod. "I will, of course." She paused before she allowed a grin. "I cannot believe Izzy will be a... a duchess," she murmured.

"I wanted you to know before she learned of it," David explained. "But I feared if I told you she was alive, you would want to know why, and then I would have to tell you the whole sordid tale, and then you would tell your friends, and then Isabella would be the topic of conversation in every Mayfair parlor, and then Craythorne would learn she was alive and demand to know where she was, and... I couldn't take that chance, Clare," he explained. "Isabella feared for her life. *I* feared for her life. I don't think I've ever seen anyone as frightened as she was the day she appeared at *The Elegant Courtesan*. She rode the entire way from Basingstoke—"

"In the middle of the night?" Her eyes widened. "She went to the brothel?" she asked in a louder voice.

"Indeed. Her horse was half-dead that morning. She was sure Craythorne would kill her because she had paid witness to what happened that day."

Settling her head onto his chest, Clarinda considered his words. Although she was disappointed to learn he thought she would share the news of Isabella's fate as gossip, she understood why he would believe such a thing. She spent her days either hosting other ladies in her parlor or visiting them in theirs. "I would have kept her a secret," she whispered, wondering if she really could have kept the news from Adele Worthington. The woman had become her best friend and confidante. "Truly."

Touched by her words, David finally allowed a nod. "Then I shall not keep such secrets from you," he vowed.

Giving a start, Clarinda stared at him. "You have more secrets?"

David blinked and struggled with how to respond. "Of course not. I just meant... I wouldn't keep *future* secrets from you," he amended. "Not that I expect to have any."

Regarding him with a bit of suspicion, Clarinda arched an eyebrow. "I shouldn't wish to learn of any after you die," she warned with a teasing grin.

David kissed her again. "I love you," he whispered.

Clarinda allowed a nod of her own. "And I suppose I love you as well."

Although she realized just then she should have been prepared for what was about to happen, Clarinda was rather surprised at David's immediate response. His intense and thorough worship of her body resulted in sensations she had never before experienced. His lovemaking had her body succumbing to a series of frissons and orgasms that seemed to go on and on until she thought she might faint. And then, just before he allowed his release and spilled his seed inside her, he made a vow never to keep another secret from her.

Clarinda fell asleep with her husband atop her, her fingers buried in his silken hair and a grin of satisfaction on her lips.

"I have a stepdaughter," were her last words before she drifted off to sleep.

Chapter 33

A LABORIOUS NIGHT

Two o'clock in the morning

Even before he heard the sharp knock on his bedchamber door, Octavius knew something was wrong. He was sure he'd heard a cry in the night, although he thought it merely a bird.

Or Jane.

She had been featured in his dreams nearly every night lately. Dreams that soon turned into nightmares that had him struggling to wake up and then too upset to return to slumber.

Hurried footsteps on the hallway's Aubusson carpeting had him sitting up in bed, and he was nearly halfway to the door before he realized he was naked. Cursing, he found his dressing gown and pulled it on before opening the door.

The sight of Isabella had him jerking back in horror. Her face, apparently streaked with tears, was smudged with what appeared to be blood. Her hair was a mass of tangled curls interlaced with bits of straw. But what frightened him the most was her night rail. Stained with a wash of what appeared to be dark red water, she looked as if she had been doused with the cook's concoction for coughs. The damp fabric clung to her torso and legs, leaving nothing to the imagination when it came to the shapely figure beneath. The lantern she dangled from one hand only accentuated the effect.

"Please, Your Grace. I've just come from the stables. Enyo needs help. I'm not strong enough," she started to say, a sob interrupting her plea as tears streamed down her cheeks.

"Jesus," Octavius whispered as he gave his head a quick shake, the remnants of his troubling dream finally leaving him so he felt a bit more clear-headed. He couldn't go out to the stables in his dressing gown, even if she had obviously worn her night rail.

What was she thinking to do such a thing?

"Wait here. I'll be but a moment," he said before he disappeared into his darkened chamber.

Isabella concentrated on slowing her breathing, mentally counting in an attempt to sort how much time had passed since she had left the stables and run up the stairs, Nelson on her heels. The dog now sat in the middle of the carpeted hallway, his tongue hanging out as he struggled to catch his breath. Isabella hadn't even realized he had followed her from the stables!

How much time had passed whilst she attempted to pull the second foal? *Twenty minutes at most,* she remembered Constance telling her. *After that, the foal will most likely have died in the womb.*

At least Enyo had been able to deliver the first on her own, a colt who was already standing on its spindly legs, wobbling about the foaling stable when Isabella realized Enyo was in distress.

The groom had confirmed just the week before that Enyo was carrying twins. *But then, so did some other dams in her line,* the man had said with a dismissive wave. Isabella remembered how surprised she had been at learning of multiple foals in Enyo's lineage, for she knew Ares shared some of the same dams as Enyo. Twins were so rare!

The pedigree charts she had managed to locate didn't include that information, though. She might have reconsidered her carefully researched plans for the two horses if she had known.

Suddenly noticing the large stain down the front of her night rail, Isabella let out a gasp and crossed an arm over her torso. What must the duke have thought when he opened his door to find her so disheveled? So bloodied?

I must look like his worst nightmare.

Movement from inside the duke's bedchamber captured her attention then, and she froze as she watched him, in profile, pull on a pair of breeches. He had been naked for that brief moment before the breeches covered his buttocks. Before his efficient fingers buttoned up the placket that strained to contain his erection. His bare chest was on full display just before it was suddenly covered in lawn, the white shirt settling over his shoulders, its bottom edge dropping to well past his waist.

Releasing her breath in a whoosh—Isabella hadn't realized she'd been holding it—she hoped he wasn't wearing one of his good shirts.

Then he was suddenly filling the doorway, the top edge of a pair of boots gripped in one hand. "What's become of Mr. Reeves?" he asked as he leaned against the door jamb and pulled on one of the boots. "Deep in his cups, is he?"

"He took the wagon to Weald for hay. He won't be back until tomorrow afternoon," Isabella replied in a quiet voice, rather surprised the duke didn't know. "And George's arms are too short. Not that I would have even woken him up for this," she added. Although he had seemed fascinated by the last foaling he had paid witness to in the pasture out back, Isabella remembered how his eyes suddenly rolled up into the back of his head, and he fell to the ground in a heap. "He fainted when Hera delivered Hermés last year."

Octavius leaned over to tug on his second boot, wondering at her reference to the stableboy's arms. And then he furrowed a brow.

Had Isabella attempted to pull a foal? It would certainly explain the condition of her night rail.

All at once he remembered the pedigree chart for Enyo and Ares' foal. There were two blank lines on the left side of the paper instead of the usual single line.

Were both foals at risk? And what about Enyo?

"But you thought nothing of waking me?" he groused as he pulled his bedchamber door shut and hurried down the hall to the back stairs, suddenly understanding the need for expediency.

"I apologize, Your Grace, but..."

"There was no one else you could awaken, I'm quite positive," he said, rather surprised to find both her and Nelson on his heels. As he descended the servants' stairs, his boots making a thumping sound as he went, he was aware of how close behind him she followed, her own half-boots barely tapping on the wooden runners while the light from the lantern cast gruesome shadows ahead of them. Nelson's bulk followed behind, the *thumps* on the treads a testament to his huge paws.

At the bottom, Octavius turned and headed out the same back door he had used to get to the stables the morning before, pausing to allow Isabella to come up alongside him. She held the lantern out in front of her as they ran, lighting the crushed granite path and flags that led to the stables. Nelson rushed on ahead.

Isabella managed to put an arm out to slow Octavius as she said, "We don't want to startle the colt," she warned, her steps slowing as they entered the stables and headed for the stall holding Enyo and her first-born. Nelson stood at guard, a slight whine sounding as if he understood the mare's predicament.

Enyo was lying on the same side she had been on when she dropped the colt. "Oh, Enyo," Isabella breathed, disappointed to see the horse still in distress. Although the second foal still hadn't made an appearance—and wouldn't without assistance—the first looked as if Enyo had already cleaned it. "He's beautiful," she whispered.

"How long has it been?" Octavius asked as he knelt to

place his hands on Enyo's belly. He was about to roll up the sleeves of his shirt, but cursed and then simply stripped it from his body. He murmured something to the horse as his hands continued to slide over her hide. Enyo knickered in response, but she didn't raise her head.

"Fifteen minutes," Isabella said as she moved to check the chronometer she had set up when she had arrived to pay witness to the first colt's birth. "Perhaps a few minutes more." She had to suppress the urge to gasp at the sight of the duke wearing only breeches and boots. The light from the lantern fully illuminated his chest, his arms, the cords of his neck, and the expression of determination on his face as one arm slowly disappeared into the mare. She realized she shouldn't have been shocked the duke seemed to know what to do, but she rather doubted Craythorne would have known despite his extensive stables.

"Everything had gone so well, I was sure the second would follow... and then... nothing. I think she was too exhausted," Isabella explained as she held the lantern.

"I've found the front hooves," Octavius said suddenly, his familiar frown appearing when he seemed perplexed.

"What about the head? I couldn't find it," Isabella said as she moved to lightly stroke Enyo's nose, ignoring Octavius' arched brow.

"I suppose that explains why you look as if you're the one who gave birth to that colt," he said as the mare knickered again, her breathing labored. The duke pushed his arm further into the horse.

Isabella gave him a quelling glance. "It's not the first time I've had to," she claimed, allowing a wan grin when the colt suddenly took an interest in her hair. At least it no longer looked as if it wanted to escape the foaling stall. "I think its head may be turned back when it should be between the knees."

"I'm well aware of where the head should be," Octavius responded between gritted teeth. Grunting with exertion, he seemed to push his arm ever farther into the mare before he sighed and paused for a breath.

"Eighteen minutes," Isabella whispered, tears once again coming to her eyes.

"I think... I think I've got it back where it belongs," Octavius said suddenly. He had used the flat of his hand to move the foal's head into place just above the knees, reaching farther to be sure the neck was in alignment. "Now let's hope the neck isn't broken," he murmured, mostly to himself. He knew Isabella had heard his comment, though, when she let out a quiet wail.

"She's having a contraction," Isabella whispered before a sob robbed her of breath. "Pull. Pull hard," she ordered.

His hand firmly gripping the front pastern, Octavius pulled, his efforts helped with Enyo's contraction. He continued to pull even after the contraction subsided, and soon his arm was completely free of the mare. Repositioning his body so he was nearly pressed against the stall wall, the duke continued to pull the entire colt free from Enyo.

"You did it!" Isabella shouted, which had the colt retreating to the corner behind her, and Enyo letting out another knicker as her body seemed to relax.

Octavius couldn't help the combination of relief and contempt he felt just then. Had she doubted him? Doubted he could at least save Enyo? He didn't expect the second foal to live. It had probably been far more than twenty minutes since Enyo had delivered the first given how old the colt in the corner seemed to be. Given how this one's neck had been turned so far from normal. Given how it lay still in the straw at his knees.

He was resigned to a stillbirth—Jesus, was he really so jaded by the loss of his son that he would think all births would end thus?—until he paid witness to Isabella's sudden determination to see to a live foaling. He watched as she crawled over the straw to the foal at his knees, tears still streaming down her face. When the filly still didn't move, Isabella stabbed a finger into the sac surrounding the newborn and broke the membrane. She peeled it away from the filly's face. "No, no, no," he heard her whisper. And then Octavius watched as she lifted a piece of straw from the bedding and tickled the filly's nostril.

When the filly suddenly sneezed, its head jerking and its hind legs attempting to straighten, Octavius closed his eyes in silent prayer.

"Yes!" Isabella whispered, new tears of happiness joining those that already stained her cheeks. "Thank you, Your Grace. Thank you."

Octavius blinked. Something inside his chest seemed to contract just then. Something he hadn't felt in a long time. Overcome at how she gazed at him—as if he were some medieval knight who had vanquished a dragon—he reached for her. His left arm pulled her body hard against his chest as he leaned his back against the foaling stall, and his head came to rest against the wooden planks.

Isabella settled her head into the small of his shoulder, one hand pressed against his bare chest. Beneath her hand, his heart beat in a staccato that soon calmed to an even tattoo. His breathing followed until he finally dropped his head so his cheek rested atop Isabella's curls.

Meanwhile, the newborn kicked its way free of its confines and struggled to stand. Enyo lifted her head and regarded the filly for a moment before she reached over and nudged it with her nose. Curious, the first colt did the same, and soon, after two or three attempts, the second foal stood up on wobbly legs.

"We need to leave them alone," Octavius whispered. "Let them get some rest."

"I'd like to be sure Enyo doesn't reject..." She lowered her head to peek between the second foal's legs. "Her," she said with a tentative grin. She angled her head up to regard Octavius for a moment. "You may have two contenders in the St. Leger," she whispered. She glanced over at Enyo, relieved to see she had already expelled the placenta.

Octavius regarded her for a moment before he suddenly

lowered his lips to hers. The first kiss was light—a bare brush of his lips over hers. But the second kiss claimed her, his tongue slipping between her lips to open them so that he could lock his own over hers. He tightened his hold on her when she responded, the hand that had been pressed against his chest moving up to rest on the side of his face.

Isabella wasn't sure what possessed the duke to kiss her just then. Perhaps it was merely the sense of relief he felt at seeing the filly come alive. Or perhaps he merely saw an opportunity to be a man for a moment, rather than the duke he was so very good at portraying every day.

Or perhaps he felt affection for her.

Isabella raised herself onto her knees, turning so she faced him, and regarded him for a moment. They exchanged no words, but after a moment, her lips were back on his, her breasts pressed against his chest, her hands moving to his head so her fingers could spear his silken hair.

When Enyo suddenly knickered and her hind legs moved, Isabella pulled away and quickly scrambled to her feet. She held out a hand to Octavius. "She's going to clean her," she said in a whisper.

Octavius regarded her hand a moment before finally gripping it. He leaned forward and pushed himself up from the straw bedding, eventually wrapping an arm around Isabella's shoulders as they both turned to watch as Enyo slowly got to her feet and began cleaning the filly.

The first foal was soon next to his mother, his head nudging her belly in an attempt to locate an udder. And while Enyo cleaned up the filly, the colt helped himself to his first meal.

Exhausted, Octavius leaned over and plucked his shirt from the straw. "Despite your hesitance to do so, we are waking George so he can see to mucking out this stall and putting in some fresh bedding," he said in a voice that belied his tiredness.

Before he could lead Isabella out of the stall, though, the stableboy appeared at the door. "No need, Yer Grace. I'm awake. I'll see to Enyo right away," he claimed, his eyes widening when he spied the two foals. "Twins?! Congratulations, Yer Grace," he said with a bow.

Octavius allowed a grin. "Thank you, although I do think most of the credit goes to her," he said as he pointed towards the mare.

"Whatever you say, Yer Grace," the boy replied with a nod. He hurried off to retrieve a pitchfork as Octavius held Isabella. They watched until the filly had located a teat not already claimed by the colt. When he was sure the filly was nursing, Octavius led Isabella out of the stall.

"Stay, Nelson," Isabella ordered as she held a hand up in the direction of the dog. Immediately lowering himself to the ground, Nelson allowed a huge yawn and then settled his head between his front paws.

Octavius was stunned to find it was still dark outside. Having left the lantern back in the foaling stall for the stableboy to use, he was about to go back for it. "Do we need the lantern?" The cool air felt good against his bare skin, the half-moon providing enough light to see the flags in the clipped lawn.

"Not at all," Isabella replied. She thrilled at how his arm gripped her shoulders as they made their way toward the house. "I need a bath, though," she murmured when they reached the crushed granite path. The darkness once again enveloped them as the roof of the east wing of the house blocked the moon's pale light.

"I've a shower bath in my chambers," Octavius murmured. "Although I do not believe I have the strength to stand under it."

Isabella sighed. "Cook has some pails of water on the stove."

Octavius frowned. "Why?"

"Because I told her Enyo would be dropping her foals tonight. She knows I need a bath after such an event."

Octavius paused before they entered the back door from which they had emerged only the hour before. "How many of my mares have you attended whilst they foaled?" he asked in surprise.

Grinning in the dark, Isabella sighed. "These are my sixth and seventh foals since coming to Huntinghurst. I attended many more in the stables at..." Her words were interrupted when Octavius' lips were suddenly covering hers again, as if he didn't want her to say the word she was about to say.

The name of Craythorne's estate.

"I had no idea," he murmured when he finally released her from his hold.

Breathless, Isabella regarded the duke for a moment. "Then I suppose we're even," she said, remembering how he had simply known what to do with Enyo.

And with that, she entered the house and headed straight for the kitchens for the pots of water.

They both desperately needed a bath.

Chapter 34

BATHING IS SUCH AN INTERESTING ENDEAVOR

A few minutes later

"This seems like an awful lot of work," Octavius murmured as he carried two pails of hot water up the stairs. In front of him, Isabella carried two more, and he was surprised she didn't seem the least bit bothered by their weight.

"I don't know if it is or it isn't," she replied in a whisper. "But it's how I do it every day."

When they reached the top with their burdens, she was about to head for her own bathing chamber, but Octavius directed her into a different bedchamber before they were anywhere near hers.

He wasn't about to be caught taking a bath in Isabella's bathing chamber should any of the servants begin their workday before he had a chance to get into bed.

A connecting door to a dark bathing chamber had Isabella stopping in her tracks for fear she might walk into something. The inky blackness seemed to swallow what little light there was in the bedchamber. *Whose room is this?* she almost asked, but Octavius struck a flint and a candle lamp illuminated a vanity and copper tub.

"Are there bubbles, do you suppose?" Isabella wondered

as she lowered her pails to the floor. Even with the room fairly dark, she didn't want the duke seeing her as she bathed.

"I can't say as how I would know," he replied. "I haven't taken a bath since I inherited the dukedom."

Already on her way to the vanity, Isabella resisted the urge to make a sound of disgust. "But you said you have a shower bath," she countered as she lifted a couple of bottles and attempted to read their labels by the dim light from the candle lamp. She finally took one over to the tub and spilled some of its contents before returning the bottle to its place on the vanity. Then she dumped one of her pails into the tub.

Having already emptied two pails of steaming water into the tub, Octavius was amazed when a mass of bubbles appeared atop the water, barely visible in the dim light. "I do have one, but it's in my bathing chamber," he replied.

Isabella regarded the room they were in, just then realizing this wasn't the duke's bathing chamber. "Would you prefer to use it? I can see to heating some more water—"

"No. This is fine."

Blinking, Isabella regarded the duke for a moment. Certainly they wouldn't be taking a bath at the same time?

Would they?

Could they?

Octavius wondered at why Isabella stared at him just then before he remembered he was still bare-chested. She probably hadn't seen a man in such a state of undress. He *hoped* she hadn't seen a man in such a state of undress. He wondered if she found him frightening or if she was simply embarrassed. Jane had claimed neither, merely saying his chest was like those she had seen in statuary. But once they were in bed together the first time, she had been frightened. She had shook and shivered and squeezed her eyes shut through most of their first experience at sexual intercourse, as if she couldn't bear the thought of being bedded. Subsequent couplings hadn't gone much better, although she no longer seemed frightened of him. His attempts to use the skills he had learned from Ava were rebuffed in favor of pleas that he simply bed her as quickly as possible.

Shaking the odd memory from his head, Octavius concentrated instead on the copper tub. He was trying to imagine how it might hold both of them when Isabella turned to retrieve a pail of water drawn straight from the chamber's pump. He intersected her hand, though, and lifted the pail himself. He dumped it into the tub.

Isabella was about to strip her ruined night rail from her body, but modesty had her regarding the duke for a moment. Ready to ask if he might leave for a few minutes—she thought to merely bathe quickly and then make her way to her own bedchamber so he could bathe—she gave a start at his next words.

"Given how tired I am, I shall give this a try," he said as he undid the fastenings of his breeches, well aware she would pay witness to his hardening manhood when the placket was loose. Despite the hour—he was quite sure it was well past three o'clock in the morning—tiredness had his mind in a jumble, and his adrenalin-robbed body was quaking. The mere suggestion of bathing with the young woman should have had him practicing chivalry. Should have had him excusing himself from the bathing chamber and returning when she was done and safely tucked into her own bed. Should have had him remembering she had been his ward.

Untouchable.

Vulnerable.

Innocent.

Instead, he found he wanted nothing more than to hold her whilst he soaked in the warm water. He gave half a thought to proposing just then, but thought better of it.

He intended to propose with a ring.

The entire experience in the stables had been so intense, so arousing despite the messiness, despite the general gore of a foal's birth, that he wondered at how his body had reacted. While he felt entirely spent—tired beyond words—he found his curiosity about Isabella too great to return to his apartments and simply wash using the pitcher of water in his bathing chamber.

"Would you mind turning around, Your Grace?" Isabella wondered, her eyes downcast as she made the request.

Octavius stiffened. "Call me 'Hunt,'" he whispered. "Or..." He allowed the alternative to trail off, rather surprised at what he was about to suggest.

"Or?" she prompted.

"Octavius is my given name," he murmured. "But only when we're alone."

Isabella blinked at hearing the Roman name. It suited him far better than 'Hunt'. "Then, do you mind turning around, Octavius?" she repeated. "I've never... I've never before bathed whilst a man watched."

"Well, I should hope not," the duke replied, rolling his eyes as he slowly turned around. He turned his head to one side, though, watching her from one eye as she stepped into the tub and quickly stripped the ruined night rail from her body. He had to resist the urge to inhale sharply at seeing her luscious body before it disappeared beneath the bubble-topped water.

When had her breasts become so full? So delectable? When had her hips rounded and her waist thinned so her figure looked like the hourglass he kept in his study back in London? Jane had never...

He closed his eyes, determined to cease thoughts of Jane just then. Jane was dead. Had been for several years. It was past time he quit mourning her. Past time he quit mourning their son.

"I'll just be a moment."

Jolted from his reverie, Octavius turned around to find Isabella completely settled into the tub. "Is there enough room in there for me?" he asked, his voice filled with doubt.

Or was that disappointment?

Isabella blinked, stunned he was considering sharing the tub with her. "I... I suppose so," she managed as she drew up her knees and slid forward, her head angled to one side to indicate the space behind her. She wrapped her arms around her bent knees, hoping they weren't too evident above the level of bubbles.

"Turn around then. I've never bathed with a woman before," he claimed in a hoarse whisper. He was sure Isabella boggled at his words, but she quickly turned her head to the right and lifted a hand as if to hide the side of her face. He couldn't help but grin when he realized she probably had a clear view of his reflection in the cheval mirror that stood against the far wall.

Octavius removed his boots and shed his breeches, a bit surprised when his cock bobbed out straight from his body. *How can I be so tired and be so aroused at the same time?* he wondered.

He moved to join Isabella by stepping into the tub behind her. Once he had his bottom down, he slowly straightened his legs along the outer edges of the tub and then snaked an arm around Isabella's waist. He felt more than heard her gasp as he pulled her body backwards until she fell against his chest, a wave of water threatening to escape the tub before settling beneath the bubbles. Isabella's curls tickled his shoulder, but he didn't have the strength or the inclination to move her. The combination of the water's warmth and her body leaning against his had a sigh of contentment escaping as he settled his head against the tub's higher back and closed his eyes.

Isabella concentrated on controlling her breathing. Although she thrilled at the thought of the duke completely naked and holding her as he was doing—hadn't she imagined a scenario much like this when she wasn't of a mind to wallop the man?—she had no idea what he intended.

I'm as good as ruined no matter what, she thought, her mind going back to the day she had burst into *The Elegant Courtesan*, desperate to locate David Fitzwilliam. At least he had ensured her identity remained a secret.

Plucking the ball of soap from the small table next to the tub, Isabella dunked it into the water. When she began stroking her arms and torso with the soap, she felt the duke shift a bit behind her. A part of him was suddenly pressed into the base of her spine, and the memory of admiring the Greek statuary in the hall downstairs suddenly had her remembering how the duke's manhood had been bobbing straight out before he buttoned it into his breeches earlier that night.

None of the statues in the hall depicted a man's member quite like that, she thought.

Well, except for Dionysius. But he was the god of wine.

Or was that Bacchus? Or were they the same? Certainly one was Greek and the other Roman...

"What ever are you thinking about right now?" Octavius asked suddenly, one of his legs bending so a knee surfaced next to Isabella's arm. She nearly let out a shout of astonishment at seeing his bare flesh rise above the water line.

"What was Dionysius the god of?" she asked, not realizing it was probably the worst question she could ask just then. She felt more than heard his burble of laughter erupt.

"The grape harvest," Octavius whispered. "Winemaking and wine. Madness." He was about to add 'fertility', but thought better of it. Despite the warm water and his exhaustion, his manhood was under the impression it was to find a new home on this night. "Why ever do you ask?"

"Didn't he have a rather large...?" Isabella stopped, her eyes squeezing shut when she realized what it was she had been about to ask the duke.

"Member?" Octavius offered, the arm around her waist giving an involuntary jerk just then. "Yes, he did," he answered calmly, daring a glance in the direction of the cheval mirror. Although it was rather dim in the bathing chamber—the flame on the single candle lamp was turned down—if he angled his head just so, he could make out Isabella's reflection. Either her reddened face was a testament to her embarrassment, or else the water in which they bathed was far hotter than he realized. "Why ever do you ask?"

About to counter his question with a comment as to

what was pressed into her back, Isabella instead let out a sigh and relaxed once again against the duke. “No reason,” she murmured. She was sure his manhood stiffened even more, nearly pushing her forward in the tub.

“Minx,” Octavius accused, his head dropping so his chin was next to her left ear.

Isabella gasped. “I am not,” she countered, bending her legs tighter so she was no longer pressed so close against his body. The ball of soap was suddenly back up on the table.

“I’m too tired to argue,” Octavius whispered.

Isabella turned her head so her chin rested on her shoulder. She regarded him from the corner of her eye. “As am I. I’m going to get out now,” she murmured. “For if I don’t do it now, I may not have the strength to do so later, and I rather rue the idea of Thompson, my occasional lady’s maid, finding me still in this tub in a few hours.” She had half a mind to continue by describing how wrinkled her fingertips and toes would be from soaking in the water too long, but thought better of it. The image wasn’t pleasant, and besides, she didn’t want to be guilty of babbling in the duke’s company.

Especially when she was bare naked.

She bent her legs and placed her hands on either side of the tub’s edges, intent on lifting herself up. But the arm around her waist tightened and her head was suddenly back against the duke’s shoulder.

“Stay with me.”

The words were said in a hoarse whisper. They sounded as desperate as they were urgent. Not a request so much as a demand.

“To what end?” Isabella whispered in reply, her breath caught in her throat.

“A good night’s sleep.”

Isabella frowned. *Is he serious?* “I hardly think—”

“Please.”

The simple word had her relaxing once again against the front of the duke’s body. “In whose bed?”

There was a moment when the bathing chamber was so quiet, Isabella was sure a water droplet's fall to the floor would have been audible. And then Octavius said, "Mine, I should think. We won't be disturbed until I ring for Cooper in the morning."

A shiver passed through Isabella's body. "Where is it? From here, I mean?" she asked, remembering they weren't in her bathing chamber, but rather one far better appointed.

"Through that door over there." His free hand lifted from the water and pointed to the door just beyond the cheval mirror.

"But, I thought this wasn't your bathing chamber," she countered in a whisper, wondering where the shower bath was located. She remembered that one of the footman had claimed to be the servant assigned to pour hot water into a container mounted above where the duke stood to take his daily shower.

"No." He didn't offer that Jane was to have used this bathing chamber. That is, if she had ever deigned to make the trip to Huntinghurst. Despite his assurances that the estate home wasn't as rustic as she imagined, Jane refused every overture Octavius had made about them spending time together at Huntinghurst.

He also didn't mention that the room through which they had come to enter the bathing chamber was the mistress suite. That every bottle on the vanity matched what Jane had on her vanity in the London mansion. That he had seen to making her rooms here as comfortable or more so than what they enjoyed in London in the hopes she might capitulate and one day make the trip with him when he checked on his horses or came to hunt.

Nor did he mention that he had been the one to purchase the bath bubbles that now barely danced on the water's surface. Bubbles that no longer hid Isabella's nakedness nor his own. "You're welcome to use this bathing chamber whenever you wish." Despite the whispered words, they sounded loud next to her ear.

Isabella turned her head slightly, a shiver passing through her entire body at the thought that his bedchamber was right next door. "Thank you for the offer," she whispered in reply.

Perhaps he mistook her shiver as a sign the water was no longer warm enough, for his next words surprised her. "The bath linens are to your right. I shall not watch as you get up."

Without a word, Isabella was suddenly up and out of the tub, her quick exit and the water sluicing from her body nearly hiding her from the duke's eyes as she reached for a bath linen. She quickly wrapped it about her body before grabbing another from the open cupboard. She held it out until Octavius took it from her.

"Much obliged," he whispered. Wondering how he would muster the energy to lift himself from the cooling water, Octavius was surprised to find Isabella still standing next to the tub, one hand held out. Much like she had done in the stables, she jerked on his hand at the same moment he pushed himself up from the tub. He was glad for the assist and not the least bit concerned she saw his entire body for the moment before he wrapped the linen about his middle.

Despite the dim lighting, he paid witness to her embarrassment. He rather liked how her cheeks pinked up, how her eyes were suddenly averted, how her head dipped. Following her line of sight, he realized she was staring at her night rail, the stained garment probably unsalvageable. "If you must wear one to bed, please feel free to return to your chambers," he said in a hoarse whisper, rather shocked at how he barely recognized his voice. *I sound as if I'm giving her an ultimatum*, he chided himself. But he didn't want to frighten her away.

Not tonight.

He *needed* her. Needed a warm body around which to wrap himself. An anchor to keep him from drifting into nightmares.

Isabella raised her eyes to meet his gaze and gave her head a quick shake. "I have no other," she replied. And with that, she dipped a curtsy and hurried off to the door that led to the duke's bedchamber.

Closing his eyes while allowing a curse, Octavius considered what he was about to do.

Take a virgin to his bed. A virgin who wasn't his wife.

Well, given his exhaustion, he had no intention of taking her virtue on this night. He merely wanted a warm body—something to hang onto—to help him get through the rest of the night. His last dream had been too real, too frightening. Surely holding onto her would fend off the terror the nightmare promised.

When he had finished drying his body, he tossed the linen over the edge of the tub, helped himself to the candle lamp, and made his way to his bedchamber.

Isabella lay in the middle of the bed, the messy linens barely hiding her torso from view. "Which side do you sleep on?" she asked in a whisper, startled to see he had shed his bath linen before making his way into the huge bedchamber. *Isn't he cold?*

"Why, the middle of course," he replied as he set the candle lamp on one of the nightstands. The glow illuminated only a portion of the room, making it seem as if the bedchamber went on forever in two directions. "I appreciate you warming the bed for me. I hope you're not cold."

Cold? How could she be cold when her entire body felt as if a furnace had been lit from the inside?

Before she could make her way to the left side of the bed, Octavius had already settled onto the mattress, one hand pulling the bed linens this way and that, as if they had been left twisted when she roused him from his slumber. She helped with the covers as best she could, realizing she was only delaying the inevitable. Despite his earlier words, he would no doubt have his way with her before he slept.

Trying to imagine how he might claim her, she was rather startled when he merely snaked an arm around her middle and pulled her body sideways until her bottom was nestled into the front of his bent body. "I would appreciate it if you didn't wake up at the crack of dawn," he whispered. "Peters says you do so nearly every day."

Isabella stiffened. *What is wrong with getting up at first light?* The stables were always the best early in the morning. "Aren't *you* an early riser?" she countered, remembering how he appeared in the breakfast parlor shortly after she did on the occasions when he had visited in the past.

"Not this morning," he murmured as he continued to wrestle with the bed linens. Suddenly, the smoothed linens, quilt and counterpane were covering them both, making the bed look as if it had been made before they climbed into it. "No earlier than nine o'clock," he whispered in warning.

Before Isabella could think of how to reply, she realized the duke had already dozed off. Half-tempted to slip from the bed and make her way to her own bedchamber, she decided she rather liked how the duke held her against his body. Rather liked his warmth and the barely-there pulse at his wrist where it rested against one of her breasts.

In worrying what he might have planned to do *to* her, she hadn't even realized he had pressed his knees into the back of hers, or that her back rested against his solid chest, or that one of his arms had found a perfect resting place around her waist.

Sighing, Isabella did her best to ignore the odd sensations that coursed through her body. The way a tingle started at the base of her spine and seemed to radiate through her torso, hardening her nipples and causing the space at the top of her thighs to throb. *What is happening to me?* she wondered. *Is this... desire*? If the duke wanted her the same way her body seemed to want him, then she now understood how easy it would be to allow him to ruin her. *Thoroughly*.

Placing one of her hands over his much larger one, Isabella allowed a sigh before she closed her eyes and finally drifted off to sleep.

Chapter 35

AWAKENED AND AROUSED

An hour later

Isabella felt as if she were floating. Or, at least attempting to float. Something heavy held her down. Something that smelled of Bay Rum and bubbles anchored her to a soft bed. When the heaviness moved and then was suddenly gone, she expected her entire body to rise above the bed. She held her breath in anticipation, willing herself to keep her eyes closed. She didn't want the sensation to go away.

Just when she was sure she was free from the bed, the air around her shoulder fluttered. A moment later, something warm touched her shoulder. Something light and feathery that moved toward her neck leaving a trail of cooling moisture behind. Her entire body shivered before the weight returned to hold her down.

"I am suffering from a quandary."

The whispered words had Isabella's eyes opening in an instant. She was stunned to discover she wasn't in her own bed—she knew it because morning light wasn't streaming into the bedchamber from an east-facing window. She was also stunned when she realized she was exactly where she had been when she first fell asleep.

Tucked into and against the duke.

She dared to lean back a bit so that she could be sure he was still behind her. Although he was no longer pressed against her back, Octavius was still abed, his head propped up on an arm. The other lie over her waist, the hand smoothing over the front of her body until his fingers reached her breasts. The shiver of delight he created beneath his fingertips nearly had her yelping in surprise, but she stilled herself. "What kind of quandary might that be?" she managed as she lowered her back to the mattress. His hand stayed on the front of her body, one of her breasts completely covered by his palm and fingers, the engorged nipple captured between the sides of two fingers.

Octavius regarded his bedmate with a wan smile. "I wish to make love to you," he whispered, his eyes darkening when his gaze took in her other bare breast. His lips suddenly covered it, and Isabella gasped as his tongue laved over the hardening bud.

His words should have frightened her. Should have had her leaping from the bed and running for her own bedchamber. But something in his voice—and the fact that his tongue was doing such luscious things to her breast just then—had her remaining right where she was. "But?" she prompted, not quite sure if it was a suitable response. What did she know, though? She had never shared a man's bed before. Never been completely naked next to a man who was also completely naked.

Blinking, Octavius lifted his head from her breast and frowned until a fold of skin developed between his brows. This time, Isabella did reach up to press her forefinger against it. "Does it hurt when it does that?" she asked in a whisper.

He seemed momentarily confused by the question. "Sometimes," he replied. He suddenly leaned over and captured her lips with his own.

Isabella's chest lifted from the bed, as if her breasts sought out the solidity of his body. His hand let go of her breast to wrap around the back of her shoulder, pulling her closer.

Breathless after a moment, Octavius let go his hold on her, his head dropping to rest on the pillow next to hers. "You should be running to your bedchamber," he whispered, his voice so hoarse he barely recognized it as his own.

Turning her head slightly, Isabella wondered what to say. "I'm not wearing any night clothes," she murmured. "And there is the issue of a rather handsome man covering most of my body." She could practically feel his frown as she moved a hand to grip his upper arm. "Octavius, if the tables were turned—if you were a lonely woman in this situation—what would you do?"

When he didn't answer right away, Isabella thought perhaps he had fallen asleep. The bedchamber was still dark, so she figured it was well before dawn.

"You think me handsome?"

Isabella grinned in the dark, rather surprised he would respond to that particular part of the comment. "I rather imagine every woman in England finds you handsome." She smoothed her hand down his arm, moving it under his wrist and over his back, her fingertips barely grazing his skin until she heard a hitch in his breath.

"No one can know," he breathed. *Especially Jane.* That Isabella's loneliness would have her choosing ruination was something he hadn't considered. He could understand the loneliness, though. He had lived with it for years. Ever since Jane's death. "You cannot tell anyone."

"Who would believe me?" She felt his head lift from the pillow, and despite the darkness, she could make out his features as he regarded her.

"Everyone in London."

"You seem to have forgotten that I have no plans to travel to London," she said with a shake of her head.

The comment seemed to surprise the duke, and he lifted himself back onto his elbow. "Craythorne is dead. You have no reason to hide any longer."

The comment gave her pause, but she wasn't about to leave Huntinghurst. Not when there were horses to train.

Racers to breed. "As I recall, I still hold the position of châtelaine for this estate," she reminded him.

Silence descended again, and the duke's stillness once again had her wondering if he had fallen asleep.

"You'll be ruined." *I don't want you to* have *to marry me.*

"Then I shan't marry."

The clipped words had Octavius grimacing. That wasn't exactly the response he was expecting. Couldn't she understand she needed to leave his bed? Didn't she know he was about to take her virtue? Claim her?

"If we do this, there will be pain," he whispered. "There will be blood—"

"Worse than what I've already experienced on this night?" she countered as she turned her head to face him.

Well, she had him there, Octavius conceded.

He squeezed his eyes shut, well aware of how his manhood throbbed, of how her body, all flushed and ripe, was ready for what could come next. He could practically smell her arousal. He could certainly feel it in how pebbled her nipples had become. In how her skin had turned to gooseflesh. In how her breaths had quickened.

She has to marry me.

He offered one last attempt as an out for her.

"If you could have anything in the world, what would it be?" he asked suddenly.

The simple question caught Isabella off-guard. She was about to chide him for changing the subject when she realized how she answered might determine what happened next. "My own stables, of course," she whispered. "With six... no, make that eight horses, and a pasture, and two stable hands..."

Her list was stopped when Octavius pressed a finger to her lips, her words so unexpected he had half a mind to call her out. But then he remembered the afternoon prior, remembered her enthusiasm for updating the pedigree charts. Remembered how she had been so frightened for Enyo and her foals. So willing to do whatever it took to see to their survival. "You are certainly not a typical daughter of the *ton*, are you?" he asked rhetorically.

She shook her head in the pillow. "Probably not, but then I know so few."

His lips settled on her hers once again as he squeezed his eyes shut. He would not be taking her maidenhood this night, he decided. Although nothing would please Norwick more than learning his daughter had been ruined by the duke, he would also see to it the two were married, probably before Octavius could see to a proper proposal and wedding arrangements.

That had been Norwick's plan all along, he realized.

Well, not on this night. He could pleasure her and then see to his own release, though. He had done that for Jane in the beginning, when she was so frightened of the marriage bed. Of his manhood. She had been so small, so frail...

He shook the thought from his head before he smoothed the flat of his hand down the front of Isabella's body. Her slight gasp came just as his fingers parted her dark curls and were about to split the folds protecting her womanhood.

Pushing a bit further and thrilling at how her back suddenly arched, he realized he wouldn't be able to stop himself given how her taut nipples begged for attention. Perhaps if he couldn't see them in the dim light... "Turn over," he ordered, his voice so hoarse he barely recognized it. He pulled his hand from between her legs and rose up on his knees.

A bit confused—Isabella was sure he was about to make her ready for his manhood—she finally rolled over but held herself up on bent arms. She let out another gasp when one of his hands was suddenly between her legs again, the other gently pushing her knees apart until he could get one of his own between them. Isabella couldn't help but hold her breath, unsure of what he was about to do next. "Are you going to...?"

His lips were suddenly next to her ear. "Lie down and relax," he whispered. "And lift your lovely bottom just a bit."

He nudged his hand up to reinforce his instructions, eliciting another gasp from her as her back had to arch to allow his hand to remain where it was. "That's it," he murmured, one of the fingers of his other hand tracing the curve of her spine until it reached the white globes of her bottom and then trailed sideways over the soft skin to her hip.

He thrilled at how her body trembled just then, of the slight gasps she made when his finger was joined by the rest of his hand so he could smooth it over her firm bottom and down to her thighs.

Her perfectly-rounded bottom, made so from how she rode astride, was nothing like any other woman's he had seen. Her thighs, long and strong and smooth, were just as captivating. He was about to imagine what they might feel like gripping the sides of his body as he drove himself into her, but thought better of it. He wasn't about to allow his own release when he hadn't yet seen to hers. "Now just relax," he murmured and he began to move his hand against her quim.

Relax? Isabella nearly repeated. How could she relax when his hand was suddenly pressed against the wet folds at the top of her thighs? When she couldn't see what he was about to do? But she slid her elbows out sideways until the front of her body was enveloped in the soft mattress. Even before she could wonder what he might do next, the pressure of his hand against her womanhood increased a bit. A most delicious sensation seemed to build just then, of anticipation and the hint of pending pleasure. She grasped the bed linens beneath each hand when a skitter of delight raced through her lower body.

When she attempted to lift her bottom higher, not to escape his touch as much as to provide more room for his hand against her quim, his other hand pressed very gently at the base of her spine. The pressure combined with what his fingers were suddenly doing against her swollen womanhood had her breaths catching, her heart racing, and her breathing labored.

"Tell me what you want me to do," Octavius whispered.

Isabella wondered at how to respond. She had no idea what to tell him. She didn't know the language to use. But every time he seemed to rub harder before softening his hold on her, before slowing his movements, she was sure *something* was about to happen. "Harder, Octavius," she managed to get out.

"Like this?" The whisper was accompanied by his hand pressing harder against her womanhood.

"Yes," she managed. "And... faster." The word was said as a plea as her fingers tightened their hold on the bed linens.

Octavius did her bidding, secretly thrilling at how her body responded to his hold, to his movements, to the pressure he applied. He thrilled at hearing his name whispered with such reverence.

Twice he had known she was on the verge of her orgasm, but he hadn't wanted to allow her the release. He nearly deprived her of it again, but thought better than to employ such exquisite torture on her—he already feared he was bruising her womanhood with his ministrations.

His movements increased in speed, his pressure against her increased, and a moment later, Isabella's entire body shuddered in his hold. Her strangled cries and his name spoken in rapture had him slowing his hand, but he kept the pressure even until her body seemed to stiffen and break before finally relaxing beneath his hand. Her sobs and cries of his name softened to quiet mewls and then finally to a purr of satisfaction.

Dropping to the mattress, Octavius rolled onto his back and gulped air, unaware he had been holding his breath in anticipation how she might react. One arm lay bent above his head as he reached out to her with the other. Given how Jane had reacted—cowering from his hold as if in disgust at what they had done—he was stunned when Isabella was suddenly pressed against the side of his body, one arm wrapped over his torso, her soft breaths washing over his heated chest.

Isabella clung to the duke, awareness of her surroundings

slowly returning. When Octavius had ordered her to turn over, she had half-expected he would mount her, much like a horse, and take her virtue. That he hadn't done so made her wonder if he merely thought better of it.

Or did he no longer desire her?

That he could create so much desire in her with what he had done with his hands had her wanting more. Wanting to do more. She slid the flat of her hand down his chest and to his curlies, well aware he was about to still it with his free hand when she whispered, "Octavius? If I do the same to you, will you be as pleasured as I was?"

Octavius took a deep breath. His arousal was evident in how his manhood stood erect from his body. "Possibly," he hedged, wondering what she had in mind.

Her hand moved farther down until her fingers wrapped around the base of the velvet-soft, steel-hard rod. It seemed to come alive in her hold, throbbing to the beat of his pulse beneath her ear. "Will you show me what to do?" she asked in a whisper, her grasp moving from the base of his erection to the tip. Her thumb passed over the wet top before sliding off the silky smooth skin. She felt more than heard his inhalation of breath, secretly thrilling at how her simple touch seemed to excite him.

His larger hand wrapped around the back of her hand, his fingers interlacing with hers, and then he guided her tight hold down his shaft and back up again. When their grip was nearly free of his manhood, he pushed it back down but made sure his thumb guided her thumb over the wet tip. He couldn't help the groan that suddenly erupted from his throat, but he felt her alarm in how she suddenly stilled her movements. "Just keep doing that," he whispered, his breaths more like pants for air as he released his hold on her hand. "Hold me as hard as you can manage."

Isabella resumed the push-pull motions, speeding them up just a bit with each round as she sensed his breathing quicken and his body stiffening in anticipation of a release it clearly needed.

Wanting to see him better—to watch as she pleasured him—Isabella slid a leg over both of his and raised up her body to straddle him, her knees tucked into the mattress on either side of his thighs. At the sudden change in how her hands gripped him, in how she held his member so his sac rested against her mons, Octavius opened his eyes. A growl erupted from his throat before the seed spilled from his manhood, the warm, thick liquid spreading over her lower torso.

Isabella watched in wonder at the change that came over the man beneath her. She felt his body go rigid, stay rigid, and then suddenly go slack. She saw how the cords in his neck strained, saw how his face displayed what looked like pain before he shuddered and then seemed to relax into the mattress. A moment later, his expression was one of peace. Isabella allowed a wan smile as she simply held his manhood and stared at a man who suddenly looked years younger.

How easy it is to pleasure him! she thought as a frisson passed through her body. The memory of what he had done to her only moments before had a wan smile touching her lips.

She frowned when she realized he probably wouldn't remember this time the same way she would. He would no doubt regret what he had done. What they had done. He would try to apologize, she imagined. Claim responsibility and offer for her hand...

Isabella blinked in the dark, giving her head a quick shake. He wouldn't propose, she was sure of that. Not that she would accept if he did, she reasoned. He was probably an impossible man to live with. Frowning all the time. Quick to anger.

Just like Craythorne, she realized, swallowing hard when a sob threatened just then. *But he's not like Craythorne*, she argued. *He's merely wounded. A bit broken. Sad.*

Finally letting go her hold on him, Isabella reached for the bath linen at the end of the bed and cleaned herself. Finding the edges of the tangled bed linens—Octavius had thrown them off their bodies at some point—she straightened them as best she could and lowered her body to rest alongside his.

She was skimming a hand over his chest in an effort to determine where she might best rest it when one of his hands suddenly fell atop hers, pinning it against his sternum. A moment later, a slight snore sounded and then he was silent.

Isabella allowed a wan smile before she lowered her lips to the corner of his and gave him a gentle kiss. "Good night, Octavius," she whispered before lowering herself back down to the mattress.

She couldn't take back her right hand, though, as the duke seemed to want it to stay right where it was.

Chapter 36

THE MORNING AFTER

Ten o'clock in the morning

Isabella awoke with a start, well aware she wasn't in her own bed. Well aware she wore no night clothes. The blanket covering her shoulder was unfamiliar as well. But when she spotted the empty pillow next to hers, the memories of earlier that morning came flooding back.

"Time to get up, sleepy head," Octavius said from where he stood looking out one of the bedchamber's windows.

Turning her body so she could sit up in the soft mattress, Isabella stared at the duke a moment before blinking away the remnants of the odd dream she had been experiencing. A dream of a huge stables filled with beautiful bay horses of every age.

All hers.

"Good morning," she managed, pushing her sleep tousled curls off of her face. She watched as Octavius pulled on a shirt. He was already wearing breeches, the Nankeen fabric hugging his thighs so close she could make out the shape of his legs without using any of her imagination.

She didn't even have to do that, she realized. She had seen those thighs wearing nothing at all. Felt their strength and seen their length when they rested on either side of her hips as they had sat in the bathtub earlier that morning.

As for the rest of his breeches, the memory of what was behind the placket had her spine tingling. She had held it in her hands. Rubbed it and cradled it and thrilled at how it throbbed in her hold. Was it any wonder her womanhood seemed to throb in response? The memory of how it had felt with the palm of his hand pressed against it—the memory of of the pleasurable waves and sharp darts of delight he had brought forth—sent a tinge of desire coursing through her lower body just then.

Despite what he had seen of her the night before, Isabella still gripped the bed linens against her bare chest. "It is already nine o'clock?" she wondered, just then remembering his edict that she not wake up before nine.

"It's ten, actually." At her gasp of disbelief, Octavius aimed a wan grin in her direction. "I was just as surprised." He moved to a tall dresser and removed something white from the top drawer. He tossed it in her direction. "Here. Something to wear until you can get to your bedchamber," he said before returning his attention to his shirt. He tucked the hem into his breeches, a mumbled curse drawing Isabella's gaze from the huge nightshirt she had unfolded and spread out on the counterpane before her.

"What is it?"

Octavius sighed. "Nothing. Rather nothing a good dousing of cold water wouldn't cure." But he was struggling with his shirt, and Isabella soon realized his hardened manhood was the reason. Once again, the memory of the night before came flooding back, and the barest hint of what she had experienced shot through her abdomen in a most pleasant frisson.

"Is it always like that?" she asked as she pulled on the nightshirt. The voluminous garment settled over her body as she climbed out of the bed, although one shoulder was left bare as the larger neckline shifted to one side.

Turning to regard her, Octavius was rather stunned at

how the sight of her in his far-too-large nightshirt would have him wishing he could simply tumble her right then and there. Her long curls, so messy and in such disarray, perfectly suited her just then. "Not usually, no," he whispered before he dropped a kiss on her bare shoulder and flicked a thumb over the silhouette of one of her nipples. The erect bud pressed into the fabric of the nightshirt, and he heard her inhalation of breath at the slight contact. "Are these always like this?"

Isabella shook her head. "Not usually, no," she replied, understanding only part of his argument. She seemed perplexed for a moment.

"What is it?" Octavius wondered, deciding he could at least pull her into a hug. A bit embarrassed at what he had done to her the night before—he'd had no intention of ever sharing a bed with her before he married her—he had thought to simply dismiss her from his bedchamber and make his way to the breakfast parlor.

"They are when I'm cold," she replied, one of her hands moving to cover a breast. "Although I certainly wasn't cold last night."

Considering her words, Octavius realized she made an excellent point. Why was it cold water could settle his arousal while it seemed to pucker her nipples was a bit of a quandary. "You were aroused," he murmured.

"Were you?" she countered with an arched brow. "Are you now?"

Octavius straightened before finally admitting, that yes, he was.

Isabella smoothed a hand over her breast again, her brows furrowing as she attempted to sort something.

The simple gesture had Octavius squeezing his eyes shut in an attempt to cast the image from his mind, but his mind's eye soon replaced it with images of her whilst they shared his bed. Of how erotic her bottom and thighs had appeared as he pleasured her with his hand. Of how erotic she looked as she sat atop him, holding his turgid manhood with both hands, her perfect breasts tipped with the nipples he had briefly suckled.

The nipples that now stood out in stark relief against his nightshirt. A nightshirt that looked as if it might be large enough to accommodate both of them at the same time. The thought of shedding his clothes and joining her in it came to mind, and a grin appeared to lighten his face.

He felt her lips kiss the corner of his mouth, and he opened his eyes to find her regarding him with the oddest expression. "What is it?"

Isabella allowed a wan smile. "You looked so young just then," she murmured. "You still do," she added as she lifted a hand to the side of his face. Her thumb brushed over a cheekbone, and her gaze followed it as she traced the space below one eye until it reached his temple.

His lips covered hers then, the kiss at first hard but then less so as he started to pull away and then thought better of it. *What would it hurt to simply kiss her like this every time we're together?* he wondered when he finally pulled away completely. He left his forehead pressed against hers for a moment. "I have to go back to London today," he whispered before taking a labored breath. He found he welcomed her mewl of disappointment when he recalled being annoyed by that same sound when his mistress of years ago employed it on him. "But I shall return. Probably within a week," he murmured.

"You will come out to the stables before you go? To check on your newest racers?" she half-asked, watching him attempt to fold a silk cravat. She took the ends from him and wrapped them around the back of his neck.

"Of course," he replied, watching as she took one end of the cravat and walked around him until she faced him again. Then she took the other end and walked around him in the other direction until she once again faced him. "Whatever are you doing?" he asked with a hint of amusement.

"Keeping it from twisting, of course," she replied as she

took the now much shorter ends and tied them into a simple square knot.

"And how, pray tell, did you know how to do that?" The cravat wasn't nearly as tight as he usually preferred it, but then it didn't feel as if it would choke him when he bent his head, either. He gazed at his reflection in the cheval mirror, noting how her knot was nothing like the tiny one his valet usually created.

"Watching my father's valet do it," she murmured. She suddenly blinked before she allowed a sigh. "My late father, I should say."

Octavius grimaced, his youthened features returning to that of an older man. "Do you wish to return to Craythorne Castle?" he asked carefully. "I rather imagine a funeral has already taken place, of course, but..."

"No," she said as she gave her head a shake. "There's nothing there for me. I rather doubt my clothes are even still there." There was something rather odd about learning she had been declared dead. That she wasn't just *missing*. At some point, she would write her brother to let him know why she had disappeared, but then she remembered the duke's recommendation to wait until after John had petitioned the Lord Chancellor for a writ of summons to the House of Lords. "Although..." She allowed the word to trail off as she realized there would be no dowry, no inheritance set aside for her.

"What is it?"

She swallowed. "Do you suppose my brother will restore my dowry? My inheritance?" she asked as she raised her eyes to meet his. "When he learns I am still alive?"

Octavius gave a shrug, hiding the fact that her sudden concern for a dowry bothered him. She wouldn't have a need for the money. "Do not concern yourself with it just now."

"But I could use that money to build my own stables," she argued. "To buy some breeding mares, and a stud, and..."

Her words were cut short when he placed a finger against her lips. "Do not fash yourself," he whispered. "You won't be five-and-twenty for, what? Five years?"

"Less than four," she murmured.

He blinked and then he attempted to do the math in his head. "You're past twenty?"

"I am one-and-twenty," she replied with an arched eyebrow, wondering at his ability to do simple arithmetic.

Feeling as if he had been punched in the gut, Octavius gave his head a shake. "How... how did I...?" He suddenly moved to his dresser again, pulling open one of the drawers. He withdrew a small pasteboard box and offered it to her. "This was supposed to be for your twentieth birthday."

Blinking, Isabella took the box, a bit hesitant as she did so. "Octavius," she murmured. "What's in it?"

"Open it," he urged.

Pulling the top off, she gazed inside and then angled her head. A gold chain made up of tiny links held a gold charm in the shape of a running horse. "Oh, it's beautiful," she breathed. She glanced up at the duke. "This is from you?"

Octavius nodded. "Yes. I apologize for its late delivery. I obviously lost track of time."

Stunned that he would have thought of her birthday, Isabella stared at the charm for several seconds. "May I wear it?"

"Of course. As often as you'd like," he replied. "Here. Let me help." He pulled the chain from its velvet bed and strung it around her neck, moving around Isabella much like she had done around him until he could fasten the catch at the back.

Her fingers moved to the charm as she made her way to stand before the cheval mirror. "Oh, I look a sight. You must have mistaken me for Medusa when you first saw me this morning," she complained when she noticed her hair's reflection in the looking glass. She turned her attention to the horse charm and bit her lip, noticing how it rested in the hollow of her throat. When she swallowed, the horse seemed to move, and she grinned.

Behind her, Octavius regarded the mirror's reflection and allowed a sigh. Medusa was the very last goddess he would have thought of that morning when he watched her emerge from his bed.

What would it be like to watch her do that every morning?

He had to quell the thought, aware of how his manhood wanted to escape his breeches in favor of a more hospitable environment.

That of Isabella.

She is one-and-twenty now.

How had he lost track of the time? Why hadn't Norwick mentioned it when he came with the news about Craythorne? Well, he had managed to extract the comment that Octavius intended to marry Isabella in exchange for assurances Norwick would tell Clarinda about Isabella.

The cur. Norwick probably expected he was proposing this very moment. But Octavius had no intention of proposing until he had a ring.

He suddenly wondered what had happened to the box he had delivered on Norwick's behalf. The box with the ring. He couldn't remember Isabella taking it with her when they went up to the salon the day before.

Isabella suddenly straightened and turned, her attention aimed at his bedchamber door. "They're looking for me," she whispered.

Octavius gave a start as he cocked his head to one side and listened. He had been completely unaware of footsteps in the hallway, of muted voices of concern passing by the door. *How could I have been so oblivious?* he wondered as he gave a nod and stepped back. He glanced around, realizing he had to find a way to get her out of the bedchamber without being seen.

"It's all well. I know a way through the adjoining rooms," Isabella whispered as she dipped a curtsy. "And the hallway behind the parlor. I'll just fetch my night rail from the bathing chamber on the way." Before she could take another step, though, Octavius stopped her with a hand. When she turned to face him, he pulled the loose ties at the top of the nightshirt and quickly pulled them into a bow, her bare shoulder disappearing beneath the fine lawn. "Oh. Thank you, Octavius."

He kissed the back of her hand and gave a nod. A moment later, he watched as she left his suite by way of the bathing chamber door.

Isabella regarded the mess in the mistress suite bathing chamber for a moment, rather dismayed at the condition of her night rail. She rolled it into a ball and tucked it under one arm before gathering the duke's few pieces of clothing and his boots and placing them on the room's only chair. With one last glance around the bathing chamber, she went through the door to the mistress suite. She passed completely through the darkened room—the drapes were never opened—and into a private salon. There, the curtains had been left open, and the light helped her find the hidden door in the room's paneling. On the other side, a thin hallway to the left led to the main hall while another to the right continued behind the first floor's parlor. Wide enough for a tea cart, it allowed a servant to deliver tea from the back of the parlor instead of having to use the main door into the room.

Once Isabella was beyond the parlor, the slim hallway wrapped again to the main hall. Pressing her ear to the door at the end, Isabella listened until she was sure no servants were about. She slowly opened the door, momentarily confused when not the hallway but the back of a tapestry appeared before her. She rolled her eyes as she imagined where she was along the hall. Her bedchamber's door was almost directly across from this particular tapestry. Peeking around the edge of the decorative wall hanging, Isabella waited a moment for a footman to disappear down the stairs before she hurried across the hall and into her bedchamber.

Only to find one of the maids staring at her from the other side of the bed.

"There you are!" Thompson exclaimed, her face

displaying a look of relief. A bucket of coal dangled from one hand.

Isabella blinked. "Good morning," she managed, wondering how long she had been missed.

"We've been so worried, my lady. You're usually up so early—"

"I was up even earlier than usual today, in fact," Isabella interrupted she she hurried to the dressing room. "At three o'clock in the morning, in fact."

The maid let out a gasp. "What happened?"

"Enyo had a bit of difficulty with her twins, but the duke pulled the second foal," Isabella explained. She felt a bit of satisfaction at seeing the maid's eyes widen. "I felt horrid waking him up, of course, but I simply couldn't do it by myself. Then, I was such a mess, I had to take a bath. Fell asleep in there, I was so exhausted." She doffed the nightshirt and quickly pulled on her chemise and corset. "Could you help?" she asked as she turned her back for the maid to tighten the corset ties.

"Of course, my lady," Thompson said as she pulled the strings. "I suppose the duke will still be abed then, too."

About to claim he was wide awake and dressed, Isabella realized she couldn't. "Oh, I've no idea. Are you sure he hasn't gone back to London?" she asked, thinking a diversion tactic might be necessary just then.

This seemed to surprise the maid before she returned to making the bed. "Oh, I'm sure I wouldn't know, my lady."

Isabella pulled on a riding habit and regarded the maid for a moment. The young woman seemed rather sad as she went about her work. "Thompson, what's wrong?" Isabella asked as she buttoned up the front of the habit's skirt.

The maid gave a slight shrug. "It's just... we was hoping you and him..." She stopped and shook her head. "Forgive me, my lady."

Isabella stilled her movements, the bodice of the habit still unbuttoned. "What?"

Thompson dipped her head. "Cook fancies herself a

matchmaker. Mrs. Cooper thinks you and the duke should marry, seeing as how he needs an heir and you love his horses so much."

Returning her attention to the buttons, Isabella allowed a grin of embarrassment. "Does she now?" The thought that she and the duke had been a topic of conversation amongst the servants was a bit of a surprise. "Well, you can let cook know the duke has made me an offer of sorts."

Her eyes widening, Thompson waited with baited breath until Isabella added, "He would like me to continue as his châtelaine here at Huntinghurst." She didn't include the reason why, of course—that Craythorne was dead and no longer a threat, or that she was one-and-twenty and able to marry should she receive an offer.

Isabella wasn't sure how she expected the servant to react, but the maid's expression of disappointment wasn't one of the possibilities. "What's wrong?" Isabella asked as she stepped forward.

Thompson merely shook her head and took a step back. She curtsied before saying, "Have a good day, my lady."

Isabella watched as the maid took her leave of the bedchamber, wondering if she had made a mistake in accepting the duke's offer to stay at Huntinghurst.

But if she hadn't, where would she go? London? It would be some time before her brother was settled in the townhouse her father occupied whilst attending Parliament. There were no stables there. Merely a mews in the back that served all the townhouses on the street. She rather doubted she would be allowed to spend her time there.

What would I do all day if I couldn't work with horses?

What did other daughters of the aristocracy do to pass the time?

Well, they probably painted tables, or created beautiful embroideries with their nimble fingers, or decorated hats and bonnets with silk flowers. Pursuits she had never pursued because, well, because she wasn't particularly gifted in the arts, she was all thumbs when it came to sewing needles, and where ever would she find silk flowers this far from London?

If it hadn't been for the Huntinghurst stables and a dozen or more horses in various stages of training, she would have gone stark raving mad. *A candidate for Bedlam, indeed.*

Once she had her unruly curls brushed out and secured with a few pins atop her head, she made her way to the breakfast parlor.

Chapter 37

A REMINDER OF A PROMISE

A few minutes later

Peters gingerly placed a newly ironed copy of the *Sussex Weekly Advertiser* next to the duke's place at the breakfast parlor table and cringed. As the area's only newspaper, it filled his master's requirement that there be one for him to read whilst eating his breakfast. As a publication that was openly opposed to the privileges enjoyed by the aristocracy, its editorial content could be offensive to the duke.

"I appreciate your concern, Peters," Octavius said as he moved to take his place at the end of the oval table. "But don't fash yourself. I'm only interested in the news articles."

The butler gave a bow. "Very good, Your Grace." He waved to a nearby footman, who immediately saw to the delivery of a pot of coffee and a plate of toast. "Cook is seeing to your eggs and ham. Will there be anything else?"

Octavius dared a glance out the room's only window, remembering too late it's south-facing view didn't include the stables. A few horses could be seen grazing in the pasture beyond the grounds of the house, though. "Any news about our new twins this morning?"

His eyes widening at hearing the question, Peters almost asked how the duke already knew about Enyo's foals. One of the scullery maids had spread the news during the servants' breakfast, saying she learned of it from George when she was gathering eggs in the hen house that morning.

Octavius noted the butler's surprise, rather pleased to know he could discombobulate the man on occasion, perhaps more than Isabella had managed to do on a daily basis her first year-and-a-half at Huntinghurst. He arched an eyebrow. "I had to pull the filly. Which reminds me. See to it the maids knows I used the tub in the mistress' bathing chamber. I didn't wish to rouse a footman to arrange a shower bath at three o'clock in the morning." This last was said in the direction of the footman who stood at attention next to the sideboard.

Even before the butler could respond, the footman nodded and took his leave of the breakfast parlor by way of the butler's pantry, apparently off to find a housemaid.

"The additions to the stables were mentioned at breakfast this morning, Your Grace. It seems all is well, according to George. Congratulations."

"Well that's a relief to hear," Isabella said as she breezed into the room. The duke set down his coffee and stood up, acknowledging her curtsy with a slight bow. "I'll wait until after breakfast to check on them," she added as she hurried up to his side and kissed him on the cheek. "Good morning, Hunt."

For the first time in a very long time, Octavius was sure color stained his cheeks. Although she had kissed him on the cheek on the occasion of his arrivals to Huntinghurst, she had never done so with a servant present. "Good morning," Octavius replied, waiting until she took her usual place at the table—Peters held her chair since the footman hadn't yet returned—before quickly reseating himself. For in the few seconds since her arrival, Octavius was suddenly aware of several things at once.

Of how his cock reacted to her arrival, stiffening as if it remembered all too well how she had held it earlier that morning.

Of how she really needed a new riding habit, for the one she wore was entirely too snug and displayed the hourglass shape of her torso.

Of how she didn't seem the least bit embarrassed to be in his company despite the fact that she had been completely naked only the hour before. Naked and sitting atop him—astride—only a few hours before that. And she was still wearing the necklace he had given her, the charm resting just inside the hollow of her throat and just above the edge of her riding habit's neckline.

"I wish to apologize again for having awakened you when I did. I knew I couldn't pull the filly," she said as a footman appeared with plates of eggs and ham.

"Apology accepted," Octavius replied. "Saving Enyo was my main concern, of course," he added, although he didn't include a hint of the annoyance he had felt at having been disturbed. His troubled sleep would have only grown worse had she not awakened him. And given how soundly he had slept until nearly ten, he knew having her to hold onto had been the reason.

Isabella leaned a bit to one side as the footman set down her plate. "Will you have an opportunity to visit the stables before you leave for London?" she asked as she stirred sugar and milk into her coffee. Although he had assured her only a half-hour earlier that he would, she was at a loss for a topic of conservation she could mention with the servants present. "I do hope one of these foals will be the racer you need for the St. Leger in a few years."

Octavius straightened in his carver and regarded her for a moment. He turned his attention to the butler and then the footman. "Leave us," he said, his manner rather severe just then.

Both servants bowed and took their leave. Octavius waited a full ten seconds before he turned his full attention on Isabella. "About... about this morning... "

A frisson shot through Isabella, his comment requiring she think about what had happened in the dark hours of early morning. Of what he had said. Of what she had promised. "I won't speak of it with anyone," Isabella said with a shake of her head. "I promised I would not."

Not exactly what he expected to hear—he had intended to ask if she made it back to her bedchamber without being seen—Octavius allowed a nod, an odd sense of disappointment settling over him. *Did I want her to be discovered leaving my apartments?* he wondered suddenly. He had slept so soundly with her pressed against him, he wanted nothing more than to have her next to him every night.

Probably for the rest of his life.

He sighed then, remembering the conversation to which she referred. Remembered his quandary. Remembered what he had done despite his promises to himself that he would never bed Isabella. His need to hold onto her—to hold onto something to quell the nightmares—had still led to behavior wholly inappropriate for a man of his stature. Of his station.

She had been his ward. Was now his châtelaine.

She might one day be his wife, but he didn't want her to *have* to be his wife.

What would Craythorne have done if he learned what had happened?

Pistols at dawn, no doubt. Or a fist to the face, and another to his ribs, and another to his groin. *I deserve that,* he thought with a sigh.

What would Norwick do if he learned what had happened?

Octavius resisted the urge to roll his eyes. The earl would probably pat him on the back and congratulate him. Buy him a drink and speak of a generous dowry. Set a wedding date.

Damn the Earl of Norwick!

The man probably hadn't yet told his wife about Isabella! Clarinda probably still believed her cousin was dead.

At least I had sense enough to leave her virtue intact, he thought, despite having ruined her in every other way.

Octavius squeezed his eyes shut for that moment when he remembered Craythorne was dead.

And then he remembered Isabella's reaction—or lack thereof—to the news that the earl had died. Did she know Craythorne wasn't her true father? Had Norwick somehow informed her? Written to her or passed the information along by way of his cousin, Constance?

He was about to ask Isabella when he noticed how she was regarding him, her eyes wide and her lower lip trembling. "What has you so troubled if not last night?" she asked in a whisper.

Octavius sighed. "You," he finally replied.

Isabella winced. "But, why?"

He shook his head. "Not here. Ride with me this morning, and we shall talk where no one can hear our conversation," he murmured, sure Peters had his ear pressed against the butler pantry's door.

Probably gloating because he thought I was berating Isabella for her inappropriate attention to my horses.

And yet nothing could be further from the truth.

"Hancock needs some exercise," Isabella replied. "I can see to the newborns later today."

It was the duke's turn to wince. "Whatever do you think you'll *see to* with those two?"

"Why, put a lead on them, of course. Walk them about a bit. Maybe even take them from their mother's sight for a moment or two. I'll have you know I do not coddle your horses," she stated.

"Obviously," he replied, rather impressed she intended to get a lead around their necks given they weren't even a day old.

"What will you name them?" she asked then.

The duke seemed to ponder the question for some time, taking a bite of his breakfast before he finally said, "Eris for the filly, certainly. As for the colt..." He finally gave a shake of his head. "If I remember my Greek mythology, Enyo was only known to have had a daughter."

"What about *Deimos?*" Isabella suggested with an arched eyebrow.

Octavius seemed to consider the name for a time. "Let me think on that for a time," he murmured.

Isabella gave a nod. "I'll fill in the pedigree chart for Eris later today," she murmured as she finished her breakfast. She held her coffee cup in both hands a moment before she said, "Please, do not be concerned that I seem... ambivalent about my father's death. I may mourn him, but it won't be right now. Not when there are newborn foals to celebrate."

The relief Octavius felt at hearing her words had him giving her a nod. He leaned over and kissed the side of her head, one hand resting on her cheek for just a moment. "One less concern, then," he said in a whisper.

Isabella wondered at his words, but decided not to ask what else seemed to have him so troubled. Surely a night spent in her company meant little to him—he no doubt had a mistress in London. He was probably used to having a woman... *how had the ladies of the evening at* The Elegant Courtesan *put it?*

A woman to warm his bed.

Yes, that was it. But if being pleasured to within an inch of her life was the cost of providing the warmth, well, it was a price she was more than willing to pay.

Chapter 38

A RIDE TO THE FOLLY

A half-hour later

The invigorating ride through the part of the duke's lands Isabella had never visited left her nearly breathless. Riding through a small forest required she follow Octavius rather than stay abreast of his mount. Although Hancock put up with it for most of the trip, he insisted on catching up to Poseidon and running neck-and-neck when he had half-a-chance.

Once they reached a clearing with a marble folly in the middle of a small rise, Isabella halted Hancock and stared in awe. "I've never been here before," she murmured.

"I should hope not," Octavius replied, rather liking how she stared at the circular structure in wonder. A series of columns held up the domed roof, and although there weren't any walls, there was a series of stone benches at the base. Around the perimeter of its round floor, a series of colorful rhododendrons made it appear as if the structure had simply been willed into existence by a Greek god. On a hot summer day, the folly would be perfect for a picnic.

Or an assignation.

"Why do you say that?" Isabella wondered before she dismounted.

The duke was quick to follow her lead, grasping Poseidon's reins so he could hobble the horse. He arched a brow when Isabella simply dropped hers, apparently trusting her horse to remain nearby. "We're miles from Huntinghurst and even farther from the nearest village," he explained as he extended one of his arms and pointed to a church steeple barely visible on the horizon. "Just beyond that are Chichester's lands," he said, referring to the Duke of Chichester. He led her down the hill a bit until an opening in the trees to the north revealed another vista. "On a really clear day, you can make out Midhurst."

Isabella's gaze swept over the horizon, her brows furrowing after a time. "Where is Boxgrove?"

The duke turned around and pointed due south. "About ten miles that way." The trees prevented them from seeing anything of the small village, but Isabella stared in that direction for a moment.

"I didn't realize Connie had to come so far to visit," she said in awe.

"She doesn't. Huntinghurst is about four miles from here. But still, it's not a quick trip for her to pay a call on you," Octavius commented. After a moment, he offered his arm. "Come. We'll be more comfortable in the folly."

Isabella placed a hand on his arm, wondering what he intended. The man's behavior was so different from his past visits, she didn't know what to expect.

Once they were under the folly's dome, he turned around, and Isabella followed his line of sight. Through a clearing in the trees to the west, the rolling hills below them displayed farm fields and forests, pastures and a village. "Oh, it's beautiful," she breathed.

Octavius watched her as she surveyed his lands below. Torn by what he wanted to do and knowing he shouldn't, he allowed her the time to ask questions as she pointed at landmarks along the horizon.

"This folly. Did you have it built? Or—?"

"My grandfather did. For his duchess," he replied in a quiet voice.

Grinning Isabella turned to regard him. "Your grandmother?"

Octavius bobbed his head and back and forth. "I suppose. She died before I was born, so I've never thought of her in that regard."

Isabella winced. "I met all four of my grandparents when I was younger. All four have since died."

"I always imagined Heath would outlast me," Octavius murmured, referring to Arabella's father. Albert Brotherton, Arabella's brother and Clarinda's father, was the current Earl of Heath. "Your uncle will certainly outlive me now." *Especially after he learns you're still alive.*

He and Norwick had only briefly considered taking the Earl of Heath into their confidence. They had merely agreed that the fewer who knew about Isabella's fate, the better off she would be.

The duke led her to the stone bench opposite of where they had been standing and turned to sit down.

"What is he like?" Isabella asked as she settled onto the gray-veined marble.

Octavius furrowed his brows, rather surprised at the question. "When was the last time you were in his company?"

Shrugging, Isabella seemed to do some figures in her head before she said, "I think I was ten... so... eleven years ago."

The duke appeared even more perplexed than he had in the breakfast parlor that morning. "How is it you haven't seen him in so long?" Surely Craythorne had brought his family to London for the Season.

"Father wouldn't allow it. My mother didn't go with him to London during the Season, so we only saw my uncle when he paid a visit to Craythorne Castle," she explained. "He was on his way to Portsmouth once. To visit a friend at the Naval Academy."

Octavius continued to frown. He hadn't noticed Arabella's absence from the seasonal entertainments, but then, his attentions had been on Jane. On courting her despite them both knowing he would eventually marry her one day.

Had Craythorne learned of Arabella's *affaire* with Norwick? Did the earl think his wife would cuckold him? Keeping her from London during the Season would have been cruel to a woman who grew up with the expectation of attending balls and soirées, routs and *musicales*. "Pardon my curse, but Craythorne was an ass," he murmured.

Isabella pinked up a bit at hearing his assessment of the late earl. "I think he believed my mother would tell her brother that he was a cruel man. I don't think she ever did so in her correspondence to him, you see, because Craythorne sometimes opened the letters before the footman saw to posting them. But if she were to have a moment of Heath's time in person, she might beg to be allowed to stay under his protection—and Craythorne didn't want to take the chance she would leave him." Her throat suddenly closed up, her mind's eyes filled with the memory of how her mother had looked with her head twisted in Craythorne's hands, with her lifeless eyes staring up at the ceiling. "And then she did. For good." She quickly swallowed in an attempt to stifle the sob that was sure to follow.

Closing his eyes, the duke seemed to ponder what to say. He hadn't meant for their trip to the folly to end in tears. After what had happened earlier that morning, he had thought to gauge her reaction. Learn her expectations. Determine a course of action for their future. He should offer for her hand while he was at it, but now was not the time. She didn't yet know everything. Until she knew the truth about her parentage, he didn't want her to make decisions that would affect the rest of her life.

At the same time, he needed an heir. He didn't want his dukedom in the hands of a regent. He wanted to raise his son with an appreciation of the responsibility of his office as well as the privilege it afforded.

Offering to keep Isabella as his châtelaine was a means of giving her a place to call home until her brother was informed she was still alive. A means of keeping her close should Norwick finally decide to pay a call and confess. A means of allowing her continued access to his horses, for he was quite sure she was onto something with her breeding choices. He might have a contender that summer, two or three next year, and even more the year after.

"Please accept my condolences," Octavius said suddenly. "I wish… I wish I knew what else to say, but I admit to being at a bit of a loss."

Isabella finally allowed a sigh, a catch in her breath due to a sob. "I have never wished to vex you," she whispered. "I never want to taunt you or test you as my mother did my father," she added with a shake of her head. "She always managed to stop just in time. Just before Craythorne would have cuffed her, or slapped her, or done something worse. She always threw herself into his arms and begged forgiveness at just the right moment."

Octavius winced at hearing her words. No wonder she had been so convinced the man had killed her mother. She probably thought all men were capable of such violence against their women.

"I never lifted a hand against my duchess," he whispered hoarsely.

"You had no reason to," Isabella countered.

Rather shocked at her response, Octavius turned to stare at her. "However would you know such a thing?"

Squirming a bit, Isabella angled her head to one side. "The servants speak of her as if she were a saint." She sighed. "As if she could do no wrong. And yet, since she never once set foot into Huntinghurst, they never actually met her." Her brows furrowed in confusion as she considered their opinion.

How had they come to think the duchess was a saint?

Straightening on the bench, Octavius arched an eyebrow. "Her public persona was well-honed," he agreed with a sigh. "No one would ever believe her true nature." He couldn't believe he was finally putting voice to his less than complimentary memories of Jane Ludlow. Memories were always kinder of those who died before their time. Especially those who died in childbirth. He *had* loved Jane, though. Had probably loved her since before he was breeched. Loved her enough to make a promise he would love no other.

The heart wants what the heart wants, Norwick had said.

Damn, but the man was right.

It was Isabella's turn to sit up straighter. "Whatever are you implying?"

The duke placed a hand over the one she rested on her thigh. He lifted the gloved hand and regarded the kid leather for a moment, wincing when he saw how worn it was, wincing again at seeing the frayed edge of her sleeve. "Jane was spoiled. She never would have worn a riding habit past a single Season. Never would have worn a pair of gloves that didn't appear new. Never would have lifted a finger to help the maids, or a horse, or..." *Spend a night with me when I needed her*, he almost added.

"She was your duchess," Isabella argued. "Would you expect her to do any of those things?"

Octavius angled his head first one way and then the other. "I suppose not," he finally agreed. Time had allowed him to remember the reasons he shouldn't hold Jane in such high esteem any longer. How she had never made the trip to Huntinghurst despite his efforts to make it as comfortable as their mansion in London. How she rarely allowed him to bed her, despite his efforts to see to her pleasure first. How she complained the entire time she was expecting his heir while at the same time, she held a hand over her belly and spoke soft words of love and affection she never put voice to him. How she made comments about the discomfort of carrying a babe and how it would be the death of her.

And it was.

"She was not a saint. Nor an angel," Octavius whispered, his gaze aimed at the horizon below them.

"Mortals never are," Isabella replied as she wiped away a tear.

Octavius turned and regarded her, his frown firmly in place. "You are," he countered quietly, remembering how he had asked that she share her bath and spend the night with him. Perhaps her shock at hearing his words had kept her from protesting, but she did as she was told. This morning, she hadn't cowered in his bed as if she were frightened of him, or gazed at him with cow eyes, or acted as if she had been thoroughly compromised, but rather behaved as if they shared a bed every night.

He squeezed his eyes shut in an attempt to wipe away the memory of what she had done to him before his cock could respond.

How had she known what to do? *Because I showed her.* How had she known how hard to hold him, and how to move her hands, and when to touch him just so? *Because I showed her.*

Well, he wanted to show her much more. Do much more with her. If she accepted his suit, then he would.

Isabella swallowed, not sure what to say. Did he think her an angel because she had agreed to share her bath? Or his bed?

Or did it have something to do with his horses?

When he remained mute, her attention went first to him and then to white pasteboard box he held.

The box in which Norwick's letter and her mother's ring had been delivered. The ring was no longer in it, though, and she lifted her eyes to find Octavius holding it in between his thumb and forefinger. He was studying the diamond in the noonday light.

"What is it?" Isabella asked in a whisper, not wanting to break the spell that seemed to have been cast over the folly just then. The birdsong was still evident, and the leaves on the surrounding trees still rustled a bit in the slight breeze, but otherwise all was quiet around them.

"It's hardly worthy of you," he said with a sigh.

"It's not paste," Isabella countered, half-tempted to add, *Is it?*

"No," Octavius said as he shook his head. He seemed to come to some decision, though, and he straightened on the bench. "I have to travel back to London. Preferably this afternoon," he said suddenly, before realizing it was far too late to make the fifty miles in just one day.

He lifted one of her gloved hands and peeled the worn leather from her fingers. Daring a glance at her before he slid the ring onto her fourth finger, he added, "Race you back to Huntinghurst?"

"I think not," she murmured then. "At least, not yet," she added as she regarded him for moment. "I have something more I need to discuss with you." She scooted a bit closer to him on the bench, and after a moment, she leaned against him.

Wrapping an arm around her back, Octavius pulled her until her head rested against the front of his shoulder, his lips kissing her forehead until curiosity had him asking, "You have my complete attention."

A half-hour later, the two made their way back to Huntinghurst, allowing the horses to set the pace.

Neither one expected callers to be waiting for them at Huntinghurst.

Chapter 39

A VISIT FROM A FATHER AND A COUSIN

A *half-hour earlier*

Clarinda stepped down from the Norwick traveling coach and stared up at the front façade of Huntinghurst in awe. "You didn't tell me it was this large," she accused.

David Fitzwilliam dared a glance at the edifice and gave a shrug. "A hunting lodge, it is not," he agreed as he offered his arm. "Come. Let's see if we can find the owner, shall we?"

Giving him a glance, Clarinda paused. "I don't know why, but I admit to being a bit nervous," she whispered, just as a stableboy appeared from the east side of the house. The boy bowed in their direction before assisting the driver with the horses. A footman suddenly appeared from the house and made his way to the trunk tied to the back of the coach.

"It seems we're expected, at least," David replied. "And as for being nervous, I am the one feeling a bit discombobulated at the moment."

Clarinda rolled her eyes, rather surprised the earl would admit to such a state. But for the entire trip from London, David had been nervous. Worried. A bit more talkative than usual.

And quite amorous.

She wondered then if his sexual advances had simply

been a means to take his mind off how he was going to tell Isabella that he was her father.

Well, no matter. Their bouts of lovemaking in between naps and a few stops at coaching inns had certainly passed the time.

A butler appeared and gave a deep bow. "Welcome to Huntinghurst, my lord, my lady. I am Peters. Although His Grace has been expecting your arrival, he isn't yet back from his ride."

The Norwicks exchanged glances. "We're actually here to see Lady Isabella. Is she in residence?" David asked.

Obviously shocked at the query, the butler gave a shake of his head. "She is riding with the duke."

"Perhaps we can wait in the parlor?" Clarinda suggested, daring a glance up at her husband.

"Of course. I'll show you to your rooms," Peters offered before he turned around and headed into the house. "And then I'll see to it tea is delivered to the parlor."

As they made their way into the house, Clarinda's gaze took in the massive great hall and the grand staircase that split in two at the first landing and then led to the first story. "Izzy is the châtelaine here?" she queried, obviously impressed by the interior of the estate home.

"She is," David affirmed. "There hasn't been a housekeeper here for a few years, so she oversees the maids."

"Can we have a châtelaine?" Clarinda asked, *sotto voce*. I rather like the idea of someone else seeing to the maids."

David frowned. "You have a housekeeper," he reminded her. "Banks is quite efficient, I should think." He didn't add that the woman had held a similar position at *The Elegant Courtesan* before he had it shut down.

"Oh! Do you suppose the duke is proposing right now?" Clarinda whispered, her attention darting about as she took in the walls of large paintings and the busts of Roman generals and the like. "Oh, I do hope he's chosen someplace romantic. Like a folly," she murmured. "I thought you might propose in a folly."

David furrowed a brow, struggling to remember just where Daniel had proposed to her. David had never actually asked for her hand but simply stepped in and made sure her affections were transferred to him before they wed. Had Clarinda been able to tell the difference between him and Daniel, he feared she would have chosen Daniel that day when they both paid a call on her.

Now, where had Daniel proposed?

Kensington Gardens.

Well, at least that could be considered romantic, he supposed with a bit of relief. "If he is proposing, he's doing so counter to his claim that I had to tell her about me first," he whispered as they made their way up the stairs.

"Are you expecting her to react badly?" Clarinda asked in surprise.

Not sure how he expected Isabella to react when told the truth, David merely shrugged. "What would you do? If you learned your father was someone other than Heath?"

Clarinda took a deep breath, made necessary as they had just reached the top of the stairs and she was a bit winded. "Weep a bit, I suppose. Then there would be screaming, and wailing, and gnashing of teeth—"

"You're not helping," David complained, just then catching her teasing grin. "You minx!" he added in a hoarse whisper.

Waving into an open door, Peters said, "This is the parlor, and your rooms are this way." He continued down the adjacent hall, finally stopping to open a door to reveal a decidedly feminine bedchamber decorated in peach and green. "For you, my lady. And for my lord..." The butler moved down to the next door along the corridor. "The master bedchamber." He opened the carved door to reveal a room done in navy blue and dark woods. "I'll see to it tea is delivered to the parlor, and the trunks are delivered here. Will your servants be joining you?"

"Their coach was still being serviced when we left *The*

King's Arm in Farnhurst," David replied. "I expect them shortly."

"Very good, my lord. I'll see to their quarters straight away."

Clarinda shed her pelisse and hat and left them along with her reticule on her bed before she made her way to David's room. "This is all far grander than I imagined," she admitted as she moved to help David remove his greatcoat.

"I don't know why we bothered to bring my valet along. You're so much better at this than he is," he murmured.

"Better at what?"

"Undressing me," he teased. He gathered her into his arms and gave her a kiss. "Thank you for not screaming and wailing and gnashing your teeth when I told you about Arabella. About Isabella," he murmured.

Clarinda gazed up at him through her dark lashes. "I thought about doing so," she admitted a bit sheepishly. "For just a moment. Two, really. But then I sorted that we weren't yet betrothed when you had your *affaire*." She sighed. "So then I wondered if perhaps *I* was your second choice."

David gave a start and then shook his head. "I don't recall having a choice at the time. If you remember, our fathers arranged the betrothal."

Arching a brow, Clarinda considered his response for a moment. "I did," she whispered.

David blinked. "You did?" he repeated, a bit confused.

Clarinda captured her lower lip with a tooth and gave a shrug. "I may have made a suggestion to Heath..." She admitted, an eyebrow arching up.

David lowered his forehead to touch hers. "How? Why? You thought me the worst possible rake at the time," he accused. To this day, she still employed a Bow Street Runner to ensure he didn't take a mistress or engage in trade. How could she have had feelings for him back when she was so young?

"The heart wants what the heart wants, doesn't it?" she replied with a shrug.

Stunned at hearing the familiar phrase, David stared at his wife for a several seconds before he pulled her into hug. "I love you, Clare." He was kissing her with a good deal of passion when he suddenly realized they were being watched. Clarinda realized it as well, for her lips pulled away from his at the same time a startled gasp sounded from hallway.

"Clarinda?" Isabella said in surprise, her hand just then dropping from having covered her mouth. "Lord Norwick? Oh, it's so good to see you!" she said with a huge grin as she dipped a curtsy.

"Izzy!" Clarinda hurried to meet her cousin at the threshold, the two hugging as they giggled.

"My lady," David said as he gave a bow, a grin appearing at seeing the cousins' reunion. A moment later, and Isabella was suddenly in front of him, giving him a kiss on the cheek.

"Oh, my lord, thank you for bringing her," Isabella said with bright eyes. "Yesterday was the most vexing day of my life, I think, with learning of Craythorne's death, and reading your letter, and the twins, and then..." She removed a glove to show her mother's wedding ring. "Thank you for sending Mum's ring. I shall keep it safe always."

David dared a glance at the ring and noticed the worn glove and the frayed edge of her sleeve. "Didn't you get the money I sent for new clothes?" he asked in concern.

Isabella gave a start and then realized to what he referred. "I did. I did use it for clothes. Your cousin, Constance, introduced me to a modiste in Boxgrove. She made me this riding habit and two others. But... I wear them far too much. So—"

"So he's just going to have to see to it you have new ones," Clarinda interrupted.

Isabella turned her attention to her cousin. "It's not really his responsibility—"

"Of course it is," Clarinda interrupted, an arched brow aimed in David's direction.

The earl blinked, realizing she had given him the perfect opening to tell Isabella he was her father. And he was just about to do so when Octavius suddenly appeared outside the bedchamber.

"There you are," he said with a grin. He gave a bow when Clarinda turned and afforded him a deep curtsy. "Peters said you'd arrived. I was about to go to the parlor, but I heard voices."

"Your Grace. Thank you for the invitation. You have such a beautiful home," Clarinda commented.

"Made so because of your cousin," he replied with a nod, waving in Isabella's direction.

David gave the duke a quelling glance, a look the duke immediately understood.

"Perhaps you'll do the honor of joining me in the parlor, Lady Norwick. I'm anxious to learn the news from Lord Heath."

Clarinda dared a glance in her cousin's direction. "Come join us when you're ready," she said in a quiet voice.

Isabella frowned and was about to follow, but David cleared his throat. "It actually *is* my responsibility, Isabella," he murmured in response to her earlier comment.

Turning her attention back to the earl, Isabella stared at him. "I hardly see how being my cousin's husband should make me *your* responsibility," she replied.

"No, but being your father does."

Isabella blinked. She swallowed. And for a moment, David was quite sure she was about to faint. "Please don't faint," he murmured as he placed a hand on her shoulder and gently pushed her so she was forced to sit on the edge of the bed.

"Oh!" Isabella managed just then. She dared a glance up at him. "You *are* 'D'," she said in a whisper, remembering the letter she had found in her mother's vanity drawer. The letter that was signed with a 'D'.

David grimaced, realizing just then she had to have read at least one of the two letters he had written to Arabella after her marriage to Craythorne. He dared not send any more. "I am," he stated with a nod.

"Oh, it all makes so much sense now," Isabella added with sigh. "It's no wonder I look so much more like Constance than my own mother." She took several breaths, as if she were fighting tears. "You must have thought me a *fool* not to have known back when I first found you. Not to have sorted it for myself."

Frowning, David sat down next to her, his head shaking from the side to side. "I thought no such thing. Arabella and I agreed a long time ago you couldn't know. She feared what Craythorne might do should he ever discover the truth, and, then, when she died, I was sure he had discovered the truth about you. It's part of why I thought we had to hide you from him. To protect you, but also keep you where I could have someone I trust befriend you."

Isabella swallowed, her brows furrowed. "Your cousin, Constance," she murmured. "She knew?"

David realized his daughter would have been incensed if she learned Constance had kept the truth from her, so he was relieved when he could could reply with, "No. At least, not until last week. I knew I could trust her to keep the secret as long as necessary, though."

Allowing a sigh, Isabella wondered if she had more family. "Do have you siblings?" she asked.

"My twin, Daniel," he replied, managing to avoid a wince as he mentioned the man. "He lives over at Norwick Park. But he doesn't know about you." Despite invitations to return to London for more than the occasional business trip, Daniel remained steadfast in his goal to remain as far from his brother and Clarinda as possible.

Continuing to frown, Isabella dared a glance up at him. "But Craythorne didn't know, did he?"

David shook his head. "I could have told him. Just before he died. But I did not. He was already... quite bereft," he whispered. "I did tell him you were alive, though. I owed him that much, I suppose."

Isabella regarded him for a time before she finally allowed a nod. "Thank you for not telling him." They sat in silence for a moment before she realized one last reality. "And the duke? He's known all along, too, hasn't he?" she asked as a tear suddenly dripped from one eye.

David wrapped an arm around her shoulders, his manner tentative as he pulled her so her head rested against his shoulder. "I told him that day you arrived at *The Elegant Courtesan*. I had to... because he kept insisting I should marry you, and I had to explain why I couldn't."

Isabella gave a start in his arms, her reaction a combination of shock and amusement. "I can imagine the frown he must have bestowed on you."

Resisting the urge to allow a bark of laughter at the reminder of just how the duke had reacted to his admission, David nodded. "Indeed. Until I told Constance and Clarinda, he was the only other person alive who knew my secret."

Isabella struggled to catch a breath as she fought back tears. "I cannot believe he didn't tell me," she whispered, tears now flowing freely.

David held a handkerchief for her as he kissed her forehead. "I would not allow it because I... because I couldn't bring myself to tell Clarinda," he admitted quietly.

Leaning away from him, Isabella gave a shake of her head. "Why ever not?" she countered, her manner rather indignant despite the tears.

"Because I fell in love with her." At Isabella's look of confusion, he added, "I didn't want her to hate me. Telling her you were my daughter meant telling her I had an *affaire* with your mother. Her aunt, if you'll recall. Now Clare is your stepmother as well as your cousin."

Isabella blinked and wiped the tears away with the handkerchief. "Coward," she finally replied, a hiccup interrupting the word.

David nodded as he bobbed his head from side to side. "I've been hearing that a lot lately," he murmured. He continued to hold her for a time, rather relieved she didn't attempt to flee or rail against him, continue to cry or beat him with her fists. He couldn't bear the thought of losing her before he'd had a chance to be her father. "I know you're of an age where you can marry without my permission, but it will be a few years before you've reached your majority," he said quietly. "I've seen to a dowry for you—"

"You have?" Isabella interrupted, straightening so she was suddenly staring at him. "Is it enough for me to buy land and build my own stables, do you suppose?"

Rather stunned at her question, David shook his head. "I expect your husband will see to all that," he countered. "You'll need some horses, too, of course."

Isabella blinked. "You expect a husband would grant me such a wish?"

The earl gave a shrug. "You wouldn't marry him if he didn't promise to fulfill your dream. Would you?" he asked with a cocked eyebrow.

A grin slowly forming, Isabella rolled her eyes and settled her head back on the top of his shoulder. "And if no man should ask for my hand? What then?"

Knowing there was a man intending to ask for her hand, and he was just down the hall, David gave a shrug. "When you reach your majority, you can have your dowry and do it yourself."

Isabella kissed him on the cheek and afforded him a brilliant smile. "Thank you, my lord," she whispered, tears once again filling her eyes.

"One caveat," the earl said as he held up a finger. "Call me 'Father', won't you? At least, when we're alone?"

Grinning, Isabella nodded. "It's the least I can do for the man who's going to help make my dream come true." She sighed and sat up straight. "Father."

David allowed a sigh of relief. "Now, for your immediate future—"

"Hunt has said I can continue to live here at Huntinghurst. To see to his horses. Make them ready for the races."

Not particularly surprised to hear the duke's proposition,

David regarded her for a moment. "Is that what you wish to do?"

Isabella nodded, a grin forming as she remembered the conversation at the folly. "Oh, yes. Very much."

He suddenly winced. "I'm going to have stiff competition at the track, aren't I?"

She nodded again, biting back a grin. "You are."

Allowing a nod of agreement, David stood up from the bed and offered his arm. "Then I suppose we should join His Grace and Clarinda in the parlor. God knows we've left them alone far too long. He's probably telling her all of my secrets—"

"And she's telling him all of mine!" Isabella interrupted, her eyes wide with mock fright.

The two raced off for the parlor, giggling and chuckling as they made their way.

EPILOGUE

March 1816 in the mistress suite at Huntinghurst

The smell of smoke awakened Octavius from his drowsy stupor. His heart racing, he quickly glanced about and then relaxed when he realized it was merely a guttering candle. The dim light left from the one candle lamp still burning shed a soft, golden glow over the woman on whose body he rested.

One of her hands made its way to the back of his head and she gently pulled him back down to her shoulder. "Just a moment more, Octavius," she whispered.

The duke heard the plea in Isabella's voice. He secretly thrilled at how she seemed so genuinely disappointed when he pulled himself from her body. "Be careful what you wish for, my sweeting, or I shall end up falling asleep completely and crushing you into the mattress."

Isabella smiled despite her own post-coital drowsiness. "I will not mind if you do," she whispered.

The quiet of Isabella's bedchamber—the mistress bedchamber at one time intended for Jane—was occasionally interrupted by the rather loud snores of Nelson, but Octavius could think of no other place he would rather be on this night—or any other. His visits to her bedchamber at Huntinghurst had become something of a nightly occurrence, his visits to his country estate much longer than the two days a month he had paid calls on her those first two years she lived at his country estate in Sussex.

Back then, he hadn't visited her with the intent of bedding her. Of making love to her. Of making her his duchess.

Of getting a child on her.

He could hardly fathom that at one time, he wanted to be rid of her.

What was I thinking?

In his drowsy stupor, he struggled to remember how he had first been introduced to his new duchess and gave a wince.

The Elegant Courtesan.

How different she had looked that morning, her curly hair in knots and her riding habit covered in mud splatters.

That had been nearly three years ago.

Her move to Huntinghurst had become a necessity once David Fitzwilliam, Earl of Norwick, informed Octavius he could no longer keep her sequestered at the brothel.

Octavius had been engaged in an especially lucrative game of hazard when Norwick approached the table and simply stood there and stared at him. A few more throws of the dice and unable to concentrate with the earl standing so near, Octavius had finally collected his chips.

"I can no longer provide protection for her," David stated in a hoarse whisper, his manner most sober despite the number of drinks he had consumed that night at Brooks's. The number of drinks he had consumed that entire week. "I can hide her no longer, Hunt."

Octavius had merely nodded, understanding the man's meaning. A witness to a murder by a man who could not be prosecuted required a hiding place, a new life—at least until the murderer was no longer a threat.

Until he, too, was dead.

"She can stay at Huntinghurst in Sussex. Small staff of

servants. Discreet and… safe," he remembered saying. "We'll move her out under cover of darkness."

And they had done just that.

Isabella was never consulted, of course. Since that fateful day when she had paid witness to what she thought was a murder, she had simply done what she was told—after she managed to get herself to London and appeared at the brothel, exhausted and in a near catatonic state.

That she should end up in the arms of a duke was a testament to her real father.

Octavius had thought she might live under his protection for a few months, but the few months became two years and would now be for the rest of their lives.

What a fool I was not to marry her then, he thought, his memories still a bit fuzzy. At least he could have promised her marriage. Saved them both years of loneliness. Months of uncertainty. Days of despair.

But back then, at his age, marrying a nineteen-year-old was out of the question. Back then, the death of his first wife had been too recent, the pain from her passing too acute to consider another to be his duchess.

I promised Jane I wouldn't give my heart to another.

Well, he had broken that promise.

Not that he could have kept it.

The heart wanted what the heart wanted, after all.

How had Norwick known to have sent for me that fateful morning? he wondered. Why not the Earl of Torrington? Or the Marquess of Morganfield? Or Devonville, even? Any of those peers would have known how to discover the truth about what had happened. But David Fitzwilliam, Earl of Norwick, had sent word to him over anyone else. Sent word that there had apparently been a murder.

Accusing an earl of murder was unseemly. Even if they had been able to prove Craythorne was guilty of Arabella's death, the man would have escaped punishment. Would have probably escaped censure.

But Norwick had known that, too. Known that despite

how sure he was that Craythorne had killed his wife, and despite his promises that he would exact revenge by killing Craythorne, he couldn't take matters into his own hands to see that justice was done.

Certainly not after he finally learned the truth of the matter.

He paid witness to Craythorne's deathbed recitation of the events of that fateful afternoon. Although he admitted to having planned to kill his fellow earl, Norwick found he couldn't when Craythorne explained how much he truly loved Arabella Brotherton. How he wanted to die for the accident that led to her death and the loss of his daughter.

Well, Norwick's daughter.

David Fitzwilliam still wasn't sure if Craythorne ever knew he hadn't fathered the girl. But to see how broken the man had become as a result of that afternoon's accident, David realized it truly didn't matter. Better to allow the man to keep his memories.

Arabella had simply slipped on the buttons of her gown and hit her head on the footboard of a bed.

Craythorne admitted he had been the one to tear the buttons from her gown. *It was all my fault,* he murmured the day Norwick had finally found where he was hiding in a cottage in Southampton and paid him a visit. *In my haste to make love to my wife, I caused her death and probably that of my daughter's.*

At least Norwick had been able to assure him Isabella was still alive, although to see the myriad of emotions the older earl displayed whilst considering the news, David wondered if he should have kept mum. No father wanted to learn their daughter thought them a monster. No father wanted their child to fear them.

Octavius closed his eyes in an attempt to push away the memories of that day he had relayed the news to Isabella. He had expected the tears, of course. The disbelief in learning the truth. What he hadn't expected was what she intended to discuss with him at the folly.

And he certainly hadn't expected she would kiss him so thoroughly when her fingers were suddenly at the back of his neck and her entire body was pressed against the front of his.

He had managed to avoid having to propose for all that time she had lived as his ward—despite the number of times he had kissed her—and in the end, he still hadn't proposed.

Because she had done so.

Once she had finally ended the kiss and allowed her fingers to grip his shoulders, she had been the one to finally allow a sigh of frustration. "Will you marry me, Octavius? You don't have to make me your duchess, and it can be a very small ceremony, but I very much wish for you to be my husband. For you to be the one who helps me make my dream come true, and for us to live at Huntinghurst for the rest of our days."

Octavius remembered blinking several times, if only because he didn't know of a way for her to not be his duchess should they marry. "It doesn't really work like that," he whispered, his forehead dropping to hers. "But if I agree to be your husband, you do realize you will have to come with me to London on occasion? We cannot stay at Huntinghurst all the time."

This seemed to have her perplexed for a moment before she finally nodded. "Most of the time?" she countered.

He screwed up his face. "Whenever Parliament isn't in session, I can be here," he countered.

She kissed him again before saying, "I accept your terms."

With half a mind to claim he needed more time to think about *her* terms, Octavius instead allowed a grin that soon turned into a smile. For the first time in years, he felt young.

And apparently, he looked it, for he caught Isabella regarding him with a most bemused expression. "What is it?" he wondered.

"You're not going back to London this afternoon," she replied with a shake of her head.

"I'm not? I was going to pay a visit to Ludgate Hill in search of a ring for you," he countered.

"Not today," she replied with a shake of her head, one of her eyebrows arching up in what Octavius realized was a blatant attempt at seduction.

A rather effective attempt at seduction, it turned out, for he found he wanted nothing more than to make love to her that very moment.

Which is why they didn't leave the folly right away.

The result of their first coupling, or perhaps their second or third, lay sleeping in a bassinet next to Isabella's bed, the two-month-old boy guarded by the massive body of Nelson. In a few minutes or perhaps an hour, Lord Tiberius would be demanding his midnight supper.

Out in the newly-expanded stables, four mares were expecting foals in a few months, and a rather small Welsh pony, purchased by Isabella just the week before at Tattersall's for only ten pounds, would begin his training in anticipation of becoming Tiberius' first horse.

As for the other horses in their stables, they had a busy season ahead of them. Three were to be entered in several races, including the St. Leger, the 1000 Guineas, the 2000 Guineas, The Oaks, and The Derby.

Despite having a newborn, Octavius discovered his duchess' interest in the beasts hadn't waned in the least. She no longer mucked stalls, of course, opting instead to train yearlings and time the horses as they were raced around the makeshift track Octavius had seen to creating behind the stables.

Although he knew Isabella could have opted to simply wait until she reached her majority to use her dowry to build her own stables and populate them with Thoroughbreds of her own choosing, Octavius was rather glad she opted instead to make him her husband.

Her dowry helped him make her dream come true.

As for having David Fitzwilliam as a father-in-law, well,

he found he didn't have to acknowledge him as such, and that was fine with both of them.

As for having the new Earl of Craythorne as his brother-in-law, Octavius found John possessed of a sound mind and the spirit of youth—even if he was his political opposite. He had responded to Isabella's initial letter in a most curious manner, his brief missive beginning with the words,

> *What a relief. I never for a moment believed you dead. However, I knew you couldn't possibly hide forever—unless it was in a horse stable.*

"Might I make a request of you?" Octavius whispered when Tiberius finally stirred and was about to wail for his midnight supper.

"What is it?" Isabella wondered, coming fully awake. She let out a moan of disappointment as Octavius pulled himself from her body and settled onto the mattress next to her.

"When it's time to teach our son patience, let's not tie him up to the orangery, shall we?"

Isabella let out a giggle as she moved to lift the babe in question from the bassinet. "Fine with me, but I'll remember you made the request when he *vexes* you in a few years," she warned with a grin.

Octavius frowned, but only for a moment. He was soon grinning ear to ear.

A NOTE TO THE READER

So you see, Gentle Reader, even the most revered duke can end up with an unlikely wife. The most rakish twin with his betrothed.

But what of the younger twin? Will Daniel Fitzwilliam ever find true love? Oh, but of course! For how he manages it, be sure to read *The Widowed Countess.*

As for Constance Fitzwilliam, know that her future is far different from what she expects. When she reaches her majority, a trip to London will have her discovering there is a man with a bit of horse sense in *The Love of a Rake.*

Thank you for taking the time to read The Dream of a Duchess. *If you enjoyed it, please consider telling your friends or posting a short review. Word of mouth is an author's best friend.*

Thank you,

Linda Rae Sande

ABOUT THE AUTHOR

A self-described nerd and lover of science, Linda Rae spent many years as a published technical writer specializing in 3D graphics workstations, software and 3D animation (her movie credits include SHREK and SHREK 2). An interest in genealogy led to years of research on the Regency era and a desire to write fiction based in that time.

A fan of action-adventure movies, she can frequently be found at the local cinema. Although she no longer has any tropical fish, she does follow the San Jose Sharks. She makes her home in Cody, Wyoming.

If you'd like to learn about upcoming releases, be sure to subscribe to her newsletter.

For more information:
www.lindaraesande.com